RO

BLIC

Zongo

Aketi   Buta   Isiro

umba

Sifa's Village   Bunia

Aruwimi River

asoko

Kisangani   Butembo

UGANDA

Lake Albert

Kampala ★

Lake Edward

Lake
Victoria

Ikela   UBUNDU RESERVE

TAYNA NATURE RESERVE

Goma   RWANDA

SALONGA NATIONAL PARK   Lake Kivu   Kigali ★

Bukavu

BURUNDI

Bujumbura ★

Baraka
Fizi

Lualaba River

Lusambo

Kananga   Mbuji-Mayi   Kabalo   Kalemi

Kabinda   Lake Tanganyika

azumba   Gandajika

Luvua   TANZANIA

Mwene-Ditu   Manono   Kiambi

River

Kamina   Pweto

Lake Mweru

UPEMBA NATIONAL PARK

Kolwezi   Likasi

ZAMBIA

Lake Malawi

Lubumbashi

MALAWI

Lilongwe ★

THE
AMERICAN
MISSION

THE AMERICAN MISSION

MATTHEW
PALMER

G. P. PUTNAM'S SONS | NEW YORK

PUTNAM

G. P. PUTNAM'S SONS
Publishers Since 1838
Published by the Penguin Group
Penguin Group (USA) LLC
375 Hudson Street
New York, NY 10014

USA · Canada · UK · Ireland · Australia
New Zealand · India · South Africa · China

A Penguin Random House Company

ISBN 978-0-399-16570-2

Printed in the United States of America

BOOK DESIGN BY AMANDA DEWEY
ENDPAPER MAP BY JEFFREY L. WARD

For Bekica, of course . . .
and, as always, for Nicky and Zoe

ACKNOWLEDGMENTS

Its reputation to the contrary, writing is not a solitary activity. That may still be true of diaries, but a book such as this one benefits from the input and support of many parties.

I want first of all to thank my father for teaching me how to write a novel and my brother, Daniel, for going first. My mother also offered keen insights as a critical reader.

Thanks to the multitalented Meg Ruley at the Jane Rotrosen Agency, this book found just the right home. Thanks also to everyone else at the agency, especially Carlie Webber, Rebecca Scherer, and—naturally—Jane herself. Nita Taublib and Meaghan Wagner have been a fantastic editing team at Putnam and the book is stronger for their guidance. Many people read the manuscript as it evolved, and I am especially grateful for the contributions of Michael and Kiki Nachmanoff, Aaron Pressman, Lee Litzenberger, Kati Hesford, and Kurt Campbell. Any mistakes, of course, are my own.

My wife, Bekica, and our children, Nicky and Zoe, offered me love and consistent support and, most important, the time I needed to write. Thanks, guys. I couldn't have done it without you.

Finally, I would like to acknowledge the men and women of the Foreign Service, who work long hours on often thankless tasks in difficult and dangerous places to advance the interests of the United States. You are terrific colleagues, and I have learned more from you than I can begin to recount.

THE
AMERICAN
MISSION

PROLOGUE

May 7, 2006
Darfur

Death came on horseback.

From the air-conditioned comfort of the brigadier's trailer, Alex Baines could just make out the black smudge clinging to the horizon like a storm cloud. Through binoculars, the picture was clearer. Ranks of horsemen clustered together, their iron lances glinting in the sun. Except for the AK-47 assault rifles slung over their shoulders, it was a scene straight out of the fourteenth century.

The Janjaweed militiamen were massing for what Alex could only assume was an imminent assault on the Riad refugee camp. He focused his attention on the one man with the power to prevent a massacre.

"General, I beg you, please defend this camp. Your peacekeepers are the only thing standing between these people and mass slaughter."

Arush Singh of the Indian Army's First Gorkha Rifles looked at Alex with heavy, owlish eyes and sipped his omnipresent cup of tea. As always, the creases on his khaki uniform were sharp and crisp.

"Quite out of the question, I'm afraid," Singh said, his upper-crust accent betraying his years of schooling at Cambridge and Sandhurst. "My mandate is limited to self-defense. I don't have the authority to shoot at the Janjaweed unless they start shooting at my men, something I very much doubt they will do."

"That is an extremely narrow reading of your authorities. There are half a dozen UN Security Council resolutions that identify Camp Riad by name as a designated safe area. We have the responsibility to protect the people who came here on that basis and with our explicit guarantee of security."

"Riad is officially a safe area. Unfortunately, however, the one resolution that specifically established my command provides a much more limited mandate. We are authorized to use lethal force only in self-defense. You know the resolution, Mr. Baines, and the reason for it. It is not an oversight or an accident. The mandate was carefully negotiated among the members of the Security Council. It's high politics, and there's nothing a simple military man can do about it."

The problem, Alex knew, was China. Beijing was allied to the Sudanese government in Khartoum and skeptical of the UN mission in Darfur. The Chinese were hungry for access to Sudan's vast oil reserves. Rather than veto the resolution that created UNFIS—the UN deployment in Sudan—and face international outrage, Beijing had quietly neutered the mission in tedious negotiations in New York over the scope of the mandate. That was the way things worked in the UN system, and it was why, despite deploying a six-hundred-man force of Bangladeshi and Uruguayan infantry, UNFIS was something of a paper tiger.

"We've checked this carefully with the lawyers in the Department of Peacekeeping Operations back at headquarters," Singh continued. "They are quite clear on this point."

"The lawyers aren't here," Alex insisted. "We are. What happens next is on us, and we can't pass that responsibility back to New York." There was a sharp edge to his voice. Dark tendrils of anger and fear clawed at his heart. He knew that he was losing the argument, and the consequences of losing were too terrible to contemplate.

"Our first priority now has to be the safety of the international staff," Singh said. "We are here to help deliver aid and assistance, not to fight a war with the Janjaweed. The situation has grown too dangerous. We need to prepare for evacuation."

"We have a responsibility to the refugees who put their faith in us. The Zaghawa could have fled to the mountains when reports of a Janjaweed attack first surfaced two weeks ago. They stayed because I asked them to, because I promised that we could protect them."

"You really shouldn't have done that," Singh sighed, sipping his tea.

When Alex opened the door to the trailer, the blast of heat hit him with an almost physical force. The cloud on the horizon had grown larger. Pulling the binoculars from his pocket, he surveyed the scene. A large man on a white horse rode across the front of the Janjaweed ranks. It was too far for Alex to see the rider's face clearly, but he would have bet a sizable sum that it was Muhammed Al-Nour. Even by the standards of the Janjaweed, Al-Nour was a murdering thug with a well-deserved reputation for brutality.

Most of the camp's ten thousand residents were members of the Zaghawa tribe. Arab Janjaweed militia had been battling the African Zaghawa for the better part of two decades. It was an unequal struggle teetering on the edge of genocide.

Pocketing the binoculars, Alex knew what he had to do next. He had to tell the Zaghawa elders that they were going to die.

As much as he would have liked to deny his own responsibility for what was about to happen, he knew that he could not. Washington had been afraid that a mass exodus from the camp would undermine the credibility of international efforts in Darfur and lead to a growing drumbeat of support for military intervention in Sudan. Moreover, the intelligence community was flatly contradicting the desert nomads' predictions of a Janjaweed attack. The government's multibillion-dollar reconnaissance satellites saw nothing that would substantiate their story. The CIA's best analysts dismissed the reports as groundless.

The State Department had instructed Alex to persuade the Zaghawa leadership to keep their people in Camp Riad. In Alex's six months in the camp, the elders had come to trust him. And when he advised them to stay, they listened to him.

Alex made his way through the squalid encampment toward the makeshift shelter where the tribal council met.

The elders were waiting.

Daoud Tirijani, de facto head of all of the Zaghawa tribesmen in the camp, stepped forward to greet him. He was a tall, thin man who looked to be in his late sixties. His sun-wrinkled skin served as testament to a harsh life in the desert. His robes were caked with the thick yellow dust that blew ceaselessly through the camp and settled in a gritty film over everything and everyone. A cloth *shesh* was wrapped around his head and neck, leaving only Daoud's face exposed to the elements. Fatima, the tribesman's principal wife, stood behind him holding one of his fifteen grandchildren. A girl. Alex bowed his head briefly in wordless apology but then looked the Zaghawa elder straight in the eye.

"I'm sorry, Daoud."

The tribesman nodded. His expression did not change.

"The Janjaweed are going to come," Alex continued. "General Singh will not fight. There may still be time for you to lead your people to the hills."

Daoud shook his head. "It is too late for that."

In a gesture of extraordinary generosity, Daoud reached out and clasped his forearm. Alex reciprocated, locking eyes with the Chief. For the Zaghawa, this was a mark of respect. Daoud was acknowledging that Alex had done all that he could. Somehow, this made him feel even worse.

"You are a great man, Daoud, a true leader. It has been a privilege to be your friend."

The ground began to rumble under their feet. The Janjaweed were coming.

Daoud turned and barked orders in Zaghawa too quickly for Alex to follow. The small knot of elders dispersed, returning to the subclans they were charged with leading through this crisis.

Fatima walked up to Alex and handed her granddaughter to him. For a moment, he resisted the responsibility, overwhelmed by what it was Fatima was asking of him and ashamed of his reluctance to accept it. Then he took the girl. He did not know what else he could do.

"Her name is Anah," she said.

Daoud's granddaughter was stick thin. She could not have been more than six years old. She clung fiercely to Alex and did not cry. Anah was a brave girl.

Wordlessly, Fatima turned away and walked to stand beside her husband.

A Janjaweed charge is a fearsome thing to see. The militiamen preferred the intimacy of the spear and sword to the impersonal killing power of automatic rifles. Nearly a hundred riders on stout horses rode through the center of the camp like an armored fist. Their leveled lances cut down scores of camp residents as they tried to flee. Alex saw one of the elders, a man he knew well, decapitated by a strike from a machete. There was nowhere to hide. The only hope for the camp residents was to stay alive long enough for the Janjaweed to sate their bloodlust.

A few peacekeepers in powder blue helmets stood and watched the slaughter. They carried their rifles slung harmlessly over their shoulders. The Janjaweed gave them a wide berth.

A few of the Zaghawa men tried to fight back, but they lacked training, experience, and weapons. Some tried to hide. Most tried to flee.

Alex saw two Janjaweed ride in parallel through the center of the camp with a chain suspended between their saddles, catching refugees around the knees and ankles, and sending them crashing to the ground. From behind a stack of crates stenciled with Australian flags, Daoud stepped out in front of one of the riders, holding a length of iron pipe. Dodging the tip of the Janjaweed's lance, he swung the heavy pipe in an arc that caught the rider on the shoulder and dumped him from the saddle. The militiaman fell hard and Daoud raised the pipe like a spear. Before he could deliver the blow, an Arab riding a white horse and wearing a black Bedouin-style headdress rode up behind him and stabbed Daoud in the neck with a curved sword. Alex recognized him from his picture in the CIA bio. It was Al-Nour.

The horse reared. The animal was so white that it seemed almost translucent in the desert sun. The muscles and veins under its skin were clearly visible. Alex recalled the passage from Revelation: *I looked and there before me was a pale horse. Its rider was named death, and hell was following close behind.*

With a speed and grace that belied his size, Al-Nour jumped from his horse and wrapped a length of cord around Daoud's ankles. Re-mounting, the Janjaweed leader dragged Daoud's body down the main road of the camp. As he rode past, Al-Nour looked at Alex and Anah with a sneer playing on his lips. He pointed his bloody blade at Alex's head but did not lift it to strike.

Alex held on tightly to Anah. He did not dare put her down. Even as he kept her safe, however, he drew strength from her. Anah had been entrusted to him. Here in the shadow of death, the survival of this one small creature was his sole responsibility.

Slowly and carefully, Alex made his way through the maze of crude shelters, moving in the direction of the trailers that housed the international staff. He whispered reassurances to Anah in English. It did not matter if she understood the words.

The killing became less efficient as the riders broke up into smaller groups and spread out through the vast camp. A few stopped murdering long enough to rape.

Alex was light-headed and dizzy. His vision narrowed to the point where he felt he was looking at the world through a long tube. Anah grew heavy in his arms as she clung to him with her face pressed tightly against his shoulder.

He had nearly reached the trailers when the cavalry arrived. A small armada of helicopters appeared in the sky over Camp Riad, and for a moment Alex dared to hope that the Janjaweed would be pushed back. The deadly Cobra gunships stayed silent, however, and circled above in lazy figure eights as four massive U.S. Marine Corps Sea Knights set down near the trailers. The blast from the Sea Knights' twin rotors sent sand and shelter material flying in every direction. Even before the helicopters had settled on their landing gear, efficient Marine rifle squads had dismounted and secured the perimeter. They did nothing to challenge the Janjaweed.

Alex assessed that the one Marine carrying a BlackBerry rather than a rifle was the mission commander. When he got closer, Alex could see the oak-leaf insignia of a lieutenant colonel and a name tag over his breast pocket that read HARROW.

"Colonel Harrow, I'm Alex Baines with the State Department. This is a UN safe area, and the Janjaweed militia are in violation of multiple Security Council resolutions. Between your Marines and the UN peacekeeping contingent, there's more than enough strength to push the Janjaweed back and save what's left of this camp."

"I reckon you might be right about that, sir," the colonel replied in a soft Georgian drawl. "But it's not in my orders. This is a NEO, a noncombatant evacuation. My orders are to get you and the UN civilian staff out of here."

"The international staff will all fit on one Sea Knight," Alex insisted. "You can evacuate at least a hundred Zaghawa on the other helicopters. We should start with the sick, the injured, and the children."

"No can do, sir. Not in my orders. Besides, we can't have refugees swarming the helos looking for a way out. It's too dangerous. I need to ask you to get on board now, please."

Alex felt the blood pounding in his temples. He fought to control his anger and failed. Without thought, he lashed out with a fist, catching the Marine colonel on the jaw and knocking him to the ground. Two young Marines stepped in quickly to defend their commander. One grunt grabbed Alex's free arm and twisted it behind his back. The other reached for Anah but stopped short when he saw the savage look in Alex's eyes.

Harrow rose from the ground and held up his hand. "It's okay. Let him go. In truth, I don't really blame him. But get this man on one of the birds. If he resists, you can restrain him . . . gently." A trickle of blood ran down Harrow's chin from his newly split lip.

"Get your shoulder into it next time," he said, before turning to greet General Singh.

Alex's guards escorted him to the door of one of the helicopters. A Marine sergeant supervising the boarding stopped him. He looked at Anah and then at Alex. "I'm sorry, sir. No locals on the helos. Colonel's orders. Internationals only, sir."

"She's my daughter," Alex replied, shouting over the noise. Even as he said it, he realized it was true.

The Marine clearly did not believe that the underfed African girl in the dirty gray shawl was Alex's child.

"Uh, do you have any identification papers for her, sir, a passport or something?"

"Her passport is in my travel bag in my trailer on the other side of the camp. Do you think we should stop there on the way out and pick it up?"

The Marine shook his head. He had real problems to deal with. Refugee paperwork was not his concern. He gestured for Alex and Anah to board.

When all of the international staff was on board, the Sea Knights rose with surprising agility from the desert surface. Two of the helicopters were flying empty.

Through the window, Alex had a perfect view of the chaos and carnage in the camp. A line of shiny white UN vehicles was pulling out onto the main road to El Genaina, carrying the well-armed peacekeepers to safety.

THREE YEARS
LATER

1

JUNE 12, 2009
CONAKRY

C heck this one out. Twenty-two years old. Absolutely stunning. Says she wants to go to Disney World, but she has a one-way ticket to New York. Why do they always say that they're going to Disney World? You'd think they'd just won the Super Bowl or something."

Hamilton Scott, Alex's partner on the visa line at the U.S. Embassy in Conakry, Guinea, leaned around the narrow partition that separated their interview booths, dangling an application for a tourist visa. The woman in the visa photo clipped to the upper corner bore a striking resemblance to the supermodel Naomi Campbell.

It was admittedly unprofessional, but Alex understood what Ham was doing. Visa-line work could be excruciatingly monotonous, and in a third-world hellhole like Conakry, the applicants would say or do just about anything to gain entrance to the United States. The vice consuls often resorted to black humor or informal games like Visa Applicant Bingo as a way to keep themselves sane.

"Do you think she'd sleep with me for a visa?" Ham asked with mock seriousness.

"Twenty-two? Isn't she a little old for you, Ham?"

"Ordinarily, yes. But this girl's exceptional. And there's no way she qualifies as a tourist."

"Qualify" was a kind of code word in visa work. The law said that anyone applying for a visa to the United States had to prove that he or she was not secretly intending to emigrate. The challenge for the applicants was demonstrating that they had strong and compelling reasons to come back after visiting the U.S. In practice, this meant money. Rich people were "qualified" for visas. Poor people struggled to overcome the supposition that they were economic migrants. In the euphemistic language of government, they were "unqualified."

Ham turned back to the applicant and explained to Ms. Hadja Malabo that, sadly, she lacked the qualifications for an American visa and should consider reapplying when her "situation" had changed. Ham's French was flawless, a consequence of four years at a boarding school in Switzerland. He was polite but, Alex thought, somewhat brusque in rejecting Ms. Malabo's application.

Ham leaned back around the partition.

"I'm almost through my stack, only four or five left. How you doing?"

Alex looked at the pile of application packages still in front of him. There were at least twenty left. He and Ham were the only two interviewing officers at post, which meant about fifty nonimmigrant visa interviews a day for each of them. Ham made his decisions with a brutal efficiency. Alex took more time with each applicant. Most would come away empty-handed, but he wanted to give each person who came into his interview booth the sense that they had had a chance to make their case and that the consul had at least given them a fair shot. For most Guineans, their brief moment with a consular officer was as close as they were going to get to the United States.

"I still have a few to go," Alex admitted.

"Give me some of yours." Ham reached over and took nearly half of the stack out of Alex's in-box. "If we can finish in less than an hour, we can grab a sandwich and a beer at Harry's bar. My treat. Gotta meet with the Ambassador after lunch to talk over the report on human trafficking I did for him last week." Ham paused for a moment. "I'm sorry, Alex," he said carefully. "You know I don't mean to rub that in."

The Ambassador had been giving Ham increasingly significant reporting responsibilities, something relatively rare for a first-tour Vice Consul but understandable given that Ham's full name was Hamilton Wendell Scott III and that both I and II had been ambassadors in half a dozen countries. Ham was just punching his consular ticket in a hardship post, something all junior officers had to do, before heading off for the salons and soirees of Western Europe and a diplomatic career with an unlimited upside. No doubt, Ham's father considered his son's stint in Conakry a "character-building" experience. He could bore future generations of American diplomats with war stories about life on the visa line in Guinea when he was ambassador to Sweden or Hungary or some such place.

For Alex, however, stamping passports looked like a permanent fixture of the next thirty years of his career. There wasn't much else a Foreign Service Officer who had lost his security clearances was good for. The contrast between Ham's upward trajectory and the flat, featureless plain that represented Alex's career prospects could not have been any starker. Both knew it, and both generally avoided talking about it.

Having crossed the invisible line, however, Ham seemed determined to charge forward.

"Have you given any more thought to the Centrex offer, Alex?" he asked with characteristic directness.

"I've written two letters," Alex replied, setting the passport he had picked up back on top of the pile. "One accepting the job and one turning it down. I've almost sent each one of them at least five times."

"It's a good job. Centrex Resources is a top-flight firm with global reach. Oil and gas is a big business in Africa now, and you'd be doing real policy work for them."

"It's a great opportunity," Alex agreed. "In truth, I'm not quite certain why they reached out to me like that. I didn't apply. It's tempting. But my appeal is pending with Diplomatic Security, and I'm hoping that they'll agree to restore my clearances." After a brief pause, he added, "This time."

"Alex, DS is like the Gestapo. They don't own up to their mistakes. And without clearances, processing visa applications is about all you'll be able to do in the Service. Head of government relations for the Africa division at a company like Centrex is just another kind of diplomacy. I think you should jump at it."

Ham's assessment of the odds DS would restore Alex's clearances was unsparing but almost certainly accurate.

Alex remembered vividly the look of satisfaction on the face of the low-level agent who had informed him that the Assistant Secretary for Diplomatic Security had decided that—as a result of both his evident issues of mental instability and his failure to seek treatment through authorized channels—Alex's access to information would be restricted to "Sensitive But Unclassified." In other words, he could use the departmental phone book and read the press guidance, but that was about it. For an ambitious young political officer, it was a professional death sentence.

What had really burned Alex was that the sanctimonious prick with an army-regulation haircut had been reading to him from Alex's medical file, including notes from his therapy sessions with Dr. Branch. The agent refused to explain how he had acquired the confidential records. Alex had told no one that he was seeing a shrink, and he had paid his bills in cash to avoid leaving a paper trail with the insurance company. Going to the State Department's doctors wasn't really an option either. Foreign Service Officers with Top Secret security clearances knew that their access to information could be "suspended indefinitely" if they sought counseling for mental or emotional trauma.

"February fifth," the agent read, "patient presents with nightmares, headaches, and trouble concentrating. Occasional panic attacks and difficulty with emotional control. Preliminary diagnosis of post-traumatic stress disorder related to service in Darfur. Prescribed Lexapro at thirty milligrams daily."

There were things that Alex had told Dr. Branch that he had never told anyone else. That this officious little martinet was somehow privy to this private information was infuriating.

"March thirteenth," the agent continued, "patient reports that the nightmares are increasing in both frequency and intensity. Vivid images of violence in Darfur coupled with feelings of inadequacy and guilt. Maybe a side effect of current medication; possible root issues with patient's loss of his father at an impressionable age. Recommend switching to Zoloft, beginning with twenty milligrams daily and stepping up to fifty depending on patient response."

The agent had read a few more entries, but it was cruelty without purpose. The judgment had already been delivered from on high. Diplomatic Security had decreed Alex Baines a dangerous risk to the safeguarding of classified information. The interview was just checking a box. At the end, the agent had handed Alex a form for him to sign, acknowledging that he had been informed that he was no longer allowed to either access or produce classified information. He instructed Alex to keep a copy for his personal files.

Maybe they were right not to trust him, Alex reasoned. Sometimes he didn't even trust himself. It had been nearly three years since the sack of Camp Riad, but not a day went by that he didn't think about it. Closing his eyes, he could see Janjaweed militia on horseback riding at full tilt through the crowded refugee camp, automatic rifles slung over their backs and polished black lances in their hands. He could hear the wet smack of a spearhead being driven clean through a human body, the incessant buzzing of flies, and, above all, the rhythmic cadence of helicopter blades beating the dry desert air.

"Alex, you still with me?" Ham asked. "You looked like you went to Bermuda for a moment there."

"No, not Bermuda." *Not by a long shot.* "Just thinking about what you said. It makes a lot of sense, but it's still a damn difficult thing to do. I know it's a bit corny, but this is an honorable profession. It's about ideas and ideals. Centrex is about maximizing shareholder profit."

Rather than laughing at him as Alex had half expected, Ham nodded thoughtfully. Under his somewhat more cynical exterior, the son and grandson of American ambassadors believed the same thing.

"Have you asked Anah what she thinks?"

Alex brightened at the mention of his daughter.

"She's not thinking about much these days except summer vacation. She can hardly wait."

"Maine again?"

"She wouldn't miss it."

One of the challenges of raising children in the Foreign Service was that the constant moving around the globe made it hard for kids to develop a sense of belonging. They grew up as rootless "third-culture kids" who did not look on the United States as home. Many families tried to compensate for this with regular visits to someplace in America that the kids could think of as theirs. For Alex and Anah, it was Alex's mother's house in Brunswick. Alex could get only a few weeks off from work, but Anah typically stayed in Maine for the entire summer. She loved the beach and the tide pools and the dark pine forests. Most of all, however, she loved that there was so much family. Alex suspected that it reminded her on some level of the big, sprawling tribal family she had come from. Anah had a score of cousins in and around Brunswick who were her constant companions for the summer months. They had embraced the black girl from Sudan as family without reservation.

The youngest of three, Alex was the only one who had left Brunswick and the first in his family to finish college. His brother had done a year at the University of Maine in Orono in forestry before dropping out and going to work for the paper company. His sister worked part-time at a coffee shop and full-time as the wife of a lobsterman. Their father had been a mechanic at the naval air station where he had worked on the P-3 Orions that patrolled the Atlantic coast looking for Soviet submarines. A longtime smoker, he had died of throat cancer when Alex was twelve.

Reluctantly, Alex and Ham turned back to the stacks of passports in front of them. The application on the top of Alex's pile belonged to an elderly man with the unwieldy name Rafiou Alfa Ismael Pascal Gushein. In Guinea, having six or seven names with a mishmash of tribal, Islamic, and French roots was not at all unusual. Gushein entered the interview booth with a young man who introduced himself in French as the applicant's nephew. His uncle, he explained, spoke neither English nor French, only the tribal Soussou language.

Alex sat on a bar stool behind two inches of bulletproof glass. A narrow slit allowed him to pass documents back and forth with the applicant. The glass wall established a psychological as well as a physical barrier between the consular officer and the applicant that was utterly intentional. It made it easier for the officers to say no.

Alex appraised Mr. Gushein while he flipped quickly through the passport. The applicant looked considerably older than his sixty-four years with his snow white hair and deeply lined face, but he stood tall and straight in the booth, and looked Alex right in the eye with an easy confidence. Alex pegged him for a village elder or headman. Someone used to automatic respect.

The passport was old and worn, but unused. A series of stamped dates on the back page indicated that Mr. Gushein had applied for a U.S. visa six times previously and been refused each time. One of Alex's Guinean staff had pulled the old applications out of the file and bundled them with the passport. Scribbled notes from previous generations of consular officers explained the reason for the refusal.

"Son living illegally in the United States," said one.

"Poor risk," said another.

Two of the previous forms said simply "214(b)," the section of immigration law that makes clear all visa applicants are assumed to be intending immigrants who must establish strong and compelling ties to their home country. Another two of the applications were blank, handled by consular officers who were apparently too busy to even explain their reasons for a decision of no consequence to them but of enormous importance to Rafiou Alfa Ismael Pascal Gushein.

"Mr. Gushein," Alex asked, "why do you want to go to the United States?"

His nephew translated into Soussou, a language of which Alex knew no more than a few words.

"My son lives there," the nephew replied, translating Mr. Gushein's response. "I have not seen him for many years."

"Where does he live?"

"Chicago."

"What does he do in Chicago?"

"He cleans the windows of very big buildings."

"Is he paying for your trip?"

"Yes."

"Do you know if your son is legally in the United States?"

"I don't know. I'm sure he would rather be, but he is a headstrong boy. He broke my rules often enough. His dream was to go to America. I know that is hard to do for poor people like my son. He would do what was necessary to make this dream real."

"Mr. Gushein, how long do you intend to spend in the United States? And how can I be certain that you will come home to Guinea?"

"I will be in your country for two weeks. I must come home before it is time to shear the sheep."

There were more questions he could ask, but Alex didn't really need any more information. It was clear to him why previous interviewers had rejected Gushein's application: They were trying to punish the son for breaking U.S. immigration law by denying the father the right to visit. Alex didn't share that philosophy. The only relevant question was whether it was reasonable to believe Mr. Gushein would return to Guinea after his visit to Chicago.

Immigration law gave consuls considerable discretion. In this case, Alex could decide to issue or not issue the visa as he saw fit. There was no appeal. Ham would certainly have said no without a second thought. Hell, he might have been one of the interviewing officers who had turned down the earlier applications.

Gushein's explanation that he would need to return to his village in time for sheep-shearing season was perfectly credible. It was the right time of year. In the villages, livestock was a rough measure of a man's wealth, and shearing was an important event on the agricultural calendar that governed rural life in West Africa.

"Mr. Gushein," Alex said, after perhaps twenty seconds of reflection. "Can you come back this afternoon to pick up your visa?"

When the nephew translated this request, Gushein nodded slowly, but Alex could see tears forming at the corners of his eyes. He had come in expecting to be rejected and had not allowed himself the luxury of hope. The Soussou elder put one hand against the wall to steady himself while his nephew gripped him by the other elbow.

"*Merci, merci,*" he said in accented but clear French, maybe one of only two or three words that he knew in that language.

Some days, Alex thought, *the job wasn't all bad.*

The glow didn't last for long. Alex had nearly finished his final interview when the Consul General shouted for him from the comfort of his leather "executive model" desk chair.

"Alex, I want to see you in my office right now."

Ronald R. Ronaldson was both Alex's boss and the embodiment of his deepest professional fears. R Cubed had once been a rising star in the Foreign Service. Somewhere along the way, however, he had fallen from grace—alcohol, it was widely assumed—and found himself at fifty commanding a small consulate in a West African shithole. He was angry about his fate and took it out on his subordinates through the infliction of petty indignities.

"Sure thing," Alex replied in as upbeat a tone as he could muster. "Let me finish with this last case, and I'll be right there."

"No, Alex. Right now."

Alex made his apologies to the last applicant, a seventeen-year-old kid with good grades at the local convent school and a scholarship offer from Wake Forest, and made his way back to the CG's office. French doors connecting his private office to the suite provided the Consul General with a commanding view of the entire section, or would have if Ron Ronaldson hadn't kept the heavy curtains on the inside drawn tight to facilitate the occasional midafternoon nap.

"What can I do for you, Ron?" Alex tried hard to keep any edge of impatience or irritation out of his voice, but he was not quite successful.

"I've been going over the statistics on visa issuance," Ron began. From the vaguely glassy look in the CG's eyes, Alex suspected that R Cubed had been conferring with either Johnnie Walker or Jack Daniel, his two most reliable confidants. "Frankly, Alex, your issuance rate is simply too high. You're nearly fifteen points higher than Ham and well ahead of the average for the region. I need you to bring that number down before it's time to send in the quarterly report."

"Why does the issuance rate matter? The real problem should be the overstay rate. There my numbers are pretty good. I may issue more visas than Ham, but in percentage terms, I don't have any more of my visa cases picked up on immigration violations than he does. Less than two percent, actually."

"I don't give a good goddamn about that. The issuance rate is the number Consular Affairs sees, and I don't want them flagging my consulate as the weak link in West Africa. We'd be seen as a terrorism risk. I'm simply telling you to get your numbers down."

"Ron, are you telling me that I need to start rejecting qualified people who traveled two days and forked over a hundred and forty dollars for three minutes of my time just to bring our numbers in line with the bell curve?" Alex knew that this approach was not going to produce the desired result, but he couldn't help himself.

Anger flared briefly in Ron's eyes before they returned to their glassy norm. "If you want to put it that way, Alex, then yes. That's exactly what I'm telling you to do. You can start with this gentleman." Ron pulled a passport and visa application out of his in-tray. Alex could see from the piles of applications and passports that the CG had been reviewing the morning's issuances. "You approved a visa earlier for a man named Rafiou Alfa Ismael Pascal Gushein." Ron mangled the pronunciation of the unfamiliar name. "The man is an obvious bad risk. When he comes back this afternoon, you tell him your decision has been overturned by a more experienced officer and that he does not qualify for a visa." Ron made no effort to hide the satisfaction he took in issuing this humiliating instruction, and Alex felt his ears begin to burn.

"I know you feel that consular work is a terrible comedown for you, Baines. And, frankly, you're not particularly good at it. You're too soft and too slow. Ham is in a different class. He's just passing through the consular universe. But you're in this for the long haul. Get used to it. Stop thinking you're better than this. Better than us."

Alex had no reply. Ron was wrong about Gushein, but not about Alex. He left the CG's office without saying a word.

That afternoon, Mr. Gushein and his nephew came back for the visa Alex had promised them. R Cubed had pulled open the curtains in his office and opened the French doors to provide a good view of Alex's humiliation.

"Listen," Alex said to Gushein's nephew. "We have a problem. The big man back there doesn't want me to give your uncle a visa. He doesn't think Mr. Gushein will come back to Guinea after visiting his son. I don't agree. I'm giving your uncle the visa, but you need to make it look like I've turned you down." Alex spoke in rapid-fire French mixed with a heavy dose of Guinean slang that he knew Ron wouldn't understand. The CG's French had never progressed much past "Frère Jacques."

"Please tell your uncle that he needs to convince the fat man back there that I've just ripped his heart out of his chest. Do you think he can do that?"

"No problem." The nephew spoke softly but rapidly to Gushein, whose face almost seemed to cave in with sadness. Alex wondered for a moment if his nephew had told him that he would not be getting a visa. No matter. He would learn the truth soon enough. Alex had printed the visa himself and placed it in the passport rather than allowing one of the local staff to do it. There was a record of the decision in the computer and Ron, of course, had access to the system, but he was generally pretty lax about administrative controls. Alex doubted very much that he would ever check.

Alex heard R Cubed slam the French doors, which was followed by the sharp hiss of the curtains being drawn. Time to celebrate his triumph with a Jack and Coke, easy on the Coke.

Gushein left the consulate leaning on his nephew for support. When he reached the door, he turned to look back at Alex and gave him an almost imperceptible nod. So he knew. The old man would have made a hell of an actor.

Alex realized that he had just made two important decisions. The first was that Mr. Gushein was getting on a plane for Chicago if Alex had to buy the ticket himself. The second was which letter he was going to send off to the Centrex people.

2

MAY 31, 2009
KISANGANI

Marie Tsiolo was nervous. It was not an emotion with which the proud daughter of a Luba principal chief was especially familiar. She had been working for this moment for nearly a year, five years if you counted her time studying in South Africa and even longer if you counted the years she had spent learning every rock and trail in the hills near her home village.

The unfamiliar surroundings heightened her anxiety. Kisangani, the third-largest city in the Democratic Republic of the Congo, was located along the last navigable stretch of the mighty Congo River. When the Belgians still ran the Congo, cotton, coffee, and rubber had made Kisangani and its colonial masters rich. Now it was a shadow of its former glories.

A few businesses still thrived in the city, and one of them was the purpose of Marie's visit. Kisangani was home to the exploration-and-engineering arm of her employer, Consolidated Mining Inc. Headquartered in New York, Consolidated was an enormous, sprawling multinational. The main office for the mineral-rich Congo was in the capital, Kinshasa, but it was out here in the wild eastern half of the country that Consolidated made most of its profits. This is where the company mined the copper and cobalt and gold that made the Congo concession so valuable.

The ultimate business of Consolidated wasn't mining; it was money. And Marie hoped that she had persuaded the company to make just a little bit less of it. Now it was time to close the deal. The future of her people hung in the balance.

The Consolidated Mining office was a far cry from the modernist glass cube the company had built in Kinshasa. The multibillion-dollar company operated out of a third-floor walk-up in a crumbling concrete building next to the Soviet-style post office. A row of small plaques announced the names of the six businesses that shared the building. Three were trading companies. One was a dentist's office. One was a brothel. Marie hit the button next to the Consolidated logo. A moment later the front door buzzed open.

There was a cracked mirror on the wall in the lobby, and Marie took a quick look at herself before climbing the stairs. She was not particularly vain, but Marie knew that her looks were an asset in negotiations. Like most of her tribe, Marie was tall, nearly six feet. Her high cheekbones and piercing dark eyes were a gift from her mother. She wore her hair in neat braids pulled back and tied off with a black ribbon. The Kisangani office was relatively informal, so Marie had dressed simply in khaki slacks and sandals with a cream-colored V-necked blouse. Her only jewelry was a single-strand necklace of polished coral beads that she had bought in Cape Town. Under one arm, she carried a black leather document case.

The door to the Consolidated Mining office was open. There was a small waiting area with a few chairs and an empty reception desk. There were three separate offices in the suite. Jack Karic, the head of the Kisangani office, was at his desk in the largest of the three, looking over the material in a thick binder open in front of him. A cigarette smoldered in a glass ashtray next to a coffee cup emblazoned with the company logo.

"Hi, Jack," Marie said, with a polite knock on the open door. The windows in Karic's office were propped open. The air-conditioning was out again.

Karic looked up from his files and glanced briefly at his watch.

"You're late."

They spoke in English. Karic's French was execrable while Marie, like many Congolese, was multilingual. In addition to French and English, she spoke Luba, Swahili, and Lingala, a trade language that served as a kind of lingua franca in the ethnically and linguistically diverse Congo. Marie took the seat directly across the desk from Karic.

"Sorry. There was trouble with the plane." In fact, all flights in and out of the city of Goma in the Congo's far east had been grounded for the better part of the day by a thick cloud of volcanic ash spewing from Mount Nyiragongo.

"No great surprise there," Karic scoffed. "They probably ran short of duct tape."

In Marie's experience, Westerners in central Africa came in two distinct flavors. Some embraced the rich cultures and accepted the hardships as inseparable from the beauties and joys of life in the region. Others, like Karic, resisted the experience, resented the hardships, and over time grew increasingly small-minded and embittered. Karic expressed his resentment over his assignment to Kisangani with a contempt for the Congo and the Congolese people that he did little to disguise.

Right now, however, Marie needed him. She let the gratuitous dig slide.

There was an air of dishevelment about Karic that mirrored that of the decaying city around him. He was taller than Marie and thin, with a pronounced Adam's apple that bobbed up and down when he spoke.

Although he had been in the Congo for nearly three years, he had never adapted to the tropical climate and his face was perpetually flushed. A halfhearted comb-over could not conceal a sizable bald spot. His oxford shirt and seersucker suit were badly wrinkled, and the sweat stains under his arms offered evidence that the office air-conditioning had been out of commission for some time.

Grudgingly, Karic offered Marie a plastic bottle of room temperature water.

"Is that my report you're reading?" she asked.

"It is."

"What do you think?"

"It's a good report."

"Thanks. You have the geology studies in there, and I brought you a proposal on the way forward for your approval. We need some heavy equipment, generators, and lots of safety gear, but nothing that the company doesn't have in excess. It's been six months since I was back in Busu-Mouli. I left plans and blueprints with my father and my uncle so that they could get a start on both the digging and refining operations. That way, we'll be able to integrate the equipment slowly as it becomes available. The initial product will be pretty crude. I'm confident that with the company's help we'll be self-financing within a year and turning an operational profit a few months after that. Ultimately, I'd like to be able to produce industrial-quality ingots on site. That's a few years down the road."

Marie's enthusiasm was unfeigned. The deal she had been negotiating with the mining company promised to transform life in her village.

Karic closed the binder. "It's a good report," he repeated. "Too good, I'm afraid. Henri tells me that he's had second thoughts about the arrangements you discussed."

Marie's heart sank. She understood immediately what Karic meant. Henri Saillard, the mining company's country representative for the

Congo, was based in Kinshasa. Like Karic's, his background was on the business end rather than the production side of Consolidated's operations. While Karic was an accountant by both training and temperament, Saillard's area of expertise was government relations. In a country as corrupt as the Congo, this particular skill was considered vital to the company's success.

"What does he want?" she asked flatly.

Karic looked at her with all the sympathy of a vulture watching a wounded animal it had marked as its next meal.

"This is a potentially big find, Marie. The company wants an open pit." He didn't need to say any more.

Returning to her village after studying at the University of the Witwatersrand in Johannesburg, Marie had recognized the honey yellow cliffs along the trails she had walked as a girl as being almost pure chalcopyrite, a mineral rich in copper and cobalt. She was determined that this potential source of wealth would go to benefit the people of her village and not the kleptocratic government in Kinshasa. The villagers were farmers and fishermen, however, not miners. Moreover, mining was a capital-intensive industry and the equipment was prohibitively expensive. Marie knew that she needed help if it was going to be done right.

With that in mind, she had approached her employer with a proposal: If Consolidated would provide surplus gear that she could use to mine and refine the chalcopyrite ore, the village would share the profits with the company, and Consolidated Mining could burnish its global image by promoting sustainable development. Marie's one condition was that the digging and the smelting needed to be conducted in an environmentally responsible way. That meant using less-efficient and therefore more-expensive techniques such as slope or shaft mining. She had no intention of allowing the lush valley where her village was located to be turned into a lifeless wasteland through strip mining.

Henri Saillard had accepted her terms, and this meeting with Karic was supposed to be a technical discussion about what equipment and material Marie needed for the project.

In that moment, Marie hated Jack Karic, Henri Saillard, and the mining company that employed them all. She tried to mask her anger with a cool and unreadable expression, but there was some undisguised heat in her response.

"It can't be open-pit, Jack. The company is not going to strip-mine my home."

"Have you looked at the price of copper? It's up over forty-five hundred dollars a ton. That's double what it was just eighteen months ago."

"This copper belongs to my people, not the company."

"You don't understand. That copper belongs to the People's Republic of China. They just haven't paid for it yet, and the only real question is who is going to collect from Beijing. If your father agrees to cooperate and relocate the village, the company can help. They'll pay a fair royalty and find a new piece of land for the village. Better land."

"And if we refuse?"

"Then Henri and I will get the government's permission to dig there anyway and you get nothing. Seems like a pretty easy call to me."

Marie was silent as she weighed what Karic had told her. He was right. It was an easy call.

"Go to hell, Jack. Busu-Mouli is our home. You can't have it. It is not for sale."

"Don't be a fool, Marie. The company will take that copper. The find is simply too rich to ignore. We're offering you a fair share, but if you fight us on this, you will lose."

"I don't think so." Marie spoke with considerably more confidence than she felt.

Karic leaned back in his chair and studied Marie intently. She could almost see the gears spinning in his brain.

"There may be a way," he suggested, "to buy yourself some time."

"How?" Marie's hostility was evident in her curt response.

"Feed the beast. Give it something else to chew on, and it might leave your village alone. At least for a while."

"What do you have in mind?"

"Coltan."

Marie was not surprised by the answer. Coltan was industry slang for columbo-tantalite, a dull black metallic ore that could be refined into tantalum. Although most people had never heard of it, tantalum was exceptionally valuable. In its refined form, it had heat-resistant properties and was capable of holding an electrical charge for an extended period. This made it the ideal material for capacitors in cell phones, laptops, and high-end stereos. The pure metal retailed for more than five hundred dollars a kilogram. The raw ore could be found in commercially exploitable quantities in very few places. Eastern Congo was one.

The oil industry recognized, but could never explain, that some petroleum geologists had a nose for oil. They could somehow "feel" the presence of big oil and could look at a data set and predict with high confidence where the company should drill. Marie had the same talent for coltan.

"It doesn't work like that. You can't find something like that just by wishing hard enough."

"I understand that. We aren't going in blind. There are site surveys in the Aruwimi Valley region that offer promising indications of a big find." His voice was oily. "The company is putting together a team to do the fieldwork. I want you to be the second geologist on that team."

"Who's the first?"

"Steve Wheeler."

Marie knew Steve Wheeler casually. He was a boisterous New Zealander with a penchant for American cowboy hats. They had been on one expedition together, looking for rubidium deposits in the south. Their first night out in the field, Wheeler had made a pass at her, but he had been a gentleman about it and accepted her rebuff with good humor. She could work with him.

"Let's say I agree, and we find coltan. Can you promise me that the company won't strip-mine my home anyway?"

Karic shook his head. "The company's resources are stretched pretty thin right now. We would be hard-pressed to take on two major new projects simultaneously, and if it came to a choice between coltan or copper, the numbers argue strongly in favor of coltan."

Marie understood the subtext to Karic's argument. He and Henri Saillard were rivals as well as colleagues. From Kinshasa, Henri had New York's ear and had arranged to keep Jack in exile in the east. If Karic could get credit for a major coltan find, he could raise his profile in New York while undercutting Saillard's efforts to seize the copper under Marie's village. Jack Karic was a snake, but she and he had a common interest in seeing Saillard taken down a peg or two. Of course, Karic would have to do something to make it unmistakably clear to headquarters that he was personally responsible for finding the coltan and critical to the expensive efforts to develop the find. Let him.

"All right. I'll do this. But this is the end, Jack. After this, the company and I are finished. When do I leave?"

"*We* leave in ten days."

"We?"

"I'm going with you."

3

Trekking through the rain forest was akin to being underwater. The thin sunlight filtered through the jungle's triple canopy reached the ground with barely enough strength left to power photosynthesis. From below, the leaves of the ancient and awe-inspiring trees shone like a monochrome stained-glass mosaic. There was little life at the bottom of this green sea. The vast bulk of the forest's biomass was located a hundred or more feet up from the floor. In contrast, the ground was covered by a thick mat of decaying vegetation. The roots of the great trunks that held up the forest roof were rotting away even before the trees reached full maturity. Stagnant pools of water covered with a scum of green algae were thick with leeches and parasites. Armchair environmentalists liked to think of the rain forest as teeming with life. Marie Tsiolo knew better. Green as it was, the forest was teeming with death.

Consolidated Mining typically sent armed guards to protect its expensively educated engineers and scientists. For this trip, the security was unusually heavy. Ten armed guards protected a core of eight company employees and a dozen porters, who carried the camp gear and survey equipment.

In addition to Marie, the expedition included two other women. Charlotte Swing was a skinny blond hydrologist from Cincinnati who chewed gum constantly and peppered her speech with the word "awesome." The youngest person on the team, she was also the expedition's unofficial high-tech wizard. The third woman, Arlene Zimmerman, worked in logistics support. She was somewhere north of fifty and having a hard time with the hiking, though she did her best not to complain. The rest of the team, beginning with Karic and Steve Wheeler, were men. Karic's number two was Wallace Purcell. As far as Marie could tell, he brought no useful skills to the team and his primary responsibility seemed to be taking copious notes in a black leather journal that he carried with him everywhere. The last two "internationals" were both mining engineers. Sven Norlund was a taciturn Swede with more than two decades of experience in Africa, much of it with Consolidated Mining. Mike Tanner was a dual U.S. and Canadian citizen from Saskatchewan who was trained as a surveyor as well as an engineer.

Marie was one of two Congolese in positions of authority. The other was Head of Security Faido Omokoko. Jack Karic was in charge of the expedition, but Faido Omokoko was in charge of the guns. A former soldier and bush fighter, the taciturn Omokoko was at least six inches taller than Marie was and covered with a network of scars. Some were the result of deliberate ritual scarring that marked his tribal identity. Others were clearly unintended. One angry scar on his left shoulder had the distinct puckered look of a bullet wound.

For three days, the Consolidated Mining party had pushed through the jungle looking for coltan. Their path was roughly parallel to the Aruwimi River, one of the Congo's countless tributaries. Satellites and ground-imaging radar had revolutionized the practice of mining geology. Sensor technology, however, was stymied by the thick roof of the rain forest. In central Congo, the modern prospectors plied their trade in the same way as previous generations of treasure hunters had: on foot.

"Why so many guards for this trip?" Marie asked Omokoko, as they picked their way slowly through a maze of twisting roots. "On earlier trips, there have never been more than two or three guards." She spoke in Lingala. Omokoko's French was good, but he was more comfortable in the trade language.

Nearly two minutes went by before Omokoko responded. That was not unusual. The former soldier was neither dumb nor slow, but he liked to take time to think over his answers.

"The company has been having problems in this region recently. Heavy equipment sabotaged, survey teams harassed. Some of our operations have been bombed, burned, or looted."

"Who's responsible?"

After a long pause, Omokoko shrugged. "The Hammer of God."

Unconsciously, Marie looked over her shoulder as if expecting to see armed men following them through the trackless rain forest. Of all the paramilitaries that prowled the jungles of eastern Congo, the Hammer of God was the most feared. Joseph Manamakimba, the Hammer of God himself, had left a blood-soaked trail that stretched from Goma to Kisangani. If the Hammer was targeting Consolidated Mining's interests in the mineral-rich east, it was very bad news for the company's shareholders. Marie was not surprised that Consolidated was trying to keep that quiet.

Suddenly, as though passing through a curtain, Marie stepped out of the dense forest and into a wide clearing. Other members of the survey team who had been walking ahead of her were standing in the field blinking in the unaccustomed sunlight.

A neat row of huts made of mud bricks and palm thatch lined a red dirt path that led in the direction of the river. Vegetables grew in small gardens between the huts, and Marie could see larger fields of manioc, sorghum, and maize on the far side of the village.

The villagers greeted the arrival of the Consolidated Mining party with obvious concern. The unannounced arrival of heavily armed strangers was rarely good news in the Congo. Shouts of alarm echoed through the village in a language that Marie did not recognize. Women and children vanished into the huts or the surrounding jungle. The men gathered in what was roughly the center of town with only primitive farm tools to use in self-defense.

Karic was hopeless as a diplomat, and he stood there looking confused. It was Marie who stepped forward in an effort to defuse the tension.

"You have nothing to fear from us," she began in Lingala. "We are engineers, not soldiers. The guns we carry are only for self-protection. We did not expect to find anyone here. There is no village here on our maps."

The carefully neutral expressions on the faces of the men in front of her did not change, but Marie thought that she detected a slight softening in the set of their shoulders, and the tension of the moment seemed to ease almost imperceptibly. An older man with nearly pure-white hair stepped forward from the cluster of villagers. He was barefoot and naked from the waist up. His smile revealed a mouth with no more than three or four teeth.

"If your appearance here is an accident, then perhaps it is a happy one," he offered. The Chief—for Marie had spent enough time around chiefs to know that he was one—held his hands to the side, palms down, and the villagers slowly lowered their wholly inadequate weapons. Grins broke out on both sides as the threat of violence disappeared, and the villagers eagerly clasped hands with the mining company employees.

Hospitality was an enormously important part of Congolese culture. The wars of the last decade had blunted that tradition, but had not yet managed to extinguish it. Marie, Faido, and the international staff were welcomed into the homes of the villagers. The porters and guards pitched their tents in the village's fields. Marie's host family was the Chief's eldest sister. Her daughter, a pretty fourteen-year-old named Sifa, was assigned to take care of her.

While most of the villagers were busy preparing the welcome feast planned for the evening, Sifa took Marie for a walk through the village. It did not take long to see just about everything there was to see. Beyond the small stretch of mud-brick huts, there were a few shelters for goats and a handful of dairy cows, a village well, and neat fields marked out by fences made of woven sticks. There was a large flat rock under a towering kapok tree that Sifa said was one of her favorite places in the village. They sat in the shade and shared a small package of Hertzog cookies stuffed with coconut and jam from a secret stash that Marie kept hidden in one of the porter's bundles. At first, Sifa looked at the cookie suspiciously. After one bite, however, any reservations were abandoned and the girl wolfed down most of the package with astonishing speed.

"What are you looking for in the jungle?" Sifa asked with open curiosity as she licked coconut crumbs from her fingers. They spoke in French, a language Sifa spoke well, with only a hint of tribal accent. "Are you searching for a place to make a village? No," she corrected herself, "that could not be it. You are traveling with white people, and white people do not make villages."

"We're not looking to settle here, Sifa, although this is a beautiful place. How long have your people lived here?"

"We've been here for three rainy seasons. Before that, we lived upriver. But the militiamen burned our village and we couldn't stay there. We walked for weeks through the jungle before we found a place where we could build a new village." For just a moment, Sifa got a faraway look in her eyes, and Marie understood that the hardships of that experience had left permanent scars. Then, as though a switch had been flipped, the slightly impish look of curiosity returned to her face.

"Don't think that I have forgotten my question," Sifa continued slyly.

"I'm quite certain that you have not. Very well. We are looking for minerals."

"Minerals?" She repeated the word carefully as though she had never heard it before.

"Certain kinds of rocks that can be made into valuable metals like iron or copper."

"What will you do with these rocks?"

"Mine them. We dig them up and sell them."

"You're in luck. We have many rocks here. Our farmers are constantly digging them out of the ground. They complain about them all the time."

"I'm sure they do," Marie said. "But not every rock is valuable. Each has a story to tell, but only a few can be used for what we have in mind."

"I see." Sifa looked at Marie thoughtfully for a moment. "And what do you do? You're quite pretty, so I thought at first that you were the woman of the big man with the rifle. But then I saw you treat with the Chief. I wasn't supposed to look. Mother said it was dangerous. But I did."

"I'm an engineer and a geologist. It's my job to find the valuable rocks from among all the others and make a plan for getting them out of the ground."

"How is it that you know how to do that?"

"Well . . . first I went to school for a long time and I studied very hard. Once you learn how to tell the rocks apart, then you have to go out and find them. That part takes practice. It's not as easy as you might think."

"Are there many girls who do this?" Sifa asked in something approaching awe.

"Not many, no." Marie well understood what lay behind the question. In village life, there were few roles for women beyond child rearing and domestic chores. Marie was fortunate in that her father, Chief Tsiolo, was unusually enlightened. She knew, however, that she was equally fortunate to be an only child. If her father had had a son, Marie might not have had the opportunities she had had: school, travel, knowledge of the world outside the village.

"How do you do it? Find the valuable rocks, I mean," Sifa asked.

"Would you like me to show you?"

The girl's beaming smile was an unmistakable answer.

Marie retrieved her field bag from Sifa's house. The porters carried the bulk of the gear, including the survey equipment and heavier scientific instruments. In a small backpack that she carried with her on the trail, Marie kept some of the basic tools of the geologist side of her training, including a rock hammer, a powerful magnifying glass, and a selection of chemicals and reagents she could use to run simple field tests.

Sifa led her down the path toward the river. The path led through a meadow of wildflowers and sawgrass to a broad, flat peninsula covered with sand and rock. The village had been built on an alluvial flood plain at the foot of a volcanic range. The volcanoes were the reason why the soil the villagers farmed was so rich and why it was mixed with a range of igneous and metamorphic rocks. Marie knelt down and picked up an irregularly shaped gray rock about the size of her fist.

"This is feldspar," she told Sifa, handing her the rock. "It almost certainly was made in one of the volcanoes upriver, and over the course of millions of years it washed down the mountain and wound up here."

"It's not very pretty," Sifa said dubiously.

"It is . . . in its own way."

"Is it valuable?"

"I'm afraid not."

"Oh. What about this one? It's quite pretty." Sifa bent over and picked up a small pink rock that sparkled in the sun. "What is it?"

"It's called quartz. It's a kind of crystal. The crystal itself is clear. The color comes from some very small amounts of metal trapped inside. Different metals make different colors."

One rock at a time, Marie taught Sifa some of the basics of geology. She showed her how to use the rock hammer to break open the small stones and how to read the story of the earth that was written inside them. Sifa was an eager student and a quick study. After a little more than an hour of exploring, the teenager found a treasure.

It was a dull brown rock about the size and shape of a potato. But something seemed special about it, and Sifa brought it to Marie for inspection with undisguised eagerness. Marie agreed that she had found something interesting.

"Watch this." From her backpack, Marie pulled out a small stone chisel and set it in the middle of the rock. Then she handed the rock hammer to Sifa.

"Hit the end of the chisel."

Sifa did as she was told.

"Harder."

Sifa hit it again, this time with considerable force. The rock split easily down the middle, exposing a hollow center filled with glittering purple crystals. Sifa picked up one half and looked at their find with an expression of sheer wonder.

"What is it?" she asked.

"It's a geode. Sometimes an air bubble in the lava will form into a rock with the conditions just right to grow crystals inside. These purple ones are called amethyst. In the cities, women like to wear jewelry made from these crystals. If you'd like, I can help you smooth and polish the edges. It'd make a nice gift for your mother."

Sifa's face assumed a look of determination. "I have made up my mind," she said with the absolute certainty of youth. "I am going to be a geologist like you and travel the world looking for valuable . . .

minerals." She rolled the last unfamiliar word off her tongue with a deliberate slowness.

Marie smiled and was about to reply when a glint of black in the corner of her eye caught her attention. Just about any other geologist would likely have missed it. It was such a small thing. But for Marie, a number of data points that she had picked up almost subliminally clicked into place. This was why Karic had wanted her on the expedition. Geology was a hard science, but successful prospecting favored intuition. Without having to look, she somehow knew what was buried there under the sand. Coltan. With a small trowel from her backpack, Marie turned over the sandy soil and inspected the silicates. The black flecks in the sand could be coltan. She separated out enough of the material to run some simple chemical tests.

After fishing around in the bottom of the pack, she pulled out a small pan with a zinc plate on the bottom and two bottles labeled PO-TASSIUM HYDROXIDE and CHLOROHYDRIC ACID. She mixed the ore and chemicals in the zinc pan. The solution foamed up rapidly with an audible hiss. This field test was far from definitive. To confirm the presence of coltan in commercially exploitable quantities, the team would need to dig a series of slit trenches and use the diesel-powered water pump that the porters carried broken down in pieces to force the material down a sluice that would separate the heavier coltan particles from the sand and clay. Karic would insist on this step. The textbooks and company operating manuals demanded it. Marie knew in her bones that it was unnecessary. She was standing on a large deposit of one of the most valuable minerals on earth.

The sun was setting and the meadow was lit by the soft light of early evening. It was, as she had told Sifa, a truly beautiful place. Because of the techniques involved, coltan mining was exceptionally destructive. For an instant, Marie had a vision of the lush clearing turned into a moonscape of craters and trenches, the river thick with mud and the soil poisoned with heavy metals. Sifa and her family would again be refugees. *Could she trade Sifa's village for her own? Could she live with herself if she did?*

"What is it, Marie? Are you all right?"

"Yes, I'm fine."

"Did you find something?"

Marie hesitated. Then she made up her mind.

"No, Sifa," she said emphatically. "There's nothing of value here. We should get back to the village. They're probably waiting on us for dinner."

She would not take the devil's bargain. If this deposit was not the answer, she would find coltan somewhere else, somewhere uninhabited.

4

JUNE 13, 2009
CONAKRY

It was a familiar dream. It had been with him for the better part of three years, a part of his life that he would gladly leave behind but knew that he never could.

He stood alone in the desert. He was barefoot, and the hot sands of Western Sudan were painful to walk on. The bleak uniformity of the landscape was broken only by the occasional scrub bush or stunted acacia tree. His feet burned as he walked toward a mountain that he could see in the distance. He walked for hours under a desert sun that never moved from its midday high. Looking down at his feet, he saw a skeleton of a man wearing the rags of the rust-colored robe he had died in. The skull was bleached white, but shreds of desiccated flesh still clung to the arms and legs. The hands were stretched out in front with the fingers digging into the sand as though the man had been dragging himself across the desert when he had finally succumbed to the heat. More skeletons appeared, rising from the sand: men, women, small children, and animals. He walked past them, intent on reaching the mountain that seemed to grow no closer.

He knew without turning around that there were people behind him. For some reason, he did not dare look back, but he knew they were there. They were following him or he was leading them. It wasn't clear which. Among them, he knew somehow, were friends, family, people he loved. Anah.

A sandstorm rose up from the desert floor, obscuring his view of the mountain. The storm took shape and form, Janjaweed riders on horseback made up of swirling sands with long lances and banners blotting out the sun. He stood still and opened his arms, awaiting the embrace of death. If he could sacrifice himself, perhaps the Janjaweed would spare those behind him. Instead, the apparitions simply flowed over and past him, filling his mouth and nostrils with choking sand and dust, and forcing him to squeeze his eyes closed. He felt the winds whipping over his body as they passed. And he knew that those behind him were dead. He could not look back. There was no point now in marching to the mountain, and there was nowhere else to go.

An insistent thumping sound filled his ears, starting low and building to an almost unbearable volume. He looked up and saw shadows sweeping through the sky like the blades of an enormous helicopter. The shadows grew larger and larger until they threatened to swallow the world.

Alex awoke with a start, the sheets soaked with the kind of sweat usually reserved for victims of malaria or dengue fever.

The air in his bedroom was thick and stale. The underpowered air conditioner had trouble keeping the temperature in the house below eighty. In the other rooms, ceiling fans helped to circulate the air, but Alex kept the one in his room turned off. The turning blades were evocative of helicopter rotors, and he knew from experience that they were potential triggers for panic attacks.

He unwrapped the sticky sheets from his body and lifted the mosquito netting to get out of bed. He was always very careful to use nets at night. No sense adding malaria on top of the PTSD. The antimalarial drug Malarone that he took to ward off the endemic disease was bad enough. Nightmares and sleep disturbance were some of the side effects of the drug.

Alex was still rubbing the sleep out of his eyes when he was tackled by a four-foot-eight dynamo who knocked him back on the bed and tangled him up in the mosquito netting.

"Good morning, sugar," Alex said.

Anah's smile immediately banished the gloomy residue of the dream. She was standing at the foot of the bed in a bright pink pajama top with matching cotton shorts. There was a strawberry embroidered on the top with SWEET THING written underneath. Alex's housekeeper, Mrs. Mabinty, had fixed Anah's hair in braided spikes with colored beads at the tips. Anah liked the way the beads clinked together when she ran. Her grin was so big that it seemed to reach all the way down to her toes, and Alex, as he did every morning, marveled at just how completely he loved her. She had big, beautiful eyes, and there was something in the set of her jaw that reminded him of her grandfather.

"Good morning, Daddy. Are you ready for our workout?"

"Sure thing, baby. But there's something I've gotta do first."

"What?"

Alex hooked his left foot behind Anah's leg and pulled her close enough to grab and tickle, which he did until she gasped for him to stop. Then she gave him a soft kiss on the cheek.

"Come on. Let's go."

Alex threw on a pair of shorts and led Anah in their twenty-minute morning yoga routine, a combination of simple positions and basic breathing techniques that they enjoyed both as exercise and as an opportunity for a little father-daughter bonding. For Alex, it was also something more. It was a part of a holistic approach to treating his

PTSD, and he clung to it like a drowning man might cling to a piece of driftwood.

When they were done, Anah looked at her father thoughtfully.

"You had the dream again last night, didn't you, Daddy? I could hear you."

"I'm sorry, baby. I didn't mean to wake you. Don't worry, okay? It was nothing. It's just a dream."

Anah looked skeptical, but ultimately decided to give her father the benefit of the doubt.

"It's Saturday," she observed. "Will you make French toast?"

"With strawberries?"

"Of course."

Alex fixed breakfast while John Coltrane played on the stereo and Anah played on the carpet with her dolls. In doll land, the little girls always had both a mother and a father and a big extended family of stuffed animals and talking cars. Having lost his own father at a relatively young age, Alex well understood the feeling of absence that Anah wrestled with. Even before she had learned any English, he had taken her once a week to see a child psychiatrist in downtown Washington recommended by Dr. Branch. Their parallel therapies were another bond between them. Although his daughter had lost so much more than he had, her youth was a distinct advantage. It was Alex, not Anah, who still seemed trapped by the past.

They rarely discussed Darfur or Camp Riad, but Anah was old enough to remember. Just how old she was neither of them knew for certain. She looked to be about five or six years old when he had first accepted responsibility for her, but poor nutrition in the camps made it hard to judge age accurately. Alex had rounded up, and as far as he and Anah were both concerned, she was a healthy nine-year-old girl. Together they had picked April 21, the day the adoption was finalized, as her birthday.

They had breakfast sitting at a small wooden table in the kitchen.

The table was oak, a tree that was most decidedly not native to Africa. It was imported from the United States, along with every other piece of furniture in the comfortable three-bedroom house the Embassy had assigned to him from the housing pool. Every one of the thirty-five houses in the pool was supplied with Ethan Allen furniture in the same "classical American" style. In fact, homes owned or leased by State everywhere in the world had the same furniture and the same inoffensive beige carpets. It was oddly dislocating for an American diplomat to visit a friend living on another continent only to find his couch and coffee table waiting for him on the other end.

Alex left the dishes in the sink for Mrs. Mabinty and took a shower in tepid water that had a slightly brown tinge. The State Department said that the water in Conakry was not safe to drink but was "probably" okay to shower in. So far, no one in the Embassy had contracted any kind of parasite that could be definitively linked to the morning shower.

By the time he had finished his shower, Anah was dressed. Already something of a fashionista, she had picked out a bright yellow skirt and paired it with a green top that had a picture of a unicorn drawn in rhinestones and sequins. Hot pink sneakers completed the ensemble.

"So what do you think about today, Anah? Do you want to make a picnic lunch and go to the botanical gardens or hop the ferry to Îles de Los and go to the beach?"

"The beach," she answered assuredly.

"The beach it is." Alex looked at his daughter and tried to imagine how his joining Centrex might change her life. It would mean moving to London, where the company was headquartered. They could bring Mrs. Mabinty with them. The questions he had were really unanswerable, and he pushed them to the back of his mind. He was absolutely certain of only one thing.

"I love you, little girl," he said.

Anah rolled her eyes. "I know that," she replied.

. . .

That night, after Anah had gone to bed exhausted from a day in the sun, Alex went to the den to work on his pet project. For nearly six months he had been trying to build a satellite system that would allow him to watch the Georgetown Hoyas play basketball. A local mechanic had cut a dish out of the hood of an ancient Mitsubishi pickup truck. Alex himself had cobbled together most of the electronics from Embassy castoffs and what he could find on the local market. The tools he used had once belonged to his father. Along with a passion for working with his hands, they were his sole inheritance.

Alex had borrowed a satellite finder from the Embassy communication section to point his Mitsu-dishy in the general direction of the Atlantic Hot Bird satellite that was hosting not only the TV broadcasts of Georgetown games but also—as he had discovered to his chagrin—a panoply of small-market channels ranging from Chinese pornography to Portuguese soap operas and Swahili game shows.

Alex almost certainly would have had better luck with the off-the-shelf components he could have shipped in from Europe or the States. It would have been faster as well. As it was, there was a real risk that Georgetown's star rookie, Greg Monroe, would make the jump to pro ball before Alex could get his contraption to work.

Without warning, the electronic snow on the TV screen was replaced by what was unmistakably an Indian Bollywood musical complete with dancing elephants. This, Alex reasoned, was a step up from the Arabic news broadcast he had found yesterday, but still a long way from the NCAA. A soccer match between Senegal and Cameroon suddenly replaced the Hindi musical.

Alex lay down on his back and stuck his head under the makeshift decoder that was supposed to translate the Hot Bird data into actual programming. For some reason, the receiver was sliding up and down the signal spectrum. He was so absorbed in the circuitry that he nearly cracked his head open on the underside of the decoder box when the phone rang.

"Hello, this is Alex," he said, picking up the receiver after nearly half a dozen rings.

"Mr. Baines." The voice on the other end was female and more efficient than friendly. "This is the State Department Operations Center. Please hold for Ambassador Spencer."

Alex was both surprised and pleased. Howard "Spence" Spencer was Alex's friend and his mentor in the Foreign Service, but they hadn't spoken in three or four months. Spence was Ambassador to the Congo now, where a complex and bloody civil war had already taken millions of lives without any sign of slowing down. This was the kind of thing that could keep an American ambassador pretty busy. Spence had been a big part of Alex's life since his freshman year in college. The Ambassador had been serving a stint as the diplomat-in-residence at Georgetown during Alex's freshman year. It was because of his course on America in Africa that Alex had graduated with a degree in African studies. It was because of Spence that Alex had gone into the Peace Corps after college and then into the Foreign Service.

Getting into the Foreign Service was a brutally Darwinian process. The year Alex joined, more than 18,000 aspirants took the entrance exam. After a grueling series of tests and interviews, and a background investigation that seemed to reach back to kindergarten, 250 candidates eventually got job offers. Spence helped Alex navigate the exam process. And when he was up for his first assignment overseas, Spence had arranged for Alex to join him at his post in Khartoum.

"Parties, you are connected. Ops will drop."

"Hello, Alex. How's everything in the wild, wild West?" Spence had the kind of deep, resonant voice and vaguely upper-crust accent that was central casting's idea of what an American ambassador should sound like.

"Ambassador, it's good to hear from you. Hope life in the Congo is treating you well."

"As well as could be hoped for. We've been tremendously busy, of course, but I'm reasonably optimistic about the way things are going here. The government has won a few tactical victories and is probably in a good position to regain control of the river." Alex knew that reclaiming the Congo River, the enormous waterway that ran through the heart of the country, would give the legitimate army a real advantage in its battles with the bewildering array of rebel groups and paramilitaries running amok in the east.

"Good luck with that, Spence. The Congo is still my first love in Africa. What's going on there right now just breaks my heart. It's a huge job, and I'm happy as hell that you're the one doing it."

"Thanks, Alex. I appreciate that. This assignment has been a really humbling experience."

Alex could hear in Spence's voice the weight of the problems he faced. The Democratic Republic of the Congo was dying a slow and painful death, and there didn't seem to be anything anyone could do to stop it. "We'll talk more shop later. Tell me first, how's the family?"

Alex had grown close to the Spencer family over the years, and he had been a frequent guest at the Ambassador's Georgetown home. The Spencers' gracious Federal-style town house was a testament to old family money. By diplomatic title, ambassadors were both extraordinary and plenipotentiary, but they were still on the government pay scale.

Spence caught him up on developments in the family. They had stayed behind when he had left for Kinshasa so that his youngest daughter could finish high school in the States.

"And how's my goddaughter?" the Ambassador asked. He and Anah had not spent much time together, but it was Spence who had pulled the strings with the immigration service that had put the adoption on a fast track. A certain senior official in Homeland Security who owed Spence an enormous but unspecified favor had taken over the case and had been exceptionally generous in his interpretation of the government's requirements for documentation. "Uncle" Spence never forgot Christmas or Anah's birthday, and he kept a framed picture of her in his office alongside pictures of his own girls.

"She's perfect."

"School's going well?"

"Yep. She's pretty much caught up with her peer group, and she finishes third grade next week. Kids adapt very quickly. From the way she talks now, you'd never know that she didn't speak a word of English or French three years ago."

After a few more minutes catching up on their surrogate Foreign Service family and trading news about mutual friends who had drifted off to the far corners of the globe, Spence arrived at the point of the call.

"So, I understand you may have a job offer pending from our friends at Centrex."

"As it so happens, I do. I'm just about to send the letter accepting the position. I expect to be finished up here in about three weeks or so. I'm also assuming I have you to thank for the opportunity, Spence. So thank you. It means a lot to me. Your support through every step of this has meant a lot. I'm grateful."

"It's been my pleasure to help out where I could," Spence replied. "Truth is, though, I'm actually calling to ask you to tear up the letter you wrote Centrex and come work for me in Kinshasa."

"What happened? Did your consul get dengue fever or did your motor pool supervisor come down with beriberi?"

"I'm serious. I don't know if you heard about what happened to my Political Counselor, Julian Wells."

"No, I'm somewhat out of the news loop here." Alex knew Julian Wells by reputation as a hard charger on his way up in the Africa bureau hierarchy.

"Julian, I'm sorry to say, was lost in a helicopter crash in central

Congo three days ago. He was on the way back from negotiating with one of the rebel groups about the terms of transit for a UN aid convoy when the helicopter went down. We don't even know the exact location of the crash site."

"I'm sorry to hear about that. I didn't know Julian myself, but we certainly had friends in common. They spoke highly of him."

"He was a good man. And we will miss him. Heartless as it may sound, however, we must also replace him. There's too much going on right now in the Congo that's too important, and Julian's deputy is just too green to take over. Alex, you know more about this country than just about anyone else in the Service. You've got the Peace Corps experience in eastern Congo that no one can match. I want you to come to Kinshasa as my Political Counselor. The AF bureau sent me a list of available candidates, including some good officers, but I want you."

"I'm not sure what good I can do for you without a security clearance," Alex replied. "I couldn't even read my own reports."

"Things change, Alex, sometimes for the better. Do you remember Evelyn Calder?"

"Sure." Calder was the U.S. Ambassador in Ethiopia and a longtime friend of Spence's.

"Well, she is taking over as Senior Director for Africa at the National Security Council. With Evelyn at the White House and that ass Gifford she's replacing out of government service and looking for a K Street paycheck, my own level of influence has been kicked up several notches. On top of that, Congo is moving up the radar screen in Washington, and AF is desperate to fill this job fast. If I call in a few markers . . . and maybe write a few IOUs . . . I think I can get DS to approve your appeal. You'd get your clearances back, and you can come work for me. What do you say?"

"What about Anah?"

"No problem. You don't think I'd bring my goddaughter into harm's way, do you? The fighting is all in the east. Kinshasa is no more dangerous than Conakry. And the international school is very good. The oil and mining companies see to that. They have kids to educate too."

Alex didn't need to ask any more questions. Centrex had offered him a good job, but that's all it was—a job. Spence had just offered him the chance to return to something he loved, cutting-edge diplomacy and peacemaking. The Political Counselor job was traditionally the number three position in an embassy after the Ambassador and the Deputy Chief of Mission. In addition to being the Ambassador's chief adviser on all political issues in the country, the Counselor had an important role in shaping U.S. policy and engaging local authorities, journalists, politicians, diplomats, and opinion leaders of all stripes to advance American interests. It was a complex, fascinating, and utterly engaging set of responsibilities.

The Congo was a huge account, and engulfed in a fast-moving war involving troops from half a dozen countries. It was also a country that Alex both loved and feared for. In truth, it wasn't even really a choice.

"When do you need me?" Alex asked.

"On the morning flight."

5

The first intimation Marie had that there was anything wrong was a red hole about the size of a five-rand coin that appeared in the center of Faido Omokoko's chest. The expedition's head of security grunted as though he had been struck in the solar plexus with a fist rather than a rifle bullet before he crumpled to the ground. For just a moment the jungle was absolutely still. Then came the distinctive stuttering cough of an AK-47. Armed men appeared as if from nowhere along the length of the mining company column that stretched back several hundred meters from Marie's position in the vanguard.

Marie threw herself flat to the forest floor and crawled as deep as she could into the brush at the base of an enormous umbrella tree. The thorny vines and tall undulating tree roots afforded poor cover, but it was better than nothing. The shooting was not random. Every man with a rifle was gunned down in short order. Faido was the only one who was truly a friend, but Marie had come to know some of the other security guards as well and felt a familiar mix of sadness and anger as she watched from her hiding spot. Although this was not the first time she had seen men die, it never got easy.

To her untrained but experienced eyes, the militants seemed disciplined and precise, not like some of the other private armies laying waste to the Congo. Most of the soldiers had tools or pieces of pipe or what looked like faucets hanging around their necks. Talismans of some sort, she supposed.

In a few short minutes, it was all over. Marie saw Jack Karic crying in pain and fear as one of the assailants pressed a rifle barrel into the back of his neck and forced him to his knees. The soldiers herded the surviving team members together into a tight group that would be easier to control.

Marie clung to the faint hope that the thin foliage would camouflage her from the guerillas. She had little doubt what they would do to her and the other women on the team. Eastern Congo was rightly regarded as the rape capital of the world. Her right hand crept down to the razor-sharp jungle knife in a sheath strapped to her calf.

It didn't take long for the soldiers to spot her. One man trained a shotgun on her while two others pushed through the thorny branches and grabbed her ankles. Marie reached back for her knife and slashed ineffectually at the hands holding on to her boots. The soldiers pulled hard and dragged her roughly out from under the bush. She scraped painfully over the ground. One of the men grabbed the hand holding the knife and pinned it to a rock, forcing her fingers open. The blade fell to the ground.

Strong hands gripped the back of her field jacket and lifted Marie to her feet. She felt hands run quickly over her body, not in preparation for sexual assault but rather a quick pat down for concealed weapons. Grabbing her arms from behind, the soldiers frog-marched her toward a group of four older men who she suspected were the officers.

A slim man with close-cropped hair, gold-rimmed spectacles, and an air of authority stepped forward and turned to face her. His features were delicate. It was the face of an aspiring poet or art student.

Marie felt a stab of icy fear. She recognized her captor. This was Joseph Manamakimba. Of all of the Congo's many warlords, Manamakimba was the most infamous. It was his reputation for callous violence that made his first words so surprising.

"Do not worry, African sister," he said in a gentle, almost soothing voice. His French was smooth and elegant. "I know what you fear and it is not to be. You will find that we are not monsters. We cherish our sisters." Manamakimba gestured to the foot soldiers holding her arms and they released her.

"But not your brothers," Marie said. "You made my friend Faido's wife a widow today." Her speech was rushed and hurried, a function of the adrenaline still coursing through her system.

"I am sorry about your friend, Marie Tsiolo. He was armed and therefore a danger to my boys. My first duty is to them. His death was regrettable, but it was also unavoidable. In the meantime, I beg you not to worry. You will not be harmed." Manamakimba's smile was genuine, but there was a glint of the predator in his eyes.

"How do you know my name?"

"Uncle Joseph knows many things. I have many friends in interesting and unusual places who see things of interest to me and help me understand what is happening to our country. I assure you that I do not mean to do you harm."

While her situation was still precarious, Manamakimba's promise that she would not be violated loosened a knot that had been tightening in her stomach. Marie knew too many Congolese women who had suffered abuse at the hands of the guerillas. Those who survived were never the same. To her chagrin, Marie recognized what she was feeling as something akin to gratitude.

"What about my friends?" Marie looked over at Charlotte and Arlene.

"If you so wish it, sister, we will extend to them the same courtesies and protections as to you."

"I wish it."

"Very well." Manamakimba turned and began shouting out orders in Lingala. One of them was to bury the bodies of the dead. This small gesture of respect was another surprise.

Marie surveyed what was left of the team. Steve Wheeler was hurt with what looked like a bullet wound to his left leg.

Wallace Purcell was dead. He had twisted his knee the day they had set out from Sifa's village, and for the last three days, he'd been walking with the aid of a tree branch. In the shadows, it was likely that one of the guerillas had mistaken it for a rifle. Now he lay on his back with his jaw slack and his eyes lifeless. He had been shot in the throat. As she watched, two of the guerillas picked up Purcell's body and carried it into the jungle to be buried alongside the company's hired guns.

Marie was one of seven people the Hammer of God had taken hostage and the only Congolese. In theory, Jack Karic was in charge, but one look at him was enough to tell Marie that someone else was going to have to step up. Karic was sitting on a rock with his knees drawn up to his chest and a wide-eyed look of panic on his face. No doubt this was Jack's first experience with violent death. He was not dealing with it well.

The injury to Steve Wheeler was the first priority. The wounded took precedence over the dead.

"Let me take a look at your leg," Marie said, as she knelt to examine the injury. A stray bullet had carved a deep gash in his thigh. It was bleeding profusely and looked painful, but it did not appear life threatening. "I've seen worse. You should be all right if we can keep the wound from getting infected. How do you feel?"

"Like someone has just laid a hot poker across my leg," Wheeler replied through gritted teeth.

"Do we have the medical kit?" she asked the group. "Steve's injury needs to be cleaned and dressed."

"We've got nothing," Mike Tanner answered. "The medical supplies were with the porters, and they've disappeared along with all the gear."

Marie turned to one of the young paramilitaries standing guard over the group.

"We need bandages and medicine for our friend," she said in Lingala.

The young man looked at her silently and then shook his head. Alongside the tools in her backpack, Marie kept a change of clothes. She ripped a cotton shirt into strips and used it to bandage Wheeler's leg. The shirt was not sterile, but it was at least clean. The tough New Zealander sat still and quiet as Marie wrapped his leg. Beads of sweat on his forehead were the only indication of just how much pain he was in.

With the one immediate task accomplished, Marie was uncertain about what they should do next. Someone should probably say something, however, and it might as well be her. At least she knew the identity of their captors. Drawing herself up to her full height, she tried her best to project a confidence she did not feel. *Come on, damn it*, she thought, *you are the daughter and granddaughter of chiefs.* Her father would know what to do and what to say. He was a natural leader. Had he not been born a chief, he would have died one. That was just the kind of man he was. His blood ran in her veins, of course, but despite all her professional accomplishments, Marie had never felt that she measured up.

She cleared her throat.

"Ladies and gentlemen," she began, for lack of a better opening line. "Let me share with you the little I know about the people who are apparently holding us hostage." Marie made a sweeping gesture with her right hand, taking in most of the guerillas. "This is the Hammer of God, and that," she said, pointing discreetly at Manamakimba, "is Joseph Manamakimba. He has promised me that he has no intention to hurt us beyond what he has already done. The important thing now is to stay calm, stay together, and stay alive." She decided not to tell them that Manamakimba had known her name.

The surviving members of the survey team looked at her wordlessly. Some were clearly in shock; some seemed on the edge of making the foolish choice to run.

"Marie." It was Sven Norlund who broke the silence. "Did our new friend give you any indication of what he was after?"

"He didn't say. It may be about money. If the Hammer of God is trying to extort money from the company, then Manamakimba has a financial incentive to keep us alive." *At least until the ransom is paid,* she added silently.

Norlund's question seemed to open the floodgates, and suddenly nearly every member of the team was clamoring with questions, all except Karic, who was staring blankly into the middle distance.

"Hold on," said Marie. "Let's take things one step at a time and let's get ourselves organized. If Manamakimba decides to move us, we had better be ready. Charlotte, do we have any kind of communications gear?"

"Not a thing. We had a sat phone and two iridium handsets, but the soldiers took those. We're down to smoke signals and ESP."

"What about food and water?" Marie asked.

Among them, the Consolidated team had about ten full canteens of water and enough food to last two or three days at the most. They had just finished dividing the supplies equally among those left alive when Manamakimba returned. With a completely neutral expression, he looked over the preparations the team had been making. He also took a long look at Jack Karic. He seemed to know who he was.

"We have wounded," Marie said. "We need bandages, medicine, and clean water."

Manamakimba shrugged. "If I had these things, I would share them with you. Alas, I do not." The Hammer of God cocked his head and gave her an appraising look. "You have done well, little sister. Make sure your flock is ready to go in five minutes. We are moving on to camp. There will be no stragglers. I will personally shoot those who can't keep up."

Her flock? Marie had no desire to be thrust into any kind of leadership position. Having started down the road, however, there seemed no way to undo the new order of things on the survey team. *Welcome to upper management. Hell of a way to get a promotion.*

The next twenty-four hours were a blur, a forced march through the jungle with no food and little water.

After the first six hours, older and weaker members of the team started to flag from both the physical and psychological strain. Steve Wheeler hobbled along on a makeshift crutch. Each step was excruciatingly painful. The bandage on his leg was already soaked through with blood.

Although she was relatively young and in good shape, the forced march was taking a toll on Marie as well. Her legs and back ached, and her face was swollen from insect bites. Exhaustion coupled with the jungle's enervating humidity was slowing her thinking, and she could almost feel her brain turning to mush. It was getting hard to form coherent thoughts. Marie wanted desperately to lie down and close her eyes. *Just for thirty seconds,* she lied to herself.

After ten hours, Arlene Zimmerman tripped over a root and landed in a heap at the foot of a fig tree. She began to cry, as much, Marie understood, out of fear and frustration as out of pain. One of the soldiers pointed his rifle at her and looked at Manamakimba for orders. The rebel leader turned toward Marie with a questioning look on his face. *What are you going to do?* he seemed to be asking. Marie didn't know the answer. She walked over to the soldier pointing the gun at Arlene and pushed the point of his rifle up into the air. "That won't be necessary, child," she said in Lingala. In truth, the soldier was probably in his early twenties, hardly a child by the standards of a typical Congolese guerilla outfit. Marie was doing what she could, however, to establish that she was in charge of this situation. Next she reached for Arlene, taking her face in her hands and then holding the elderly scientist's head against her breast. Marie stroked her short gray hair. "It's okay, Arlene," she said. "We're gonna make it. It's just another ten minutes. It's okay. You can lean on my shoulder till we get there. It's just a little farther." None of this was true, but that hardly seemed important.

For lack of anything better to say, she repeated her reassurances in French and Lingala. Arlene spoke neither language, but Marie was speaking as much to the guerillas as to the American. *You do not need to kill her* was the message she hoped to send.

When Marie turned Arlene's face up to her own, the American's eyes were red and filled with tears, but she was once again in control. "Thank you, Marie," she said, before rising to her feet and retrieving the branch she had been using as a walking stick.

Jack wasn't so lucky. He had never recovered from the shock of the initial assault. The expedition's nominal leader could be utterly ruthless in negotiating a contract, but he had no experience with physical violence. At about the twelve-hour mark, Jack Karic sat down to die.

Steve Wheeler tried in a somewhat desultory fashion to pull Karic to his feet. Manamakimba walked toward them, cradling a pistol in one hand. A tall shirtless guerilla carrying a rifle walked alongside him. Marie hurried to Karic's side.

"Come on, Jack," she said, kneeling beside him in the mud. "You've got to get up. They're going to kill you if you don't."

"They're going to kill us all eventually, Marie. It might as well be now. We're all dead." Karic's voice was flat and his face was without affect. He seemed indifferent to his fate.

"You can't know that, Jack. Stay alive, keep moving, and pray for rescue. That's all you can do, but it beats being shot like a dog and left here beside the trail. Just a little farther." Although Marie understood that her embrace of Arlene had been instrumental in getting the elderly scientist back on her feet, she couldn't quite bring herself to touch Jack Karic. This was the man who had threatened her village with extinction and used that threat to gain a measure of control over her. On some level, Karic seemed to recognize this.

"I'm sorry, Marie," he said.

About what? Marie wondered silently. *About failing his colleagues? About lying down to die? About threatening my village and my family?*

"It's okay," she said.

"Is it really?" Manamakimba asked from over her shoulder, his lips not more than six inches from her ear. Marie jumped nervously. Manamakimba continued in English and addressed himself to Karic. "Is it okay, Mr. Karic?"

"No, I suppose it's not."

"You suppose?"

"No, it's not," Karic corrected himself. He pulled himself onto his knees and made as if to stand. The guerilla leader pushed him back down.

"John Karic, you stand accused of rape and murder, the rape of our dear lady Africa, and the murder of untold numbers of her children." Manamakimba pulled his glasses down close to the end of his nose, giving him the air of a schoolteacher. "How do you plead?"

"Does it matter?" Karic asked.

"Probably not." Manamakimba raised his pistol and pointed it at Karic's temple.

"You don't have to do this," Marie said, moving to place herself between Karic and Manamakimba. The young soldier at the guerilla leader's side used his rifle to bar her way. "Please," she added, looking Manamakimba in the eye.

Karic looked up at Marie. "I'm sorry, Marie," he repeated.

"You already said that, Mr. Karic," Manamakimba observed patiently. "Do you think you can be a little more . . . specific?"

Karic looked down. "What we did to you—what I did to you—was wrong. I'm sorry. I truly am. I am not a deeply religious man, but I do believe in God, Marie. I would ask for your absolution."

Manamakimba cocked his pistol. The message was plain enough: *Time's up.*

"You are forgiven, Jack," Marie said, and wondered if it was true.

The sound of the single gunshot was unbearably loud.

6

Alex did not leave the next day, and Spence had not actually expected it. Moving between countries and cultures was an inevitable fact of Foreign Service life, but it was still enormously dislocating and logistically complicated. Life before Anah had been much simpler. Alex had had few material attachments and was free to pull up stakes at a moment's notice. The place where he lived at any particular time was little more than his address. Anah changed all that. In building a home for his daughter, Alex had inevitably accumulated a houseful of possessions. Moreover, his was no longer the only voice that mattered in planning for the future. After hanging up with Spence, Alex spent a few hours thinking about how best to raise the issue with Anah of an imminent move to Kinshasa.

Sunday breakfast was always pancakes, with Alex and Anah doing the cooking together.

"Anah, there's something I need to talk to you about," Alex began, as his daughter was tearing through her second stack of silver-dollar pancakes with grim determination.

"What is it, Daddy?" Anah asked through a mouthful of pancakes.

"I got a call last night from Uncle Spence. He wants us to move to Kinshasa so that I can work for him there."

"Okay." Anah seemed completely undisturbed by this news.

"It means leaving right away, honey, like, in a couple of days."

Anah's eyes narrowed and she put her fork down on her plate.

"What about Maine?" she asked accusingly. "Is this going to mess that up?"

"Maybe a little," Alex admitted. "You can still go, but I may not be able to spend any time with you and Grandma this summer. Mrs. Mabinty can take you there, and I'll ask her if she'd be willing to stay with you and Grandma at the house."

"Will I stay the whole summer?"

"Do you want to? You don't have to."

"No, I want to."

The thought of nearly three months separated from Anah was depressing, but Alex knew that she would be happier in Brunswick than in Kinshasa for the summer months, especially as he had no idea what kind of hours he would be working. It would be different once school started in the fall and she had friends and activities.

"I'll Skype with you every day," Alex offered, somewhat nonplussed that his daughter seemed to accept the idea of a summer apart so readily.

"That'd be nice, Daddy. Billy promised me that he'd take me camping this summer, and Uncle Leo said I could go out on the boat with him and catch lobsters. I don't really like lobster, but the traps are cool and sometimes there's crabs inside too."

Alex's heart filled with love for his little girl, and he felt it press against his chest as though it had suddenly grown in size. The smile he offered her had a slight tinge of melancholy.

"I'm going to be sad without you, sweetie."

"I know you will," she said innocently.

Alex's farewell call on his ambassador was similarly easy. The Ambassador, a veteran Africa hand named Stephen Fry, already knew about Spence's offer. Ambassadors were usually deferential to each other and rarely went poaching personnel without permission. Although he had a quick and incisive mind, Fry—a short, round man with a bulbous nose and receding hairline—looked more like an insurance adjustor than a U.S. Ambassador. He had to crane his neck at a sharp angle as he stood to shake hands and congratulate Alex on what both of them agreed was a tremendous opportunity.

The next day, a cable came from Washington announcing that the Bureau of Diplomatic Security had reinstated Alex R. Baines's Top Secret clearance, including access to Special Compartmentalized Information, the most sensitive human and technical intelligence. Although written in dry bureaucratic language, the memo oozed grudging reluctance from every line. There were caveats. Alex's clearances were interim and subject to immediate revocation at the discretion of the DS Assistant Secretary. Moreover, the clearances were not automatically transferable. His eligibility for a Top Secret clearance would be reviewed upon completion of his assignment in Kinshasa. He had never seen a message like it. Department cables were negotiated documents. The language reflected, he understood, a bloody interdepartmental battle that Alex's side had won, but only by a whisker.

The following days were a blur of activity, preparing the consulate for his departure, supervising the pack-out of his household effects, and finding someone to buy the twenty-year-old Land Rover he had been driving since the week he had arrived in Conakry. Four jam-packed days after his conversation with Spence, Alex drove Anah and Mrs. Mabinty to the airport. As he had suspected, Mrs. Mabinty had jumped at the chance to spend the summer with Anah and Alex's mother in Maine. The grossly overweight housekeeper had packed a heavy carry-on bag full of Guinean treats, including chips made of fried taro root, dried plantains, and an enormous plastic tub of peanut soup.

"U.S. Customs will never let you bring that into the country," Alex warned her.

"Don't worry," Mrs. Mabinty replied confidently. "I'm going to eat it on the plane."

He hugged his daughter tightly at the gate and kissed her forehead. Anah hugged him back fiercely. Her eyes were shining with tears that she refused to shed, and for a moment Alex thought about tossing their tickets to Augusta in the trash and booking them both on his flight to Kinshasa. He knew, however, that that was selfish. He was thinking more of his feelings than of Anah's.

"Take good care of Grandma and Mrs. Mabinty, okay?"

"I will. I'll miss you, Daddy."

There was a lump in his throat, but Alex put on a brave face for his daughter.

"I love you, Anah."

The next day Alex was back at the airport, this time to catch his own Air France flight to Kinshasa. The four-and-a-half-hour flight was uneventful, but when the pilot announced that they had been cleared for descent to Kinshasa airport, Alex felt a sharp, electric thrill. He was getting back into the game.

Conakry was a city of some two million people, but it was a small town in comparison with Kinshasa. The arrival terminal at N'djili International Airport was packed wall-to-wall with a mass of humanity that moved—if it was moving at all—in currents and tides rather than with any kind of linear purpose. It was just how he remembered it when he had landed on the Sabena flight from Brussels as a green Peace Corps volunteer more than ten years ago.

Almost magically, the crowds parted in front of him and Alex was confronted by two Congolese men, one short and heavyset, the second tall and almost comically thin. The shorter man was wearing a garish Hawaiian shirt with one too many buttons open at the top, khakis, and leather sandals. He also sported a thick gold chain around his neck and a gaudy gold watch on his wrist. The second man was dressed simply in jeans and a plain white T-shirt. His clothes hung on his bony frame as if from a wire hanger.

The shorter man smiled broadly and stuck out his hand.

"Mr. Baines," he said. It wasn't really a question. Alex was almost certainly the only white person in the terminal.

"Alex. Are you with the Embassy?" Alex shook hands with the two men. The taller man's hands were thickly calloused like a farmer's.

"Yes," said the shorter man, who was clearly the boss. He fished an embassy ID card out of his pocket to establish his bona fides. In truth, his flawless American accent was almost as good as the ID. "My name is Leonard. I'm your fixer."

Everywhere in the world, American diplomats relied heavily on the guidance, experience, and local knowledge of Foreign Service Nationals. In the more chaotic environments, FSNs were essential for helping the American staff maneuver through complicated and unfamiliar bureaucracies. The practice was known as "fixing." A good fixer could minimize, but not eliminate, the arbitrary inefficiencies inherent in the third world.

Leonard had Alex give his claim checks to the tall man along with five dollars in cash for the dollops of baksheesh that would ensure his bags made it from the airplane to his new house on time and intact.

They swam through the crowd to immigration control, where Leonard led Alex to a window on one side with a sign above it in faded yellow letters that said DIPLOMATIQUE. The unsmiling middle-aged man in the booth looked at his passport suspiciously before applying a sudden flurry of rubber stamps to the inside pages.

"Welcome to Kinshasa, Mr. Alex," Leonard said, when they were outside the terminal.

"Thanks, Leonard. It's good to be back."

"You've been here before?"

"I was a Peace Corps volunteer in Goma before I joined State. We used to come in and out through Kinshasa, and the volunteers in the east would take R & R here."

Leonard seemed impressed. "Goma, huh? Things have been very bad out there over the last years. It's gotten much worse since the *geno-cidaires* came."

The *genocidaires* were Rwandan Hutus who got their name from their role as the perpetrators of the 1994 genocide. When the Tutsi had retaken power, thousands of Hutu had fled across the border into eastern Congo, which they used as a base camp for their proxy war against the new Tutsi-dominated government in Kigali. The *genocidaires* had also fought against their Congolese hosts, and the fighting they instigated in the Congo's far east had tipped the country into civil war.

"When I was there, it wasn't as bad as it is now. Mine was the last class of Peace Corps volunteers in the Congo. It was just starting to get really dangerous. I've kept in touch with some friends there over the years, and I've tried to keep on top of what's happening. It's enough to break your heart."

"It is that, Mr. Alex. But the Congolese people still have a lot of heart left in them. You'll see. Come on. We're parked over here."

Alex didn't need to be told which car it was. The enormous Suburban sitting heavy on its wheels from the armored plates that Alex knew were welded in the door panels practically screamed "U.S. Embassy."

Leonard drove like a lunatic, weaving in and out of Kinshasa's incredible traffic, which mixed cars, trucks, buses, bicycles, scooters, pedestrians, and various forms of animal transport into a single anarchic mass. It was impossible to tell from the traffic alone whether the Congolese drove on the left or right. All the while, Leonard kept up a running monologue on Congolese politics, the U.S. Embassy, and Alex's great good fortune in working for "Ambassador Spence."

"It sounds to me like you have spent some time in the States," Alex observed, when Leonard paused for a brief moment to catch his breath and dodge a motorcycle that seemed as though it were being driven by fifty chickens.

"Graduated from the University of Michigan in economics. I had to come back when my father got sick. Now I'm head of my family. Not a position I can easily fill from Ann Arbor. I miss the U.S., of course, but home is where the family is."

Leonard's colloquial American-accented English was so good it was almost disconcerting. Alex could easily see him at a frat party in Michigan with a plastic cup of beer in one hand and an arm around a pretty sorority girl.

Leonard pushed the Suburban through a gap in the traffic that Alex would have sworn was barely large enough for a Volkswagen Beetle, passing an open army truck carrying heavily armed teenage conscripts.

"What's the security situation like?" Alex asked, nodding toward the truck.

"Not so bad in Kinshasa, at least during the day. Outside of town is something else. Don't go anywhere alone. Don't go anywhere without armor." Leonard rapped his knuckles affectionately on the thick Plexiglas fitted over the Suburban's side-panel windows. "If a cop tries to pull you over, don't stop. At a minimum, it's a shakedown. More likely, it's a kidnapping attempt. Don't kid yourself into believing they're just enforcing traffic laws." He waved vaguely at the absolute anarchy around them.

It was about a forty-five-minute ride in bumper-to-bumper chaos from the airport to Gombe, Kinshasa's diplomatic district. The American mission was as immediately identifiable by the concrete jersey barriers that circled the building as by the enormous flag that flew overhead or the Great Seal that decorated the gate. The Embassy building dominated the neighborhood, a pink granite monster surrounded by dingy three-story concrete-block houses. A long line of Congolese families snaked around the compound, waiting for their opportunity to interview for a visa.

Leonard pulled the Suburban through a gap in the jersey barriers and stopped in front of an enormous metal gate painted a bright yellow. He killed the engine and popped the hood. Three local guards in sky blue short-sleeved shirts and dark blue slacks searched the car for explosives. One walked around the vehicle with a mirror on a pole looking at the undercarriage. A second checked out the engine while the third opened the rear hatch and shone a flashlight into the wheel well. Two black-clad members of the Special Police stood to one side with AK-47s held at port arms.

When they got the all clear, Leonard started the engine. The heavy gate rolled open, and Leonard drove forward fifteen feet before stopping at a second gate. Only when the first gate closed behind him did the second one open.

"Here we are," Leonard said, as he pulled through the gate and onto the driveway in front of the chancery building. "Home sweet home."

A slim Asian man in a light charcoal gray suit and maroon tie was waiting for Alex at the front door.

"I'm Mark Fong," he said, as they shook hands. Fong looked like he was barely out of school. Kinshasa was likely his first tour of duty. "I'm your deputy in the political section. Good to have you on board."

"Even better to be here," Alex replied. "I'm looking forward to getting to work."

"That may be sooner than you had planned. Ordinarily I'd show you around and let you get settled, but I'm afraid we have something of a situation. The Ambassador wants you to come upstairs first thing."

Mark handed Alex a laminated Embassy ID on a cheap metal lanyard. His picture and name were framed by a gold border, indicating that he was cleared for classified information and had unrestricted access to all parts of the mission. His ID badge in Conakry had had a blue border. He slipped the lanyard around his neck.

Now just don't blow it, he thought.

The Ambassador's office was on the fourth floor, behind layers of security that included a Marine Security Guard who controlled a heavy mag-lock door from behind a screen of bulletproof glass, a badge reader in the elevator that activated the button for the fourth floor, and a cipher lock on the door to the executive suite.

The Front Office was spacious and plush, with thick carpets and leather armchairs. Two secretaries sat at desks positioned just in front of the private offices for the Ambassador and Deputy Chief of Mission. The secretaries, both overweight middle-aged women with short gray hair and glasses, looked as if they could have been sisters.

"Hello, Peggy," Alex said to the Ambassador's secretary. She looked up from the spreadsheet on her computer screen and smiled when she saw who it was.

"Well, look who we have here. Come give your Aunt Peggy a kiss." With a visible effort she got up from the overmatched Aeron chair and hugged Alex. Peggy Walker had been Spence's assistant for the better part of twenty years. She went everywhere with him and did just about everything for him. Alex had known her since his first week in the Service and had tremendous respect for both her sheer competence and her obvious devotion to Spence.

"It's good to have you back, Alex," Peggy said when she finally let go. Her eyes were shiny with tears. "I'm glad that you're getting another chance."

"Thanks, Peggy. It's good to see you too." Alex was not surprised that Peggy knew about his troubles with DS. Ambassadors had few secrets from their secretaries.

Peggy sat down heavily in the Aeron chair, which let out a thin squeak of protest. Back in command of her desk, she was all business. "The Ambassador is expecting you, Mr. Baines," she said. "Please go in."

Spence was sitting at a long oak conference table deep in conversation with a group of half a dozen people when Alex entered. On the center of the table, he could see a detailed map of what looked like a stretch of the Congo River. Most of the group at the table wore conventional business attire, but the one woman in the room was wearing an army uniform and the man next to her was dressed in what looked like a white linen suit with a red silk tie emblazoned with some sort of crest. This was definitely not standard State Department issue. The body language of the group was tense. Only the slight man in the tropical suit looked unruffled.

Even so, Spence smiled broadly when he saw Alex enter the room. He stood up and gave Alex a firm handshake, clasping Alex's shoulder with his left hand. At just about an inch over six feet tall, Alex was not a small man, but Spence was at least two inches taller and built like a bear. It had been more than a year since they had seen each other and Alex was struck by how much Spence had aged. His hair was now more gray than black and there were deep creases around his eyes.

"Spence, you look like hell."

"You don't know the half of it, Alex," he laughed, shedding at least five years in doing so. "Let me introduce you to the team."

Turning to the group at the table, Spence announced in his deep ambassadorial baritone: "Colleagues, allow me to present Alex Baines, the new head of the political section and a dear friend. Alex, I think you know Bob Jeffries, my DCM." Alex and Jeffries had worked together on a crisis action team in Washington following a failed coup attempt in Uganda.

Alex remembered Jeffries as a technically competent but cautious officer, more inclined to focus on potential danger than opportunity.

Alex nodded at Jeffries. "It's good to see you again, Bob," he said. "You too."

"Next to him," Spence continued, "is Deborah Fessler, our Defense Attaché." The Attaché was a brassy blonde with the broad shoulders and compact build of a power lifter. The eagles on her shoulders marked her as a full colonel.

"On the other side of the table, we have our Station Chief, Jonah Keeler; our Regional Security Officer, Rick Viggiano; and Henri Saillard from Consolidated Mining."

Keeler was a slim black man who looked to be in his mid-forties. He wore stylish tortoiseshell glasses that gave him a vaguely professorial air. In contrast, Viggiano looked like an enforcer for the mob, with thickly muscled arms, slicked-back hair, and a bushy mustache that was vintage seventies. His hands were the size of dinner plates. Saillard was the dandy in the white suit. He sported a carefully trimmed goatee, and his dark hair contrasted sharply with his Nordic blue eyes. His presence in the conversation was something of a surprise. Not only was he an outsider, he was clearly a foreigner, French or Belgian Alex guessed by his name. His presence would necessarily restrict what it was that the group could discuss.

Spence no doubt had his reasons for wanting him in on the conversation. It was his mission and therefore his call. Alex moved to stand behind the one empty seat at the table. "Looks like I've arrived at something of an interesting time."

"That's for damn sure," Deborah Fessler said without irony.

"Alex, I'm glad you're here," Spence said, as he sat back in his seat at the head of the table. "We've got a problem that we need your help with. Seems a survey team working with Consolidated Mining got jumped out in the bush by the Hammer of God. They're holding hostages, including as many as six Americans."

"Hammer of God? Pretty theatrical name," Alex commented. He had never heard of the group. The international press rarely covered developments in the Congo, and the Hammer of God had yet to make the *New York Times*. Alex had his clearances back, but it would still take time to get up to speed. There were new players on the scene since the last time he had been in the country.

"Maybe a bit self-aggrandizing," the colonel replied, "but not entirely undeserved. The Hammer is the private army of Joseph Manamakimba, who is a no-fooling sociopath with a history of murdering hostages. His soldiers don't just follow him, they worship Manamakimba as a living god. They are supposed to have some kind of magical protection in combat, and they win most of the time so who's to say it isn't true? In all seriousness, Manamakimba has some skill. The Hammer is still a paramilitary and its organization is somewhat ad hoc, but the officers seem to know what they're doing. We think Manamakimba has had some professional training, maybe from the Cubans in Angola."

Spence motioned for Alex to sit. "Colonel Fessler and Jonah can bring you up to speed on the situation."

The colonel pointed to a spot on the map near a bend in the Congo River. This is the last known position of the Consolidated team. Intelligence from intercepts of Hammer of God communications indicates that the hostages are being held in the same area.

"We can't get any pictures through the jungle canopy, but the level of chatter is consistent with a force of approximately thirty fighters. If Manamakimba himself is there, and we've listened in on a couple of conversations that lead us to believe he is, this is likely a group of some of his toughest, most experienced jungle fighters."

"What do we know about Manamakimba? What kind of man are we dealing with here?" It was essential, Alex believed, never to forget that you were negotiating with a person, not an organization or a country. Understanding that individual, what he valued, how he viewed the world, and what kind of personal stake he had in the discussions was often the difference between success and failure. Spence had taught him that.

It was the CIA Station Chief who responded. "In truth, Manamakimba is something of a cipher. He's been one of our top targets for intelligence gathering over the last couple of years, but we haven't been able to get close to anyone close to him. The intelligence is almost all second- or thirdhand. We don't know where he's from, what his goals are, or even what he was doing before the Congo went to hell. We do know that he's smart, ballsy, and successful. This war was made for a guy like him."

Keeler was refreshingly matter-of-fact about what he did not know. This was not a common attribute among station chiefs.

"We don't even have a particularly good picture of him," Keeler continued, handing Alex a red folder with a SECRET cover sheet. Inside was the standard Agency bio on Manamakimba with a slightly blurry head shot that looked like it might have been a passport or visa photo. Even in the fuzzy photo, however, Alex could see that Joseph Manamakimba was strikingly handsome. He did not look like a mass murderer, but the scant text of the biography painted a different picture.

"The guy hardly looks like Genghis Khan," Alex observed.

"No contest," Keeler replied. "Manamakimba would make the khan look like the social secretary at a church picnic."

"Has he made any demands at this point?"

"Yes, he's asked for thirty-five million dollars and the complete withdrawal of UN forces and all Western oil and mining companies from eastern Congo."

"That's interesting."

"Ain't it?"

"Is it possible that Manamakimba was deliberately targeting this group? That he didn't just stumble across them in the jungle by chance?"

"What are you getting at, Alex?" Spence asked.

"What he's asking for is impossible . . . and all out of proportion to the leverage he has," Alex explained. "According to our Agency friends, Manamakimba is smart and effective, so it seems unlikely that he doesn't understand that."

"So?'

"So, it means that this is a political act and not opportunistic blackmail. It sounds to me like he's trying to draw attention to a cause rather than effecting a particular outcome."

Alex looked across the table at Henri Saillard. "Have you had other run-ins with the Hammer of God recently? Consolidated Mining is the largest operator in eastern Congo. It's logical that you would be a magnet for Manamakimba if he's targeting the extractive industry."

"No," Saillard replied dismissively. "This is an isolated incident perpetrated by a greedy thug. This is a criminal not a political act."

"I wouldn't be so certain of that," Jonah Keeler chimed in. "What Alex is saying makes a lot of sense to me. There have been a spate of attacks on mining operations in the same area where the Consolidated team was hit. Nothing definitive links the other attacks to the Hammer of God, but it wouldn't surprise me at all if they were responsible. I suppose we'll find out soon enough what Manamakimba's after."

"How so?" Alex asked.

"They've asked for a parley," Fessler explained. "Based on the demands on the table, we don't think that there's a deal to be had, but there may be a chance to buy some time. There's a group of Pakistani UN peacekeepers moving into position to execute a raid to secure the release of the hostages. They need at least twenty-four hours to deploy, however, and Manamakimba is threatening to shoot one hostage every hour beginning at dawn if we don't meet his terms. We're hoping negotiations can go on long enough for us to get the Pakistanis in position. It's a gamble, but it's likely the only chance this group has."

Alex could envision the risks, not only for the hostages but for the negotiating team as well. A hostage rescue operation was complex and difficult under the best of circumstances. Factor in the lack of operational intelligence and the peacekeepers' lack of experience and appropriate training, and the most likely outcome of this exercise would be massive loss of life on all sides. It could work, though, with the right negotiator. The negotiator would need to string Manamakimba along, selling him on the idea that there was a deal on offer if he kept talking a little longer. It was a difficult and dangerous task that fell somewhere between the role of bait and sacrificial lamb. Alex did not envy whoever drew the short straw for that assignment.

"Who's doing the actual negotiations?" Alex asked Spence. "The mining company or the UN?"

"I thought that was clear," the Ambassador replied. "You are."

7

The first obstacle was the helicopter. The Congo was vast, about the size of Western Europe, and there were few paved roads. Air transport was the only practicable means of traveling the long distances. In central and eastern Congo, most of the air links were controlled by UNSAF, the unfortunate acronym for the UN Security Assistance Force that was inevitably mispronounced "unsafe." An UNSAF charter plane flew Alex, Jonah Keeler, Rick Viggiano, and a few of the RSO's local security people to Bumba in north central Congo. From there, they would have to take a Russian Mi-8 helicopter to the UN resupply base near the confluence of the Congo and Aruwimi Rivers. The tough and reliable Mi-8 was the workhorse of African air transport.

For Alex, the challenge was not a fear of flying, or even a fear of crashing. It was a fear of ghosts. Since Darfur, the sight and sound of helicopters had been enough to trigger panic attacks and flashbacks to the butchery in Camp Riad. Dr. Branch had helped him understand these episodes as symptoms of an underlying condition rather than as a sign of weakness or moral failure. PTSD was a subtle disease that responded to changes in the environment. It was possible to identify the triggers, however, and develop effective coping strategies. Yoga was part of Alex's regimen. So was avoidance. The Sea Knight flight out of Western Sudan was the last time he had been on a helicopter.

Deplaning, he could see three Mi-8s clustered on the runway. In repose, the massive rotor blades drooped precariously close to the tarmac. It was only when they were spinning that the blades would straighten out and stabilize into a flat disk. As the team walked across the tarmac toward the helicopters, the rotors of the lead Mi-8 began to turn, cutting through the humid air with a characteristic rhythmic thrum.

Alex's heart rate soared and a trickle of sweat ran down the back of his neck. He could hear his breathing grow heavier and faster, and he made a conscious effort to control it. The yoga was supposed to help with this. He tried *ujjayi pranayama*, a technique that integrated breath control with low-frequency vocalizations. It was almost a humming sound, and Alex hoped that the rotor noise would mask it from his colleagues. The breathing exercises helped. His pulse rate dropped slightly, and the surging sense of panic began to recede somewhat. Just in case, he patted his pocket to make sure that the plastic bottle of Zoloft was still there. That was his insurance policy.

As Alex climbed through the narrow hatch into the Mi-8, his chest tightened and it became harder to concentrate on the *pranayama*. It felt as though there was not enough oxygen in the aircraft's cramped interior.

The Mi-8 was primarily a cargo carrier, and seating was limited to a bench made of canvas-strapped aluminum tubing welded to the hull. Alex took a seat and buckled up the restraints. He concentrated on his breathing and struggled to maintain an outward appearance of equanimity. Jonah Keeler leaned over in his direction and said something that Alex did not catch. He nodded in agreement, hoping that the Station

Chief would leave it at that. It was evidently an adequate response, as Jonah turned to his other side to talk to one of the UNSAF officers traveling with them.

The rotor volume increased, and the aircraft shuddered slightly as it lost contact with the ground. As they rose up, Alex looked out of one of the small portholes at the ground below. Rather than verdant jungle, his mind's eye saw a blood red desert and Janjaweed horsemen riding with leveled lances. He knew it wasn't real, but the image below him was so powerful and haunting that he pulled up hard against the restraints. The webbing dug into his shoulders.

He looked away from the window and bit the inside of his cheek hard enough to draw blood. The pain helped to beat back the vision of the past. Without conscious thought, he reached for the bottle of Xanax in his pocket, grasping the top lightly with two fingers. The flight would be so much easier if he was mildly sedated. The side effects of the drug included irritability, memory problems, and drowsiness. None of these were particularly attractive attributes to acquire in advance of negotiations with a homicidal sociopath. Instead, he took a picture of Anah out of his shirt pocket. It was her most recent school picture, and she was sitting in front of a plain blue background smiling at the camera.

Alex held his daughter's picture in the palm of his hand, stealing occasional glances at it throughout the eighty-minute flight. But it was not until he was back on solid ground at the UN peacekeepers' advance base on the shores of the Aruwimi River that he felt fully in control.

The normally sleepy outpost was bustling. The UN soldiers had already exchanged their sky blue berets for jungle-pattern Kevlar helmets. The young Pakistani conscripts who had arrived in the Congo as peacekeepers had been told to prepare for war.

This was as close to the rendezvous point as they could get by air. Manamakimba had been clear that he would shoot at any helicopters approaching his camp. According to the CIA assessment, the guerillas had collected just enough shoulder-fired missiles to make the threat credible.

There was only one road upriver, and it was about an eight-hour drive from the UN camp to the bend that Manamakimba had identified as the meeting place. The peacekeepers-turned-warriors would give the negotiators a two-hour head start and a total of six hours from first contact in which to make a deal. At zero hour, and assuming as nearly everyone did that the negotiations would fail, the Pakistanis would assault the camp in strength and, at least according to the plan, secure the freedom of both the hostages and the negotiators.

The negotiating team traveled in a convoy of five lightly armored Toyota Land Cruisers. The UN's fully armored Humvees were significantly heavier and tended to sink up to their axles in river mud.

Alex rode shotgun in the lead vehicle. The driver, Nduku, was a shift supervisor on the Embassy's local guard force and a former paramilitary from an outfit that had battled frequently with the Hammer of God. Viggiano liked to have at least a few people on his payroll who knew something about killing. Two armed Pakistani soldiers sat in the back, Sergeant Irfan Chaudry and Private Ali Sharif. To Alex's chagrin, the head of the UN operation had assigned them to Alex as his personal bodyguards. Neither looked old enough to shave, and their oversize helmets merely exaggerated their youthful appearance. The Pakistanis were armed with wicked-looking Heckler & Koch G3 assault rifles. On the seat next to him, Nduku had an auto-racing magazine and a chocolate bar. In a fight with the weapons at their disposal, Alex would have put his money on Nduku.

Chaudry and Sharif took their responsibilities seriously, however, and Alex was glad of the company. It kept him from brooding too much about either the upcoming encounter with Manamakimba or the unsettling vision of Sudan he had seen through the helicopter window.

Alex popped Miriam Makeba's jazzy *Pata Pata* into the Land

Cruiser's CD player. Pretty soon, Chaudry and Sharif were bobbing their heads in time to the rhythms sung in the soft but powerful voice of South Africa's folk legend.

For the next few hours, the conversation wandered widely over the usual topics of general interest to young men: family, sports, food, and girls. Even as he was chatting idly with Nduku and the UN soldiers, however, a good part of Alex's mental energy was occupied with the task in front of him. He sifted through the variables, looking for an angle or an edge, anything that might improve the prospects for success. Risk could not be avoided, but it could be managed. Having a daughter, he discovered, had changed the way he thought about risk. The risks he took for himself he was now taking for Anah as well. If the worst came to it, his brother had agreed to be Anah's guardian, and Alex's will was up-to-date and on file with the State Department's central personnel office. It would be better for all concerned, he reasoned, if that option remained theoretical.

The road they were traveling followed a rambling route through mostly dense jungle. When the road intersected a river, there was often a small village, usually nothing more than a scattering of huts. Twice they drove through villages that had been pillaged by one or more of eastern Congo's multitude of armed groups. One village looked as though it had been abandoned for months. The jungle was already moving in to reclaim the land that had been cleared for crops. In the next village, however, thin wisps of smoke wafted into the air from huts that had only recently been burned to the ground. There was a lull in the conversation as Alex and his companions considered the significance of this particular portent.

About a kilometer from the rendezvous point, an armed soldier stepped into the middle of the road and waved for the convoy to stop. Alex had to look closely to see the other paramilitaries waiting expectantly in the jungle on either side of the road. This was the first potential tipping point. If Manamakimba was intent on provoking a major confrontation with the UN, wiping out the convoy would be a good place to begin. The soldier standing in the road with his arm out-stretched like some kind of traffic cop had his rifle slung across his back. He was wearing a black tank top and jungle camouflage pants tucked into heavy combat boots. The handle of an impressively large knife protruded from one of the boots. Sweat glistened on his shaved head.

Most striking, however, was what seemed to be a kitchen faucet dangling around the guerilla's neck from a piece of manila rope.

"Nduku, what's with the plumbing supplies?" Alex asked the driver. Having fought for years in the jungles of eastern Congo before deciding to peddle his trade to the other side of the security equation, the former irregular was a wealth of information on the Congo's myriad paramili-tary outfits.

"Magic," Nduku answered. "All the Hammer of God fighters wear them. Manamakimba himself has blessed each totem. It makes the wearer immune from bullets. This is true. I swear it is. I have seen it myself. The bullets go right through them and leave no mark."

Nduku crossed himself reflexively as he spoke.

Alex had experience in Sudan negotiating with warlords and their subchiefs. It was always tricky and the consequences for getting it wrong could be severe. When the guerilla approached the jeep, Alex had to open the door to speak. The windows in even semi-armored cars do not roll down. After the air-conditioned comfort of the Land Cruiser, the jungle air was fetid and humid with a pervasive odor of rot and decay.

"You are the Americans?" The soldier spoke in Lingala rather than French.

"Yes, we are," Alex replied in the same language. In his Peace Corps days, Lingala had been the language of choice for communicating across tribal lines. Like most trade languages, it was relatively simple and easy to pick up. Alex's Lingala was nearly as good as his French.

"We walk from here. You come alone. No others. No guns."

Without looking away from the guerilla, Alex spoke in English to his Pakistani bodyguards. "Boys, I'm going to get out of the car. I want you behind me and to one side. Keep your rifles in your hands but don't point them at anyone. Keep some distance between yourselves so he can't target you both."

The Hammer of God fighter stepped back when Alex and the UN soldiers got out of the car. The guerilla was built like a wrestler, but he was shorter than Alex. Instead of looking down at the American seated in the Land Cruiser, he now had to look up. It was a subtle shift, but the dynamic was clearly different. Similarly, the Pakistani soldiers visibly under his command meant that, at least as far as the guerilla was concerned, Alex was now armed. Alex leaned forward slightly to underscore the man's failure to intimidate him with a show of force. "*Te*," he said, using the Lingala word for "no."

"Let me explain to you how this is going to work. We are here to secure the release of our people from your custody. These are the cars in which we will transport them to safety. Refusing to allow them through indicates to me that Mr. Manamakimba is not serious about reaching an agreement. If that is the case, we should turn around and leave now. If that's not true, then the cars are coming with us. These men," he said, inclining his head in the direction of Chaudry and Sharif, "are my personal bodyguards. They will not leave my side. Mr. Manamakimba is expecting us and I believe he would strongly prefer us to be alive."

There was a look of uncertainty in the guerilla's eyes as he wavered between two very different decisions. Grudgingly, he stepped aside and gestured to Alex to follow him. The tightness in Alex's chest eased as he took a deep, controlled breath. The approach he had chosen had been a calculated risk, but a real one nevertheless.

The soldier who had only moments ago been threatening Alex stepped into the jungle and emerged riding a Kawasaki dirt bike with a noisy two-stroke engine. Without a word, the guerilla gunned the engine and took off down the riverside road. Nduku followed.

They bounced down the rutted road for slightly more than a kilometer. Suddenly the jungle opened up on both sides into a wide, flat clearing. Large, dun-colored canvas tents stood in a neat row on the far side of the clearing. The small convoy of white Land Cruisers parked alongside the road. The Americans and their UNSAF minders got out of the cars and stretched surreptitiously to work out the kinks from the long and uncomfortable trip. Nduku stayed behind the wheel. Alex took the opportunity to survey the camp.

Guerilla fighters were engaged in a variety of tasks. Some were standing guard on the camp perimeter. Some were cleaning their weapons. A few were sleeping in hammocks strung between trees. Many had a faucet, a piece of copper pipe, or some other mundane tool of the plumbing trade hanging around their necks. Most of those carrying guns looked to be adults, but Alex saw a number of children working in the camp. One group, in which the oldest could have been no more than twelve, was cooking a one-pot meal over a sizable fire. Another group was kicking around a soccer ball.

In the middle of the field, Alex saw the hostages. A quick head count gave him a total of six captives. Most were obviously foreign, but there was one woman who looked Congolese, and Alex suspected that she was Marie Tsiolo. The company's files had her listed as the second geologist on the survey team. It looked like most of the internationals had survived their ordeal. *Let's hope their luck holds,* Alex thought.

Not far from the hostages, Alex saw Manamakimba sitting in a canvas folding chair next to a flat rock the approximate size and shape of a coffee table. Alex strode purposefully toward the guerilla commander. *Slow and steady. You have all the time in the world.*

Yeah, right. Alex looked at his watch. It was 11:15 AM. Keeler would radio their exact arrival time back to the base. Alex had until 5:15 PM to broker some kind of deal. After that, the shooting would begin.

By prearrangement, Keeler and Viggiano stayed with the vehicles. They had decided to mirror Manamakimba. If the Hammer of God leader came to the table with a bevy of advisers and attendants, Jonah and Rick and the Pakistanis would join Alex to play the same role. If Manamakimba wanted to do the meeting alone, however, Alex would accommodate him. Alex hoped that if he could establish some kind of rapport with Manamakimba, however psychotic he might turn out to be, it would up his chances of winning the release of at least a few of the hostages.

Manamakimba was dressed in almost identical fashion to the hulking soldier who had escorted them to camp. He was leaning back in his chair with his face turned up toward the sun. His legs were stretched out in front of him, crossed at the ankles. He seemed completely at peace. A glass of what looked to be some kind of fruit juice rested on the rock beside him.

As Alex approached, Manamakimba opened his eyes and stared at him intently. He lifted a single finger and one of the camp boys rushed over and set up another canvas chair so sun-faded it was impossible to tell whether the original color had been orange or yellow.

Manamakimba stood up and extended his hand. His grip was firm and cool. The Hammer of God leader wasn't quite Alex's height, but his charisma was immediately obvious. The eyes behind the delicate-looking glasses were sharp and fiercely intelligent.

"Welcome, Mr. Ambassador," Manamakimba began. He spoke in French. "I extend to you my protection and my hospitality for as long as our conversation lasts."

"Thank you, Mr. Manamakimba. My name is Alex Baines. I am not the Ambassador, but I am here with the full authority to represent the United States. I am hopeful that we can reach an understanding that avoids further loss of life."

Manamakimba gestured for Alex to sit. A camp boy who could have been no more than nine or ten appeared with a second glass of fruit juice, which he set down on the rock next to Manamakimba's. The boy was dangerously thin and his wide eyes had the yellowed whites that were a warning sign of one or more of the host of tropical diseases to which young people in central Africa were vulnerable: jaundice maybe, or yellow fever, or some kind of parasite. He wore a rusty valve around his neck on a frayed boot lace, a sign of Manamakimba's favor.

"I share your desire for a common understanding and a peaceful outcome to this dispute," Manamakimba continued. "I have something that belongs to you." He gestured toward the hostages some fifty yards away who were watching them with undisguised interest. "Understandably, you want it back. I am sympathetic. I too have lost something. My country. It is currently in the possession of a group of thieves, murderers, and slavers who call themselves the government of the Democratic Republic of the Congo. They enjoy the support in this conceit of important players in the international system, including the United Nations, the mining companies, and the government of your own country. This support must end."

This speech, delivered with poise and practiced smoothness, was not at all what the Agency bio had led Alex to expect from the Hammer of God. He wondered what else the CIA had gotten wrong about Joseph Manamakimba.

"The first thing I would like to do is to speak with the hostages," Alex said. "I want to make sure that they have not been harmed, and I need to assess the extent of their medical needs."

"This is not unreasonable," Manamakimba replied magnanimously. "You may do so. I assure you that they have been well treated in our care."

Alex walked over to what remained of the Consolidated Mining survey team. A few of the hostages stood up when Alex approached, but one man remained flat on the ground. Two women knelt at his side, tending to their colleague as best they could.

As a group, they seemed frightened but not panicky. This was positive.

"Hello. My name is Alex Baines. I'm from the U.S. Embassy in Kinshasa, and I'm here to discuss with your captors the terms of your release. I promise you that we are doing everything we can to get you out. Can someone give me a quick update on your status? It looks like at least one of you is hurt. Is everyone else okay? Is there anyone missing? Anything you can tell me would be helpful."

"Except for Steve, we're basically in good shape. Steve was shot. The wound has gone septic and he's in shock." It was the Congolese woman who spoke up. Her English, he noted, was flawless.

"Marie Tsiolo, I presume."

She nodded almost imperceptibly.

"Is this everyone, or were there other team members who might have been taken somewhere else?" Alex asked.

"No. This is everyone."

"Is Jack Karic here?"

"Jack didn't make it," Marie said. "Neither did Wallace Purcell. The Hammer of God killed them both. I've been representing us in our conversations with Manamakimba. Temporarily, at least, I suppose that puts me in charge."

Alex had read Marie's personnel file. She was a relative newcomer to the company, and she had one of the thinnest files. Her evaluations had been stellar, however, and it was clear that Consolidated saw her as a rising star. That had made the letter of resignation in her file all the more puzzling. Only three days before heading into the jungle, Marie Tsiolo had given her notice. This was to be her last expedition with Consolidated.

"What can you tell me about Manamakimba?" Alex asked Marie.

"He's complicated," Marie replied. "Not the mindless killer that the newspapers make him out to be. He's smart, surprisingly thoughtful, and he seems to believe absolutely in his cause."

"What is his cause?"

"His country. Our country, I suppose. He sees himself as a patriot battling the greed of the mining companies."

"Is there anything you can think of that might help me to negotiate with him?"

"Yes," Marie replied. "Me."

Alex looked at her quizzically.

"Like it or not, and I assure you I don't, this team is my responsibility. At this point, Dr. Wheeler's life is measured in hours. We don't have a lot of time, and I don't intend to sit here while you make a hash of the negotiations with Manamakimba." Looking Alex right in the eye, Marie added in Lingala, "He eats pretty little white boys like you for breakfast."

"In that case, he might find that he's bitten off more than he can chew," Alex replied in the same language.

"All the same, you'll want me with you when you talk to him," Marie said, shifting smoothly back to English. If she was at all impressed by Alex's command of Lingala, she hid it well. "I understand him in ways that you cannot."

Alex considered this for a moment. Marie had a point. She also had established a relationship with Manamakimba that would take Alex valuable time to replicate, if, in fact, he ever could. As a Congolese, Marie might have credibility with the Hammer of God that Alex could never hope to match. It was unusual for hostages to participate in the negotiations for their own release. As a rule, they had an obvious incentive to overpromise. Marie Tsiolo seemed cool and collected, however, and it seemed a risk that was worth taking.

"Come on," Alex agreed. "Let's go get this done."

8

Marie did not want to give Manamakimba the opportunity to reject her participation in the negotiations, so she sat in the chair the American diplomat had vacated. Manamakimba said nothing, but he gestured to one of his aides and a boy came running over with a third chair for Alex.

The three negotiators sat facing one another over the flat granite slab that served as a table.

"I see you brought reinforcements," Manamakimba observed dryly.

"Do you have any objection to Ms. Tsiolo's participation in our discussion?"

"None whatsoever." Manamakimba settled back comfortably in his chair. "Are you satisfied with the condition of our guests?" he asked Alex.

"The *guests* are not satisfied with their condition," Marie said before Alex could respond. "My colleague, Steve Wheeler, is dying. His wound has festered. He needs a hospital urgently. I want you to let him go before we discuss terms for the release of the rest of the team."

"Many of my children are also sick or injured." Manamakimba's expansive gesture implied that he used "children" metaphorically to include all of his Hammer of God fighters. "They have no access to doctors or hospitals. The treatment available to your Dr. Wheeler is no better than what I can offer my own people, but neither is it any worse. Surely you don't mean to imply that your white friend is somehow more deserving than your African brothers and sisters."

"White or black is immaterial to me. What concerns me is the color of his leg. It is red and swollen and cold to the touch. I'm no doctor, but I know enough to recognize gangrene."

"I could have the leg cut off," Manamakimba offered. "Some of my boys have considerable experience with that."

I bet they do, Marie thought.

"He's too weak. The blood loss would kill him. He needs a hospital and medicine."

"What's one more death in the Congo?" Manamakimba asked. "Millions of our countrymen have died in these wars . . . wars that have been fought at the behest of companies like yours, Ms. Tsiolo. If he dies, Dr. Wheeler will be just one of many victims. If his death serves to advance the cause of liberation for our people, then it is a death more valuable than most."

"It will do the opposite," Alex warned. "I am here to negotiate at your invitation, but if you are serious about reaching a deal that can benefit both of us, then we will have to establish a degree of trust. Ordinarily, that takes time, but it is time that Dr. Wheeler does not have. If you allow him to die under your charge while trying to score debating points, it will make it exceedingly difficult for us to develop any kind of trust or confidence in you. We have made a gesture in agreeing to meet here in your camp. You should reciprocate and let Dr. Wheeler go now. You will still have enough hostages to justify continued negotiations, and you eliminate the risk of losing one of your guests on a timeline that you don't control."

Marie liked that the American was appealing to Manamakimba's self-interest rather than his humanity. The Congo had a way of hardening one to the suffering of others. Self-interest was timeless.

"Surely you don't expect to get something for nothing in the case of Dr. Wheeler," Manamakimba replied. "Goodwill frankly seems somewhat abstract at this point. Perhaps we could discuss the terms for the professor's release."

"What did you have in mind?" Alex asked.

"I propose a statement on behalf of Consolidated Mining, the United Nations, and the United States of America accepting responsibility for the violence in eastern Congo . . . and, shall we say, one million dollars to cover the Hammer of God's expenses."

Marie was again struck by the juxtaposition of the high-minded and the venal in Manamakimba's rhetoric.

"That seems a bit steep for a single hostage," Alex observed.

"Ah, it is good to see that you are not above bartering for lives. You will find that an invaluable attribute in our country."

"Then let's negotiate in a serious way. What you are asking for is out of the question. Dr. Wheeler has little time. We cannot negotiate on terms that would require messages to be relayed back and forth to Kinshasa, much less to New York or Washington. We need to work with what we have at hand. There are certain commitments I can make now, but only in exchange for Dr. Wheeler's immediate release."

"What would you suggest then?"

"A straight-up trade. Release Dr. Wheeler and you have my word that I will stay in this camp as your . . . guest . . . until we have reached agreement on a deal that will free all of the members of the Consolidated Mining team. In reality, you'd be trading up. You'd have the same number of hostages, but you'd be giving up a dying man for a healthy one, and a U.S. official at that."

"You are not a coward," Manamakimba offered, after a moment's reflection. "That is something. But what do I gain by this when I could simply keep you both."

"I don't believe you will do that. You gave us your word that we would have safe passage for these talks, and unless I misjudge you, I think your word is something that you take seriously. I assure you that I take my word seriously as well, and if I offer myself freely as your hostage, it is without intent to deceive."

Manamakimba hesitated, then nodded his agreement. It was a good deal and the guerilla leader knew it.

"Very well. I accept your offer, Mr. Baines."

"No," Marie interrupted. "It is not enough."

The two men looked at her. They both seemed somewhat surprised at her intervention. Manamakimba, she noted with irritation, also seemed bemused.

"You think our American friend values himself too highly?" the Hammer of God asked.

"I think he sells himself short," Marie offered. "He is an American diplomat. The local representative of the most powerful country in the world. Surely he is worth more than an old and injured geologist. It is not a fair trade. In addition, Dr. Wheeler is gravely ill and will require care on the trip back to Kinshasa. The two women, Arlene and Charlotte, have been looking after him. Let them go as well and you can keep the American diplomat. Otherwise, I reject your deal as insufficient."

Manamakimba laughed. There was nothing malevolent in it. It was a genuine laugh, full of warmth and humor.

"Two women seems extravagant," the guerilla leader said. "A man should be satisfied with one good woman. You, Ms. Tsiolo, would be more than enough for any man, I expect. But I am not unreasonable, and I recognize the value that your American friend offers. You may have one of the women to nurse the doctor on his trip back to . . . civilization." The last word dripped with sarcasm. "They may leave immediately. But you must choose which one it is to be, Ms. Tsiolo. You are their leader. The decision is rightly yours."

Marie's stomach turned over. This was not a responsibility she wanted. Whichever one she picked was likely to survive this experience. The other would share the collective fate of the rest of the team, and Marie was realistic enough to know that their future did not look bright. It was quite literally the power of life and death.

"How does it feel," he asked, "to hold the fate of another in your hands? It is true power. Many men become addicted to this. Do not grow to love it overmuch, Marie Tsiolo. Power is a harsh mistress."

Marie looked over at what was left of the Consolidated Mining survey team. Steve Wheeler was thrashing in a fever-racked dream. Charlotte lifted his head and cradled it in her lap. She tried to get him to drink from the clean water in her canteen, but the geologist was too dazed to swallow.

That small act of kindness was enough.

"Charlotte Swing will go with Steve," she announced.

"The blond one?" Manamakimba asked.

"Yes."

"Too bad. I was looking forward to getting to know her better."

Manamakimba turned to Alex. "You may have Mr. Wheeler and Ms. Swing. You may take them immediately and then you may take their places . . . as my guest."

Alex nodded and left to make the arrangements for their transport.

Manamakimba looked at Marie with such intensity it was as though he was trying to see inside her.

"You drive a harder bargain than the American."

"I have had more time to take your measure."

Marie watched as two UN soldiers and two Hammer of God fighters moved Steve Wheeler onto a stretcher and placed it in the back of one of the Land Cruisers. Charlotte Swing hugged the other members of the team and got into the vehicle. The Land Cruiser pulled out and started down the dirt track toward the UN base. Marie offered a silent prayer to her ancestors for Steve Wheeler.

When Alex returned, the negotiations began in earnest.

"Dr. Wheeler and Ms. Swing represent a decent beginning," Alex said. "Shall we discuss terms for the release of the remaining members of the team . . . and for me, of course?"

"Shall we? I believe that I have put my terms on the table. Thirty-five million dollars and the withdrawal of all foreign forces from eastern Congo. This applies in particular to the mining interests, but to the UN forces as well. They serve the occupiers and they are not welcome. If you'd prefer to pay in euros," Manamakimba added, "I can offer you a favorable exchange rate. I'm afraid that I can't accept Congolese francs."

"That's not a terribly realistic offer, Mr. Manamakimba. Only the UN Security Council can order the withdrawal of UNSAF. I can offer you a meeting with the UNSAF commander. An opportunity to bring your grievances right to the top. Perhaps if you had a chance to observe some of the UN operations, it would help alleviate your concerns. In addition, it might be possible for me to facilitate an amnesty deal with the government if you release the hostages immediately and agree to verifiable disarmament."

"Now who's being unrealistic, Mr. Baines? In this neighborhood, disarmament is death. I will not ask that of my children. I will not trade the soldiers I hold for empty promises."

"The people you are holding—me included—are civilians, not soldiers. They are scientists and engineers. They have no part in the war."

"That is where you are wrong. The mining companies and the officials who protect them are the essence of this war. They provide both the reason and the means for violence. They are modern conquistadors disguised as free-market capitalists in the service of their lords and masters in Kinshasa, London, New York, Beijing, and Pretoria. I have studied your Western civilization, Mr. Baines." Manamakimba again made the word derisive. "I am not an uneducated savage skulking through the forest. I studied mechanical engineering at the University of Liège."

Marie was not surprised by this. She had concluded early on that the guerilla leader had considerable formal education.

"I learned many things in Belgium, including the history of my own people. The Kingdom of Kongo was a great empire, but it was built with gold and spears rather than steel and guns. The Belgians made us slaves. We were not even a colony. We were a company, the private company of King Leopold II. The people of the Congo were just so many machine parts. We collected the Belgians' rubber and dug their copper and slaughtered our elephants for their ivory. Millions of us died. If a village failed to meet its quota, the white officers of Leopold's enforcers, the Force Publique, took their hands in compensation. Baskets of severed hands flowed back to Europe along with the plunder. When the Belgians finally left, we were so weak and divided that we turned on one another. For the last fifty years, the West has worked to keep us weak so that we might continue to feed their industrial machine.

"So do not tell me, Mr. Baines, that these are innocent civilians I have in my possession. They are every bit the foot soldiers of the conquerors. Just ask my pretty African sister what her own employer wants to do to her family, her village. Uncle Joseph knows." Manamakimba pointed a long bony finger at his own chest. "Why don't you?"

When Alex looked at her, Marie turned away. Although she could not accept Manamakimba's methods, his passion and conviction spoke to her. He was certainly right about the way in which the company had betrayed her. She had been naïve.

"I did not ask you to fight my battles," Marie told the guerilla leader. "We can take care of ourselves."

"Can you now? That is not how it looks from the outside, Ms. Tsiolo. Remember that what is happening to you is only a small taste of what is happening to our country."

There was a lull in the conversation as though the participants by mutual consent had paused to consider where they were. It was the American who broke the silence.

"I appreciate the history of this country and I'm sympathetic to what you're saying. The Congo and its people have suffered terribly over the last century. If you are looking to educate me, I assure you that you have my complete attention. If you're looking for justice, this isn't the way."

The guerilla leader had an intense look in his eyes. "Let me show you both something," he said, as he pulled a small stack of photographs out of a cargo pocket on the thigh of his jungle camouflage pants. "These are pictures of my family. My wife, Serena, our two sons, and our daughter."

Marie and Alex leafed through the photographs. Manamakimba's wife was a graceful woman with a warm and welcoming smile. In one of the pictures, she was standing in front of a small, well-kept house wearing a simple yellow skirt and a cotton T-shirt. She was lovely. The three children stood in a knot on her right side holding hands. They were wearing what looked like school uniforms. The other pictures were of Serena and the children playing in the yard, cooking, and doing other ordinary things. The guerilla leader appeared in only one picture. This was a more formal shot, with Manamakimba and his wife sitting on a bench, their children arrayed in an arc in front of them. In the picture, the ruthless Hammer of God looked like nothing other than a proud husband and father.

"They are beautiful," Marie said sympathetically, knowing what was coming next.

"My family is dead. They are all dead. Serena and my daughter, Claire, were killed by Rwandan *genocidaires*. My sons starved to death. The Rwandans came to fight wars and stayed to make money. It is the same with the South Africans and the Zambians. These are our neighbors, but they are the newcomers. The Europeans and the Americans, they have been at this for a hundred years. I lost my first family. I am not going to lose my second."

He motioned to one of the camp boys, who ran over immediately. Manamakimba pulled off the boy's hat and rubbed his head affectionately. Marie could see a line of bright red welts on the boy's neck, the unmistakable marker of schistosomiasis, a dangerous, even potentially fatal, parasitic infection. The boy already looked weak and malnourished. He was going to have a hard time fighting back against the parasitic worms burrowing into his lungs and liver. Treatment for the condition was relatively cheap and painless. It was also, Marie was certain, unavailable to the Hammer of God. There wasn't a pharmacy or a doctor this side of Kisangani.

"Charlie is sick," Manamakimba said simply. "It is likely he will die. It is not my intention to allow that."

"Nor should it be," Marie said. "But taking the life of others isn't going to do this boy any good."

Manamakimba said nothing. But he patted Charlie on the head and sent him away.

Four hours later nothing had changed. As the negotiations dragged on, Marie noticed Alex glancing surreptitiously at his watch. She wondered what he could possibly be waiting for. Out here in the jungle, time was an almost meaningless abstraction.

Meanwhile, the guerilla leader was clearly warming to his theme of the Hammer of God as the real defenders of the Congo, forced into battle against an array of national enemies both foreign and internal. He required little or nothing in the way of feedback to encourage his monologue. "By branding us as criminals and outlaws, the puppet government in Kinshasa has pushed us into a corner. The Hammer of God is my family. They are all I have left. I love them and they love me. I provide for them as a father. I give them food and shelter. There is little enough I can do about medicine, but we care for the sick and injured as well as we are able."

"What if we could do something about medicine?" Marie asked impulsively. "What if there was a way that we could provide treatment to your sick and wounded? What might that be worth to you?"

"It might change things. It depends."

Marie thought she saw an opening, but she needed to explore the options privately with the American first.

"Give us a minute to talk," she said to Manamakimba.

"Of course," the Hammer of God said, rising from his chair. "We have plenty of time." He looked at Alex as he said this.

When they were alone, Marie turned to Alex and asked with a fierce urgency, "Is there something you can do to get medical care for the Hammer of God? A doctor and some medical supplies. I think he'd be willing to do a deal if we can come up with the right incentives."

"It wouldn't take much to make a difference," Alex agreed. "You and I both know what's wrong with Charlie. Schistosomiasis. It's easy enough to treat. There's a State Department doctor in Johannesburg. I could potentially persuade him to offer the Hammer of God his services, but there's not enough time to set it up now."

"What do you mean? Why do you keep looking at your watch? What's going to happen?"

Alex told her about the UN rescue operation that was scheduled to get under way in only forty-five minutes. Marie was appalled.

"This is going to cost a lot of lives," she observed. "Yours and mine not least among them."

"In all likelihood," Alex agreed.

"Then we had better close this deal, hadn't we?"

"Indeed. And remember, if the shooting starts, get low and flat and stay there."

Manamakimba returned and took his seat. One of the camp boys brought fresh glasses of juice and set them on the rock.

"Well," Manamakimba asked. "What do you have in mind?"

"In exchange for the immediate release of all of the hostages, I can offer you the services of Embassy medical personnel for a week to tend your sick and injured," Alex said. "I can also offer you whatever medical supplies are necessary for him to provide treatment."

"Two weeks," Manamakimba said. "And I want a doctor, not nurses."

Marie was encouraged that Manamakimba seemed to accept the basic outlines of the deal.

"Understood and agreed."

"And medicines, whatever is needed."

"Also agreed."

"Good drugs, not the expired castoffs that some of the missionaries have been trading for souls."

"Of course."

Manamakimba wasn't quite finished bargaining. "And one more thing . . ."

"Yes," Alex asked cautiously.

"By releasing you and my other . . . guests, I am taking your commitment to this bargain on faith."

"You'll have to trust that I'll make good on my word, yes."

"I want a token of your commitment up front."

"What are you thinking about?"

Manamakimba looked over at the line of Land Cruisers parked on the far side of the field. Off the assembly line, they retailed for nearly sixty thousand dollars. Fully armored, the vehicles were worth somewhere in the low six figures.

"I'll take one of your jeeps," Manamakimba said. "I can put it to good use."

Alex stood and walked over to the UN convoy. He was back in less than five minutes. Almost casually, he tossed a set of keys to Manamakimba.

"I threw in half a tank of gas," he said. "It will take me a little time to arrange for a doctor. How can I get a message to you when I have that set up?"

Manamakimba reached into his pants pocket and pulled out a short stack of rectangular white cards. He handed one to Alex and one to Marie. The top line read JOSEPH MANAMAKIMBA, and under that COMMANDER, HAMMER OF GOD. There was an eleven-digit satellite phone number in the lower left corner, and a Gmail address. In the upper right corner, a red hammer was superimposed over an outline of the Congo.

"Call me anytime," Manamakimba said. "E-mail is hit or miss. There are not many Internet cafés out here."

"The Hammer of God has a logo?" Marie asked. This was beyond bizarre, something akin to Al Qaeda advertising for an administrative assistant in the classifieds.

"Sure. I may have trained as an engineer . . . but I took a couple of marketing classes at university."

He turned to Alex. "Now may be a good time call your Pakistani friends in their new helmets and tell them they do not have to die today." He checked his watch. "You have a little less than half an hour."

9

Alex read through his report again, just to be sure he hadn't missed anything. It didn't make any sense. Negotiating the freedom of the Consolidated survey team had been an impressive piece of diplomacy, the kind that should make an embassy immodestly toot its own horn in cable traffic back to Washington. Moreover, Alex had spent most of a day talking one-on-one with Joseph Manamakimba, who was himself a Class A intelligence target.

Alex had written a substantial report on the negotiations with Manamakimba immediately after getting back to Kinshasa, being careful to share the credit for the success with Marie Tsiolo. He worked through the night and by morning had a solid ten-page cable with a comment paragraph at the end that challenged the conventional wisdom of Manamakimba as a simple-minded killing machine.

Inexplicably, Spence had sat on the report for nearly a week. He knew as well as Alex did that immediacy added punch to any report. A week was a lifetime in diplomacy. Cables that sat around too long lost their edge and their audience back home.

Finally, and after considerable prodding from Alex, the cable came back from the Front Office. It had a single note on the front in red pen, the color traditionally reserved in U.S. embassies for the Ambassador. Alex read it again, hoping that the words would offer him some insight into the thinking behind the message. "Good report, but I don't want to stir up a hornet's nest over this. I'll back-channel the appropriate people to keep them in the loop."

That was it. It didn't make any sense.

He allowed himself the luxury of disappointment. In the hard, cold calculus of life in the State Department, the only accomplishments that counted were the ones that people knew about. Saving six lives was obviously the most important thing and that was enormously gratifying, but Alex was also eager to reestablish his reputation in the Africa Bureau. The report he had written would have gone a long way toward doing that. This was true even though Alex had been careful to downplay his own role. The FSOs and intelligence analysts who would have read the cable were experienced enough to understand how it had played out.

Mark Fong stuck his head into Alex's office.

"I'm going down for a cup of coffee. Do you want anything?"

Alex put the report in his shred-box. In the greater scheme of things, this was no big deal. The Congo was a big, fascinating place. There would be more opportunities.

"I'll come with you," Alex said. "I could use a break."

The cafeteria was on the ground floor and looked out onto the Embassy courtyard. French doors opened up onto a patio that held some plastic tables and chairs. It had a definite cut-rate flair, but the coffee was decent. A half dozen or so Embassy staffers were in the cafeteria for a midmorning break. Jonah Keeler was sitting by himself at one of the outside tables, and he motioned for Alex and Mark to join him.

"Morning, gentlemen." Keeler had been reading *L'Avenir*, Congo's paper of record. He folded up the paper and put it on the chair next to him to make room for Alex and Mark. "How's everything on the political front?"

"Not too bad," Mark said.

"I've been waiting eagerly for your report on our adventures last week, Alex," said Keeler. "I haven't seen anything in the traffic yet. What's the holdup?"

"Just got the word from the Front Office," Alex replied. "Spence doesn't want to report this front-channel. He's going to send some e-mails, but otherwise I think we are going to play this like it never happened." Alex was pleased that there was no hint of disappointment in his response.

"Well, that's a damn shame. You did a hell of a job out there, and any insights into Manamakimba's thinking are worth sharing. If you'd like, I'd be happy to scavenge from your report and send it back in my channels. The trolls in the basement at Langley would eat that stuff up."

"Thanks for the offer, Jonah, but I think that's exactly what Spence is looking to avoid."

"I can appreciate that, but I think it's a mistake. *Que será, será*. Hey, did you happen to the check the score of the Georgetown-Temple game?" Keeler had graduated from Cornell, but he had grown up in Philadelphia and was a huge Temple fan.

"Was there a game?" Alex asked innocently. In truth, he had checked the box scores that morning online and knew that Keeler's Owls had upended the favored Hoyas on national television.

They talked basketball for a few minutes, and then Mark Fong excused himself. He was on a deadline. He had also made clear on more than one occasion that he considered sports talk an indescribable form of torture that merited its own entry in the annual human rights report.

"There's something I've been meaning to ask you about since our trip last week," Alex said when Mark had left.

"I'm listening."

"It's about Marie Tsiolo. I think she could help me get a better handle on what's going on in the east. Also, Manamakimba seemed to know an awful lot about her. There's something going on that he hinted at, but he didn't offer details. Something that involves Consolidated Mining. I'd like to know more about what it is."

All of this was true, but it was not, Alex admitted to himself, the whole truth. His interest in finding Marie was at least as much about her stunning brown eyes and her daunting aloofness.

"Do you think you could help me track her down?" Alex continued. "There's nothing in Consolidated's records about what village she is from. I think she's Luba, but I could easily be wrong about that."

"Why not just ask Spence's new best friend, Henri Saillard, how to get ahold of her?"

"I'd rather that Consolidated Mining not know I'm looking for her." Alex somehow doubted that Marie had parted amicably from her employer.

"So, you want the seventy-five-billion-dollar-a-year intelligence community to help you get a date for the prom?"

"Something like that."

"I'll see what I can do," Keeler replied.

That evening, Alex Skyped with Anah in Brunswick from the unclassified computer in his office. Internet connections in Kinshasa were spotty at best, even for the Embassy of the United States. The picture was a little jerky, but Anah's voice came through clearly. She sounded happy, Alex thought. Brunswick was now her home as much as his.

"I made a picture of you today, Daddy," she said with a shy smile. "Gramma bought me a new art set and some big sheets of paper. Let me show it to you.

"What do you think?" she asked, holding the picture up to the camera.

It was a picture of the two of them walking hand in hand in what Alex supposed was a park. His daughter was well past the stick-figure stage. The people in the drawing were recognizably Alex and Anah. She had some real natural talent, he thought, even allowing for the blinders of parental pride. In the picture, they were holding hands, her dark brown fingers curled tightly around his peach-colored ones. The pastels smudged together in a way that felt more true than strict anatomical accuracy would have allowed for. In the drawings of her family that Anah brought home from her art classes at school, it was always the two of them together. Hers were invariably the smallest family portraits in her class. No mother, no brothers or sisters, not even any pets. Just Anah and her father.

"That's fantastic, sweetie. Will you save that one for me? I think it's too good for the refrigerator. We can put it in a frame and I can hang it up in my office."

Anah's smile broadened at the thought.

"I'd like that," she agreed.

Instead of going home after the call, Alex headed across town in the red Toyota RAV4 that he had inherited from his deceased predecessor. It was a little unsettling to drive a dead man's car, but Julian's next of kin, a semi-estranged brother, had not wanted to hassle with shipping the vehicle back to the United States. Alex did his best to follow the map on the seat beside him. He had only the sketchiest directions from Leonard, and the neighborhoods he was driving through were gradually getting worse and worse.

Half of the buildings in this part of town looked abandoned. Trash blew through the streets or accumulated in rotting piles. A lone, one-legged drunk tottered uneasily on his crutch, a plastic bottle of home brew in his free hand. *Nina Simone Sings the Blues* on the RAV's stereo was the perfect accompaniment to the dismal scenery. Almost imperceptibly, Alex felt the black dog of depression creeping up on him. Quite likely, he recognized, this was a function of coming down off the high of the hostage talks. He fished a pill bottle out of the glove compartment and shook a single white tablet onto his palm. He washed it down with a quick swig from a bottle of water.

After a few wrong turns, Alex found the place he was looking for, a church with unadorned concrete walls and a tile roof. A sign in front identified the church, rather grandly he thought, as ST. MARY'S OF THE ASSUMPTION. This was definitely the place.

Alex's second impression wasn't much better. He drove through the gate and parked. There were two other cars in the lot. Both were up on blocks and neither had an engine. They seemed to have been built primarily out of rust. The church was actually located inside a small compound enclosed by a crumbling brick wall. In addition to the church, the compound included two blockhouse-style buildings and a stone and wood structure that looked like it might once have been a barn or a stable.

Alex locked the car and went into the church.

Inside, the church was well lit and pleasantly clean. A young boy was sweeping the aisle with a broom made of rough straw. An enormous plasticine Christ smiled down on him from the cross hanging on one of the side walls.

"Hello. Can you tell me where I can find Father Antoine?"

The boy nodded. He took Alex's hand and led him to a door at the back of the church, near the altar. Alex knocked.

"*Entrez.*"

Father Antoine was sitting at an ancient wooden desk piled with books and papers, and he was running a finger down a column in an oversize ledger bound in red leather. He was wearing a white cassock and a matching skull cap. A pair of bifocals perched at the end of his nose.

"Hello, Father."

The priest got up from the desk and embraced Alex, kissing him on both cheeks.

"Kill the fatted calf," he said, pulling back from the hug and clapping Alex on the shoulder. "For the prodigal son has returned. Welcome home, my dear friend, it's been . . ."

"Eight years," Alex finished.

"Too long," Father Antoine agreed.

"I'm sorry I've been out of touch, Father. No excuses. But I've tried to keep up with things, and I heard that you had moved from Goma to Kinshasa. It didn't take long for me to find you. Everyone in town seems to know about this place. It looks like you're doing good work. The kind of work that you always talked about."

"We are doing the Lord's work. My flock is growing and we take in children—war orphans and AIDS orphans mostly—who have nowhere else to go. The facilities are still a bit rough, mind you. We could use the services of a good carpenter."

"If I meet any good ones, I'll be sure to give them your card."

It was an old joke. Alex and Father Antoine had worked together on numerous Peace Corps–sponsored construction projects in the Goma area. They had quickly discovered that the priest and power tools were a potentially lethal combination, and Antoine had contented himself with offering a steady stream of encouragement and unsolicited, and usually erroneous, advice.

"So, are you back on a visit? I understand that tourists are getting some terrific deals at Kinshasa's finest hotels."

"More than a visit, actually. I'm working at the U.S. Embassy. I should be in town for the next two years at least."

"Well, that should certainly give us plenty of time to get caught up."

"And enough time to wear out my welcome, I expect."

"Come, let me show you around. I know it's supposed to be a sin, even if only a venial one, but I'm really quite proud of this place. I get few chances to show it off. And then I hope I can persuade you to join us for dinner. The children would love to meet you."

"That would be nice. I have an adopted daughter myself that I'm hoping you'll get to meet soon. Her name is Anah and she's nine. Plus, I'm never one to pass up a free meal."

"Oh, it won't be free, I assure you. But you'll pay for it later. Congratulations on becoming a father. It's a weighty title, more important than king or ambassador or even"—his voice dropped to a conspiratorial whisper—"pope. But please don't tell Rome."

Father Antoine turned and retrieved a wooden cane next to his desk chair.

"Land mine," Antoine explained, when he saw Alex looking at the cane. "It happened only a couple of months after you left. I was lucky, actually. I got to keep my leg. Many others aren't so fortunate."

"I'm sorry," Alex said. "Land mines are evil things. Bury one and it'll wait patiently for years for the opportunity to hurt someone."

"That's the truth of it. I have no idea whose weapon it was, or even which war it was from. We've had so many."

Inside the church, Antoine motioned to the young boy still sweeping the floors to join them.

"Jean-Pierre," he said, "go back to the house and get ready for dinner. Make sure the house is in order. We have company. We'll be by in a few minutes."

Jean-Pierre nodded but did not reply.

"He's a good child," Antoine said, after the boy had run off, "but he won't speak. He hasn't said a word since he came here two years ago. He was a soldier for one of the rebel groups, I can't remember which one now. Before they took him, they murdered his family in front of him—his father, his mother, and his two sisters. As far as I know, he hasn't spoken since then. I'm quite concerned for him. Since he can't speak, he can't confess; and unless he confesses, he cannot be absolved.

"We have nearly thirty boys staying with us at the moment. Most are orphans, a few have parents too poor or incapacitated to take care of them. A just society would not require parents to surrender their children because of penury. But there are more children who need our help than we have beds."

"Where do the kids stay?" Alex asked.

"In the buildings behind the church. It's starting to get a little crowded, and I'd like to renovate what used to be the stables and turn it into a dormitory. That's a pretty big project, however." Antoine sighed and looked up briefly. "God will provide in good time."

He glanced slyly at Alex. "Maybe he already has."

"Maybe."

"I told you you'd end up paying for dinner."

In truth, Alex had been hoping that Father Antoine would give him an excuse to strap on a tool belt and do some building. Diplomacy could be an extremely creative profession, but it was by nature somewhat abstract. Alex welcomed whatever opportunities came his way to descend from the ethereal world of statecraft and build real, physical things.

"Come, let me take you to the dormitories. You can meet the children."

"Lead on."

Alex surveyed the stables as they walked past. He could see right away that this was going to be a big job. The building would need plumbing and electricity as well as basic structural repairs, a new roof, new windows, and a real floor. Alex couldn't do it alone, and he knew from experience that Father Antoine would be no help. He hoped the kids were up to the job.

The blockhouse dormitories were crowded, but there wasn't the frenetic madness that Alex would have expected from a similarly large group of American kids packed together in a tight space. The house was two levels. Half of the downstairs was taken up by rows of bunk beds with thin mattresses. The other half was dominated by a long table with wooden benches that was already set for dinner. The plates and cups were made of cheap, unbreakable plastic. A small lounge area in the back corner held a television set, a few books, even fewer toys, and a couple of wooden chairs. Some of the younger kids were watching what looked to Alex like a Mexican soap opera on the television. All of the children wore dark gray shorts and white, short-sleeved shirts with button-down fronts and an elaborate seal over the left breast.

A door off the side led to the kitchen, where Alex could see the older boys preparing the evening meal. The distinctive odor of boiling cassava root wafted from the room.

"Gentlemen, we have a guest." Father Antoine drew himself up to his full height. He was, Alex suspected, quite an imposing figure to the young children, many of them fresh from the bush. One boy turned off the television set. All of the children stood up and faced the priest with their hands held behind their backs. A few of them stared at Alex in wide-eyed amazement. It was possible that he was the first white person they had seen other than on television. Alex noticed that Jean-Pierre had appeared at his side and stood very close, establishing a special claim on their guest.

"Mr. Alex is volunteering his time to help us rebuild the stables next door. It is my expectation that you will assist him in every way you can. If he asks you to do something, it is as though it were coming from me. Is that clear?"

The children all murmured their assent, with the exception of Jean-Pierre, who simply nodded in agreement. Alex was amused at how easily Father Antoine had transformed his "maybe" into a "yes." He had not changed much since Goma.

"Mr. Alex, please join us. It's a simple meal, of course, but there is enough for all."

"I would be honored," Alex replied.

Over dinner, Alex had an idea that he shared with Father Antoine.

"Father, maybe we can start our repair work with that television. I can't imagine the kids really want to watch *Maria Loves Carlos*. How about we see if we can't find the cartoon channel on this thing."

"I'm afraid that's not going to work," the priest replied. "We don't have any satellite equipment. This old set is all we have. It only gets the one channel and that irregularly."

"You may not have a satellite dish, but you do have a couple of cars in that lot out front."

"With no engines," Antoine observed, "they aren't worth very much."

"I don't need an engine, Father. I only need a hood."

10

Alex's phone rang on the dot of 8:30 on Monday morning, the start of the Embassy's official workday.

"Hello, this is Alex Baines."

The voice at the other end was abrasive and demanding. "This is Viggiano. I'd like to see you in my office right now."

Calls like this from the Regional Security Officer were almost never good news.

"Actually, Rick, I'm working on the morning press summary for Spence. Can we do this at about ten?"

"No, I want to do this right now. It shouldn't take more than five minutes."

"I'll be down in a minute."

Although he had told Viggiano he would be right down, Alex took another fifteen minutes to finish summarizing the latest news on the domestic political front, including rumors of a cabinet reshuffle, a burgeoning feud between the Minister of Defense and the Minister of the

Interior, and the latest raft of corruption scandals in the Ministry of Communications. A fairly typical day. Having reached a convenient place to stop, he headed down the stairs to the security office, which was on the ground floor of the chancery next to Post One, the duty station manned twenty-four hours a day by one of the Marines from the Embassy's Marine Security Guard detachment. Alex waved hello to Sergeant Martinez on duty. Martinez saluted smartly.

Viggiano's door was open.

"What can I do for you, Rick?" Alex asked, as he sat down.

Viggiano got right to the point. "Did you make contact on Friday evening with a Catholic priest named Antoine Mitifu?"

"Yes. I know Father Antoine from my Peace Corps days. He and I are friends and I'm going to do some work with him sprucing up the orphanage he runs at St. Mary's."

"I want you to stay away from Mitifu."

"Why?"

"He's a known communist agitator."

"A what? Do we even use that phrase anymore? It seems so sixties."

"You heard me, Baines. He's a commie. You may remember them. The enemies of freedom and democracy."

"What makes you think he's a communist? For that matter, how do you know that I even met with him? Are you following him . . . or are you following me?"

"It doesn't matter how I know. What matters is that you are associating with a known communist." With visible effort, Viggiano tried to shift to a more conciliatory tack. His smile, however, looked more like a snarl. "Look, Alex, you just got your clearances back, interim clearances at that. I'd hate to see you put that at risk."

Alex knew this was the RSO's idea of the soft sell, but it still came across as an outrageous and naked threat.

"Just so I understand. Is this in the category of friendly advice, or is this an order from the Ambassador?"

"For now, let's just call it friendly advice."

"Thanks, Rick. I'll keep that in mind."

That afternoon, Alex received a last-minute summons to join the Ambassador for a meeting in the Bubble. Peggy could not tell him the subject of the meeting, but she made it clear that it was a command performance.

The secure conference room—really a room within a room—was on the fourth floor of the chancery, down the corridor from the Front Office behind an inconspicuous unmarked door with its own cipher lock. At the appointed hour, Alex keyed in the combination, one of a dozen or so that he had had to commit to memory. A second door, this one steel rather than wood, led to a large room. A small set of steps led up to the hatch of the Bubble, a self-contained conference room suspended six inches off the floor by thick bands of an elastic composite to reduce vibrations. It was the only place in the Embassy, in the whole country, for that matter, where it was possible to talk openly at a Top Secret level.

The room holding the Bubble throbbed with the combined sound of the chillers and the white-noise generators. Alex lifted the heavy arm bar that locked the hatch shut and stepped across the Bubble's raised threshold. The space inside was surprisingly small, an indication of the thickness of the walls. A long conference table filled the room. There was just enough space to squeeze between the chair backs and the side walls to make it down to the far end. The walls were lined with noise-reducing foam panels. With the hatch closed and locked, the ambient noise was reduced to a tolerable level.

Jonah Keeler was already there, along with Bob Jeffries, Colonel Fessler, Viggiano, and the Embassy's Economic and Commercial Counselor, Angela Constantinos. The ECON office was responsible both for reporting on the economic situation in the Congo and for advocating on behalf of American business. In the DRC, that meant primarily resource-extraction industries: oil and gas, mining, and logging. Outside of that, the country really didn't have much of an economy to speak of.

Alex nodded hello to the group at the table and took his seat immediately to the right of the DCM. Although the only assigned seat was the Ambassador's, which was at the head of the table, the country team in just about every embassy developed its own informal seating chart. Alex had not only inherited Julian Wells's office, house, and car, he had also inherited his seat at the conference table. In bureaucratic terms, it was a good chair, reflecting Alex's relatively senior position within the mission hierarchy.

"Anyone know what we are talking about?" Alex asked the group. Most of them shook their heads. Viggiano ignored him. Jeffries was conspicuously silent.

"Haven't got the foggiest," said Deborah Fessler. "I suppose we'll find out when the Ambassador gets here."

The arm bar on the hatch made a sharp clapping sound as it snapped up. Ambassador Spencer strode in, followed by the diminutive Henri Saillard, looking natty in a lightweight charcoal gray suit. His pocket square matched the yellow and blue squares on his expensive-looking tie. Saillard was carrying a three-foot-long mailing tube. Everyone at the table stood up when the Ambassador entered the room. This was long-standing State Department protocol. No one at the table seemed particularly surprised or unhappy at the appearance of Saillard. No one without a security clearance was supposed to be inside the Bubble. No one without a clearance was even supposed to know that there *was* a Bubble. This was Viggiano's patch, however, not Alex's. He wouldn't want the RSO analyzing election results, and Alex had no intention of playing security officer.

Saillard sat to Spence's left, a seat that ordinarily would have gone to the head of the public affairs section, had she been present. It was a desirable chair.

"Thank you all for coming on such short notice," Spence began. "And I apologize for the secrecy. Henri and I have had a couple of meetings this morning about a potentially significant development that I have only just learned about. I want to get your input and develop an action plan. Henri, why don't you bring the team up to date."

Saillard pulled the cap off one end of the mailing tube and pulled out a map, which he unrolled on the conference table. Weighted corners held the map flat.

"Our survey teams have recently identified an extraordinarily rich deposit of copper ore in the Mongala River Valley region. There are also preliminary indications of exploitable quantities of rubidium and tungsten." Saillard pointed to a spot on the map not far from the confluence of the Mongala and the Congo Rivers. "We estimate that full production at the Mongala site could produce approximately one hundred thousand tons of refined copper annually. That's nearly half a billion dollars at current market prices.

"The Mongala River Valley lies outside the area of Consolidated Mining's current concession. Exploiting this deposit will require reaching agreement with the government to extend our exclusive mineral rights into this region. The initial outlay will be considerable and we can only do this if we can lock in an exclusive arrangement for at least the next fifteen years."

"Have you done the research for the environmental impact statement?" Angela Constantinos asked. "That's now a World Trade Organization requirement."

"Which can be waived by national governments," Saillard replied. "We will be soliciting your help in getting Kinshasa to agree to waive the impact statement."

"What kind of operation do you have in mind for this deposit?" Constantinos asked.

"Open-pit with on-site refining."

Constantinos grimaced. "That means essentially chopping off the tops of at least two of these peaks. That's going to produce considerable rubble as a by-product of operations. It's going to be hard to get an environmental waiver for something this big."

"We are confident you will be able to carry this off," Saillard replied. "Consolidated Mining will also be making its own approach to the government on this particular issue." Alex knew that this "approach" would likely involve thick envelopes of cash. Nobody would say this out loud; it was a violation of U.S. as well as local law. But it was also de rigueur for big business deals in the region.

Alex took a hard look at the map. "I see at least half a dozen villages inside the zone you have blocked off for mining operations. How do you propose to handle that?"

"Three of the villages can be converted into work camps for the miners. Three of the villages will have to be relocated. Consolidated is prepared to assist in that admittedly painful process. The villages are not large. The largest village, I believe it is called Busu-Mouli, has maybe fifteen hundred residents. In total, we anticipate that no more than four or five thousand people will be affected by this." Saillard was matter-of-fact about the need to uproot thousands of people to make room for the mine. It was clear that he had done this before.

"Of course," he continued, "it will be easier if we can get the local authorities to recognize that it is ultimately in their own interest to cooperate with us. The mining operation will create jobs and opportunities. We can also help provide security against the activities of some of the more unpleasant paramilitary groups in the region."

The Ambassador spoke up. "This will actually be your job, Alex. I'd like you to serve as the liaison with the local chiefs and convince them to support this project."

Alex nodded, but didn't say anything. He understood the need to support U.S. business interests. It was one of the core missions of every embassy. But he hated what the mining company was planning to do.

The group spent the next thirty minutes analyzing the political, economic, and security aspects of the deal. This was just a preliminary set of ideas. There were a thousand hoops to jump through before an agreement could be signed. But at the end of the session, they had fleshed out a rough strategy. One of the elements of their approach called for Alex to travel to the region to meet with the local chiefs and lay out the benefits of cooperating with Consolidated. Spence asked Angela to write up a synopsis of the agreed strategy and called an end to the meeting.

"Alex, would you stick around for a few minutes?" he asked, as the mission staff began to file out of the Bubble.

"Of course."

After a moment, Spence and Alex were alone in the Bubble. With only the two of them in the room, the noise from the machinery was all the more noticeable.

"I just wanted to make sure that you understood the reasons why I elected not to send in your cable on the Manamakimba mission. You did an absolutely fantastic job, Alex, and it was an excellent cable. I decided to hold off sending the front-channel report only because I didn't want to raise too many red flags in Washington right now about mining company operations in the Congo. If this rises too high on the radar, it'll bring the White House and Commerce into the picture, and they'd almost certainly find a way to screw up the Consolidated deal. This is too big an opportunity to lose because of ham-fisted handling from Washington."

"Thanks, Spence. I'm grateful for your confidence. This is your mission. Ultimately, it's your decision as to what we report. I have no problem with that."

"Even so, it must be somewhat disappointing. I understand your desire to get back in the game, and I promise you that by the end of this, you are going to be back in the middle of things. I'm just about at the end of my string in any event. I expect to be looking for some cushy academic job or consulting position when I'm done here. You have another thirty years ahead of you."

"You make it sound like a sentence."

Alex and Spence both laughed.

"In some ways, maybe it is."

It was only after Alex got back to his office that he realized there was something odd about what Spence had said. He had told everyone at the strategy session that he had just learned about the Consolidated find. How could that have factored into his decision last week not to send Alex's report?

Just as Alex was closing up for the evening and sweeping his office for any stray classified documents that he might have forgotten to lock in his safe, Jonah Keeler stuck his head in.

"Hey, Alex. You got a minute?"

"Sure thing. What's up?"

"Well . . . I ran Marie Tsiolo's name by some friends in the local services. They found her for me."

"Hey, that's excellent. Thank you."

"Don't be so quick to thank me."

"What do you mean?"

"Alex. She's from Busu-Mouli. Your new friend, Saillard, wants to bury her village beneath a million tons of crushed rock."

"Shit."

11

Marie couldn't shake the feeling that all she had done was to buy a little time. Her village was, she feared, doomed.

It was hard, however, to be too gloomy on such a beautiful morning. She sat on the porch of her father's house drinking instant coffee sweetened with condensed milk and watching the village children play soccer with a ball she had brought back from South Africa. It had been only five days since she and the American had negotiated the freedom of the mining company team, but it already felt like something in the distant past.

Her father was awake now. She could hear him puttering in the kitchen area. A few moments later he joined her on the porch, a wooden mug of goat's milk in his hand. He was getting on in years, Marie thought. His hair was now mostly gray and there were new lines in his face that could only be partially ascribed to the burden of leadership. He was wearing a pair of faded canvas pants with a rope belt. The pants reached only as far as his calves. He wore no shoes. Marie thought of the trim black capri pants she had purchased on her last trip to Johannesburg and smiled softly. Her father was naked from the waist up. At nearly sixty, he was still wiry and strong, but his ribs were more prominent than Marie remembered. He was losing weight. This was worrisome.

Like more than a million other Congolese, Chief Moise Tsiolo was HIV-positive. Unlike most, he had access to medications that had so far kept him alive. His daughter had made sure of it.

"Good morning, Papa," Marie offered in the Luba language.

"Good morning, daughter. You're up early." Her father replied in French. He had always insisted on speaking French to her, having observed once that there were no great universities holding their classes in Luba.

"Busy day. I need to bury a big hole."

Her father laughed.

"Don't be hasty, my sweet girl. You've only just gotten home. And don't make any decisions just yet. There have been some changes while you were away."

"I'm sure. I hadn't expected that you would all just sit around and wait for me."

"Some have been waiting. And some things don't change. Jean-Baptiste has been asking for you. He knows you are home."

Marie frowned slightly at this. She and Jean-Baptiste A Nyembo had been briefly involved nearly a decade ago. Papa liked Jean-Baptiste and had not understood why Marie had broken it off. That Marie herself did not fully understand why had made it difficult to explain.

"And just how did he find that out, Papa?" Marie asked.

"It's a small town, Marie. People talk."

"Tell me about it."

After a breakfast of fruit and *liboke*, a whole river fish wrapped in banana leaves and grilled over hot coals, Marie kissed her father on the cheek, grabbed her backpack, and set off across the village. She had almost forgotten how much she loved this place. The village was perched on a hillside along the Mongala, one of the Congo River's major tributaries. Villagers fished for perch in the Mongala River and raised yams and corn in terraced fields built into the hill.

The village was not wealthy, but Marie had seen an opportunity for Busu-Mouli to build the clinics and schools and fishing fleets that would transform the lives of the freehold farmers who served as the backbone of the community. Copper and rubber were the traditional sources of wealth in the Congo, and Marie had hoped that the chalcopyrite deposit she had found would liberate her people and allow them to achieve their full potential. But it was not turning out as she had planned.

Marie climbed the steep and narrow path that led up to the mine site. She stopped to chat with a number of friends and neighbors along the way. The unhurried pace of village life was one of its greatest appeals. It took her more than an hour to make the trip. By the time she reached the mine, the day's work was well under way. Young men were attacking the cliff face with steel tools and filling wicker baskets with raw ore. Marie recognized many of them. Two of them were her cousins. The men carrying the ore baskets downhill to the smelter balanced the load on their backs and carried the weight with a rope or knotted cloth stretched across their foreheads. Their bulging trapezius muscles testified to the grueling demands of the job. There was a hole in the cliff face approximately three meters across. Marie could hear the dull slap of metal on rock and the curses of tired men coming from inside.

An older man stood to one side watching the younger men toiling in the sun. He saw Marie approaching and a grin spread across his face. He walked over to meet her, wrapped her in a tight hug, and kissed her violently on both cheeks. Thomas Katanga was her mother's brother. He was also her father's right-hand man and now the pit boss for the mine. Marie's mine.

"Welcome home, my dear Marie. I heard that you had come back to your father's house. This is a blessing. We prayed to so many different gods for your safe return that there seemed a risk of setting them against each other."

"It's good to be back. I missed you all terribly." They spoke Luba together, and for Marie, the language was a taste of home.

"So tell me, Uncle Thomas," Marie continued, "how's my baby?"

"On balance, pretty good. The tunnel is reasonably stable and the roof seems to be holding. We are using timber to shore it up. It's your design and so far it is working well. My carpenters can build it. We are just going to have to trust your math."

"I've always been good with numbers, Uncle. Don't you worry about that."

"Do you want to see it?"

"You're damn right I do."

Thomas Katanga led Marie on a tour of the mine she had conceived and midwifed but had never seen. The path up to the mine entrance was strewn with broken pieces of ore. Marie picked up a stone and held it close. The rock was a dull yellow, but the brassy metallic streaks of pyrite running through the stone caught the sun and glowed. Even in its raw form, it was clear to Marie just how rich a vein this was.

The mine entrance itself was a perfect half circle. Timber supports formed an inverted V inside the tunnel, theoretically minimizing the risk of a cave-in. It was a simple design that Marie had seen in her textbooks but never in stone and wood.

"We've taken most of the easily accessible ore from the face," Katanga observed. "Now we need to follow the richer veins into the mountain. It was slow going at first and we had a couple of accidents, but the boys are learning a few tricks. Most important, they are learning to be careful. This is never an easy thing to teach young men."

"What kind of progress have you been able to make?"

"Maybe two and a half meters a day. Our real bottleneck is the smelting. There's no point bringing out the ore faster than we can process it. Our total daily output is about one hundred kilograms of pure metal. Not bad. But we are hoping some of the equipment your mining friends have will let us quadruple that."

Marie pretended she hadn't heard the last point. "Let's go inside," she said, as she pulled two headlamps out of her backpack. She gave one to Thomas and slipped the other over her own head.

The walls and floor of the tunnel were rough and uneven, nothing like the smooth finish of the established mines she had worked at in South Africa and Botswana. The shaft sloped gently downward, and Marie could see that Katanga had done a creditable job of following the richest vein of ore as he built the main tunnel. The tunnel led into the cliff for about three hundred meters. Marie knew that the men wouldn't be able to dig much farther without some kind of ventilation. The air was already thick with carbon dioxide. At the base of the tunnel, miners were hard at work hollowing out a large room. Most just nodded hello. A few called out to Marie by name.

"This is about as far in as the vein goes," Katanga observed. "We are following two lesser veins that run parallel to the floor, but the richest ore starts to go deep here. We need to start digging down. Until we get some real equipment, it'll be slow going. I estimate our production will peak sometime in the next week and then start dropping off as we start building down. The boys will have to work short shifts as the air gets stale, and hauling the ore up to the top of the hole is going to add another layer of effort to this."

Marie knew Katanga was looking for reassurance. He wanted to hear that Consolidated Mining was riding to the rescue with a barge full of jackhammers and explosives, ventilators and powered winches. This was not going to happen. Katanga had a right to know that. But she couldn't bring herself to tell him.

"Come, girl, let me show you our smelter."

Marie followed Katanga out of the mine and down the winding

path to the Mongala River. On the bank of the river, there was a large building with a frame made of palm logs and walls made of a collage of various materials. The roof was corrugated tin, a relatively expensive luxury that spoke to the importance of keeping whatever was inside dry. Black smoke belched from the single chimney that protruded from the middle of the roof. A simple wooden dock stuck out into the river and served as a boat landing.

A hand-lettered sign over the front door read UNITED LUBA SMELT-ING. It was true, she realized. This project was already too big for her village to handle on its own. Her father had made deals and alliances with surrounding Luba villages to loan labor, materials, and seed capital to get the mine and smelting operations going. The mine would inevitably reshape the political as well as the physical landscape of the Mongala Valley.

Katanga was visibly proud as he gave her a tour of the "factory." At one end of the single large room, a group of women was sorting and washing the ore to remove dirt and other impurities. Nearby, three men were trying to fix a complex but clearly makeshift machine that seemed designed to function as a rock crusher. Marie saw that it was powered by two truck engines linked together with a single driveshaft. The gears of the crusher were heavy-duty propellers, probably stripped from the fishing boats and ferries that plied the Congo River.

Marie's background was in mine engineering rather than mineral processing. She had put together the schematics for the smelter operations, but her diagram had said simply "put rock crusher here." She was in awe of what the villagers had accomplished.

"This is absolutely amazing, Uncle Thomas. You've done so much."

"It hasn't been easy," Katanga replied. "There have been setbacks. Look at the crusher. One of the engines has burned out again. It happens fairly frequently, but we've been able to keep it running most of the time. The propellers were your father's idea."

"Papa always had a gift for making do. Remember when you and he reconfigured the motors in the fishing boats to run on palm oil when there was a diesel shortage? The fleet smelled like fried plantains."

A clay kiln sat in the middle of the building, radiating heat from the charcoal fire burning beneath it. This was Marie's design, based on kilns that Luba tribes had been using long before the Europeans came to central Africa. Two men worked a large bellows to stoke the fire and create the heat necessary to melt the crushed chalcopyrite into copper metal. As Marie watched, one of the men abandoned the bellows and opened the door to the kiln. He used a metal rod with a hook on one end to extract a large steel pot. Using both arms, he shifted the pot to a hook hanging from the ceiling and used the pole to pull down on an edge of the lid. A shimmering orange liquid spilled out of the pot and into a series of rectangular molds on the floor. Metallic brown bricks from earlier castings were piled next to the molds. This was matte, a crude mixture of molten sulfides. The matte would need to be converted into "blister" copper and then refined by heat and electrolysis before it could be sold on the open market.

This was a low-tech operation. They were skipping a couple of key steps that would have drastically improved the purity of the copper matte. Each step of the smelting process added value to the finished product. The equipment to do this was pretty basic for an operation like Consolidated Mining, but difficult to jury-rig out of boat parts and truck engines. The more sophisticated and expensive equipment was well beyond anything an operation like this could aspire to. The bosses at Consolidated had promised to provide a converter for making blister copper, along with the other specialized machinery that made modern mining the voracious mountain-eating beast it had become.

"I'm blown away by this. I never dreamed you'd move this fast."

"You underestimate us, Marie. You have been away a long time. You have forgotten just what we are capable of. What your father is capable of."

"You're right. I do sometimes forget." Marie swallowed hard at what she had to say next. "Uncle Thomas," she said, after a moment's pause. "They aren't going to help us. The mining company, I mean. What you have accomplished is extraordinary, but we made our plans based on the idea that Consolidated Mining was going to back us with money, equipment, and technical support. I found out just before the last trip . . . the one that ended badly . . . that they aren't going to do that."

Although she had promised herself that she wasn't going to cry, Marie felt her eyes fill, and Katanga's face shimmered slightly as she looked at him through her tears.

He reached out and took hold of both of her arms, clasping her biceps firmly and urgently. "We know that, child. In truth, your father and I, we never expected that they would. We are prepared; we do not need your mining friends."

"It's worse than that," Marie continued. "It isn't that they are going to leave us alone. When the big bosses in New York saw the test results on the ore samples I brought them, they got greedy. Then the Chinese started snapping up every ton of copper and steel and manganese and you-name-it that came on the market. This is a rich find, maybe the richest in the Congo. They want it for themselves. It was one thing to offer us help when it looked like there was little at stake. The ore samples changed that picture for them. The company is negotiating its own deal with the Ministry for Mines and Metals in Kinshasa. Consolidated will buy the usual army of politicians and bureaucrats, and through them, they'll get exclusive mineral rights to the valley. They are going to chop the top off the mountain, fill in the river, and leach the tailings with acid to extract every last damn molecule of copper. And it's my fault, Uncle. I'm sorry."

"It's okay, Marie. I understand. Your father understands."

"He told you already, didn't he? You knew all the while you were giving me the grand tour."

"He told me last night after you went to bed. It's a difficult situation, but perhaps not as desperate as it might seem. We have options."

"Yes, we do. We can bury the mine. We fill in the entrance to the mineshaft and cover the scars with brush. Then we lose the charts and burn the smelter to the ground. We can pull up the survey stakes and relocate them on the other side of the river valley. In the meantime, we can think of something else."

"We already have. Your father, that is. Come. Let me show you."

Katanga led Marie back toward the village. In the field just on the edge of Busu-Mouli where Marie and her friends had once played soccer, a group of young men was training with rifles. Twenty men—boys really, Marie realized—were taking turns charging four at a time with fixed bayonets at dummies made of straw and wrapped in canvas. Another group of boys was practicing marksmanship, firing at wooden targets oriented so that stray rounds would land harmlessly in the forest. Other small groups were practicing a range of military skills. A few were marching. Some were disassembling and cleaning rifles. Nearly all of the "soldiers," and Marie put imaginary quotes around the word even as she thought it, were barefoot. A few carried tree branches rather than rifles.

"We have been investing some of the profits from the mining operation in our army," Katanga explained. "Copper for guns. Jean-Baptiste has been in charge of that. Your father has appointed him Captain of the Guard."

Marie almost laughed at the grandiosity of the title. But she took a moment to observe the tall, well-built man leading the riflery training. Jean-Baptiste seemed comfortable in command.

Katanga pointed out an older man in a military uniform who was teaching some of the younger boys how to strip and clean a Kalashnikov. Marie recognized her father's old army uniform even before recognizing her beloved papa. Chief Tsiolo smiled when he saw his daughter and beckoned her and Katanga to join him on the field.

"Well, Marie. How is your mine?" he asked.

"My mine, Papa?"

"If it isn't yours, then who does it belong to?"

"All of us, I suppose. How are your soldiers doing?"

"How do they look?"

Marie thought about the disciplined and battle-hardened troops that Manamakimba had led against the Consolidated Mining team. Then she surveyed the young boys just becoming familiar with the seductive power of the gun. There was no comparison.

"Magnificent, Papa," she answered.

12

It was an unlovely, ungainly contraption—Marie would not go so far as to call it a machine—but it was getting the job done. Her home-made rock drill was never going to take the market by storm. Instead of hydraulic pumps, Marie's drill used a system of sandbag counterweights and the muscle of three of the village's young men. Another villager on a modified bicycle powered the chain drive that turned the drill bit. The Chinese-made tricone bit at the bottom of the shaft was the one honest-to-God piece of mining equipment she was using. Katanga had traded for it, and it had cost nearly two days of production. It was worth every ounce of copper. The saving grace of the project was the depth she was drilling to. By Marie's math, she and her crew had to drill down no more than fifty feet through solid stone before intersecting the mine. She had surveyed the site carefully to make absolutely certain that she would hit the target. Now they were very close.

"Not much longer, Uncle, I can feel it," Marie said.

"I hope so. The air in the mine is getting pretty stale. There's not enough oxygen to keep a candle lit."

Almost on cue, the sandbags pushed the metal pipes through the roof of the mine and crashed to the ground with a heavy thud.

"We're in," Marie shouted. Katanga wrapped her up in an affectionate hug.

"That's my girl," he said.

Marie put her hand over the end of the pipe and could feel the warm, foul air rushing up from below. Cool, oxygenated air would be forced in through the mouth of the tunnel because of the change in pressure. At some point a fire underneath the vent might help to hurry things along, but for now Mother Nature should be able to handle the load.

Once she was satisfied that the hole was clean and solid and in no risk of collapsing in on itself, Marie supervised the dismantling and storage of her rock drill. If everything continued to go well, they would need it again at some point.

Then she went back to her baby, the smelter.

Marie and Katanga had agreed on a rough division of labor. He would oversee the mining operations, calling on Marie for assistance when he encountered a particularly challenging technical problem such as ventilating the mine shaft. Marie, meanwhile, would take over the smelter and look for ways to improve the quality of the finished product.

She had taken to sleeping most nights in the back room of the smelter that she had converted into an office. Before Marie's return, Katanga hadn't bothered to keep any records on production. Whatever came in as raw ore was processed as quickly as possible. Whatever came out as metal was sold or traded. It was simple. No one had thought to write it down.

Marie surveyed the charts and graphs she had tacked up on the walls behind her desk, which was nothing more than an old door laid across two oil drums. The charts tracked only the last ten days of production, but she could see that there had been a noticeable rise in both the quantity of metal produced and the purity of the copper. Some of the refinements she had initiated were already paying dividends. It was a start, but it wasn't enough. *There is more I can do*, Marie thought. *I am sure of it.*

Flora, one of the older villagers who served as an unofficial shift leader, stuck her head into the office.

"Marie, one of the belts on the rock crusher snapped again. We had to shut the machine down."

Marie sighed. The crusher was the most temperamental element of the smelter operations. Nearly every day, something went wrong.

"Get Omer or one of his boys to look at it. If he has to scavenge a belt from one of the fishing boats, so be it."

Flora nodded, but looked none too happy. Marie knew that if Omer Mputu couldn't get the machine up and running in short order, Flora would browbeat him until the screws were spinning again and happily crushing big rocks into small rocks.

At first, Marie thought that the crusher had jammed and the drive shaft was stripping the gears. But it was the middle of the night, and she quickly realized that what she was hearing was gunfire. Instantly awake and alert, she threw off the thin blanket covering her and jumped to her feet. It was dark in the windowless office where she had been sleeping on a straw pallet. The generator had been shut down for the night, so there were no lights to turn on. She fumbled for the flashlight she kept on the desk, hoping that the batteries were still charged. She breathed a little easier when she hit the button and a dim brown glow lit up the room.

Marie reached under the desk and pulled on the strip of duct tape that held a pistol in place. She stripped the tape from the handgun, a Yugoslav Zastava, and made sure the safety was off. The red dot on the side was clearly visible. *Red is dead*, she remembered from one of the security training courses they had put her through at Consolidated. Marie had fired the gun maybe three or four times in that course.

There was another round of gunfire, closer this time. Marie's first thoughts were for her smelter. One of the changes she had implemented after taking over was to put a night watchman in place to prevent looting. When Marie had turned in, a sixteen-year-old boy named Kamba had just started his shift.

"Where the hell is he," Marie whispered to herself.

She moved slowly and carefully out of her office and into the main hall of the smelter. She held the pistol in her right hand and the flashlight in her left. The beam was too weak to illuminate the far side of the facility. The flashlight cast a half circle of brown light extending out about six feet. Beyond that, the room was in darkness.

"Kamba," she said softly. And then a little louder. "Kamba, are you here?"

There was no response.

The pistol felt heavy and awkward in her hand. Marie checked again to make sure the safety was off. *Red is dead. Red is dead.* Another chattering round of automatic-weapons fire. This time, she could see the muzzle flash framed in one of the windows. Closer than before.

Marie made her way carefully to the door on the far side. She stepped across the threshold, making almost no sound in her bare feet.

"Kamba, where are you?" She was whispering again.

Outside the door, Marie shone the light to her right and swung it in a wide arc. As she was doing so, she stepped back away from the door and stumbled over something soft and sticky. She knew immediately what it was and had to consciously stifle the sob that welled up unbidden from inside her. She turned the flashlight onto the body of the young boy. His throat had been slit.

There was a distinct odor of gasoline in the air, and Marie could hear muffled noises coming from around the corner of the smelter. Her smelter.

She turned off the flashlight and placed it gently on the ground beside Kamba's body. With its weak beam, it was more of a liability than an asset. It would not help her find the intruders, but it would give them something to shoot at. Pressing her body flat against the side of the building, Marie moved slowly and carefully to the corner. A three-quarters moon emerged from behind the clouds and cast enough light to see by. She looked around the edge of the building. She saw three men. One was kneeling by the side of the smelter pouring the contents of a jerry can of what could only be gasoline onto the walls. The other two stood behind him, watching him work.

"You finish up here," she heard one of them say in slightly accented French. "Juvenal, come with me and we'll take care of the inside." Marie recognized the accent. It was Rwandan. These were almost certainly Hutu *genocidaires*. What the hell where they doing here and why did they want to burn down her smelter?

Marie was damned if they were going to do that without a fight.

Without a clear idea of what she was going to accomplish, Marie aimed the heavy pistol at the only man not carrying a heavy can of gas on the assumption that he was the leader. She squeezed off three shots in rapid succession. All three shots missed. Shooting a man, she realized, was not the same thing as shooting paper targets.

The *genocidaires* seemed uncertain which direction the shots had come from. The man she had shot at was carrying an assault rifle and he sprayed an entire magazine in a wide arc. Most of the rounds sailed harmlessly into the jungle, but one bullet slammed into the smelter wall near Marie's head. She jerked her head back from the corner.

The Rwandans were experienced. They spread out to make themselves a more difficult target and moved aggressively toward Marie's side of the smelter. Marie fired two more rounds around the corner without even aiming and ran back to the door.

Inside, the smelter was almost pitch-black. The pale moonlight that filtered through the door and the few small windows did little more than define several different shades of darkness. For a moment Marie was afraid that the *genocidaires* were not going to follow her; that they would simply burn the building down with her inside it. But they did come after her; maybe they were still uncertain about how many opponents they were facing and unwilling to turn their backs on a potential danger. Unlike Marie, the Rwandans had decent flashlights, and they swung their beams around the room looking for someone to shoot.

"Split up," she heard them say. "Find whoever it is and kill them. No prisoners today."

Marie huddled behind the furnace, her mind racing as she looked for a way out. She could hear her breath coming in rapid gasps and she struggled for calm.

A shaft of light swept through the air over her head. She could tell from watching the beam that one of the Rwandans was moving from the back end of the furnace toward the door. In front of the door, Marie knew, a heavy steel cauldron used for smelting copper ore was hanging from a chain. It was almost directly above her. Maybe just a couple of feet to the right. She tucked the pistol into the waistband of her pants. When the *genocidaire* was almost exactly across from her, Marie rose and pushed the heavy cauldron forward with both hands. It slammed into the Rwandan's face with a satisfying crunch of bone. The flashlight went skittering across the floor, and Marie heard both the soldier and his rifle fall to ground.

Marie pushed herself deep into the shadow of the machinery and listened carefully. She could hear one *genocidaire* across the room, probably next to the rock crusher. The other seemed to be moving carefully toward the office, where she had been sleeping less than fifteen minutes earlier.

"Juvenal. Forget this. Let's just finish the job."

There was no response. Juvenal, Marie realized, must be the one sleeping the sleep of the cracked skull.

"Juvenal. Can you hear me?" The voice came from the area near the tables where the village women sorted and washed the copper ore before it was smelted. Marie could see the flashlight beam of the third *genocidaire* panning across the far wall near the office. There was no one between her and the door. It might yet be possible to live through this. Live through this and save her smelter.

Marie crawled carefully toward the door. She stayed low to the ground, using every shadow to her advantage. Once outside, she planned to empty the jerry cans of gasoline into the river and then go for help. It was the best she could do on short notice.

The door frame was only about twenty meters away, but it seemed to take forever to cover the distance. Marie was close to the door, no more than five meters away, when she suddenly found herself impaled at the center of a bright circle of blue-white light. She froze. The light felt like an actual weight pressing on her spine. It was as though she could feel the individual photons holding her in place like a bug pinned to a mat.

"Well, look at that. It's just a girl." The speaker was the one Marie had tentatively identified as the leader. She recognized his voice. He had been waiting for her, Marie realized. He knew that she would try for the door.

"There must be others." The voice of the remaining *genocidaire*— the arsonist—came from her left. He had covered the distance from the office quickly and quietly, closing the door of the trap that Marie now found herself in.

"I don't think so. I think the girl is all there is. I'll take care of her."

With the flashlight beams shining into her face, Marie couldn't see so much as an outline of the Rwandans. She had heard stories about what the Hutu had done to the Tutsi in Rwanda. Crimes so awful the perpetrators could never go home. She reached carefully for the pistol in the waistband of her pants.

"Don't do that, little girl." It was the leader's voice. "It'll be easier for you that way."

The Rwandan raised his rifle and the shadow of the barrel fell across Marie's face. Involuntarily, she closed her eyes.

The staccato chatter of automatic-weapons fire was the last sound Marie expected to hear in her young life. It was followed almost immediately by a scream that she realized with some surprise was not her own. She opened her eyes.

The arsonist still stood to her right, but his head was cocked at an unnatural angle and much of it seemed to be missing. The leader was lying on the floor. The flashlight lying next to him cast monstrous shadows of his profile onto the far wall of the smelter. The *genocidaire*'s screams grew weak and raspy. Marie saw a stream of blood flowing from his chest, following the dips and valleys in the uneven floor.

She was still uncertain about what had happened. She reached down and touched the barrel of her pistol. It was tucked into her waistband. She hadn't shot them. Marie carefully shifted first onto her hands and knees, and then into a kneeling position behind the rock crusher. She could see a flashlight beam searching back and forth through the smelter. Whoever had shot the two Rwandans was looking for more targets.

"Marie, are you there? Are there any others?"

"Jean-Baptiste?" she called hopefully.

"Yes. Are there any others?" he repeated.

"There's one more over by the furnace, but I think I broke his skull."

Jean-Baptiste did not waste a moment. He moved quickly, holding his rifle with one hand and running the flashlight back and forth across the floor with the other. Suddenly he stopped. Marie heard two quick shots. Only then did Jean-Baptiste come to her, smelling of gunpowder and killing. Without another word, he took her in his arms. Marie clung to him and began sobbing violently into his chest.

13

I t's a hell of a country, ain't it? Primordial, even." J. J. Sykes had to shout so Alex could hear him over the prop noise. Sykes nudged the controls of the de Havilland DHC-3 Otter to keep the aircraft on course as the Congo River below them began to curve north. Sykes had been in the Congo for the better part of three years, flying around central Africa for Ibis Air Cargo, a company that was almost, but not quite, a wholly owned subsidiary of the Central Intelligence Agency. In addition to being a pilot, Sykes was an aspiring poet, which was why he tried to slip words such as "primordial" into his conversation. "I mean, it's like the country is a living thing," Sykes continued when Alex failed to rise to the "primordial" bait. "It's like a single organism, with the rivers serving as veins and arteries. The jungle is like the lungs. You know what I mean."

"I suppose I do, J.J.," Alex replied resignedly. They had been flying for nearly two and a half hours now, and J. J. Sykes hadn't stopped talking for more than five minutes of the flight.

"I always thought of her as a woman. The Congo, I mean. Some of the other countries we fly in are male. Namibia, for example, is a strapping young lad, all rock and desert and heat. Namibia calls you out. Namibia has balls. Namibia will kill you like a man. The Congo, though, she's a sneaky, seductive bitch. She'll wait till you ain't looking and then stick a knife between your shoulder blades into your heart."

"That's an interesting theory." Part of Alex hoped that they would be landing soon so that he could escape the incessant yammering of J. J. Sykes. A larger part of him was so unhappy with what he had been tasked to do in Busu-Mouli that he might just as well circle the village in the single-engine Otter for the next week or so.

"It's a shame that there are so many things down there that want you dead. It looks beautiful and healthy enough from up here, but that is one wild-ass place at ground level."

Alex just nodded. He studied the terrain below. Sykes was operating just on the edge of sanity, but Alex had to admit that he had a point, at least about the Congo's rivers. They were the country's vital arteries. The late afternoon sun reflecting off the surface of the water set the extraordinary network of rivers and lakes into sharp relief against the dark background of the jungle canopy. Occasional towns and villages lined the banks of the Congo River, but the vast majority of the land they were flying over was wilderness.

"We're coming up on the confluence of the Mongala and Congo Rivers," Sykes reported. "Busu-Mouli should be about five miles up the Mongala on the right bank. There should be a couple of smaller villages nearby, but Busu-Mouli will be the big one."

"Can we take a pass over the village before we land?" Alex asked. *Might as well get a good look at it before we bury it.*

"I don't see why not. Hey, this baby is equipped with external speakers. You want me to cue up 'The Ride of the Valkyries' when we do the flyover?"

"I'm pretty sure that *Apocalypse Now* hasn't made it to the Busu-Mouli multiplex yet."

Alex pointed toward a large building, the largest they had seen since leaving Kinshasa, right on the edge of the Mongala River. A handful of fishing boats were tied up along one side of a dock next to the building.

"What's that down there?"

"It looks like a warehouse of some kind," Sykes answered. "But it isn't on any of the charts and I didn't see anything like it in the satellite photos our mutual friend Jonah shared with me."

"How old were the photos?"

"Six months or so, I suppose."

"Is that Busu-Mouli?"

"The cluster of buildings upriver from the big one should be Busu-Mouli, at least by the map. I'd say a thousand people . . . maybe two thousand maximum . . . in that village. Maybe another two or three thousand in the various villages scattered around."

"Let's go check it out."

For the first time in the flight, Sykes stopped talking. He lifted the nose of the Otter to bleed off airspeed and lose some altitude. For all of his quirks, Sykes was a smooth and accomplished pilot. He flew low and slow over Busu-Mouli, giving Alex a chance to survey the town and the landscape. The town had a clear main street, a wide avenue of red earth lined with a hodgepodge collection of buildings. A few side streets radiated off the main drag. There were quite a number of people in the streets. Most were looking up at the plane, shielding their eyes from the sun for a better look.

"J.J., can you bring us in a loop around the hills to the north of town." Alex wanted to check out the site that Consolidated had identified as the source of copper ore.

"No problem. We've got plenty of gas for the round trip."

The countryside was stunningly beautiful. Carpets of thick jungle mixed with a patchwork of farm fields. The Congo was still the wildest country in Africa, maybe the wildest country in the world. But underneath the Congo's fragile green shell there was a wealth of riches that greedy men would be unable to ignore for much longer. Civil war or no, Alex knew, the outside world was coming after the Congo's mineral wealth.

From his bird's-eye vantage point, Alex saw a wide, well-tended track that led from the unexplained warehouse on the river's edge up into the hills. As Sykes gently rolled the Otter around the first hill, Alex saw that the path disappeared under what looked like a broad swath of camouflage netting. Alex pointed it out to Sykes.

"Can you get me any closer to that?"

"I can try. But the winds will get tricky if we get too close to the cliff."

"Don't do anything crazy. But see how close you can get us without one of those 'unscheduled landings.'"

"Man, you shoulda seen some of the shit we used to pull back in the 'Nam with Air America."

Sykes put the Otter into a sharp banking turn and flew parallel to the jungle track that led up from the warehouse. At the closest point, the wingtip was no more than ten feet from the camouflage net. Alex couldn't make out what was underneath. Whatever it was, however, it seemed that it must be important to someone who was unhappy with the interest they were demonstrating in the site.

"Holy shit, that's ground fire." Sykes immediately rolled the Otter away from the cliff and kept low to the ground as he slipped the plane back toward the river.

"To be fair, they did just catch us sneaking a peek through the bedroom windows. Let's go knock on the front door and see if that improves the mood. Can you set us down in the river and pull up to the dock by the warehouse?"

"You sure you want to do it that way? This Otter is unarmed, but I got some other planes back at the field that pack a bit more of a punch."

"I'm sure. Let's do it this way. You catch more flies with honey."

"You'll catch even more with a corpse."

"Let's try not to test that out."

Sykes brought the Otter down gently on the wide Mongala River and pulled alongside the dock opposite the fishing boats. He cut the power to the prop, but left the engine running as he hopped out to tether the aircraft. Sykes was leaving open the possibility that they were going to have to leave in a hurry. By the time Alex scrambled across the pilot's seat and out onto the dock, there was a welcoming committee waiting for them. Five men wearing civilian clothes but carrying military-grade firearms stood between them and the shore. Alex stepped forward. He did not want to appear either weak or uncertain in approaching this conversation. He stopped quickly, however, when the men pointed the muzzles at his chest.

"You are trespassing in Busu-Mouli," a tall man at the front of the group said in French. "You are not welcome here. Get back in your plane and we will allow you to leave unharmed."

"Please let me explain why we're here. My name is Alex Baines. I am with the American Embassy in Kinshasa. I have some information that I would like to talk over with the headman of Busu-Mouli. If that's you, let's talk. If not, I'd welcome an opportunity to meet with the Chief."

"You have thirty seconds to get back inside your airplane." All five guns seemed to zero in on a spot in the middle of Alex's chest.

"Let's come back with something with a chain gun attached," said Sykes in an exaggerated stage whisper.

Alex was stumped. He didn't want to go back empty-handed, but he would be damned if he was going to get himself killed defending the interests of a publicly traded mining company. Before either party was forced to back down, a woman came sauntering down the path that led from the dock to the warehouse. Alex could tell even before she was close enough to see her face clearly that it was Marie Tsiolo. She was wearing green cotton pants with a trendy alligator belt and a yellow top.

Back at Manamakimba's camp, Marie had worn her braided hair pulled back into a ponytail. Now it hung loose down to her shoulders. She looked good. She was also in no hurry. She called something to the men with guns in a language that Alex could not understand but that he assumed was Luba. She took her time descending the hill and surveyed the scene carefully before speaking. Despite Alex's role in helping to secure her release from captivity, she looked at him without even a hint of welcome.

"What's going on, Jean-Baptiste?" she said in French to the tall man who had been doing the speaking for the group. "Is this what Busu-Mouli hospitality has come to in my time away? We should at least ask Mr. Baines what he's doing here."

"You know him?" Jean-Baptiste looked away from Alex and focused on Marie. His gun didn't move.

"Yes. He helped negotiate the release of the mining party from Manamakimba."

"So?"

"So I'm inclined to give him the benefit of the doubt. And I would prefer that you not shoot him without first finding out why he is here."

"You know why he is here and so do I. He's after our copper."

"Maybe so. I suppose you could try to beat the truth out of him. On the other hand, we could just ask him." Marie reached out one hand and pushed the barrel of Jean-Baptiste's gun down toward the ground. He didn't resist. As the weapon dropped, his men disengaged their muzzles from Alex's midsection. There was a palpable easing of tension. Jean-Baptiste shot Alex a look that was at least as devastating as the bullet in the chamber.

"So, how about it, Mr. Baines," Marie said, turning from Jean-Baptiste and taking a hard look at Alex. "What brings you to our humble village?"

"There are some things that are happening that you should know about, Ms. Tsiolo. Whether they're good or bad, I'm not in a position to say. But they are important and there will be choices to make. There are some options . . . possibilities that I would like to discuss with your headman or the village council."

"You mean my father, Chief Tsiolo."

"I suppose I do." *Damn. Keeler hadn't told him that part, and it certainly had not been in her file.*

"Well then. Let me take you to him."

Alex grabbed his briefcase out of the plane and followed Marie up a steep path that led toward the town he had surveyed from the air. It was a dirt track, but it was both well built and well maintained. Logs set into the ground at regular intervals formed a rough stairway. Marie said nothing as they hiked up the hill. She seemed more aloof than she had been during the long negotiation with Manamakimba.

"You look well, Marie." Alex used her first name, hoping that it would help break through the crust of ice that seemed to lie between them. "Have you been in touch with Dr. Wheeler? I understand that he's out of the hospital and back in the States."

"I heard the same thing, but I haven't spoken to Steve myself," Marie said in her lightly accented English. "In fact, I haven't been in touch with anyone from Consolidated Mining since our captivity. Have you?"

This last sentence came out as much an accusation as a question, but Alex elected to take it at face value. He lengthened his stride slightly so that he could catch up to Marie and walk alongside her.

"Arlene Zimmerman sent me a letter from Johannesburg. She asked for a transfer. Can't say that I blame her. Charlotte is out of the business altogether. Arlene told me that she was joining some sort of Silicon Valley start-up. Mike Tanner, I understand, is taking a job in the oil fields in Alberta. And Sven is already back in the field with Consolidated. Arlene said that he was looking for rubidium in the south, somewhere near Bukama. The only one Arlene didn't know anything about was you. The Consolidated people in Kinshasa told me you resigned. Have you moved back here permanently?"

"I never truly left. This is my home. I went away for school and for a little work experience on top of that, but I never gave up my place in my father's house."

"I can see that. I left home at seventeen, but my mother still keeps my old bedroom pretty much as I left it, right down to the basketball trophies and the algebra books. My daughter's sleeping in it right now."

"How old is your girl?"

"Anah's nine. I adopted her in Sudan a couple of years ago. She's spending the summer with my family in America, but she'll be here in Kinshasa in time to start school in September. I hope you get a chance to meet her. I think that she would like you."

"I'm afraid there aren't very many mementos from my childhood in my room. We didn't have very much."

"And now?"

"Things are better now. My father is a good leader. It's been hard for everyone, of course, since the wars began." Marie had used the plural and Alex supposed that was fair. The ten-year-old civil war was so complex that it was like a dozen wars laid on top of one another.

"You all seem pretty capable of defending yourselves," Alex observed.

Marie laughed. "You mean Jean-Baptiste and his boys. That was another one of my father's ideas. I admit I was skeptical at first, but they have proven themselves. We have the *genocidaire* graves to prove it."

"Rwandans?" Alex was surprised by that. "What were they doing this far west?"

"I don't know. The ones who came here are all dead. There have been no more."

Marie lapsed into silence. Alex had the impression that she felt she had somehow said more than she should have. They walked side by side for another few minutes before the jungle opened up to reveal the town of Busu-Mouli. By the admittedly low standards of Congolese villages, Busu-Mouli seemed a relatively prosperous place. The streets were smooth and free of trash, the houses looked to be in good repair, and there was an unmistakable atmosphere of positive activity. There were no cars or motorcycles in the village. The only transportation of any kind seemed to be the ubiquitous *chukudus*. These were essentially oversize wooden scooters made by hand. Strips of rubber wrapped around the wheels helped smooth the ride. The *chukudus* looked primitive, but they were durable and, in the hands of an experienced driver, surprisingly fast. They could also carry a heavy load, and Alex saw stacks of firewood, baskets of cassava, and even three live pigs being carted about the village.

Chief Tsiolo's house—Marie's house—was at the far end of the town's main street. The walls were straight and the steps that led up to the front porch were new and the roof freshly thatched. A coat of white paint and a couple of flowerpots on the porch made the house look almost like a country cottage. Chief Tsiolo was sitting on the porch. He was dressed in khaki shorts and a blue shirt that he wore unbuttoned, exposing his thin frame and ropy muscles. He watched Alex and Marie approach, but his face remained impassive. Alex climbed the steps up to the porch and extended his hand. Tsiolo rose from his chair to take it. His grip was firm and he had the rough calluses of a man who made his living with his hands. The Chief didn't speak, but he gestured for them to take a seat at the small table. Alex had hoped that Marie would introduce him to her father, but she seemed to be in no hurry to do so.

"Chief Tsiolo," he began, after a brief hesitation, "my name is Alex Baines. I'm with the U.S. Embassy in Kinshasa. I have some information that I believe would be of value to you."

Tsiolo said nothing in response. It took a real effort on Alex's part not to rush to fill the gap. Americans in general were uncomfortable with silence in conversation. Over the years, Alex had gotten used to the slower rhythms of Africa. He was less impatient than he had once been, less impulsive.

After a minute or two of quiet, during which he seemed to be thinking through the various implications of Alex's identity, Chief Tsiolo offered his response. "I know who you are. I know why you have come. The answer is no. Can I offer you some palm wine? It's been cooled in the river."

All in all, a very unpromising beginning, Alex decided.

14

JUNE 30, 2009
BUSU-MOULI

Marie had to admit that she was impressed with how Alex had handled his presentation. He was articulate, engaging, persuasive, and ultimately unsuccessful. Throughout the afternoon's long discussion, Marie had said little. Her father was Chief even if he was barely literate. Instead, Marie had taken on the role her mother would have played had she been alive, serving palm wine and food to the men as they talked.

Alex, she understood, had not been fooled by this little charade. He looked to her for reactions as much as to her father. In fact, he looked at her often. Almost unconsciously, Marie found herself straightening her back and smoothing her hair. She caught herself doing it and scowled slightly.

Alex made his points, and he made them well. They were the same points she had made to herself in her own internal dialogue on the risks and rewards of the course she had charted for her village. Work with

150

the mining company and you at least get something. Oppose the company and you risk coming away with less than nothing.

Alex had illustrated his argument with examples from Botswana and South Africa, where genuine partnerships between local communities and multinational corporations had worked out to everyone's benefit. He spoke confidently, but without the typical American bravado that too often risked crossing over into arrogance. At the same time, there was something profoundly sad about this American, even if Marie couldn't quite put her finger on what it was.

In the face of Alex's presentation, Chief Tsiolo was unmovable.

"You seem like a reasonable young man," he said. "You are at least polite to your elders. Too many of your generation cannot be bothered. They won't take the time to pay their respects to an old man. But you have come to me with a proposal that I can never accept. You would have me abandon my home, sell our future—the future of my people— for a truckload of promises and thirty pieces of silver. I am all too aware of what the promises of Consolidated Mining are worth. The Luba people do not need to rely on Consolidated's generosity to benefit from the wealth that lies beneath our feet. We do not need their permission."

"I understand that, Chief," Alex replied. "But you should know that there are powerful players, some foreign and some Congolese, that have fixed their sights on the copper that they can find in your mountains. This gives you the leverage you need to negotiate a fair deal. If you reject this, others will make the decision for you, and these others will have no particular interest in protecting either the Luba heritage or the Luba people."

"We will take our chances. We are not completely defenseless." Tsiolo gestured to Marie, who refilled Alex's glass of palm wine from the jug on the table.

"Do you mean Jean-Baptiste and his militia? I don't think they play in the same league as our mutual friends from Consolidated Mining."

"Maybe not. But we have more at stake. Never underestimate a man who is defending his home."

"Sound advice."

"We are a warrior people. The Luba empire once extended as far as the shores of Lake Tanganyika. Failure to resist would dishonor my ancestors."

"Respectfully, Chief. That's not entirely true." Alex spoke slowly, seeming to choose his words with care. "The Luba were—and are—great warriors. But the empire was built on trade and commerce, not conquest. Your greatest kings, Ilungu Sungu and Kumwimbe Ngombe, expanded their reach to the north and east by trading salt and copper and gold. They were never afraid to fight, but they knew that was rarely the best way to defend their interests."

"You know our history," Chief Tsiolo acknowledged, somewhat grudgingly. "Do you know your own? Do you know what you Europeans have done to my country and my people?"

"Yes." Alex looked at Marie and then turned to lock eyes with her father. There was something in his expression, a powerful emotion that she could not quite interpret. It seemed somehow both very sad and very far away. "I know this all too well. I will not forget, and I know that you cannot. I love this beautiful country and I have enormous respect for the Luba people. I understand your fears about Consolidated Mining. In truth, I share them. I cannot tell you that I trust the mining company or that you should. All I can do is promise that I will do absolutely everything in my power to make sure that the company abides by the terms of whatever agreement you reach. That is all I can offer. It has to be enough."

There was a long pause as Chief Tsiolo considered what Alex had said, and Marie thought for a moment that her father might be softening. Then the Chief shook his head, almost as though he were trying to shake the doubt from his mind.

"I believe we have reached the end of our official discussions. I have heard you out as courtesy dictates and you have my answer. Now I hope that you will join us for dinner and spend the night in my house as my guest."

Marie looked sharply at her father. She knew him too well to believe he didn't have a reason for doing this, but it was hard to fathom what that might be. The American diplomat seemed a genuinely decent man, but he was on the other side. There was no room in Marie's world or her father's to accommodate that kind of choice.

"What about my pilot?" Alex asked.

"Do not worry," Tsiolo responded. "He will be well looked after."

"I would be pleased to accept your invitation."

"We have several hours before dinner," Tsiolo observed. "Marie, why don't you show our guest around the village. Show him the mine and the smelter. Let him see what we have accomplished on our own and how little we need the guiding hand of his mining friends."

Marie bowed her head slightly. "Of course, Father."

Marie gave Alex almost the same tour that Katanga had given her when she had arrived home. They started with the mine, and she indulged Alex's probing questions about the technical details of mining operations. She was proud of her mine and she enjoyed showing it off. From the top of the bluff where she had set up the drilling equipment, they had a sweeping view of the valley. The valley floor was green and vibrant and the whitewashed houses in the village stood out in sharp relief. The neatly square cultivated fields of maize, yams, and barley contrasted with the sprawling green chaos of the forest.

"If Consolidated has its way," Marie said, "all of this will be buried under the rubble tailings from the mine."

"What happens with the waste rock from your own mining activities?" Alex asked. "Won't those present the same challenge?"

"Not at all. We're doing what's called slope mining, following the natural path of the richest veins of ore deep into the mountain. It's a lot of work, particularly without machines, but it produces minimal tailings. What Consolidated wants to do is to cut the mountains in half, feast on the innards, and dump what's left into the river. It's easier and cheaper than slope mining and infinitely more destructive. It maximizes Consolidated's profits, but this valley won't be habitable for hundreds of years after they're through with it. And you're going to help them do it, Alex." It was only after she said it that Marie realized she had called him by his first name.

"I hear what you're saying, Marie. I really do. In truth, I'm still hoping to find a way that everyone can win. I don't work for Consolidated Mining. It's an American company, but I work for the American people. They're not the same thing. I'm pretty sure the people I work for would like to see this work out so that Busu-Mouli and Consolidated can help each other."

"That's just not going to happen."

"Look, you've done amazing things here, all of it without power and modern tools. Isn't it possible that with a little financing and technical help from Consolidated, you could benefit from increased production and the mining company could turn a fair profit as well?"

"It's not only possible, it's optimal," Marie said. "But it's not going to happen."

"Well why not?"

"Because Consolidated has already rejected that deal. It's exactly what I had proposed when I discussed this site with Jack Karic and his overboss, that jackal Henri Saillard. Saillard accepted the deal, led me on for a while, and then had Karic tell me that it was all off only a few days before the exploration trip that Manamakimba and the Hammer of God cut a little short."

"*You* told Saillard that there was copper here? That's how they know about this deposit?"

Marie bit the inside of her cheek to keep her lips from trembling, but there was no disguising the sadness in her eyes. "Yes, I did. You can say this is all my fault if you want. I thought we needed help. I thought it would be too hard. That we couldn't do it on our own. I underestimated my father and my people. I won't do that again. I suggest you don't make the same mistake."

"How long has Saillard known about this place?"

"More than six months now."

"Six months? Jesus, we just heard about this a few days ago. And Saillard told us that it was a brand-new find."

"Well, then he's been playing you for a fool too." Marie shook her head in disgust. "Let's go," she said, looking for a way to change the subject. "I'll show you the smelter."

The smelter was hot and busy. About twenty villagers were hard at work, carrying the raw ore, tending the fires, and pouring molten copper into the steel molds. As the villagers gained experience, they had grown more efficient and Marie was proud of just how far they had come in a very short time.

"Were you trying to improve the ventilation in here?" Alex asked, pointing to the bullet holes on the south side of the building.

"We had a little incident the other night. Some *genocidaires* thought they could shut us down. They're dead now, so I guess they were wrong. The holes aren't in anything structural so there's no rush to fix them. We'll get around to it eventually, but there's still a lot to do."

"This is a pretty impressive setup," Alex observed, looking around the crowded room. "What are they working on?"

Three men were bent over one of the few actual machines in the enormous open room with a box of tools at their feet.

"That's the rock crusher. It does the job, but it's somewhat fragile. Our mechanics have to break it down at least once a day."

Alex walked over to the machine. The men had taken the machine apart and were in the process of rebuilding it. They smiled at Marie, nodded dismissively toward Alex, and continued working. Alex watched them for a few minutes.

To Marie, it seemed pretty clear what the problem was. The metal shaft that held the repurposed boat propellers in place was warped. It was a chronic problem that the village's best mechanics had not yet been able to fix.

"Have you given any thought to using something other than propellers to crush the ore?" Alex finally asked in Lingala.

None of the men responded to Alex. The older man looked at Marie for some kind of signal.

"It's all right, Mputu. He's a friend . . . I think," she added after a moment's hesitation.

"Mputu is our chief mechanic," Marie explained. "These boys are his apprentices and his sons.

"This is Mr. Baines," she continued, gesturing at Alex as though there were someone else she might have been speaking of. Mputu had known everyone else in the room his or their entire lives. "He's a guest of my father's."

"Pleasure to meet you," Alex said. "And thank you for letting me watch you work. I admire good engineering. I'm an amateur mechanic of sorts myself."

Mputu nodded but said nothing.

"This is a beautiful machine you've built, but I wonder if the crusher could benefit from a stronger piece of steel on the business end. The blades of the propeller are trying to cut the rock rather than smash it. It looks to me like they're bending from the force of the cuts and this is putting too much pressure on the driveshaft. It might make sense to try the gears from the . . ." He paused and looked at Marie. "What's the Lingala word for transmission?" he asked in English.

"It's transmission." Despite herself, Marie laughed.

"The gears from the transmission are heavier and flatter than the propellers," Alex continued, "and they should grind the ore into smaller pieces. It would also put less stress on the shaft. It might mean fewer repairs."

There was an awkward moment of silence. Then the older man nodded thoughtfully. "You know, that's an idea," he said. He looked at Marie, who nodded. "We'll try it out and see if it helps."

The meal at the Tsiolo home that evening was an achievement. Busu-Mouli was far from wealthy, but Chief Tsiolo knew how to put on a show. The village women had outdone themselves in preparing a feast worthy of their chief. The first course was a fiery *muamba nsusu*, a kind of chicken soup in a thick peanut-tomato sauce. Next, the women selected for the honor of serving the meal had brought out platters heaped with capitaine, a perch with delicate white flesh sautéed in palm oil with hot *pili-pili* peppers, and *mboto*, a long, skinny river fish smoked and flavored with sorrel. Packets of baked banana leaves piled on another plate contained a mixture of beef and *mbika*, a kind of flour ground from the seeds of pumpkins and squash. A covered ceramic dish decorated with hand-painted birds and flowers held *saka-saka*, steamed cassava leaves with eggplant and garlic. There were also platters of rice, yucca, fried plantains, and sweet potatoes.

Chief Tsiolo sat at the head of the long wooden table in the only chair with a back. The other guests sat on benches running along both sides. Alex, the guest of honor, sat on the Chief's immediate right. Katanga sat next to Alex. Marie and Jean-Baptiste sat across from him. There were a few other village elders at the table, and Alex was introduced to them in a formal and ritualized process.

Chief Tsiolo himself served Alex from the platter of spiced capitaine.

Like a dutiful daughter, Marie served Katanga and Jean-Baptiste before helping herself. Capitaine was her favorite fish. These were perfectly prepared and expertly seasoned. She savored the taste.

"So I understand that you were doing some work on our temperamental rock crusher today," Chief Tsiolo said as he dropped a generous helping of steamed beans onto Alex's plate.

"Not really. I didn't even get my hands dirty. I just had an idea that I thought might help make the machine a little more reliable."

"Are you an engineer by training?"

"More a mechanic. Cars mostly, and some electronics. But an engine is an engine. The principles are the same whether it's a car or a boat or Mputu's troublesome rock crusher. If my ideas help Mputu and his boys get the most out of the machine, I'll be pleased with that."

"And why would that be?" Jean-Baptiste asked, with an air of open hostility. "When your very presence here is an effort to destroy our way of life." The tendons on his neck stood out in bold relief. Marie was glad that she had insisted that the guests leave all guns on the front porch.

Alex held his hands out, palm open, in Jean-Baptiste's direction. "I understand why you think that. But it isn't true. You have a problem here that you need to deal with that isn't my creation. It's not an American creation either. Even so, I think I can be helpful in solving it and I'd like you to hear me out. I have a proposal for you to consider and I'd no more insist that you take it than I insisted Mr. Mputu take his cues from me in fixing the rock crusher. He's open-minded enough, however, to listen to other people's ideas and take from them what he likes. Are you?"

"And if we refuse you and your corporate masters? I, for one, will not give up what is rightfully mine without a fight."

As he said this, Jean-Baptiste looked at Marie, who was sitting on his left. It was clear to her that he was talking about more than mining rights. Marie glanced at her father at the head of the narrow rectangular table. He was smiling. *You bastard, you're enjoying this.*

"That may not be your choice to make," Alex said calmly.

Marie spoke up, hoping to give Jean-Baptiste's anger a chance to cool.

"Jean-Baptiste is right," she said, as she speared another *mboto* from the platter in front of her. "At least about the security situation. The Rwandans have been moving farther west, but this is the first time they've been seen in the Mongala Valley. The *genocidaires* are only the most recent problem. We have the Hammer of God to contend with and an alphabet soup of pretenders who would all like to take Manamakimba's place at the top of the pyramid. The government, meanwhile, is sucking more and more tax money from the villages. But you can only get so much blood from a stone."

"What does that have to do with Consolidated Mining and its interest in Busu-Mouli?"

"It has everything to do with it. Who do you think backed President Silwamba's rise to power? Consolidated Mining and CentAf Petroleum picked him and then helped him fix the election."

"Most people in Kinshasa think it was the army that put Silwamba in power in exchange for a free hand in the east."

"And a healthy dose of money, courtesy of the extraction industries. Nothing happens in this country that isn't connected somehow back to mining and drilling. It's all we have to offer."

"It's the resource curse in operation," Alex agreed.

"What do you mean?" Chief Tsiolo asked.

Marie answered. "It means, Papa, that if a country has a wealth of resources like oil or gold and a weak government, it may never develop naturally. People don't make things, they just dig money out of the ground, and it's too easy for big men to come along who think it all belongs to them by right."

"I understand that problem all too well," her father replied. The Chief looked at Alex. "So what would you suggest we tell our new friends from Consolidated Mining?"

"Chief Tsiolo, your people need a secure home. The wealth locked in these mountains means that this village is no longer that place. If what Jean-Baptiste says is true, that only adds urgency to the problem we all understand. Only you can know what's right for your people. But if I were in your position, I would ask for land on the river where you could build a new village. Not far from Busu-Mouli because you will want to keep an eye on the mine, which should be operated by a joint partnership between Consolidated and the Luba people. You can use your share of the profits to build a school and a health clinic. You can also buy a generator and a new fleet of fishing boats to keep your economy diversified and avoid becoming overly dependent on the price of copper. It will be a hard transition, but I believe your people can prosper under a fair arrangement."

"Perhaps you are right," Chief Tsiolo conceded. "But I think I have a better idea."

"I'm all ears."

"We stay in our homes and Consolidated provides the equipment and technology we need to mine and smelt the ore without destroying the valley."

"That would be better for the village. But isn't that the deal that Consolidated already rejected?"

"This time will be different," the wizened chief replied.

"Why?"

"Because this time you are going to convince them."

15

They came for Alex in the middle of the night, moving quietly to the large bedroom at the back of the house that ordinarily was Chief Tsiolo's. It was the only room in the village with floorboards, a sign of the Chief's wealth and prominence. One of the men stepped on a loose board that creaked loudly in the dark room. Alex, lying on a thin mattress on the floor, woke with a start and sensed that he was not alone.

"Chief?" he asked, rising onto one elbow and peering into the inky darkness.

Several figures rushed at him in the dark. Alex swung his fists, connecting with the side of one man's head and another man's rib cage before strong hands grabbed hold of his arms and legs and pinned them to the mattress. He tried to shout for help, but a sharp punch to his solar plexus knocked the wind from him. A gag was stuffed in his mouth. One of the attackers slipped a canvas bag over his head and tied it around his neck with a thick cord. The bag was damp and smelled of mold and fear.

Alex tried once more to get away, twisting his body for leverage and freeing his right arm. He lashed out blindly, hoping to connect with a face or a throat. Instead, his fist glanced harmlessly off a muscular shoulder, and he was quickly wrapped up in the bedsheet with his arms pinned at his sides.

He flashed back on the hostage survival training course that the State Department had made him take before sending him to Khartoum. The instructor had been an unassuming middle-aged man with a walrus mustache named Walter Hurd, who, along with fifty-one colleagues, had spent 444 days in Tehran as a guest of the ayatollah. Rule number one, he had stressed to the group of twenty or so Foreign Service Officers headed out to difficult and dangerous places around the world, was to stay alive. "If they are going to kill you," he said, "they are most likely to do this in the first ten minutes. Make it through the first couple of minutes and you have a very good chance of surviving the experience." Rule number two had been, when the time came, to die well as a representative of the United States. There was no rule number three.

Alex consciously relaxed his body and did what he could while hooded and gagged to make sense of what was happening. He guessed that there were six people carrying him, three to a side. They carried him through the middle of the Chief's house without any effort to disguise their presence. Once outside, they turned right and walked for about twenty minutes over irregular ground. Most of the time the path seemed to be going up. No one spoke and he had no way of knowing who had taken him hostage. Even the exchange of a few words might have answered this question for him. The language they spoke or their accent if they spoke French would have been a giveaway. For Anah's sake as well as his own, he hoped like hell that his captors were not Rwandan *genocidaires*. If so, he was almost certainly as good as dead.

After a time, the air grew still and the footsteps of his captors seemed to echo. Alex sensed they had gone inside some kind of structure. After a few minutes he was stood upright. The sheet was unwrapped from his body, the bag was removed from his head, and the gag was loosened. Alex saw that they were in a cave. It looked like a natural cavern with a dry sand floor and elaborate stalactite rock formations hanging from the ceiling. A large fire filled the cavern with a dull red light. A man stood near the fire wearing the skin of a leopard and carrying a short wooden staff mounted at the top with what looked like a monkey's skull. He was bent forward and Alex could not see his face. In the dim light he seemed to have the head of a leopard. The man straightened and the hollowed-out leopard's head fell onto one shoulder. He looked Alex straight in the eye. It was Chief Tsiolo.

Alex was shirtless and he wore only a pair of loose cotton pants. The fire, however, kept the cave from feeling cold or damp. He looked quickly around at the others in the cavern. As near as he could tell, they were all men. Jean-Baptiste was standing ten feet away looking intently at his Chief. Alex saw the mechanic Mputu from the smelter and at least one of his sons. He also saw Tsiolo's brother-in-law, Katanga, who had been at the dinner. The rest were strangers to him.

There were approximately fifty men in the cavern standing in a half circle around the fire. All of the men were naked from the waist up. Many had elaborate decorative scars or tattoos that crisscrossed their torsos. There were at least a dozen conversations under way, some lighthearted and some intense. Some were in Lingala, some in Luba, at least one in French, and others in tribal languages Alex didn't recognize. Whatever this was, it was not a strictly local event, he realized. A good percentage of the men gathered in the cavern were from different villages, even different tribes.

A few moments later, Tsiolo called out in Lingala for silence, and the babble of conversation halted abruptly.

No one was looking at Alex. They were focused on Chief Tsiolo.

The Chief reached into a leather pouch at his waist and pulled out a handful of powder that he threw into the fire. The flames glowed green and purple, and a sweet-smelling smoke suffused the air of the cavern.

A group of four men with drums of various sizes began to beat out a steady rhythm. The Chief led the men in a chanted counterpoint to the drums that started low and soft but began quickly to build in pitch and intensity. Alex didn't recognize the language, but he knew what he was looking at. This was a ritual ceremony of a secret society. Before Islam, before Christianity, secret societies were the storehouse of tribal lore and ritual practice. The vast diversity of Africa produced thousands of variations on this theme. Some societies were focused on hunting rituals, others on fertility or the passage into manhood. Many involved ritual sacrifice: animal or, in the distant past, human.

Some of the men watching were clapping their hands in time to the drums. Others were swaying from side to side. As the chanting rose to a crescendo, a man wearing a carved wooden mask with a protruding snout jumped out in front near the Chief. He had patches of what Alex took to be zebra skin wrapped around his waist. The man crouched low near the fire, and he and Chief Tsiolo began a delicate and graceful dance. The Chief advanced and the masked man retreated with a series of spins and twists. It was a hunt, Alex realized, with the leopard in pursuit of what he now understood was an okapi. The "leopard" was circling his prey now, forcing the "okapi" into a narrow stretch of ground between the fire pit and the far-right flank of the audience. Chief Tsiolo feinted left with the skull-mounted staff and then moved right in one fluid motion, grabbing the bare shoulders of the okapi dancer and guiding him gently to the sandy floor of the cavern. The man lay still. The hunter was victorious.

The chanting stopped abruptly.

Another man stepped out of the circle of watchers into the open space in the center. Alex thought he recognized him from the smelter. The man was leading a large bullock by a white rope wrapped around its neck. He held the rope in his left hand. His right held a gleaming machete with a three-foot blade. It looked wickedly sharp. The man presented the rope to Chief Tsiolo and clasped his left hand over his heart. Tsiolo raised his staff over his head and gave a high piercing cry. Slowly and deliberately, the man raised the machete over his head and, with a shout, brought it down. The blow was strong enough and the blade sharp enough that the bullock's head was nearly severed from its body. Black blood spurted from the neck. The animal staggered forward on spindly legs before collapsing to the sand floor of the cavern. It was a clean kill. The approving murmurs from the crowd marked this as a good omen.

Two younger men stepped forward from the crowd with knives and began butchering the animal. They worked quickly and with practiced skill.

Suddenly, Alex felt strong hands grip his arms from both sides and push him into the center of the circle. Looking over his shoulder, he could see it was Katanga and Mputu who had him firmly in their grip. Together, the two men marched him forward to face Chief Tsiolo, who looked every inch the king in his ceremonial regalia. They forced Alex to his knees in front of the Chief. Mputu pulled a thin-bladed knife from his belt and handed it to Chief Tsiolo. The Chief ran the blade across his forearm to test its edge. He seemed satisfied. Alex thought about what he had just seen happen to the steer. Then he thought about rule number two.

Acting on some invisible signal, the drums and chanting abruptly stopped. A preternatural silence fell over the cavern.

Tsiolo raised both arms over his head. His left hand held the staff. In his right was the knife. He shouted, in a language that Alex could not understand, at the assembled members of the secret society that he led. He spoke in short bursts of speech, and the circle of men responded with appropriate grunts of agreement or hoots of derision.

Tsiolo paused and looked at Alex, who could see neither anger nor compassion in the Chief's face. He seemed completely impassive. Tsiolo turned back to the assembly and resumed his address, this time in Lingala.

"This man," he said, pointing the skull toward Alex, "tells me that the people of Busu-Mouli and the other villages in the valley must leave their homes. That the rich and powerful from Kinshasa and Europe and America will not let us stay. He tells us that we have no choice. Does he even have a heart?" The onlookers hooted and jeered.

"Should we find out?" he asked, brandishing the razor-sharp blade in his right hand. The men in the cavern laughed and cheered.

"I think maybe yes," Tsiolo said, stepping forward and raising the knife. Alex didn't flinch. He looked Tsiolo square in the eye. Even at that moment, he could not bring himself to believe that the Chief meant to kill him.

The knife stopped halfway and Tsiolo looked at the blade in mock surprise. "But wait," he continued. "This man does have a heart. I have seen it. I saw it when he rescued my daughter, your sister Marie, from the demon in human form, Joseph Manamakimba. He did not have to do this thing. He could have freed only his own countrymen, but he did not. He saved my Marie as well and for this I owe him a debt.

"So why then," Tsiolo continued, "would a good man with a big heart plot the death of our village and our way of life? I can only believe it is because he does not know us and he does not know the Luba people or the Chokwe or the Kasai. He does not know that we are worth saving. Tonight that will change." He looked at Alex. "*You* will be changed."

Tsiolo moved close to Alex and lowered the knife to his chest. "Alex the American," the Chief said, speaking to Alex but directing his speech to the onlookers. "You see your mission as the protection of your own tribe. So be it. But in saving my daughter's life, you have also chosen to join the Luba people. As Chief, I recognize you as a citizen of Busu-Mouli and a brother to every man in this room."

Before Alex could react, Tsiolo brought the knife to his chest and cut a nearly perfect two-inch circle in his pectoral muscle just above the right nipple. The cut was so quick and the blade so sharp that at first Alex felt nothing. This was quickly followed, however, by a searing pain that brought tears to his eyes. He did not cry out, however, or struggle against the men holding him down.

Mputu's enormous hand slapped red clay onto the fresh wound, and the Luba mechanic drove the dirt into the cuts with a powerful twisting motion. The cool clay offered some relief from the pain of the incision, but Alex understood that the clay was intended to leave the permanent raised welts that were critical to ritual scarring. That was when Alex noticed that among the various scars on his body, Tsiolo had the same nearly perfect circle that he had carved into Alex's chest. Others did too, he noticed, including Mputu and Katanga.

Alex relaxed somewhat. Rule number one was to stay alive and it looked increasingly likely that he would clear that bar. There was no point in carving this kind of ritual mark into a corpse.

Tsiolo hauled Alex to his feet and embraced him. His slender arms were surprisingly strong. "All who look upon you will know you for what you are," he whispered fiercely in Alex's ear. "One of the Anioto . . . the leopard men . . . a member of the Brotherhood of the Circle. Your tribe, your people are in danger. You must help us. It is your duty."

"You are a manipulative son of a bitch," Alex replied in English. "But you have a point. I'll do what I can."

16

"Hand me the screwdriver, please, Jean-Pierre. The big one with the yellow handle." Alex was lying flat on his back with his head inside an access panel on the wall of the stable that he hoped would eventually become a dormitory for Jean-Pierre and the other boys living with Father Antoine. The stable was wired for electricity, but the lights did not work. Alex thought he had just found the source of the problem. Jean-Pierre found the correct tool and put it in Alex's outstretched hand. The young mute boy had attached himself to Alex and had proven to be both a quick study and a hard worker. He was older than Anah, but small for his age. Alex hoped the two of them might become friends after a fashion once Anah moved to Kinshasa.

Alex used the screwdriver to tighten the bolt holding the cable that had come loose when the fitting had rusted through. The part he was using for the repair was not quite the right size, but it would probably serve.

As he cranked hard on the screwdriver to ensure the tightest possible fit, Alex felt a stab of pain in his chest where the wound inflicted by Chief Tsiolo four days earlier was beginning to heal. The experience in the cavern in Busu-Mouli still had something of a dreamlike quality about it. If he did not have the circular cut in his chest, he might have wondered whether it had even happened at all.

When he was satisfied that everything was firmly locked in place, Alex slowly pulled his head out of the hole in the wall and coughed some of the dust out of his throat. He took a swallow from a bottle of Bonaqua water.

"What do you think, Jean-Pierre? Do you want to try it out?"

The boy nodded but said nothing.

They walked over to the fuse box on the other side of the stables. Alex pointed at the master switch.

"Go ahead," he said.

Jean-Pierre stepped forward tentatively, taking the switch in both hands and pushing it up into the "on" position. Two of the three light-bulbs set in sheet-metal fixtures dangling from the ceiling came on, casting a dull brown light through the room. Alex put both of his hands on Jean-Pierre's thin shoulders and gave them a squeeze. The boy looked up at him and smiled.

"That's good enough for today, J.P. We've got the place cleaned out and the electricity back on. I'll come back on Thursday and we can start taking the stalls apart. We'll need to be careful with the wood, though. I have plans for it. I think you and I can use it to build bunk beds for the boys. How does that sound?"

Jean-Pierre nodded in agreement.

After Alex had cleaned himself up, he joined Father Antoine at a small table under the shade of a palm tree in the church courtyard. The priest was dressed casually in light slacks and a short-sleeved dress shirt. His cane hung from the back of the chair. One of the boys brought them a tray with two cold Turbo King beers. The smell of wood smoke wafted across the courtyard from the kitchen, where the older boys were preparing the evening meal.

"To the future Alex Baines Memorial Dormitory," Antoine suggested, raising his beer.

The beer was darker and heavier than Alex might have liked for such a warm afternoon, but it was delicious.

"How long do you think it will take to finish this project?" the priest asked. Alex noted that the way he had said "this" project implied that there would be others to follow.

"With just me and the boys, and assuming that we can get all of the material, it'll probably take at least four months. It's a pretty sizable job."

"What if I rolled up my sleeves and helped out?"

"Then it'll take six months." Alex smiled.

"Touché."

The two sat in the heat in a companionable silence.

"So," the priest said carefully, "I hear that you may have been visiting our old neighborhood."

Alex was not surprised that Antoine knew this. There were few countries with intelligence services more adept at procuring information than the Catholic Church.

"I was out east for a couple of days, but I didn't get as far as Goma. How'd you hear about that?"

"It's a small town. People talk, especially to priests."

"There are eight million people in Kinshasa."

"And I'm on a first-name basis with nearly all of them. How was the trip?"

"Unsettling." Alex was glad he had a friend with whom he could talk over the experience. After asking him to treat the conversation like something that he had heard in confession, Alex told him about the trip, including Consolidated's plans for Busu-Mouli, Chief Tsiolo's rejection of the mining giant's demands, and his own unwilling induction into the secret society that Tsiolo had called the Brotherhood of the Circle.

When Alex finished, Antoine leaned back in his chair and looked at the darkening sky in contemplation. He pushed his gold-rimmed glasses back up to the bridge of his nose.

"So what are you going to do?" he asked.

"I don't know. I've tried to push the idea with the Ambassador of Sustainable Development for the region, but the mining company seems hell-bent on bulldozing the area flat and digging down from there to see what else they can find. It's an astonishingly beautiful place and it would be a crime to destroy it."

"Can you stop them?"

"It's hard to say. I know Ambassador Spencer well, but he seems to have changed somehow. Then there's a man named Saillard who heads up Consolidated's operations here in the Congo. There's something vaguely creepy about him, but Spence seems to trust him. I'm frankly a little uncertain about how to handle it."

"Put your trust in the Lord."

Alex knew from their time together in the Goma region that Antoine's faith was deep and unshakable. The terrible things he had seen in eastern Congo had done nothing to alter his fundamental belief in the glory of the Almighty. Alex's own faith had been considerably more tenuous than that to begin with. After Sudan, he had none.

"The Lord and I are not really on speaking terms these days, Father."

"I know that, Alex. Or at least I suspect it. I remain confident, however, that this will change. You are part of His plan after all. In the meantime, you have some pretty serious moral and ethical issues to wrestle with."

"Tell me about it."

"If you can't change your Ambassador's mind, is there someone else you can appeal to, either here or back in Washington?"

"I doubt I'll make much headway in Kinshasa. Consolidated is well plugged in here and I am confident they have a network of political patrons on their payroll. In theory, I could go back to Washington on my own and make the case that we should be opposing Consolidated Mining's plans for Busu-Mouli rather than advocating for them. It wouldn't do much good to go back to the Central Africa office at State. They don't have enough clout to overrule the Ambassador on this. I suppose that I could send in a dissent channel message."

"What is that?"

"It's something that goes back to the last days of the Vietnam War. About fifty American diplomats quit their jobs to protest the bombing of Cambodia. The way they saw it, the bombing campaign was both immoral and bad national strategy, and a public resignation was the only way they could get anyone in power to pay attention to their views. It cost the Service a lot of experienced officers and was something of an embarrassment for the administration. So Henry Kissinger, who was Secretary of State at the time, decided that we needed a vehicle for expressing what he called 'disciplined dissent.' The dissent channel is a way of letting the higher-ups know that we aren't happy about something without having to make a public stink."

"How does it work?"

"It's pretty simple, actually. All I have to do is write a cable to Washington and send it out with some special captions. I can write anything I want and send it myself without having it approved by anyone else in the mission. By regulation, the Secretary of State is required to read it and respond personally. Most of the time it's pro forma, but a couple of times dissent channel messages have actually resulted in a change in policy. Not often, mind you, but it's happened."

They had both finished their beers, and the boy reappeared with two more icy Turbo Kings.

"Sometimes," Antoine observed, "it's important to do the right thing even if it doesn't materially change the situation."

"I know that's true, Father, but there's also the issue of my relationship with Spence. He went out pretty far on a limb to get me this job and bring me back from professional purgatory. Going over his head would be a betrayal of that confidence."

"That seems a small issue when compared to the future of an entire village."

"Is it? I don't know. That relationship means something to me. And the Congo's problems, Africa's problems, are so vast that what happens to Busu-Mouli seems almost incidental. Millions of people have been killed in this war already, and there's no end in sight. The Congo War is the worst, but it's hardly the only one in Africa."

"There are some people working for a better future for the Congo, including your new friends in the Brotherhood of the Circle."

Alex looked up in surprise, and his eyes narrowed slightly as he considered what his friend had just told him.

"What can you tell me about the Brotherhood?" Alex asked. "The rituals seemed typical of a secret society, but I've never heard of one that was pan-tribal. They're supposed to be vehicles for bonding kinsmen and passing on tribal knowledge."

"The Brotherhood is different," Antoine asserted. "The very fact that they welcomed you into the fold should at least make that clear. Your story isn't the first time I have heard about this group."

Antoine paused as though considering his next thought. Alex knew better than to rush him.

"There are those across the Congo who are angry about what has happened to our country and the collective failure of our political leaders to set it right. They have built a network that spans the breadth of the country and integrates people of vision from all levels of society. They are chiefs and truck drivers, teachers and soldiers. They are deliberately trying to break down barriers of class and tribe that have contributed so much to the Congo's suffering. They are modeled on the secret societies that you and I both know, but they are looking forward to the twenty-first century rather than back to an ideal golden age in the past. The group is secret because some in power would see them as a threat. To the extent they know they exist, they do see them as a threat.

"This group has many names. One of them is the Brotherhood of the Circle. The hierarchy is looser than in many of the more traditional secret societies. From what you tell me . . . and from what little I know . . . it sounds like Chief Tsiolo is a fairly important man in the Brotherhood."

"You call them men of vision. What is the vision? What are they working for?"

"Peace, first and foremost. An end to tribal violence. Then justice. Beyond that, democracy of a sort, development, a place for the Congo in the region, and a position on the global stage that is something other than supine."

"Sounds appealing. But how do they plan to carry that out? Some local leaders and a few intellectuals can't really take on the army and the political class in Kinshasa. President Silwamba and his supporters are at the heart of the Congo's problems. They have made themselves enormously rich at the public's expense, and they have done nothing to bring an end to the wars in the east."

"Not all politicians are cut from the same cloth."

"Who are you thinking of."

"Albert Ilunga."

Alex almost laughed. "Ilunga? Is he even a politician anymore? He hasn't been part of the political scene in years. It's like he went into hiding when he got out of prison. I'm afraid Silwamba broke him."

Albert Ilunga and his Congolese Freedom Party had won a surprise victory nearly six years earlier in the last reasonably democratic elections that the country had held. He had never taken office. While the votes were being counted, the establishment organized to protect itself. Before the official results were announced, Ilunga was accused of "sedition" and "conspiring with foreign forces against the government." The charges against him were obscure and the evidence gossamer-thin, but Silwamba controlled the security services as well as the courts, and the protests organized by Ilunga's supporters were quickly snuffed out. The trial of Albert Ilunga was held in secret, but his sentence of twenty years at the notorious Makala Prison in the jungles of central Congo was public knowledge.

After three years, Silwamba released him from prison. By then, however, Ilunga was a visibly broken man. Mistreatment, malaria, and isolation had taken a toll on him. As a condition of his release, Ilunga had agreed not to run for office or head a political party. He seemed to have dropped off the map and Alex had trouble imagining him making a political comeback.

"I assure you that Ilunga hasn't gone into hiding . . . and he's far from broken. It's true that he hasn't been politically active, at least in public, but he is still engaged in helping the less fortunate. He and his organization are doing the Lord's work with wounded war veterans, helping them reintegrate into society. There are many who still view Ilunga as the legitimately elected president and Silwamba as a usurper."

The boy who had been waiting on them reappeared and informed them that dinner was ready. Dusk was beginning to settle over the city. The sky had turned from blue to purple, and the buzz of insects competed with the sounds of Kinshasa's traffic coming from the other side of the courtyard walls.

"I'd like you to meet Ilunga, Alex. I know him reasonably well, as our work sometimes overlaps. I think that you might find he restores some of your faith in what you call the political class."

"What makes you think that?" Alex asked gently.

"Because Ilunga has one of these." The priest pulled open his shirt with his right hand to show Alex a raised scar on his chest in the shape of a perfect two-inch circle.

17

The massive armored Cadillac with the Stars and Stripes flying from each front corner pulled into the circular drive in front of the presidential palace. An honor guard of Congolese paratroopers in jungle camouflage and black berets snapped to attention. These were members of the Black Lions, Silwamba's own praetorian guard. There were persistent rumors in Kinshasa that in addition to providing for the President's security, the paratroopers also took an active role in eliminating his political rivals.

A single massive flagpole dominated the center of the circle. Rather than the Congolese flag, the giant cloth flapping in the breeze was the President's personal flag. It featured an outline of Silwamba's profile framed by a pair of stylized Kalashnikovs and surrounded by a gold disk that was unmistakably a halo. *Even by regional standards,* Alex thought, *this is a bit over the top.* The Black Lions were flying the national flag. One of the soldiers held a large Democratic Republic of the Congo flag on a polished mahogany pole. The flag was electric blue with red and yellow stripes at a diagonal and a single gold star in the upper left. To Alex, it looked oddly futuristic, like some Hollywood image of a flag of an imaginary galactic federation. In honor of the visitors, a second soldier displayed a considerably smaller American flag.

The Caddy, known affectionately as the Dragon to the Embassy community, stopped in front of the stone steps leading up to the massive metal doors of the palace. A reception committee was waiting on the lower steps. An attendant in a red jacket and white gloves opened the door of the Cadillac and Ambassador Spence exited at a deliberate pace. Alex hustled around from the other side of the car and stood on Spence's right about half a step back as the Ambassador greeted the President's Chief of Protocol.

"Welcome, Mr. Ambassador. It has been too long since you had the occasion to visit us. President Silwamba is looking forward to today's meeting."

"Thank you, Minister," he began, as the Chief of Protocol in the DRC system was formally a part of the President's Cabinet. "We're grateful that the President was able to make time in his schedule on such short notice."

The Embassy had received a cable from Washington two days earlier instructing the Ambassador to seek an urgent meeting with the Congolese government at the highest possible level to deliver a message on a U.S.-led initiative to establish a new sub-Saharan security organization focused on counterterrorism. All of the embassies in Africa had received the same instructions, and there was something of a competition among the U.S. missions in the Africa bureau to see who had the best access. The posts that came in the earliest and at the highest level would be acknowledged as the winners of this informal contest. Two days to get a meeting with the President of your country was the gold standard, and Spence was demonstrating to his colleagues across Africa that he was a force to be reckoned with.

The Chief of Protocol led Spence and Alex up the red-carpeted stairway. The entryway was lined with marble and onyx, and the stairs were flanked by sweeping balustrades that ended in a spiral at the base. Their footsteps echoed against the marble walls as they climbed to the second floor. French doors at the top of the stair's led to the presidential suite, and President Silwamba was there to greet the Ambassador.

"Spence, my friend," he said, enfolding the Ambassador in a bear hug. President Silwamba was Spence's height, but he must have outweighed him by at least 150 pounds. His thick neck lopped over his collar and threatened to blow out the buttons of what looked to Alex like an extremely expensive hand-tailored shirt. The dark suit he wore was almost certainly Savile Row. The silk tie and shoes were Italian. The watch on his wrist was a Rolex Oyster, the timepiece of despots. Even in a five-thousand-dollar suit, the corpulent Silwamba bore more than a passing resemblance to Jabba the Hutt.

"It's good to see you, Mr. President. It's been too long. Let me introduce my new Political Counselor, Alex Baines."

"Yes, I heard about what happened to young Mr. Wells. My sympathies to his family."

"Thank you. I'll pass that along."

"Where are you coming from, Mr. Baines?" Silwamba's gaze was baleful, like that of a cobra contemplating a potential meal.

"My last assignment was in Conakry, Mr. President."

"Wonderful. Then Kinshasa is something of an upgrade for you, no?"

"More than you know, sir."

"Is this your first time in my country?"

"No, sir. I was a Peace Corps volunteer in the Goma region about ten years ago."

The President's eyebrows shot up at that. "And what did you think of the girls there?" he asked in the copper-belt Swahili common to eastern Congo.

"They are very pretty, Mr. President," Alex replied in the same language. Along with Lingala, he had picked up a fair amount of the pidgin Swahili that was one of the region's many trade languages.

"I'm going to keep an eye on you, young man," Silwamba said, with a smile that did not quite reach his eyes. Alex was not certain whether he should read that simple statement as a compliment or a threat.

Silwamba introduced his "plus-one" for the meeting, a young Congolese diplomat on loan to the presidential staff. In diplomatic parlance, meetings were defined as the principal plus whatever agreed-upon number of advisers, notetakers, and bag carriers would be let into the room.

The President ushered them through a set of heavy wooden doors into his private office, a large room with a sweeping view of the grounds and pictures of himself decorating every wall. There were photographs of Silwamba delivering a speech, meeting with the premier of China, and receiving a bouquet of flowers from a young girl. There were oil paintings of the President staring contemplatively off into the middle distance and even one of him in full military uniform riding a white charger. *It was good to be the king,* Alex thought, *up until the day when it wasn't.* Few of Silwamba's predecessors had died in bed, and maybe half of those had simply been sleeping when they were murdered.

Alex and Spence sat down on a plush couch covered in soft brown leather. Silwamba and his notetaker sat in matching chairs on the other side of a heavy marble-and-mahogany table. Two attractive young women in uniforms that would not have looked out of place at a Catholic prep school served tea from silver trays and glided off wordlessly.

After a few minutes of broad-brush conversation about Congolese politics and the fighting in the east, Spence turned the conversation to the purpose of the meeting.

"Mr. President, my government has instructed me to ask for this meeting in order to preview our proposal for a new partnership between the United States and sub-Saharan Africa in the ongoing struggle against terrorism and violent extremism. As you know, some of the first shots in what became the global war on terror were fired not far from here in Nairobi and Dar es Salaam. The bombing of our embassies in Kenya and Tanzania took 212 lives, the vast majority of them African. Terrorism has been decoupled from territory, and terrorist cells will infect any state too weak to defend itself. We are in the process of driving Al Qaeda out of Central Asia, and we know for a fact that they are looking for an alternative home. Bin Laden lived in Khartoum before the Sudanese ultimately kicked him out. Al Qaeda's new leadership might well be looking to return to Africa."

Silwamba nodded thoughtfully. Or sleepily. Alex was not entirely sure which.

"The United States would like to propose a standing body in the African Union devoted exclusively to counterterrorism and focusing on sub-Saharan Africa. The U.S. would provide intelligence support to the organization and work on developing a coordinated response to the threat of terrorism incorporating all elements of state power: diplomatic, intelligence, military, political, and economic. We are prepared to provide fifty million dollars in seed money to support the start-up costs of this organization. We hope that Kinshasa will back this initiative in Addis and encourage other sub-Saharan member states to do the same." The African Union was headquartered in the Ethiopian capital of Addis Ababa, which nearly everyone referred to as Addis.

Spence had done a solid job laying out the U.S. position, even if it did not seem to Alex that his heart had been in it. The Ambassador had been good but not as brilliant as he had been so often in the past. By diplomatic protocol, Spence had made his presentation, and it was now the President's turn to respond. After that, the two men could ask each other any questions they might have and call it a day.

"Mr. Ambassador," Silwamba began, after taking a moment to sip his tea and adjust his collar, which was pinched between two rolls of fat on his neck. "Thank you for the proposal. We will give it the consideration it deserves. Terrorism is a terrible scourge that must be wiped out without mercy."

Silwamba evidently considered that this discharged his obligation to respond to Spence's proposal. He looked expectantly at Spence.

"Oh, yes. Alex, would you excuse me for a moment. There are some issues I'd like to discuss privately with the President."

"Of course, Mr. Ambassador." Alex and Silwamba's plus-one both rose and left the room. The young Congolese diplomat continued through the French doors and, Alex supposed, back to his office to write up an account of the meeting in which the President was sure to feature as the star. Alex took a seat in a wingback chair in the anteroom and waited for Spence to conclude whatever private business he might have with the President. This was extremely unusual. Spence had never before asked him to leave a meeting, and for the life of him, Alex could not imagine what it was he needed to discuss with Silwamba one-on-one. Doubtless, Spence would tell him when they got back to the Embassy.

One of the efficient and beautiful young women who had served tea in the President's office reappeared with a smaller tray and left a glass on the side table. Alex sipped the tea and mulled over the problem in front of him: What to do about Busu-Mouli. He had tried to talk to Spence about it, but the Ambassador had made it clear that his goal was getting the village to cooperate with the mining company rather than vice versa. While Alex understood all of the arguments, he had reached a different conclusion. Embassies were supposed to support the business interests of important American companies. Nevertheless, he was confident that Embassy Kinshasa was on the wrong side of this conflict. There was simply no way that bulldozing the Mongala Valley was in the best interests of the United States, no matter how much copper ore was in the ground. The money that greased the skids for the big business deals underpinned the fundamentally corrupt political system in the

Congo. This promoted instability, retarded long-term development, and ultimately made the Congo a harder place to do business. There had to be a better way. He needed to make Spence see that. Maybe if he could see him outside the office, sit down together for a drink like they had done in the old days. The days before Darfur.

The sound of the French doors opening snapped Alex out of his reverie. Henri Saillard walked in wearing a natty pin-striped charcoal suit and carrying a black crocodile-skin briefcase in his right hand. *What the hell is he doing here?* Alex wondered. He had considered Saillard a bit foppish before, even prissy, but now he saw him as cold, calculating, and manipulative. Saillard, for his part, was all smiles to see Alex, and he came over to shake his hand.

"Mr. Baines, I have not had the opportunity to thank you properly for the good work you did in negotiating the freedom of my colleagues. Consolidated Mining is grateful to you, and I am in your debt."

"Just doing my job," Alex replied coolly.

"And doing it extremely well. Let me know when you have had enough of government service. I promise you that we pay much better."

"I have no doubt."

"I would welcome a chance to hear about your visit to Busu-Mouli and your meeting with the village leadership. My organization is quite anxious to get started on the project."

"There are some issues related to your plans for the village and the valley that I'd like an opportunity to discuss with you as well."

"Excellent. Are you free for lunch tomorrow by any chance?"

"That would be fine."

"Wonderful. Let's say one o'clock at Le Caf' Conc'."

Alex knew the place. It was perhaps the most expensive restaurant in Kinshasa.

"I'll be there."

"Superb. Well, I must be off. I'll see you tomorrow." And with that, the head of Consolidated Mining's central Africa operations opened the door to the President's private office and let himself in. *What the fuck?* Certainly Spence's private business with Silwamba was not connected to Consolidated Mining. *Was it?*

Alex worried this over in his mind for the next fifteen minutes, trying to ignore the kernel of anger he felt at Spence for shutting him out of the conversation. When the doors to the private office finally opened, Alex stood up like a shot. Silwamba, Spence, and Saillard came out of the office laughing at some private joke. Saillard, Alex noticed, was no longer carrying the briefcase. Whatever was in it, he had left it behind. The only question was whether Saillard conducted business in dollars, euros, or Congolese francs.

Alex, Spence, and Saillard walked out together. Saillard's silver Mercedes S-Class was parked behind Spence's Cadillac. The red-jacketed attendants opened the doors for them.

They rode back to the Embassy in silence.

That afternoon Alex asked Peggy for some time in the Ambassador's schedule. Spence had half an hour starting at six before he had to get ready for a reception at the Dutch Ambassador's villa in Gombe. Alex spent the intervening hours working on his report to Washington. It was a short cable, he reasoned, as he had missed what had undoubtedly been the most interesting part of the conversation.

Spence was sitting behind his big oak desk reading Alex's report of their meeting with President Silwamba when Alex walked into the Ambassador's office a few minutes after six.

"Good report, Alex," he said, signing his initials in the upper right corner indicating that the message was okay to transmit. He put the cable in his out-box. "What can I do for you this evening?"

"I'd like to know what happened today at the presidential palace."

"What do you mean?"

"What did you and the President have to discuss that needed to be kept from me, and what the hell . . ." Alex paused to make sure that his anger did not dictate his next sentence. "What was Henri Saillard doing there?"

Spence did not seem surprised at Alex's obvious irritation.

"Silwamba and I had some private business to discuss. If I wanted you to know what it was, I wouldn't have asked you to leave. As for Saillard, I didn't invite him. The President did. It was just as much a surprise to me as it was to you. He wanted to talk over the terms of Consolidated's copper concessions in the south and east. It seems the President doesn't believe that his treasury is being adequately compensated. Saillard had drawn up a new proposal with terms slightly more favorable to the government. He left the contract there for the government's lawyers to look over. It was all perfectly innocuous."

"Spence, I have to tell you that I don't trust Saillard. I think he's crooked and potentially dangerous."

"How so?" Alex's mentor seemed more amused than concerned by the suggestion.

"He and the company are up to their eyeballs in Congolese politics. You don't get the kinds of favorable trade terms in this country that Consolidated has without buckets of under-the-table money. On top of that, Saillard has been spinning us something fierce. We know for a fact that he lied about the Hammer of God attack on the Consolidated survey team as being a one-off event. There have been a whole series of attacks that he elected not to share with us. That kind of information could have been critical in the negotiations. He lied about how long he had known about the copper deposits near Busu-Mouli, and he neglected to tell us that he and the company had reneged on a deal to develop the site in partnership with the village. The villagers negotiated that deal in good faith."

Spence said nothing, and Alex knew that he was being given enough rope to hang himself with. *The hell with it.*

"We are on the wrong side of history here, Ambassador. I've seen what the villagers in Busu-Mouli have been able to accomplish on their own. It's truly impressive. With just a little help from the outside, it could be a new model for sustainable and environmentally responsible development. If Consolidated Mining's not interested, we should be. This is exactly the kind of project that the Agency for International Development has been looking for in central Africa. We should be backing the village in this, not the mining company. What they're doing may be good for Consolidated's quarterly report, but it's a disaster for the Congo."

He decided to stop there. He had already crossed a number of likely red lines.

Spence seemed lost in thought for a moment as though he was digesting what Alex had to say.

"I agree with you that Henri is something of a slippery character," Spence offered finally. Alex knew full well what he was doing. It was Spence, after all, who had taught him to begin a disagreement by picking out something benign that the other person had just said and agreeing with it wholeheartedly. It was disarming.

"And I certainly wouldn't want him to marry one of my girls," he continued. "But the company he represents is a major American enterprise that employs thousands of people and provides our country with the raw materials we need to maintain our nation's extremely expensive standard of living. I appreciate that what Consolidated wants to do in Busu-Mouli is unappealing, but it's really no different than what a dozen coal companies do every day in West Virginia. That kind of environmental damage should be reserved only for the most valuable and important deposits. Busu-Mouli, regrettably, sits atop one of them.

"This isn't a case of one standard for America and one for Africa. If this deposit were in the Adirondacks, the mining companies would be doing exactly the same thing. Look. Our goal . . . our mission . . . is to advance the interests of the United States. It's not always terribly pretty.

But it pays the bills that allow us to continue to operate as a great nation that accomplishes great things. So I understand where you're coming from. I really do. I just don't agree with you."

"Spence, there's something about all this that doesn't look right," Alex insisted. "Saillard has unprecedented access to the mission and to you personally."

"Be careful where you take this, Alex." There was a hint of warning in the Ambassador's tone.

"Just look at the facts. I've never heard of someone without a clearance being let into the Bubble. He has too much influence over not only what we do but how we do it. On policy, he has us pushing a plan that most Americans would find abhorrent. There's a chance here to partner with the local community and develop the resources in a sustainable way. We should be jumping on this opportunity rather than pushing the villagers to abandon their homes. We're better than this, Spence."

"Are you certain this doesn't have anything to do with an attractive mining engineer who has undue influence over certain parts of this embassy?"

Alex flushed but kept his cool. Sykes must have reported on him back up his chain. *Either that,* he thought, *or Consolidated has a spy in Busu-Mouli.*

"I don't think so. I think this is about trying to do the right thing."

Alex had never seen Spence angry. He had seen him shout and badger, but he had always been under control and always in the service of a calculated aim. Now he saw him angry.

"Goddamn it, Alex. Don't get all high and mighty with me. I've been trying to do the right thing in Africa since you were in goddamn grade school. I've sweated blood for this continent and its people, and I will not have my motives impugned by a psychologically fragile subordinate, even if I do look on him as family.

"I saved your ass and your career when DS was ready to throw you on the scrap pile. I think I deserve a little respect from you as the beneficiary of my efforts, and I think, damn it, that I deserve the benefit of the doubt."

Alex realized that he had taken this issue as far as he could—and then some. It was time to get out.

"I understand. Thank you, Ambassador. I appreciate your time."

18

L e Caf' Conc' was the kind of place that was redolent of European empires. Dark wood paneling and lush carpeting contributed to a quiet, subdued atmosphere while white-gloved waiters attended to the needs of a clientele that included diplomats, business executives, senior government officials, and, inevitably, spies. It was an establishment that prided itself on grace and discretion. As he stepped into the cool interior of the restaurant, Alex glanced at his watch and half expected it to tell him that it was 1892 rather than five minutes after one o'clock.

The maître d' informed him that Monsieur Saillard was already waiting at the table. Saillard rose when they approached and he shook Alex's hand. He was wearing a bespoke light gray double-breasted suit with an expensive-looking tie and silver cuff links. His hair was gelled securely into place. Alex was dressed more casually in a blazer and tan slacks.

"I'm so glad you could make it today," Saillard said, as they took their seats. "We have much to talk about." Their table was tucked back in the corner of the main dining room, affording them privacy for the conversation.

"I suppose we do."

"But let us order first. If you haven't tried it, the chateaubriand is magnificent."

There were no prices on the menu. Le Caf' Conc's clientele did not need that information. Alex ordered a simple fillet of sole and a salad. Saillard went for the chateaubriand with the crab soup and a side of caviar. He also ordered a bottle of vintage Bordeaux that by itself probably exceeded Alex's representational allowance. *Corporate guys lived well.*

The waiter uncorked the bottle at the table and offered Saillard a small taste. The mining executive nodded his approval.

"Tell me about your adventures with Mr. Manamakimba," Saillard began, after the waiter had filled their glasses with the excellent wine. "I'm so grateful that you were able to get all of our people out safely."

Alex offered a brief description of the negotiations with Manamakimba.

"It's odd, though," Alex observed. "From what you told us, you seemed persuaded that this was a random event. That there was no pattern in the Hammer of God's targeting Consolidated's interests in the east. But that doesn't seem to be the case. I came away from my time with Manamakimba believing that he had chosen his target very carefully."

Saillard seemed unconcerned by this. "Well, it is impossible to know what happens in the mind of a man as brutish as Mr. Manamakimba. I assure you, however, that our operations in eastern Congo—which are very important to my company—are quite secure."

"And what about your plans for Busu-Mouli? Has your thinking on this changed at all on the basis of my reports?"

"I'm afraid not. We do appreciate your recommendations, of course. But you are asking us to surrender significant profits in a difficult economic environment. Our first responsibility, of course, is to our shareholders."

"On its website, Consolidated Mining trumpets its commitment to corporate social responsibility. This seems like a golden opportunity to put that principle into operation."

"If it were a minor find, I would agree with you. If all that we were looking at was a small deposit of low-grade ore, we would be more than pleased to provide some surplus or refurbished equipment, take a few pictures for the website, and . . . what is that expression you Americans are so fond of . . . give something back? It's quite charming really, if a tad self-aggrandizing."

The waiter brought Alex's salad and Saillard's soup. The Belgian tucked his napkin into his collar to avoid staining his tie.

"As I understand it from the Tsiolo family, you did more than decide to decline assistance. You reached an agreement with the village and then pulled out when you realized how much money there was to be made there."

Saillard shrugged. "That's one way of looking at it, I suppose. Another is that the company adapted its position in light of new information that came onto the market. It's normal business practice really."

"That may be true, but I also believe it represents the triumph of short-term thinking over long-range strategic planning. Look, Henri. We both know that the Silwamba government is fragile. Consolidated enjoys a privileged position for the time being, but you risk losing that position when political change comes to the Congo. If you have a different and less exploitative relationship with the people of this country, your longer-term position will be more secure."

"You may be right. And I can see how you were so effective in persuading Mr. Manamakimba to cooperate. It is a calculus that revolves around just how much profit Consolidated Mining can make in the

Congo before the political climate changes in a way fundamentally inimical to our interests. We have . . . crunched, is that the right word? . . . crunched the numbers, and as a matter of business, we are quite confident that our decision here is the correct one."

"And what if the villagers refuse to leave?"

"If we have the necessary government approvals to take possession of the land, we will take possession of the land." A few drops of crab soup fell off his spoon and stained the napkin.

Alex looked at him quizzically.

"The government's reach outside of Kinshasa is pretty shaky. It's unlikely you could get the police to enforce a court order."

"Out there," Saillard observed, "the law operates quite differently. We do have ways of exercising our rights in eastern Congo, and we have considerable experience in dealing with the unique challenges."

One waiter removed the empty salad and soup plates, and a second server delivered the main course. Next to Saillard's steak, the waiter placed a small silver dish of caviar and a plate of toast points. Alex took a bite of the sole without really tasting it. He thought through what Saillard had just told him. The threat of violence was implicit, but it was there. *Just how far was Consolidated Mining prepared to go in pursuit of profit?* It was worth pressing a few buttons, Alex decided, to gauge the reaction.

"Henri, I appreciate that Consolidated Mining has very specific interests in eastern Congo and, in particular, Busu-Mouli. You are an American company, and we owe you a measure of support. At the same time, I represent the United States, and our interests as a nation are significantly broader than yours as a corporation. Tying ourselves too closely to your venture in Busu-Mouli risks undercutting long-term U.S. interests in Congo. I'm going to recommend to the Ambassador that we cease acting as Consolidated Mining's representative in this matter. Ultimately, of course, it will be the Ambassador's decision, but that will be my recommendation. How's the steak?"

Saillard's knuckles tightened on the wooden handle of the steak knife, and for a brief moment it looked like he might be ready to cut into something other than chateaubriand.

"I'd think very carefully before doing anything so rash," he said, abandoning all pretense of bonhomie. "I understand that your position in your own service is not absolutely secure. I would hate to see a promising career snuffed out before it had really even begun."

While it was infuriating, Alex was not surprised that Saillard had access to information about his struggles with Diplomatic Security. He suspected that Viggiano was the source.

They finished the meal largely in silence. Saillard did not suggest that they linger over coffee.

Alex stayed late at the Embassy that evening to finish up some paperwork. At about eight o'clock he went to the cafeteria to get a Snickers bar out of the vending machine. Jonah Keeler was sitting at a table by himself nursing a cup of coffee.

"I hear you've been making some waves."

"News travels fast."

"Not as fast as gossip. Listen. A little friendly advice. You watch your ass. There are folks in this city—hell, in this embassy—who would like to see you go down. Don't give them the opportunity."

"Thanks, Dad. I'll be careful."

"I'm serious, boy. You have no idea what you are getting into."

"No," Alex agreed. "But I'm starting to."

19

The mine and smelter had become Marie's obsession. Copper was money, and money was what Busu-Mouli needed if the village was to have any chance of survival. She was more skeptical than her father that Alex could deliver Consolidated Mining, no matter how sincere he might be. She understood the scale of the challenge better than her father. Consolidated Mining was an enormous operation, and it was so thoroughly intertwined with the government in Kinshasa that it was hard to tell where the one stopped and the other began.

Only money, Marie believed, could change the calculus and potentially save the village. With money, the Tsiolo clan could engage in the same kind of influence-seeking that now threatened to destroy the village. Money would also buy the weapons the villagers could use to defend themselves. The central government exercised little effective control outside the major cities. Kinshasa could cede Busu-Mouli to Consolidated Mining, but the company would still have to muster sufficient force to take control in fact as well as in law.

Marie stood facing the rock wall at the business end of the main shaft. She ran her fingers over the rough stone surface, tracing the outline of the chalcopyrite and malachite veins visible in the rock. The yellowish chalcopyrite glistened like gold as it reflected the light from the mining lamp hanging from a hook on the wood-reinforced ceiling. The malachite deposits were a smooth, deep green that spoke of copper riches reaching far back into the earth.

The men who worked at the face of the shaft did their best to follow the twisting veins of copper as they wound their way through the mountain. There was an art to it, however, and Marie had an almost intuitive feel for which path the veins would follow that her male compatriots could not match. The rock was a living thing that would whisper its secrets to you if you were open to its message.

"Slant the tunnel to the left and angle it down another ten degrees," she finally said to the shift supervisor, a muscular twenty-two-year-old named Yves who looked like he could have been cut from stone himself.

Marie could not be absolutely confident in the guidance she had given Yves, and her instructors at the Witwatersrand School of Mining in Johannesburg would have been horrified by her methodology, but so far she had been right more often than she had been wrong. Yves and his work crew hefted their picks and prepared to attack the rock face. A pile of wicker baskets stood along the wall, ready to be filled with the raw ore and carried up to the surface. Marie clapped Yves on the shoulder and made her way up the shaft toward sunlight and fresh air. The rank air here at the deepest part of the shaft had left her slightly light-headed.

She had been underground for only about two hours and it was already early evening. Even so, the colors of the outside world seemed shockingly vivid in comparison to the muted hues of the subterranean. Marie stood at the mouth of the tunnel breathing in the sweet, clean air. She took a swallow of water from the canteen on her hip and headed down the narrow mountain track to the smelter. Katanga was there, overseeing repairs to the furnace.

Her uncle had proven to be indispensable to the operation. He was organized, dedicated, and inspiring to the younger villagers, whose labor, freely given in support of Busu-Mouli's future, made what they were doing possible, even mildly profitable. For now, the proceeds from the sale of copper ingots were sunk back into the mine, with a small percentage diverted to support Jean-Baptiste's village guard. Eventually, the profits from the mine would be used to improve the quality of life for all of the inhabitants of the valley. If Marie had her way, that day was coming soon.

She retrieved several rolls of schematic diagrams from her office in the back room of the smelter and spread them out on a table near the rock crusher. The crusher was silent for now, as a broken furnace had created a bottleneck that was being felt back up the line of production. The crusher itself was in good working order, and Marie was pleased that Alex's design suggestions had resulted in a more reliable and efficient machine. She liked the American's mechanically inclined mind. He made things with his hands that made a difference in the real world. For Marie, that meant something.

She weighted the corners of the oversize diagrams with pieces of copper ore scavenged from the floor. Then she called for Katanga to come offer his opinion.

"I'm worried about B shaft, Uncle," Marie said, pointing to the place on the diagram that had drawn her attention. As they had advanced into the mountain, the main tunnel had sprouted several branching side shafts that tracked different veins of copper ore. B shaft had been a problem from the beginning. The ore was of lower quality and the surrounding rock was soft and brittle. A cave-in had injured two miners three days earlier, one of them seriously, and Marie was no longer sure if B shaft was worth the cost.

"What about adding more reinforcements?"

"We can try, but there are already so many beams in place that it's difficult to move. Even so, the ceiling is unstable. If we keep digging that vein, eventually we are going to have a major cave-in. Boys will die. I'm thinking that we close down B shaft and shift the focus to C. We can keep things going at the main face as well, and we should have enough raw ore to keep us in business. Assuming, of course, that you and Mputu can get the furnace fixed." She smiled at Katanga to show that no criticism was intended.

Katanga took no offense.

"Don't worry. A few more hours and we will be back to normal. Even with the problem with the furnace, the smelting operation is still able to stay ahead of the miners. Your American boyfriend did us a real favor in helping us to redesign the crusher."

"He's not my boyfriend," Marie said automatically.

"That's not what Jean-Baptiste thinks."

"Jean-Baptiste is an arrogant—" Marie didn't finish the sentence. She and Katanga froze as the frantic clanging of a bell cut through the conversation. The village bell was reserved for emergencies. The sudden chatter from an AK-47 confirmed her worst fears. Busu-Mouli was under attack.

Since the earlier attempt by the *genocidaires* to burn down the smelter, Marie had installed a gun rack on the wall near her office. She took a Kalashnikov off the rack and slipped the heavy Zastava pistol into her belt. Katanga took an AK-47 for himself that he slung over his shoulder. He held a machine pistol in his beefy right hand. Some of the other men, including Mputu, armed themselves as well.

Marie took charge.

"Uncle, if these are *genocidaires,* they probably put in upstream and took the Lisala road. That means they will have to pass right through the village. I'll take Mputu and his sons and see if we can circle around them on the goat track to the north. I'd like you to take the rest of the boys and guard the path along the riverfront. If they make it to the smelter and burn it down, we've lost the village whether or not we win the battle."

Through their work on the mine together, Katanga had gotten used to taking orders from his niece.

"Very well, Marie. But remember that what you just said about the smelter applies to you as well. Without you, we are lost. Don't do anything foolish."

"I wouldn't dream of it."

There was another burst of automatic-rifle fire followed by the crack of aimed shots and an explosion that might have been a rocket-propelled grenade.

"Mputu," Katanga said, turning to the village's chief mechanic. "Keep her alive."

The mechanic nodded his acceptance of the charge. In the lamplight, beads of sweat gleamed on his bald head.

Katanga led a group of five armed men out the door and down to the river. Other than the river itself, there were only two paths leading to the smelter. Katanga's team would cover one, and Marie and Mputu would take the other. A roundabout route connected the smelter to the mining area and back to the village, but it was a lengthy path that followed the easiest terrain. A steeper, rockier goat path served as a shortcut and this was the track Marie intended to use.

Mputu insisted on leading the way, and Marie did not try to argue. To make doubly certain that he was making good on his promise to Katanga, Mputu instructed his oldest son, Kikaya, to shadow Marie and protect her with his life.

Scanning the jungle on either side, alert for danger, they moved carefully along the narrow trail until they reached the edge of the village. The sun had set and the deep twilight shadows made it hard for

Marie to get a sense of the scale of the fighting. At least two houses were burning. She could see defenders scattered in small groups returning fire that was coming from the direction of the Lisala road.

Busu-Mouli was essentially a crossroads. One road, really no more than a wide path in parts, ran east-west and led down to the river and then up through the hills around the village. The north-south axis led to the Lisala road, Busu-Mouli's primary overland connection with the outside world. To the south, the road came to a dead end on the far side of the farmland that stretched for the better part of half a mile from the last house in the village. The Chief's house was set on a small rise toward the southern end of town, but the real heart of the village was the well at the center of the crossroads.

Marie could see that small teams of villagers were spread in a loose arc at the northern end of town. Occasional bursts of gunfire from attackers hidden in the jungle kept the defenders in place, but this was not yet a determined assault.

Jean-Baptiste, surrounded by a phalanx of armed young men, had taken up a position by the well in the center of town. Marie crouched as she ran across the open ground between the jungle and the minimal cover afforded by the well. She anxiously anticipated the whine of bullets, but no shots were aimed in her direction.

"Jean-Baptiste," she said breathlessly, when she reached his side. "Where's my father?"

"On his porch with the damn shotgun. I told him to stay inside. And what the hell are you doing here? You should have stayed with the smelter." Baptiste was dressed in olive drab fatigues with a pistol strapped to one thigh and a machete strapped to the other. His Kalashnikov leaned carelessly against the well.

"Well, I'm here now and I've brought reinforcements. What's going on?"

"Rwandans. There's a fair number of them, but not enough it seems to take us head-on. The boys are fighting well and for now we are holding. If we can discourage them, maybe they'll go look for an easier target."

Marie was skeptical. Busu-Mouli had not been chosen at random. The *genocidaires* had been sent here for a purpose.

As if to confirm her suspicions, a rocket-propelled grenade flew swiftly overhead and punched a hole through another house on the far side of the square. The mud-brick-and-wattle construction simply fell over on its side. An elderly man climbed out from the rubble, calling for help. His wife, he shouted, was trapped under the corrugated tin roof. Two of Jean-Baptiste's militia ran to his aid.

"They are not going away," Marie said insistently. "You may have surprised them, but they're going to come in after us."

"You might be right," Jean-Baptiste admitted. "Wait for the bastards," he shouted to the defenders. "Don't waste your bullets on the trees. You," he said to Marie, "get someplace safe."

Marie, trailed by Mputu and Kikaya, ran to her father's home, where she found the Chief of the Luba sitting on a carved ceremonial stool, cradling an ancient shotgun. Three men from the village had been left there to guard their chief. Marie ran to her father and kissed him on the cheek. "Papa, go inside."

"No, my only child. I am Chief. My people must see me as they fight for their homes. I will not cower in the kitchen like a woman. These Rwandans are womanly. They thought they would have an easy night of it. Now they have to work up the courage for an attack against men."

Marie recognized that this was not the right moment to try to push her father's thinking on gender roles in a more progressive direction.

"I think they are about ready."

"I think so too."

They didn't have long to wait.

A red flare went up over the village, bathing the town in an eerie light. All along the tree line, Marie could see the white flashes from the muzzles of the attackers' Kalashnikovs. A scream of defiance from one of the defenders served as a counterpoint, and the village guard returned fire. Some were disciplined in their use of ammunition. Others just sprayed a full magazine into the jungle. If they hit anything, it would only be by blind luck.

From the porch, Marie had a good overview of the battle and, for the moment at least, was relatively safe. Teams of Rwandan guerillas appeared from the jungle and moved toward Busu-Mouli in a leapfrog fashion, with the teams up front giving covering fire to those coming up from behind. Although the *genocidaires* were more experienced than the village guard, they were assaulting entrenched positions manned by people defending their homes and families. None of the defenders had any doubt what would happen to them if they were overrun.

Marie saw one *genocidaire* cut almost in half by a burst of fire from a machine pistol. Another collapsed when a bullet slammed through his right eye and out the back of his head. The defenders too were taking casualties. A teenage boy ran past holding a bloody shirt to his arm.

The porch was a good firing position, and when the attackers got close enough to be within range, Marie switched her AK to semiautomatic and started shooting at the guerillas. Mputu, his sons, and the three guardsmen followed suit. Not being under direct fire themselves and standing above the attackers, Marie and her kinsmen were able to keep up a withering assault. She saw at least four *genocidaires* go down almost immediately, although it was impossible for her to tell whether it was her shots that had hit home.

For a moment it looked like the Rwandans might break. They were killers but not real soldiers. The *genocidaires* preferred their targets helpless and unarmed. Then one of the Rwandan teams managed to make it around the far side of one of the houses on the right flank of the defenders' line. When the guardsmen realized that they were being shot at from behind, they panicked and broke cover. *Genocidaire* guerillas flowed through the gap in the lines. Busu-Mouli was on the verge of being lost.

Suddenly, Tsiolo leaped off the porch, shouting a piercing and incomprehensible war cry. Marie, Mputu, and the others followed, racing to keep pace with their much older chief.

"Luba, to your king," Tsiolo cried, as he closed in on the gap in the lines.

One Rwandan attacker turned to face this new threat just in time to have his face blown off by a blast from Tsiolo's shotgun. The Chief shot a second attacker in the back. Without any time to reload, he swung the now useless gun like club, catching a third attacker across the bridge of the nose and driving him to his knees.

Marie and the others were only a few paces behind, firing from the hip to keep the attackers back from their chief. But Tsiolo had gotten too far out in front and a burst of fire from an AK-47 hit him in the shoulder and the belly. The Principal Chief of Busu-Mouli fell to the ground and lay still.

"Papa!" Marie screamed. She tossed her rifle aside and ran to her stricken father. Mputu led his sons in a counttercharge that pushed the Rwandans back. The defenders had seen their chief fall and attacked the *genocidaires* with a previously unknown ferocity. Now it was the Rwandans' turn to run, and they broke for the jungle pursued by the citizen soldiers of Busu-Mouli hell-bent on vengeance.

Marie knelt in the dust, cradling her father's head in her lap.

"Don't die, Papa," she pleaded, as tears streamed down her cheeks. "You can't die." She choked back a sob.

"Kikaya," she called. "Get the red medical bag from my house. Hurry."

Mputu's oldest son leaped to obey. Within moments, he was helping her unpack the limited stock of basic medical supplies from the first-aid kit. There was no doctor in Busu-Mouli, and the traditional healers with their herbal remedies and sympathetic magic would be of little use in treating gunshot wounds. Most did as much damage to their patients as the conditions they were supposed to be treating. Marie's basic first-aid training with Consolidated Mining had made her probably the most accomplished medical professional in a hundred-mile radius.

She did what she could, but Marie was painfully aware of the limitations of both her skills and the contents of her medical kit. Mercifully, the bullets had passed in and out. There was a pair of clamps in the first-aid bag, but she did not relish the idea of poking around inside her father's body, hunting for pieces of a spent bullet. The most important thing was to control the bleeding. She directed Kiyala to hold a clean pad of gauze firmly against the wound in her father's shoulder while she did the same for his abdomen. The shoulder injury was of tangential concern. It was the wound in the abdomen that she knew was life-threatening.

"Do not worry, daughter," her father said, and she could hear the pain in the strain of his voice. "Your Uncle Katanga hit me harder than this when he caught me kissing your mother in the manioc field before we were married. I hit him back too. Just as hard. I'll bet your mother never told you that story."

"Yes, she did. I believe it ended with her grabbing you both by the ears until you shook hands."

The Chief closed his eyes.

"I think I'm going to rest for a few minutes," he said.

"Yes, Papa. Get some rest."

Slowly, they got the bleeding under control. Mputu and his sons carried the Chief into the house, where Marie made him as comfortable as possible with clean sheets on the bed and a traditional herbal concoction that she knew from experience actually did help manage pain. The bleeding had stopped. There was no way of knowing, however, what kind of internal damage the bullet might have done. As a precaution, she had started her father on a course of amoxicillin. The drugs in her medical kit were all well past their expiration dates, but they were all she had.

Her father slept for fourteen hours, and Marie had begun to fear that he had slipped into a coma until he awoke and asked to see Katanga.

Marie waited in the front room while her uncle and father spoke for nearly two hours. When Katanga emerged from the Chief's room, he looked grim. There was a determined set to his jaw, as if he were a man who had just shouldered a heavy burden.

"What did you do to poor Katanga?" Marie asked her father, as she changed his bandages.

"I gave him a job. A difficult job, but one I am sure he is up to."

"Do I want to know what it is?"

"You do not." Her father tensed abruptly as a sudden stab of pain made him draw a deep breath. The area around the hole in his belly was tender and swollen, and his skin felt hot to her touch. Marie feared that despite the antibiotics, infection had already set in.

"Marie," the Chief continued, after the pain had subsided. "When I am gone . . ."

"Stop that, Papa," she interrupted. "You are not going to die. I won't allow it." Marie could hear the fierce urgency in her own voice as she blinked back tears. "We need you. I need you."

The next day, Katanga brought a visitor to see the Chief. Mbusa Lamala was one of the major subchiefs, and the Lamalas had an alliance with the Tsiolos that stretched back generations. Mbusa was one of her father's strongest supporters on the tribal council. Marie was excluded from the conversation, but she had no doubt what the three were discussing: succession to the position of Principal Chief. Over the next several days, Katanga brought three more subchiefs to the house to call on Chief Tsiolo. Marie knew them all well. She had known them since she was a girl. It did not escape her notice that those summoned to see the Chief were among the most powerful personalities on the council.

Despite Marie's best efforts, her father's condition continued to worsen. He developed a fever that neither the limited supply of Western medicines in her kit nor the traditional healers' best herbal remedies could control. The wound in his belly began leaking a mixture of pus and blood. Her father was dying before her eyes, and there was nothing Marie could do to help him.

On the fourth day after the *genocidaires* had attacked Busu-Mouli, Marie sat at her father's bedside, holding his hand and telling him stories about the exploits of legendary Luba warriors, the same stories that he had told her when she was a young girl. It was nearly midnight when the fever broke and her father looked at her lucidly.

"Daughter, I am dying."

"Yes, Father."

"Katanga will need your help for what I have asked him to do."

"Of course. Anything."

"You are quick to promise. What will be asked of you is not easy."

Tsiolo took Marie's hand and pressed it against the raised circular scar on his chest.

"When the time comes, remember this. Trust this."

Marie grasped his wrist lightly with her fingers, and she could feel his pulse, weak and thready.

"I love you, Marie."

"I love you, Papa." She laid her hand across his chest.

Chief Tsiolo, the last male in his line, coughed once, closed his eyes, and died.

Marie buried her father in the family plot next to her mother. There were two days of mourning in the village, followed by a feast. On the third day, the subchiefs from the surrounding villages who had sworn fealty to her father gathered in Busu-Mouli to choose a new principal chief.

Katanga served as the host of the tribal council, acting in his late brother-in-law's stead. He sat in Tsiolo's traditional seat at the long dining table in the Chief's house. Marie's house now. Jean-Baptiste sat on his left. Marie sat on Katanga's right, studiously ignoring the mutterings of those who believed that women did not belong at a tribal council. There were about a dozen subchiefs present or represented by proxy, most of those by their eldest sons.

"Good afternoon, chiefs of the Luba people," Katanga began. "We gather today in the wake of a tragedy, the untimely death of our principal chief. This is a difficult time. We are all of us under siege and none of us more so than Busu-Mouli. But we cannot wait to choose a new leader. Who among us is fit to lead?"

The bargaining began in earnest. One by one, the most ambitious of the subchiefs put forward their candidacy. One by one, their rivals shot them down. Food and copious amounts of alcohol were served as the afternoon stretched into the evening.

Finally, Mbusa Lamala rose to speak. "I propose that Katanga be appointed Chief of Busu-Mouli and elevated to Principal Chief. He has proven his leadership abilities in his oversight of the mining operation that his brother-in-law championed to such great effect. The young men look up to him and they will, I believe, follow him willingly." Mbusa sat, and there was a generally positive buzz among the subchiefs. The choice of Katanga seemed popular. This is what Marie had been expecting. A tribal council, her father had once explained to her, was an elaborate stage play. If the leader was wise and capable, the outcome was known in advance, not to all, of course, but to those whom the Principal Chief could count on to make it so. Her father had done his usual thorough job in laying the groundwork for Katanga.

Katanga rose and raised one hand palm outward to ask for silence. "Chief Lamala, you honor me. But it is an honor of which I am not worthy. A man should know his limitations, and I am not meant to be Chief. Fortunately, there is one among the citizens of Busu-Mouli who, I believe, is ready for that responsibility. One who has demonstrated the skills and character of a true leader."

This was not at all according to the script that Marie thought

Katanga and her father had written. She saw Jean-Baptiste straighten in his seat. He was evidently confident that Katanga was speaking of him. She felt a momentary flash of anger at the thought, but kept her face expressionless. *Could this be what her father meant when he told her that she would be asked to do something difficult?*

"I would follow this person to hell," Katanga continued. He paused as though for effect. "I speak, of course, of Chief Tsiolo's daughter, Marie."

Jean-Baptiste scowled and looked fiercely at Katanga, but he bit his tongue. Marie simply looked startled.

The chiefs murmured among themselves angrily. One of the minor subchiefs blurted out, "A woman as Chief? It's an affront to the ancestors." Some of the older and more conservative chiefs noisily agreed.

"Hold on a moment," said Kabika Abo, the chief of the small village of Ikonongo and one of those who Katanga had brought to see her father before he died. "Have you forgotten the *vilie*, the first female spirit? Is she not the founder of the Luba clan? Is she not the guarantor of the fertility of our chiefs and the guardian of our lineage? I believe she is still with us. I believe she has been incarnated in Marie Tsiolo, who I know to be a true avenging angel." Abo was not normally an especially eloquent speaker, and Marie was certain that he had practiced this speech many times before he delivered it. He spoke well, however, and it was an argument that would carry weight with the clan leaders.

"I realize that it is unusual," Katanga said, "but these are unusual times. The outside world presses in upon us as never before in our history. Who among you knows this world? Didier?" he asked, pointing at the chief who had objected to Marie's gender. "Have you ever been as far as Kinshasa? Marie has studied at one of the finest universities in South Africa. She is a trained engineer and it is she—not I—who designed and built the mine and the smelter that represent the future of our people. Tsiolo himself wanted Marie to take his place. It is admittedly a modern idea, but if we insist on clinging to our old ways, I assure you that the modern world will destroy us."

Mbusa Lamala again took the floor. "Katanga is right," he said. "And I recognize the wisdom in the words of Chief Abo. I am persuaded. This is the best course for our people. I second the call for Marie Tsiolo to be made Principal Chief and I exercise my right to demand a vote."

Katanga and Lamala were moving quickly in lockstep. It was clear to Marie that the fix was in from the beginning. Lamala's original nomination of Katanga was a tactical ploy, a bit of misdirection. It was a classic move on the part of her father. She also understood why the Chief had kept her in the dark. She did not want her father's job, and both he and Katanga knew it.

"Chief Lamala has the right to call for a vote," Katanga agreed. "The vote will be by secret ballot. Red stones for yes, black for no."

Most of the chiefs were illiterate, making written ballots problematic. The Luba tradition was to cast secret ballots with colored stones. One at a time, each chief rose and approached a simple wooden box on the table in front of Katanga. One at a time, each chief put a pebble into the box. Katanga held eye contact with each as they voted. Finally Katanga cast his vote as Tsiolo's proxy.

Jean-Baptiste counted the stones. There were eight red stones and five black stones in the box.

One at a time, the subchiefs came forward to greet their new leader and pledge their loyalty. Marie Tsiolo was the new Principal Chief of Busu-Mouli.

Now what the hell am I supposed to do? she wondered.

20

Antoine's enthusiasm was infectious. It always had been. Now he was pitching Alex on Albert Ilunga as a possible savior for the Congo. He argued with both passion and logic, and Alex thought that the priest had missed his calling. He should have been a Jesuit. Despite the cane, or perhaps because of it, Antoine enjoyed walking, even in Kinshasa's tropical heat. Ilunga's house, a comfortable villa that was all he had left of a once-considerable family fortune, was in the Kintambo district, not too far from the church. Antoine had insisted they walk.

The streets were crowded with cars, motorcycles, and just about every other conceivable form of wheeled transportation. Even the sidewalks had their own frenetic energy. Stalls on the side of the road hawked everything from Coca-Cola to dried bonobo penises, which were marketed rather literally for their alleged "medicinal" properties. Women in bright print dresses with matching head scarves badgered them to buy fruit from wicker or plastic containers piled high with guava, bananas, pineapple, and grapes. Victims of the Congo's wars, many missing arms or legs, begged for spare change. Antoine gave a handful of francs to one young boy whose left leg had been amputated below the knee. The boy had a crutch made from a forked tree branch. A strip of car tire was tied to the fork for the boy's armpit to rest on, and a stick bound to the branch with thick twine served as a handgrip.

"Land mine?" he asked the boy.

"Yes, Father."

Antoine tapped his leg and showed the boy his cane.

"Me too," the priest said softly.

The boy nodded his empathy for their shared plight and pocketed the priest's money.

"I'm still not sold on this idea," Alex said, picking up the conversation where they had left off. "I accept that Ilunga is an admirable man. He tried to lead his country in a different direction. And he paid a price for it. But Ilunga has been out of politics for more than six years. How can he lead the Congo out of this mess?"

"There are many who still look on him as the legitimate ruler of a truly democratic Democratic Republic of the Congo. There are many who believe we wouldn't be in this predicament if Ilunga had been allowed to take the office that he won in a fair election."

"But that's exactly the point. The army didn't let him do that. Instead, they arrested Ilunga, sent him off to Makala Prison, and that moment was lost. He spent three years in solitary confinement. As long as Silwamba retains the loyalty of the security services, I don't see why that wouldn't simply happen again. Silwamba may not be popular, but he has the guns. That still counts for too much in this country."

"The people are with Ilunga. All that is needed is a spark and they will rally to his cause."

"What kind of spark are we talking about?"

"The Lord will provide," Antoine responded with assurance.

"I wish I could be certain of that."

"Me too."

Antoine stopped abruptly.

"Here we are," he said.

Kintambo was a relatively green and leafy part of the city. Mature shade trees planted along the sidewalk offered a welcome break from the heat. Ilunga's villa was larger than Alex had expected, with a two-story house and a couple of smaller outbuildings visible from the street. It had, however, seen better days, and Alex hoped that the villa's faded glories did not represent an ill omen for Ilunga's political future. The house was set back from the street behind a tall stucco wall with a single gate. Shards of broken glass set in concrete on top of the wall were meant to discourage unwelcome evening visitors. In case that was not enough, a guard sat to one side of the gate on a low stool in the shade of a mahogany tree. As Alex and Antoine approached, the guard looked up from the magazine he was reading. Although he was unarmed, it would have taken an exceptionally brave thief to challenge him. The man would have looked right at home guarding the gates to hell. The right side of the guard's face was a mass of scar tissue, and he had only one eye. He seemed to be expecting Antoine, however, because he nodded and returned to his magazine.

There was no sign on the building, just a small bronze plaque by the gate that gave the address as 36 RUE LUKENGU and then in slightly smaller letters HEADQUARTERS OF THE CONGOLESE FREEDOM COALITION. Underneath those words was a perfect circle about two inches in diameter. Alex touched his chest and rubbed his finger over the scar that had healed as a raised ridge of flesh.

"Is this really the headquarters for the Freedom Party? I thought the party was outlawed? It seems kind of dangerous to advertise it this way."

"The Freedom Coalition isn't a political party," Antoine explained. "It's a civic organization that offers vocational training and job placement to wounded veterans, whether they fought with the regular army or the militia. The house is all Ilunga has left. The government seized all of his other assets. But he still has some well-off supporters and they provide him with some resources to run this center. Ilunga lives here, but he has also offered lodging to some of the veterans. As long as he stays out of the public spotlight and away from active politics, the regime tolerates him."

Antoine opened the wrought-iron gate and ushered Alex through. A slightly built man came out of the main house to greet them. When Alex had been a Peace Corps volunteer, Albert Ilunga had been an up-and-coming political leader looking to challenge Silwamba's leadership. Alex had left the Congo some years before the election that had resulted in Ilunga's arrest, but the man's face was familiar to Alex from television and newspaper accounts at the time. Even so, had he not been expecting to meet him, Alex would not have recognized the man walking down the front steps. Ilunga looked to have aged twenty years in the last six. He wore his gray hair cut short and his face was lined by both the sun and his years in the jungle prison. He was dressed simply in a short-sleeved white dress shirt and gray slacks. His shoes were inexpensive and in need of a polishing. There was something about him that bespoke a deep humility. Alex wondered just how an unjust prison sentence changed a man, particularly when most of the time was spent in solitary confinement.

His greeting was warm and welcoming, and Ilunga clasped his left hand onto Antoine's shoulder as they shook their hellos. Then he turned and looked at Alex. "So this is the young man you were telling me about. I am pleased you brought him here.

"Hello, brother," Ilunga said, extending his hand. "Welcome to my home." His grip was firm and his handshake emphatic.

"My pleasure, Mr. Ilunga. I just learned that this is also your office."

"Call me Albert, please. Yes. This is where the Freedom Coalition does its work. It's a terrible thing to work and live in the same place, you know. It's more like living in your office than working in your home. Plus, I can't seem to stay out of the refrigerator. I'm afraid I've been putting on weight." Ilunga could not have weighed more than one hundred pounds.

"Well, you have the satisfaction of doing important work."

"It's mostly social work, but I do agree that it is of some value. The veterans need help, and most of the international aid agencies don't want to have anything to do with ex-militia. The Freedom Coalition helps them find productive work, teaches them skills. More importantly, we try to convince them that their lives have value."

"The men live here with you?"

"Some do, but most come and go. Some tell me where they go. Others choose not to, and I don't ask. All I offer is an opportunity. Come, let me show you."

Ilunga led Alex and Antoine into the building. He walked with exaggerated care, and Alex remembered reading somewhere that the prison guards had beaten him so badly that he suffered from chronic back pain and could no longer raise his arms above his shoulders.

The first floor of the main building was divided into classrooms. Most were in use. As far as Alex could tell, the students were all men, but there were a few female instructors. In one room the students were learning about HIV/AIDS. War had killed millions in the Congo over the last decade, but AIDS had proven an even more efficient instrument of death. The instructor was an older woman in a yellow cotton dress wearing heavy stone jewelry. She was slipping a condom over a banana with the ease of considerable practice and trading ribald comments with the men.

"Do you carry those in a larger size?" one of the students asked.

The instructor held the banana up in front of her face.

"If you have more to offer than my little friend here, I'll marry you right now," she said to riotous laughter from the class.

Next door, a middle-aged man was teaching three other middle-aged men to read from a dog-eared copy of a Honda Accord repair manual. Across the hall, a group of mostly younger men were learning computer skills. There were five ancient-looking computers set up in the room, but they were connected to the Internet and the instructor clearly knew what he was doing. A blackboard along one wall was filled with charts and diagrams and symbols. It looked to Alex like the students were learning to design websites and code in HTML.

Ilunga led them through a side door into the garden and toward the largest outbuilding, a cinder-block structure about the size of a double-wide trailer.

"We're fortunate enough to have several skilled instructors in the computer courses," Ilunga commented. "These are primarily for the younger veterans, however. They are still adaptable. Some of the older men have never so much as seen a computer. We have them learning more traditional vocational skills."

Inside the cinder-block building, a group of some twenty former soldiers were practicing carpentry, metalworking, and other blue-collar trades. Most stopped working when they saw Ilunga enter. More than a few bowed their heads in silent thanks. Ilunga introduced Alex, and he shook hands with most of the men and asked them about their projects.

Lunch was served outside in the garden in the rear of the building. The three men sat at a small café table while students from Ilunga's school served them a simple but filling meal. Ilunga ate sparingly, mostly rice with a little beef and chili sauce. The lemonade was fresh and tasted incredibly good as the noonday sun pushed the heat index up well over one hundred. They kept the conversation light. Alex and Ilunga discovered a shared love of music, particularly African jazz. Antoine mostly listened, clearly pleased that his two friends seemed to be hitting it off.

When the meal was finished, Alex shifted the conversation in a more serious direction. "Do you ever think about getting back into politics? I expect that the work you are doing with the Freedom Coalition is personally pretty satisfying. But is that enough for you? I'm struck that the name of your operation here echoes the name of your political party. It feels a little bit like unfinished business."

"You have a point," Ilunga agreed, "although I don't know that I've ever thought about it in such explicit terms. I still have ambitions for political change in this country. The current regime is well entrenched but not invulnerable. Everywhere in the world, power has a structure. Power in the Congo is concentrated in only a few hands. That is a strength, but also a vulnerability. The fewer the players, the deeper the suspicions. The power centers in this country distrust each other. If they can be set against each other, the regime cannot stand."

"The system runs deeper than a few people at the top. How do you keep the new people in power from taking over where the old ones left off?"

"The affairs of the Congo should be run by the people of the Congo. I would expel the soldiers of our neighbors. We have Rwandans, Ugandans, Zambians, and Burundians fighting on our soil. They must leave. I would ensure that the mineral wealth of my country benefits the people of my country. The big foreign firms would be welcome as partners but not as masters. And finally, I would ensure that the government speaks with the voice of the people, a real democracy with real representative government and checks on those in power."

"Nothing important was ever accomplished by men who lacked ambition," Alex replied. "But what about the mechanism for change? The elections, when they bother to have them, are rigged. Last time around, Silwamba dispensed with any opponent and extended his term in an up-or-down referendum in which he took . . . what . . . ninety-seven percent of the vote? The media is under the control of the government. The security services are loyal to Silwamba. How do you bring about your vision of the future?"

"When the time for change comes, the Lord will show the way," Ilunga replied, and Alex noticed that he touched his chest in the place where Antoine had told him the coalition leader carried a circular scar similar to his own.

"It's a little surprising to me that the government lets you do even this. They thought you were dangerous enough to lock you up for three years. You still have a popular following, even if you don't maintain a public presence. There haven't been any threats to shut you down?"

"I suppose I have managed to persuade them that I am harmless. In jail, I was something of a celebrity and a constant thorn in their side. Amnesty International wrote letters about me. Your Hollywood stars called for my release from prison. Now I am just an eccentric old man teaching other old men how to read and how to make furniture or repair motorcycles. It would cost more to oppress me than they stand to gain."

They had to walk through the main house to get to the front gate. Almost in the exact center of the building, Alex noticed one door that seemed oddly out of place. It was made of steel, where the other doors were wood, and it looked brand-new. A large dead-bolt lock set in the middle of the door marked it as guarding something of some importance.

"What's in there?" Alex asked.

Ilunga looked thoughtfully at the door for a moment and then inquiringly toward Antoine. The priest nodded once.

Ilunga pulled a large key out from under his shirt. It was hanging on a metal chain around his neck. The lock turned easily.

The door opened outward, and Ilunga had to use all of his strength to pull it open. Alex resisted the temptation to step in to help, something he knew would have been humiliating for the older man.

Behind the door was a set of stairs.

"The basement," Ilunga explained. "We keep some of our . . . school supplies . . . down there."

It seemed unlikely that the Freedom Coalition was storing pencils and copier paper behind a five-thousand-dollar door.

Ilunga hit a light switch inside the frame and closed the door behind them when they started down the stairs. The light was set right over the stairs so most of the basement room was still in shadow when they reached the bottom. Ilunga touched another switch on the wall and the room was bathed in a bright incandescent light.

Racks of AK-47s, grenade launchers, and other small arms reflected and amplified the light. The basement was packed almost wall-to-wall with weapons of various types and calibers.

Albert Ilunga was building a private army.

21

That night he had the dream again. It was the first time the dream had visited since he had come to Kinshasa. The dream, like the illness that spawned it, was patient and adaptable. It bided its time. It evolved. This time, the Tsiolos appeared in the dream. Father and daughter. Anah was there with him as well. Father and daughter. And when the riders came on horses the size of mountains, there was nothing he could do to save them. Waking, Alex found the sheets wrapped tightly around him like a cocoon. He untangled them and stripped the sodden mass from the bed.

It was early. The sun was just coming up, so Alex decided on *surya namaskara*, the sun salutation, for his morning yoga. He felt immeasurably better after the workout, and a shower and shave helped to further clear his mind. He had a decision to make that he had been putting off since his visit to the headquarters of the Freedom Coalition—whether he was going to report to Spence and Washington what he had learned about Ilunga's private armory.

The answer to that question eluded him throughout a day of meetings and reports. The Silwamba administration was stepping up its attacks on Congolese civil society. He and Leonard had coffee with the head of the Center for Public Integrity, a local organization working to expose political corruption in Kinshasa. The center had just been raided by the police, and Alex promised to see what he could find out from a contact at the Interior Ministry. It was clear that the regime was growing nervous and looking to reassert its dominant position. There was no telling how Silwamba and his security services would respond to reports that one civil-society leader was stockpiling weapons.

It was easy to imagine what the Congo might be like with someone like Ilunga in charge rather than the loathsome and avaricious Silwamba. Ilunga's leadership qualities and the force of his personality were compelling. There was something about his passion for justice that reminded Alex of Marie Tsiolo. He had been thinking about her quite often since his visit to Busu-Mouli two weeks ago. She was stubborn and opinionated, but also smart and compassionate. She was also, he admitted to himself, extremely attractive. He wondered idly what kind of excuse he might be able to manufacture to make another visit to her village.

Alex wrapped up his work at about seven and chatted with Anah for twenty minutes. Skype had helped to take some of the sting out of the enforced family separations that were an inescapable part of diplomatic life. Anah seemed bubbly and happy, showing off a starfish that she had found on the beach that morning. He missed her terribly, and it felt like there was a hole in the pit of his stomach after he broke the connection to Brunswick.

Before leaving the office, Alex ran a stack of classified traffic through the shredder, then removed his hard drive from the computer with a special key and locked it in the safe. The Marines swept the office every night looking for unsecured classified material. Alex's newly restored clearances were still provisional, and Viggiano clearly had it out for him. He could not afford any security violations. When he was satisfied that there were no loose confidential papers anywhere, he punched the exit code into the alarm system to secure his office.

He did not feel like going home to brood further on his dilemma. Instead, he drove to a jazz bar that he remembered in the Ngaba section of Kinshasa near University City. At one time it had been a popular hangout for Peace Corps volunteers on their infrequent visits to the capital. The Peace Corps was long gone, but Leonard had told him that the Ibiza was still there and the music was still good.

He parked on the street in front of the bar, a nondescript concrete building painted a cheery canary yellow and wedged between a block of apartments and a small supermarket. A date palm growing in a pot by the door was hung with colored Christmas lights.

It was still early by Kinshasa's standards. Even so, there was a pretty good crowd at the Ibiza, including a handful of Westerners. The four-piece ensemble on the stage at the far end of the room was covering Joseph Kabasele's "Indépendence Cha Cha."

Alex took a seat at the bar and ordered a Stella Artois on draft and a plate of *gambas*, freshwater shrimp from the Congo River grilled and served with garlic and chili paste. The beer was cold, the shrimp were fresh and succulent, and the music was sublimely beautiful. In a moment of clarity, he realized that there was simply no way he could justify reporting what he knew about the collection of weapons in Albert Ilunga's basement. Something was happening in Congolese politics that needed an opportunity to evolve. Alex would not take responsibility for crushing it. There had really never been another choice.

The band launched into a Miles Davis arrangement of "On Green Dolphin Street." The saxophonist was pretty good, Alex thought, and the keyboard player was exceptional. He closed his eyes and let the music wash through him, draining the tension out of his body. When he opened his eyes, Jonah Keeler was sitting on the stool next to him, eating one of the shrimp from his plate.

"Good band," he said.

"Not bad. Not the most adventurous playlist, but they're pretty tight."

Keeler raised a finger to get the attention of the bartender.

"Jack and Coke, please."

"*Oui, monsieur.*"

The band wrapped up "On Green Dolphin Street" and started on Abdullah Ibrahim's "African Suite." The bartender brought Keeler his drink.

"I don't suppose this is . . . what are the kids calling it these days . . . a coincidence?" Alex asked.

"Nope."

"How did you know I was here?"

"Please. We spend billions of dollars a year on intelligence. Now admittedly, all that money can't seem to find bin Laden. But it sure as shit can find you."

"What are you interested in? Music lessons?"

"There's something I'd like to show you."

"Something we couldn't talk about in the office."

"Most definitely."

"Can you tell me what it is?"

"I'd rather show you."

"When?"

"You gonna finish those shrimp?"

Keeler put two five-thousand-franc notes on the bar to cover the bill. He left his drink untouched. When they got outside, Keeler gave Alex his instructions.

"Go home. Park in your normal spot. Go inside and wait for one hour. Then leave by the back door. Walk two blocks south to Batatela Street. I'll meet you at the northwest corner by the kiosk. Wear comfortable clothes."

"What is this about?"

"Tradecraft."

Alex followed his instructions and by ten o'clock he was standing on the corner of Batatela and Rue Ouganda. The kiosk sold newspapers, magazines, snacks, soda, and, if you knew to ask for it, locally grown cannabis. This late, the kiosk was closed. A plywood shutter was locked shut to protect the dusty Fantas and a few ounces of low-grade pot. There was little traffic on the street.

A black Honda CR-V pulled up to the corner. Alex noticed that it had regular Kinshasa license plates rather than the *corps diplomatique* plates that identified Embassy vehicles.

"Get in," Keeler said, from behind the wheel.

"Nice wheels," Alex said, when they were under way. "I thought you drove a Beemer, though."

"I do. This is a Company car. Tonight, we're on Company business." Alex could hear the capital letter in Company. The CIA.

For about twenty minutes Keeler drove in a seemingly random pattern around the city, circling blocks, doubling back on his route, and keeping as much as possible to the smaller side streets.

"More tradecraft?" Alex asked.

"Nah, I'm just lost. But I'm too much of a man to stop and ask for directions," Keeler replied.

"Who are you afraid is following us, our side or the bad guys?"

"Are you absolutely sure there's a difference?"

When Keeler was satisfied that they were on their own, he took a sharp turn without signaling onto the on-ramp for the N1 and they drove south for about forty-five minutes to Dibulu. There were a few other cars on the highway, but traffic was moving swiftly. Right outside Dibulu was an exit with a sign that read AUTHORIZED VEHICLES ONLY. VIOLATORS ARE SUBJECT TO PROSECUTION. For the less literate drivers, there was a picture underneath the warning of a guard with a rifle shooting an intruder in the back. Keeler did not take that exit, but he did turn onto an unmarked gravel road about two miles farther on that curved back in the direction of the threatening road sign.

"I don't suppose that we constitute an authorized vehicle," Alex commented.

"Probably not. Although you never know what you can talk your way out of until you have to."

Keeler killed the headlights. For a moment everything outside was dark, and Alex was sure that they were about to drive into the ditch by the side of the road. Suddenly the windshield came to life, projecting an image of the road ahead in which objects were outlined in eerie green light. A yellow line ran down the middle of the road. Other than that, it looked almost like driving in the day. The techie part of Alex's personality loved it.

"Very cool. How do you do that?"

"Heads-up display with a fourth-generation active night-vision system. I told you, it's a Company car."

"You guys get much cooler toys than we do. The State Department gave me a laptop."

"Does it come with a death ray?"

"Does Windows Vista count?"

"Well, it sure sucks the life out of you."

They drove slowly down the gravel road for about fifteen minutes. Then the yellow line veered off the road into the scrub-covered hills. Keeler followed the line. "GPS," he explained. After a short, bumpy ride, the yellow line ended with an icon of a red flag projected onto the windshield.

"Where are we?"

"A small military airfield near Kasangulu. It's a secondary field, rarely used by the DRC Air Force. I have a reason to believe that it's going to be used tonight."

"By whom?"

"Patience. You'll see."

Keeler opened the back of the CR-V. He pulled out something heavy and handed it to Alex. It was a black flak jacket. Alex put it on and Keeler helped him cinch it tight. It weighed about twenty pounds. The Station Chief donned a similar vest and slung a black duffel bag over his shoulder.

"Jonah, what the fuck are we doing?"

"We're going for a look-see. Don't worry. We're not going to get close, and we aren't going to do anything but look. I think you need to see for yourself what I believe is about to go down."

"And the guards?"

"They mostly don't bother. Remember, this is a reserve airfield. They don't use it on a regular basis."

There was enough moonlight to navigate by. It seemed to Alex that Keeler had been here before as he threaded his way confidently between the hills. A ten-minute walk brought them to a chain-link fence with three strips of barbed wire at the top. Keeler pulled a large set of clippers out of the duffel bag and cut a man-size hole in the fence in less than a minute.

"In you go, lad. Keep low."

Alex crawled through the hole and kept himself flat on the ground. A moment later, Keeler was beside him. He looked at his watch, cupping his hand over it before pressing the button that illuminated the time.

"Fifteen minutes," he whispered.

They waited.

Alex heard it before he saw it. It was the insistent drone of a turbo-prop. He looked up, but he could not see the lights of an incoming aircraft.

"They're landing without lights," Keeler explained, when he saw Alex look up. "Really not terribly safe, you know. Let's go take a look. Keep right next to me. Do what I tell you. Don't stand up unless somebody's shooting at you. Got that?"

"Let's go back to that somebody-shooting-at-me part."

"Follow me."

Keeler led Alex up to the top of a small rise. There were a few sizable rocks at the top that they used for cover. From the top of the rise, they had a view of the airfield below. In the moonlight, Alex saw a large twin-engine aircraft land and pull up alongside two trucks and a car parked by what had to be the control tower. The Station Chief pulled some equipment out of the duffel and set it up on top of one of the rocks. It looked to Alex like a telescope with a parabolic dish on the end.

"Is that a microphone?"

"Best in the world. We're gonna see if we can both look and listen. This thing is a little temperamental. Next time, I'm buying Japanese." He handed Alex a large pair of binoculars and took one for himself.

"Moon's so damn bright we almost don't need the night vision, but I want to get a good clear look at this."

Through the binoculars, they watched the crew lower the rear door of the cargo aircraft and begin removing large crates strapped to wooden pallets. They worked carefully and efficiently. A group of six African men stood by the trucks. Two of them were carrying rifles.

"That's an Antonov An-26," Keeler said. "No tail number. No registry. It's a ghost aircraft. There will be no record that it was ever in this country." Keeler trained the parabolic mike on the scene below them and plugged two earphones into a splitter on the back of the device. He handed one to Alex, who slipped the single earpiece over his right ear.

A man in a suit stepped out of the back of the sedan and walked over to the crates. He was noticeably shorter than the others, and although his back was turned to them, Alex was quite sure that this was Henri Saillard.

Sure enough, Saillard turned and looked almost straight at them. Alex ducked instinctively.

"Don't worry," Keeler assured him. "We're too far away to be spotted without night-vision equipment and high-quality optics. We can see him, but he can't see us. Why, I do believe that that is your new friend, Henry. Hello, Henry."

"I wouldn't have thought this was his scene. He seemed more like a take-a-meeting-then-lunch-at-the-club kind of guy."

"Don't let him fool you. He's one tough bastard. I've done a little spadework on him. Before getting into the mining business, he flew attack helicopters for the French Foreign Legion. He saw action in the Balkans and in the wars in West Africa in the nineties. Won the Legion of Honor for heroism under fire in Chad."

Without warning, Alex heard Saillard's voice in his ear. He was speaking in English. "Right on time as always, gentlemen. It's a pleasure doing business with professionals."

"Good." The accent of the crew chief was Slavic of some sort. "We want to unload quickly and turn around. We need to be back home and under cover before light."

"Of course. Do you mind if we inspect the goods?"

"Please, but do it quickly."

Alex saw the crew chief nod at one of the other Europeans, who used a crowbar to remove the lids from the dozen crates parked on the tarmac. Through his earpiece, Alex could hear the sound of the wood splitting. The CIA microphone was really a remarkable piece of technology.

Saillard motioned to the men by the truck, who took their time sauntering over. Their deliberate pace seemed intended to send a message: We are not under your orders. The African men reached into the crates and pulled out samples of the contents. Alex was not surprised to see that they were weapons. Some crates held standard assault rifles that looked like AK-47s. Other crates held more exotic weapons, including something that Alex was pretty certain was a surface-to-air missile. He pointed it out to Keeler.

"Yep. That, my friend, is the Russian SA-16 Igla-1E man-portable air-defense system. Not top-of-the–line, mind you, but not too far back. I can also see what look like .50-caliber sniper rifles, RPG-7 grenade launchers, and a couple of machine guns. I'm not sure of the make on those from here. That is pretty serious firepower for the Congo."

There was a new voice. "This is very good. It is certainly better equipment than what we have been working with. But it is not enough. We will need many more crates if we are to do what is expected of us." Alex could see through the binoculars that one of the tall African men was speaking. He was dressed in camouflage pants and a light-colored shirt. It was hard to judge colors through the night-vision equipment. There was something about him that made clear he was used to command. Most strikingly, however, he spoke French with a distinct Rwandan accent.

"That guy isn't Congolese," Alex told Keeler.

The Station Chief did not seem surprised.

"There will be more shipments, I assure you," Saillard said. "But this should be enough to take care of that little problem you have been having in the east, *non*?"

The Rwandan nodded. "Yes. This should be sufficient."

"Do you recognize him?" Keeler asked Alex.

"No, I don't. But I do know he's Rwandan. Probably Hutu. Almost certainly one of the *genocidaires*."

"Very good, Mr. Baines. That is the very poorly named Innocent Ngoca. He is the commander of the Democratic Front for the Liberation of Rwanda. They go by the French initials FDLR. The locals call them the Front. I call them the rat bastards. These are the boys behind the Rwandan genocide. They killed 800,000 people in about three and a half weeks, mostly with machetes and farm tools. Then they got beat and ran into the jungle one step ahead of the vengeful mob. They've been plotting to get back in power in Rwanda ever since, but a girl's gotta make a living and in the meantime the Front has been selling its services to the highest bidder in the Congo's wars. We have a pretty thick file on this guy back in the office."

"I hope it's better than the file you had on Manamakimba."

"Funny you should mention that. When Manamakimba didn't turn out to be like his jacket says he should, I started digging into that a little more. Seems like your friend Joseph has been the victim of a well-orchestrated PR campaign designed to pin on him responsibility for very bad deeds that most properly belong to Mr. Ngoca down there."

"Who's behind that? It seems a bit sophisticated for a group of psychopaths holed up in the rain forest."

"Sure does. And that's a very interesting question."

"You have something else for us?" Ngoca asked.

"But of course," Saillard replied.

Saillard retrieved a briefcase from his car, opened it, and pulled out a leather bag. He emptied it inside the briefcase.

"Some is in cash and some in diamonds. The diamonds are concentrated value. Easy to carry around and they won't rot in that forest home of yours. I trust you will know how to turn them into cash when necessary."

Ngoca laughed.

"Yes. We have some experience in that."

Saillard gave him the briefcase. The Africans and the aircrew began loading the crates into the back of the trucks.

"Wait a second," Alex said to Keeler. "That doesn't make any sense to me. Saillard is giving the arms to Ngoca. If he's running guns, shouldn't he be the one getting the money and diamonds in return? It's like he's paying him to take the weapons. Why is he doing that?"

"Isn't it obvious?"

With only a moment's reflection, Alex realized that Keeler was right.

"Ngoca works for Saillard. And it's payday."

The Station Chief nodded in agreement.

"Sure looks that way, doesn't it?"

22

Marie had never imagined that being Chief could be so tedious. Her father had made it look effortless, and her respect for him grew with each of the seemingly endless decisions that she was called on to make. Her people needed her to be strong and brave, but a large part of her wanted nothing more than to run away and hide and cry over the loss of her father. The official mourning ceremonies had done nothing to help her. She had been expected to lead the rituals, not to weep like a little orphan girl. Orphan. She was a grown woman, educated, and now a chief chosen by her people to lead them. But she was an orphan now as well. Alone in the world. No mother, no father, no brothers or sisters to share the pains and joys of life. No children of her own. She had known, but hadn't truly understood, how much she had relied on her father's strength. How close they had grown since they had lost her mother. His death had blown a hole in her life as large and deep as the mine Marie was carving into the mountainside. Filling that hole would take time, Marie realized.

For now, there was work to do. Her face would betray none of her internal turmoil. The rage and grief she would hide beneath a mask of calm and wisdom appropriate to a chief. She would bear this burden silently. Of this, she knew her father would be proud.

Today she was holding court. Village disputes that could not be resolved between neighbors were put before the chief for adjudication. Her word was absolute and there was no higher authority. Because she was Principal Chief, Marie had to hear the petty complaints and entreaties not only from the residents of Busu-Mouli but from neighboring Luba villages as well. She tried not to think about all of the work on the mine and smelter that was not getting done because she was listening to two village women contest the ownership of a goat.

But this dispute, she had to admit, was kind of interesting.

"This woman's son stole my daughter's virginity. She is a good girl, never any trouble. She was led astray by this devil. Now he must make amends by marrying her and paying a bride-price equal to what she would have been worth with her maidenhood intact."

The plaintiff was a middle-aged woman in a dress that would probably have been tight on her ten years earlier. Her name was Beatrice and Marie had known her all her life. Of course, she knew the defendant equally well. That was one of the strangest things about being Chief. It was like being both the father and the mother of a large extended family. Some days she was the nurturing mother who looked after the sick and the needy. Although the villagers called her Chief Marie because there was only one Chief Tsiolo, today she was the father.

"Is what Beatrice says true, Zawadi?" Marie asked. The defendant was thin and somewhat sickly looking. She had never recovered completely from a bad case of dengue fever that she had contracted three years ago. She had four sons with reputations that ensured no mother wanted her daughter spending time in their company.

Zawadi glared defiantly at Beatrice. "It is true that my son had relations with this girl, Nanette. But he was hardly the first. Many boys and not a few men have been where my son has gone. He has taken nothing from her that was not taken long ago."

Beatrice shook with fury at the insult. "That is a brazen lie," she shouted. "This cow would dare accuse my Nanette of such behavior? She was innocent of such things, Chief Marie, before this boy ruined her forever."

This situation would have been farcical if it had not been so deadly serious. Family was a significant financial investment in the Congo. Marriages were alliances between families, and a good bride-price for a prime daughter could be the difference between a comfortable old age and starvation. No one in Busu-Mouli would starve as long as Marie was Chief, but for the women involved in this dispute, the stakes were high.

"What do the children wish to do?" Marie asked. The two women looked slightly befuddled. *Who cares what they want?* Marie read in their expressions. *This doesn't concern them.*

It was Zawadi who spoke up. "My son would marry this girl if I let him. He claims to love her. But he can do much better than Nanette, I am sure of it."

"You would not be saying that if your Patrice had not so dishonored my daughter."

Marie held up her hand and the two women broke off the exchange before it became too heated.

"And what of Nanette?" Marie asked Beatrice. "What are her wishes?"

"She would marry this scoundrel, Patrice. She also claims it is love. I support her in this now only because I fear that what was done to her will become widely known."

If it wasn't going to before, Marie thought, *you certainly made sure that it would.*

"Very well," Marie announced, "it is my decision that Patrice and Nanette are to be married, consistent with the wishes of the two young people involved. It is also my judgment, however, that Zawadi's family will be asked to pay only one-half of the normal bride-price of twelve goats. This is to acknowledge the family's loss of opportunity to negotiate the best possible arrangement for Patrice. So it is decided."

These last words were the ritualistic close to a ruling by the Chief that meant he—or in this case, she—would brook no opposition and no further argument. The women nodded respectfully. Neither seemed dissatisfied with the decision. Marie did not know whether her ruling was just, but it certainly was expedient. Old King Solomon had had the right idea, even if his methods may have been somewhat extreme.

Her chiefly duties done for the day, Marie headed up to the mine to check out the progress the team had made. B shaft was still a concern. The rock in that section of the hill had proven to be exceptionally brittle. She had wanted to close the tunnel, but Katanga had persuaded her that the rich vein of ore that B shaft was tracking was worth the risk.

She was still nearly a kilometer from the mine when she heard three short, sharp blasts from an air horn. The harsh sound of the horn carried all the way down to the village. She and Katanga had set up a simple system of communication. One long blast was a summons for Katanga or Marie. Two blasts announced an equipment failure requiring the attention of Mputu or one of his sons. Three short blasts was a disaster: a fire, a serious injury, or a cave-in.

Marie ran.

Katanga was standing at the mouth of the mine. A cloud of copper-colored dust hanging in the air hinted at a collapsed tunnel.

"What happened?" she asked, gasping for breath after the run up the steep final section of trail. "Is anyone still in there?" Marie was gripped by a double sense of responsibility. As Chief Engineer, the mine was hers to run. As Chief of Busu-Mouli, all of the villagers were hers to protect. She had failed in both responsibilities.

"There are three boys inside, two miners and Mputu's eldest son. The generator seized up and he was trying to get it working again."

"Do you know what happened?"

Katanga spread his hands helplessly. "It looks like the ceiling collapsed in B shaft. Four other boys were working the face of the main tunnel and they made it out."

Behind Katanga, Marie could see the four miners who had just survived a close brush with death. They were caked in yellow-gray dust so thick that they looked more like ghosts than men.

Marie called to them. "Boys, quickly," she said, with a clear undercurrent of urgency in her voice. "Tell me what happened in there."

"We're not sure, Chief Marie," one of the men replied. "We were digging the rock when we heard a loud crack, like splitting wood, and then a roar. Next thing we knew, the tunnel was full of dust and smoke, and we got out as fast as we could."

"Did you see a rockfall?"

"Yes, Chief," said another boy. "The tunnel is almost entirely closed up. There were men in there."

"I know," Marie replied. *They are my men.*

She used a knife to cut a piece of cloth from her shirt that she wrapped around her mouth and nose.

"Uncle, bring a hammer and a metal pipe," Marie said to Katanga, as she strode purposefully toward the tunnel entrance. If those boys were still alive, she would dig them out with her fingernails if she had to.

Katanga gathered the tools and, as he had promised, followed his niece into the jaws of Hell.

Inside the tunnel, the dust was thick and choking. The flashlight that Marie had taken from the emergency locker struggled to cut through the cloud of dust. A thin, feeble beam illuminated the tunnel ahead for maybe ten feet. Beyond that was just a fog of yellow-gray.

She knew where she wanted to go. She had the mine's schematics committed to memory. B shaft was approximately 150 meters in on the left. It was about half as wide as the other shafts. Marie had ordered this as a precaution against just the kind of cave-in they had suffered. The rock here was rotten and treacherous. B shaft should have been abandoned weeks ago. She had been greedy.

Rock dust stung her eyes and worked its way through her makeshift mask into her throat. Marie coughed convulsively and steadied herself with a hand on the tunnel wall. She was about where she thought B shaft should be. She nearly walked past it. There was no longer an entrance to the side tunnel, just a gap in the wall of the main tunnel that was filled to the top with rubble. The light from Katanga's flashlight joined her own. Marie took the heavy hammer from her uncle and banged it against the rockfall three times. Then she paused to listen. She heard nothing. She tried again and this time pressed her ear up against the wall of the tunnel. She heard three notes that sounded like metal on stone. At least one of the miners had survived the collapse. That meant there was an air pocket of some sort behind this wall. They had some time, but without knowing the size of the fall, it was impossible to know how much time.

"Uncle, try to drive that pipe into the rubble pile. See if we can make a hole into the air pocket where our men are trapped."

Katanga located a gap in the stones and tried to force the pipe through with repeated blows of the heavy sledge. Marie heard a clatter of steel against rock. She turned her light toward the sound and saw that she and Katanga had been joined by the four men they had left at the entrance. Two were simple laborers, but the other two were experienced miners who would be a real asset if the only answer proved to be digging out the poor souls trapped in B shaft. These men had themselves just escaped being buried alive. On their own, they had come back underground to help their less fortunate brothers. Marie was immensely proud of them.

"Good boys. We need you. You two," she said to the inexperienced laborers, "see if you can help Katanga get that pipe pushed through the rocks. He'll tell you what to do. You boys," she said to the miners, "start taking the pile apart. Be careful. We can't afford a secondary slide. I'd rather you take more time and get the job done without an accident. If we work together, we'll get those men out. I promise."

Imitating Marie, the miners tied strips of cloth around the lower half of their face and attacked the rock fall with picks and crowbars. Marie directed their efforts at first, instructing them to start in one of the upper corners and work their way down at an angle to the fall. They were not trying to dig the trapped miners out. They were simply hoping to open a hole to the outside world before the men inside ran out of air.

It quickly became clear that Katanga was not going to be able to drive the pipe into the pocket behind the cave-in. The fall was just too dense. Marie thought back to her schooling, trying to dredge up some idea or insight that would help her here. There wasn't much. The mandatory emergency-management course at Witwatersrand had been geared toward the high-tech environment of a modern mining operation.

Marie's mind was racing and she made a conscious effort to slow both her thinking and her pulse rate. She would make better decisions calm. The boys trapped in B shaft deserved no less from her. Closing her eyes, she sought to visualize the schematics of the tunnel system. B shaft angled up slightly and was almost perpendicular to the central shaft. The longer C shaft was about fifty meters back and curved sharply as it followed the twisting path of the richest veins of ore. At some point, B shaft was supposed to actually cross over C shaft, and Marie had ordered that section of C shaft reinforced as insurance against the roof's collapsing. How far had the tunnel progressed? Had it reached its intersection with C shaft or were there still unknown meters of rock ahead?

Marie explained what she was thinking to Katanga. Her uncle was not certain that they had dug far enough for her plan to work. Moreover, there was a risk that they could make things considerably worse.

"I know that, Uncle. Is it worth the risk?"

Katanga paused as he weighed the unpalatable options. "It's worth it."

The dust was starting to settle and it was a little easier to see. Marie made her way carefully back to the main entrance. She wanted to run, but she did not dare risk being injured. Outside, it was already getting dark. The trapped miners were running out of time.

There was a small shed built up against the cliff wall. Inside, Marie found what she had come for. Explosives. One wall was lined with military hardware, including small artillery shells and land mines. Commercial blasting material was hard to come by, but the Congo was awash in weapons, and military-grade explosives were as common as stray dogs. Katanga and Mputu had been working together on adapting these weapons of war to a new purpose. Their initial tests had been encouraging. Even so, these tools were nowhere near ready for regular use. They were too unpredictable. Marie found what she was looking for, a bulky antitank mine with a simple timing fuse grafted to it. She also took a roll of duct tape from the supply chest.

Marie was grateful to find that the entrance to C shaft was clear of debris and looked undamaged. Katanga was already inside, knocking down the timber joists in the section of the tunnel that in theory was directly below B shaft. There could be as little as a meter of rock above them, but the reality of the tunnel complex was likely different than the paper plans. Marie tried not to think about everything that could go wrong.

Katanga pointed at the land mine in her hand.

"We don't know what the explosive force of that charge is," he observed. "If it's too strong, we could bring the whole tunnel down."

"I know. We don't have time to do the math. It's either this or those boys die."

"Okay, Chief. I hope you know what you're doing."

"Me too."

Katanga found a timber that was nearly as tall as the ceiling. Marie used the duct tape to affix the mine to the top of the timber. Katanga lifted the timber to press the business end of the mine flat up against the ceiling while Marie jammed broken pieces of wood underneath to shim it firmly in place. Without resistance from below, the explosive force of the charge would be spent driving the land mine back to the floor. There was also a risk, of course, that the charge would be too strong and the miners trapped above would be killed by either the pressure wave or stone shrapnel. Having made the preparations, Marie now had to make a decision. They could wait until the teams working on B shaft had worked their way in from the front, which could be many hours, or they could set off this charge and pray for a decent outcome. For a moment, she was racked with uncertainty.

"Make a decision, Marie," Katanga ventured. "We will support you no matter what you choose and no man will hold you to blame for the outcome."

"What would you do, Uncle?"

"I am not Chief."

"You are my family. You are all the family I have."

"If it were me in there, I would not want to wait while the air grew thick and foul. If it is fated to be my time, better a quick death than a long, slow one."

"Evacuate the others."

She waited a few minutes to give Katanga time to get the villagers outside to safety while she examined the mechanics of the land mine's new triggering system. Mputu had deactivated the pressure fuse. The timing device that would trigger the explosion was a switch attached to a cheap Chinese-made alarm clock. Marie set the timer for three minutes and scrambled down the tunnel.

They clustered together a safe distance from the tunnel entrance and waited. The minutes ticked off slowly, painfully slowly. Exactly three minutes after she set the charge, they felt the rumble of an explosion and a few seconds later a fist of sound and dust leaped out of the tunnel mouth. Marie rewrapped the cloth around her face and went back underground. The others followed close behind their chief. They picked their way through the rubble and collapsed beams to the site of the explosion. A hole at least two meters wide had been punched in the ceiling. Katanga helped lift one of the miners up into the hole. No more than a minute later, they heard his whoop of joy.

"They're alive," they heard him call.

The three men who had been trapped in B shaft were hypoxic. Another twenty minutes and they almost certainly would have been dead. Mputu's boy had been slightly injured by stone chips generated by the explosion. The two miners were untouched. All three would survive. It took them nearly half an hour to get the men through the hole in the floor and out to fresh air. Night had fallen and the cool evening breeze stood in blessed contrast to the stale air of the tunnels. Marie's ears were ringing. It took her a moment to realize that this was not a result of the explosion. She was hearing bells, the warning bells of the village.

"Oh dear God," she said, sprinting down the footpath to where she had a clear view of the village below. Her knees went weak when she saw the orange glow coming up from the forest floor.

The village of Busu-Mouli was on fire.

23

On most nights in most embassies, the lights stayed on late in a few offices, including the CIA station, the executive office, and the political section. At ten on a Tuesday night, however, Alex was all but alone in the chancery. Spence was long gone and Jonah Keeler's office door, a monstrous piece of steel with a coded cipher lock and an elaborate system of dead bolts, was alarmed. At this hour, the only other person in the mission was the Marine guard on duty, alternating his time between the guard booth at Post One and patrols through the mission to sweep for unsecured classified material.

Alex was sitting at his computer, staring at a blank cable template and trying to think of how to begin. What he had seen last night at the airfield had persuaded him that he needed to take action. Consolidated Mining was dirty. The company was partnered with some of the most murderous thugs in history, the perpetrators of the Rwandan genocide. Alex could not bring himself to accept that Spence was part of this. Somehow, the mining company was misleading the Ambassador, taking advantage of his commitment to U.S. security. At the same time, it was painfully clear that the Embassy was at least enabling Consolidated in its predatory behavior.

From his desktop, Alex could send a cable to any post in the world. This one had only one addressee, SECSTATE, WASHDC. On the template, the next line down was called the caption line. There were a variety of captions indicating special handling instructions for the message. NODIS or EXDIS captions, for "No Distribution" and "Executive Distribution," meant that only a select few should be permitted to read these cables. DG channel meant that it was a sensitive personnel issue for action by the Director General of the Foreign Service.

The caption line on the cable template on Alex's computer screen read in capital letters "DISSENT CHANNEL." Alex had never sent a cable like this. *Hell,* he thought, *he didn't even know any FSOs who had.* For the better part of an hour, he had been sitting there looking at the blank template and trying to shape his thoughts into a coherent argument. He knew what he wanted to do. He also knew what he had to avoid. He wanted Washington to understand what was happening here and launch an investigation into Consolidated Mining and its activities in the Congo. He also wanted to protect Spence, to make clear that he was not accusing his ambassador—his friend—of complicity in what for all intents and purposes amounted to murder on a grand scale.

What he was doing was extremely perilous. In theory, officers could not be punished for anything they might send in through the dissent channel. It was protected communication between career diplomats and the political leadership of the State Department. In practice, some officers who had made use of this vehicle for "disciplined dissent" had been labeled whistleblowers, traitors who had violated the department's own unwritten code of omertà. Moreover, Alex's run-in with Diplomatic Security meant that his career was already on the bubble. Spence's patronage was one of the few tools Alex could rely on to hold off the security goons who would take personal pleasure in stripping his clearances.

"Mr. Secretary," he began. "A single American company, Consolidated Mining, has joined forces with the remnants of the militia responsible for the Rwandan genocide to plunder the rich natural resources of the Democratic Republic of the Congo. The United States government is enabling these activities. Consolidated Mining's behavior is not only wrong and shortsighted, it is criminal. It is in our interest that the DRC develop as a prosperous, stable, and democratic nation. What is happening in eastern Congo cannot stay secret. Eventually it will be exposed to the world. If we do not change course and launch an investigation into Consolidated's operations here, we risk being labeled as accomplices to genocide in Africa's third-largest country."

Alex wrote for another two hours, building and honing his argument until it was as clear and compelling as he could possibly make it. While he left nothing out, he was careful not to speculate. He wanted a reasoned argument, not a conspiratorial screed that risked being dismissed as a paranoid fantasy. It was just after midnight when he finished the final draft. He read it over one more time and decided that he was, in fact, satisfied.

All he needed to do now was hit the "send" button. Within hours, it would be printed and placed in front of the Secretary of State. There was no technical reason to seek anyone's clearance or authorization to send the cable. He moved the cursor to "send" and paused.

It was hard to know what impact this cable would have on himself and his mentor, much less on the situation in the Congo. As hard as he had tried to avoid it, it was certainly possible to read the message as accusing Spence of actively supporting Consolidated's corrosive actions. *Didn't he owe it to Spence to discuss it first?* Alex hesitated. It did not seem fair or right to simply blindside the one man who had consistently stood up for him in his darkest times.

He moved the cursor to a different option: "forward message." He clicked the icon and entered Spence's e-mail address. "Let's discuss tomorrow," he wrote in the dialogue box.

There was no message from Spence waiting on Alex's computer when he arrived at the office the next morning. In truth, he had not been certain what kind of reaction to expect. He had prepared himself mentally and emotionally for anger, accusations of disloyalty, or a reasoned effort on Spence's part to explain why Alex was simply wrong. What he had not anticipated was radio silence, no acknowledgment that Spence had even read the message.

Unable to concentrate, Alex spent most of the day working in a fairly desultory fashion. At about four, Mark Fong stuck his head in the office.

"Alex, I just e-mailed you the latest version of the human rights report. It's due today. Do you mind taking a quick look at it?"

"No problem," Alex said, without much enthusiasm. "If it looks okay, I'll just send it in. No reason to bother the Front Office with it until it's in final form."

"Sounds great. Let me know if you have any questions."

The human rights report was a standardized yearly report that embassies all over the world prepared on their countries. The report on the Congo was particularly complex because the ongoing violence had contributed to massive violations of human rights in addition to a staggering loss of life. There was a new section this year on rape as a weapon of war that included gruesome stories and statistics. An hour later, Alex had made a few minor edits and the report was ready to send back to Washington.

The document was already set up in Cable Express. Once Alex had made his changes and checked that the format was correct, the message was ready to send. He slid the cursor over the "send" button and clicked.

Nothing happened. Ordinarily a dialogue box would pop up with a re-assuring "Your message has been sent" and a cable number that made it easy to find the message in the database. Alex hit "send" again. This time, an error message appeared. It read, "Code 704." Alex was familiar with some of the more common error codes for mistakes in formatting or addressing cables. It was a fairly arcane art even for experienced offi-cers, and it was easy to make a minor error that would force the per-snickety software to reject the message. Code 704 was a new one, however. Alex checked the formatting of the cable again, but could not find an obvious mistake.

He picked up his phone and dialed the commo room.

"Schefultowski," said a gravelly voice. Drew Schefultowski was the Embassy's head communicator. He spent all day in a windowless room on the top floor of the chancery surrounded by computers and commu-nications equipment. The commo room was the most sensitive part of the Embassy. There were parts of the facility that were off-limits even to the Ambassador.

Schefultowski had joined State after twenty years in the Navy. He drank too much, smoked too much, and had a generally curmudgeonly view of life. Alex liked him tremendously.

"Hey, Drew. It's Alex. I'm having some trouble with Cable Express that I'm hoping you can help me sort out."

There was a long pause before Drew answered.

"What kind of trouble?"

"Uh. Some weird code that I've never seen before. 704. Do you know what that means?"

"Listen, Alex. There's nothing I can do to fix this. You'll have to take it up with the Front Office." Drew sounded distant and uncom-fortable.

"What's this about, Drew?"

"Talk to the Ambassador about it, would you?" Schefultowski hung up.

Alex stared at the receiver, uncertain of what to make of the conversation. Whatever Drew was talking about, it did not sound like a simple technical glitch. A feeling of unease started to creep up his spine. Somewhere he knew the office had a Cable Express operating manual that should include a list of all the codes and an explanation of their meaning.

After a few minutes of rummaging through his office, he found what he was looking for in the bottom drawer of the safe. It was a bound manual of about a hundred or so pages. There was a picture on the cover of two vaguely attractive people bent over a keyboard who looked extremely happy about something. The appendixes included a list of error codes. Alex looked at 704 in disbelief. He checked the dialogue box on his screen again to make sure that he had the number right. He did. Code 704, the manual said, was for "accounts disabled by administrator." Alex's authority to send and receive cables had been suspended.

His phone rang. It was Spence's extension.

Alex picked up the receiver.

"Spence?"

"Would you come upstairs, please, Alex. We need to talk."

A lex knew something was wrong the moment he walked into the Front Office suite. There was a distinct air of tension and Peggy would not make eye contact with him.

"You can go in," she said coolly, without looking up from her typing. "They're expecting you."

"They?"

"Yes."

Inside the office, Rick Viggiano and Jonah Keeler were waiting along with Spence and the feckless Deputy Chief of Mission, Bob Jeffries.

"What's going on, Spence?" Alex asked.

"Why don't you sit down. We have something we need to talk to you about."

"Okay." Alex sat on the couch with Keeler. Spence and Viggiano sat across from them in armchairs. Jeffries stood behind Spence with his arms folded across his chest. Viggiano had a black legal briefcase crammed with papers that he set down next to his chair. A conspicuous bulge in his jacket indicated that he was carrying a gun. That was nothing out of the ordinary, at least not for Viggiano. Most RSOs stored their firearms in the safe in their office with a trigger lock securely in place. Viggiano would wear his piece to the swimming pool.

Spence did not waste time on small talk. "It is my opinion, Alex, that your behavior over the last few weeks has become increasingly erratic. Frankly, I was concerned for you. You have a history of instability, and I was worried that you were getting into something over your head. I asked Rick Viggiano to investigate. This morning he searched your residence."

"He broke into my home?" Alex asked, incredulous.

Viggiano scoffed. "Broke in with the extra key in the admin office if that's what you mean."

"I'm sure you understand," Spence said pedantically, "that your residence is not your personal property. It belongs to the Embassy and we have blanket authority to search it when the Chief of Mission deems it necessary."

"That's a pretty technical defense for what seems a clear violation of privacy."

"And why is privacy so important to you?" Viggiano pressed. "Got something you want to hide, maybe?"

"No, that's not the point."

"Oh, that is precisely the point." The former cop pulled a thick buff-colored folder out of his briefcase and laid it on the coffee table between him and Alex.

"Okay, I'll bite, Rick. What's in the file? More notes from my shrink?"

"Secrets," Viggiano replied. "But not your secrets . . . our secrets."

"What are you talking about?"

"Take a look."

Alex picked up the folder and opened it. Inside was a half-inch stack of documents. He flipped through them quickly. It was a mix of State cables, Defense Attaché reports, and CIA HUMINT, or human intelligence, reporting. The lowest level of classification that he saw was confidential. There was at least one document that was Secret/NOFORN. The NOFORN stood for "No Foreigners," meaning that it was sensitive enough that it could not be shared even with America's closest allies. Most of the documents seemed to have something to do with either Russia or China.

"I found this in your house," Viggiano said, clearly relishing the moment. "This file was taped to the underside of a dresser drawer in your bedroom. You know, I wouldn't have taken you for a boxers guy. I would have thought tighty-whiteys. You are aware, aren't you, about the rules governing the handling of classified information and the consequences for willful mismanagement of the same?"

The muscles in Alex's neck and shoulders tensed and a sudden rush of adrenaline pushed up his heart rate. Alex did not understand what was happening, but he knew that he was in some serious trouble.

"I know the rules, Rick. But I've never seen this file before. I don't know what's going on, but if you found this file in my house, then it's a plant. Somebody put it there."

"Now who would want to do something like that?" Viggiano asked innocently.

"I honestly don't know."

"What about these?" Viggiano pulled a small, brown leather bag out of the briefcase. He untied the drawstring and emptied it onto the table with a dramatic flourish worthy of a TV detective. The pile of brilliant crystals on the table could only be one thing. Diamonds. Alex was no expert, but it looked like there was an easy half a million dollars in stones, some raw and some cut and polished, sitting on the coffee table.

"I found these in your sock drawer," Viggiano continued. "Not the most original hiding place, I gotta tell you. Everyone uses the sock drawer. Like they were the first one to think of it. It's a stupid place to hide shit."

"I didn't hide anything. I told you—"

"Alex," Spence interrupted. "You should think very carefully about what you say next. There's no point denying the reality of the evidence in front of us. I'm just hoping that you can explain this to me. I'm not going to leap to any conclusions. I want to hear from you what this is about. Are you selling secrets, Alex? To whom? And why? Go ahead and tell me you aren't. I want to believe that. I'm ready to believe that. But please don't tell us that we don't have what we have."

"I'm not saying that, Spence. I'm simply saying that none of this is mine."

"That's not good enough."

"What do you want from me?"

"The truth. That's all."

"Spence, does this have anything to do with the cable I sent you last night?"

"I don't know what you're talking about," the Ambassador replied calmly.

Alex looked to Jonah Keeler for help. The Station Chief did not even acknowledge his glance.

"We'll get to the bottom of this eventually," Spence said, after a few moments of awkward silence. "In the meantime, I can't have you in my embassy. I've asked Mike and Jonah to remove you from your position."

"Remove me?"

"I'm sorry, Alex."

"Alex Baines," Viggiano said. "You have the right to remain silent . . ."

The RSO tied Alex's hands behind his back with a yellow plastic strip. As he and Keeler marched him past the secretaries on their way out of the Front Office, Alex felt his face grow red and hot with shame. An armored Land Cruiser was waiting in the Embassy garage with the engine running. Viggiano hustled Alex into the right rear seat. He put his hand on the top of Alex's head to keep him from resisting, like he had done for thousands of other suspects he had bundled into the back of squad cars in the course of his career. Keeler sat up front with the driver. Viggiano joined Alex in the back.

It was impossible for Alex to find a comfortable position with his hands tied behind his back. He couldn't imagine why Viggiano thought he needed the restraints. Alex suspected that it was pure sadism that informed that particular choice.

"Where are you taking me?" he asked.

"The airport. We've got a charter flight just for you and me back to Washington and ultimately federal prison. Don't worry. It'll probably be someplace cushy."

"What the fuck is this really about? Are you on Saillard's payroll? Why are you setting me up like this?"

"Why, I take exception to those insinuations. I am an honest, upright representative of U.S. law enforcement, a simple man doing a difficult job."

"Jonah, help me out here," Alex pleaded. "What is going on?"

The Station Chief said nothing. He did not even look over his shoulder into the backseat.

The Land Cruiser pulled out of the Embassy's underground garage, through the "airlock" at the front gates, and then out into the chaotic Kinshasa traffic. Alex found that it was tolerably comfortable if he shifted to face the window so that he was not putting too much pressure on his wrists and shoulders. He pressed his chin to his chest and breathed in and out in a slow regular pattern.

At this time of day, the airport was at least an hour from the Embassy. There were only a few roads that led to the airport, and UN peacekeepers manned checkpoints at key intersections to keep the various militia groups from attacking the airfield or international passengers. Embassy cars were usually waved through the checkpoints, but this time the soldiers flagged them over. Alex thought he heard Viggiano curse under his breath.

The driver had to open the door to speak to the peacekeepers.

"Hey, Alex," the soldier said, when he got a look inside the vehicle. "It's me, Chaudry. Ali is here with me as well."

Alex looked up hopefully. These were the Pakistani peacekeepers who had been his bodyguards for the meeting with Manamakimba. Maybe he could use this chance in some way. Viggiano patted his chest and whispered, "You say anything stupid and so help me I will blow your fuckin' head off right here. Don't try me."

"Hello, Irfan. It's great to see you." He did not try to disguise the fact that his hands were bound behind his back.

Chaudry seemed not to notice.

"Sorry we had to stop you guys. We got a tip a few hours ago that some bad guys had planted explosives on a diplomatic vehicle. Nothing more specific than that. I'm afraid we are going to need to sweep the car."

Ali Sharif appeared with a mirror mounted on the end of a pole with a flashlight clipped about halfway down. The peacekeeper walked around the car holding the mirror underneath and using the flashlight to illuminate the undercarriage. When he reached the front passenger-side door, he froze and gestured for Chaudry.

"Gentlemen, I'm going to have to ask you to get out of the car, please."

"Don't even think about it," Viggiano muttered to Alex. The RSO got out on the left side of the Land Cruiser. Keeler got out from the front and opened Alex's door. Alex stepped out and felt a sharp tug on his plastic restraints. He looked down in time to see the Station Chief place a folding knife back into his pocket. He pulled his wrists apart just enough to be certain that the bonds had been cut.

"Run," Keeler whispered in his ear. "Run for your life."

Alex understood what Keeler was saying, but he found it difficult to grasp. He was not supposed to survive the trip "home."

He took a quick look around. They were in a busy market district. On Alex's side of the car, several square blocks of stalls and kiosks were set up, with traders hawking everything from secondhand clothing to tires to live river shrimp.

Alex ran.

He bolted for the marketplace. Looking over his shoulder, he saw Viggiano draw his gun and aim it straight at him in a two-handed grip. Chaudry knocked his arm down just before he fired, and the 9mm slug from the RSO's Sig Sauer automatic punched a hole in the pavement rather than between Alex's shoulder blades. Viggiano pushed the Pakistani peacekeeper roughly to one side and ran toward the market. Alex went into a sprint.

A crash and an exchange of curses behind him told Alex that Viggiano had run into something, but he did not dare to turn back and look. Instead, he ducked through the shop of a spice merchant, ran down an alley lined entirely with retreaded tires, and popped out inside a courtyard where men sat drinking beer at white plastic picnic tables. Multiple alleyways fed into the courtyard and Viggiano appeared at the far end, having followed a different route to the same destination. Alex dashed across the courtyard for another of the narrow alleys, this one dominated by fruit and vegetable stands. Viggiano ran after him, stumbling over tables, chairs, and beer-drinking patrons who did not quite bother to get out of the way.

The covered market was sprawling and complex, and Alex took as many quick turns as he could in an effort to shake his pursuer. The concrete floors were cracked and slick with rotten fruit and vegetables. He slipped on a patch of oil on the ground and nearly went sliding into one of the stalls. He stopped to catch both his breath and his bearings. Through a gap in the stalls, Alex spotted Viggiano. The RSO was about three alleyways over, scanning the market in every direction. Alex sank lower to the ground and tried to keep out of Viggiano's view as he edged closer toward one of the market's numerous exits. He lost sight of Viggiano in the crowd and made a panicked beeline for the closest way out. Before he could reach the street, the RSO appeared about fifty feet in front of him, blocking his path. Viggiano raised his gun and Alex was torn between giving himself up and making a break for another of the small side alleys.

Suddenly whistles started blowing, and the market filled with uniformed Kinshasa police, who surrounded Viggiano and forced him to lower his weapon. With the arrival of the cops, merchants began sweeping their goods into boxes and locking up their stalls. Alex seized on the disruption caused by the police to turn his back on the scene and simply walk away. Within a few minutes, he was out of the market and on the streets of Kinshasa.

He didn't know where to go; he only knew that he needed to get as far away from Viggiano as possible. Dusk was beginning to settle over the city and Alex was grateful for the concealment it offered.

It was an oddly dislocating feeling to walk the streets of an African city without the weight and support of the U.S. government and the American Embassy behind him. He had spent his whole career in a protective bubble of diplomatic immunity, Western medicine, money, and the ultimate trump card, evacuation by the U.S. Marine Corps in the event everything went south.

Now he had nothing. He was homeless, jobless, broke, and alone on the streets of the capital city in a country at war.

24

It was not easy for a tall white man in Kinshasa to be inconspicuous. Europeans were not objects of curiosity in Kinshasa as they were in other parts of the country, but they did stand out. Walking down a side street near the market, Alex passed a pair of uniformed policemen on foot patrol. For the first time in his life, he felt a thrill of fear run through him at the sight of the police. It was a reminder that he was now on the wrong side of the law.

He turned onto Avenue de la Victoire, one of Kinshasa's major thoroughfares, and started south. He had no particular destination in mind. He just wanted to keep moving. Although he wanted desperately to run, he knew that would be a mistake. Instead, he willed his jaw to unclench, forced himself to take a few deep breaths, and maneuvered down the crowded sidewalk with as little urgency as he could muster.

A white UN jeep sped down Victoire at high speed. Alex flinched, certain that they were looking for him. An alley between two crumbling concrete apartment buildings seemed to promise safety, even though it was exactly the kind of place he would have consciously avoided just a few hours ago.

This late in the afternoon, it was already quite dark in the warren of backstreets. The stench of rotting garbage filled his nostrils. Two feral dogs fought over some scraps of meat. A one-legged and shoeless man lay alongside the wall.

As creepy as it was, the alley seemed as welcoming a place as any he was likely to find in the city right now. So he pressed himself into the shadows and waited for it to grow dark. With nothing to distract him, he thought back on the events of the day and tried to figure out what the hell had happened to him. Saillard was behind it, he was sure, but it was hard to escape the conclusion that Spence had knowingly cooperated in framing him for espionage. His cable message to Spence was the obvious trigger. It was possible that Viggiano was monitoring his computer. It would have been easy enough for the RSO to do that. Perhaps he had intercepted Alex's message to Spence last night. The Ambassador might have been telling the truth when he said he never received the draft of Alex's dissent channel cable. Even as he framed the thought, however, he knew that it stretched credibility. His friend and mentor had set him up.

A little more than two hours later, Alex edged out of the alley onto Avenue Kabu-Vasu. It was completely dark. The only lights came from the passing cars.

There was really only one place he could go.

It would take him hours on foot to get across town to Father Antoine's church, and the odds of getting mugged along the way were considerably better than even. Kinshasa did not have regular taxis. Instead, an elaborate ride-sharing system had grown up organically, with unmarked cars carrying multiple fares across town, and this often required passengers to change cars several times to get to their destinations. The locals had developed a complex system of hand gestures to signal the gypsy cabs where they wanted to go. Alex had not taken a cab in Kinshasa since he had visited the city in his Peace Corps days, but he still remembered some of the basic signals. He stood on the corner of Avenue de la Victoire and Boulevard du 30 Juin and held three fingers sideways, indicating that he was headed to Kintambo.

After about fifteen minutes, a beat-up Honda Civic that was missing the passenger-side door pulled up to the curb. There were already two people in the backseat. He negotiated a price with the driver, paying only about twice the going rate for a local. He had to change cars twice to get to where he wanted to go. This was still five blocks from the church, but he did not want the cabdriver to know his destination and he wanted to approach the church on foot on the off chance that it was being watched.

His watch read ten-fifteen. Antoine would be up, but the boys had a strict nine-thirty bedtime. In this part of Kintambo, the streets were not crowded after dark, and Alex figured that he should be able to spot anyone loitering in front of the church. He could not see any police cars or unmarked vans on the street, but he was painfully aware that he had only the vaguest notion of what he should be looking for.

When he was satisfied to the extent possible that the church was not under surveillance, Alex walked around the corner and down a side street until he came to a low door built into the wall that surrounded the church compound. One of the bricks alongside the door frame was loose, and he pulled it out to retrieve the key that was kept there. The door opened up behind the stables.

The priest was awake in his study, and Alex found him with his feet up on the desk eating peanuts and watching MTV South Africa on a small television set perched on the side table.

"Hello, Antoine."

"Alex," the priest replied with warmth and enthusiasm. "What an unexpected pleasure. Care to join me for peanuts and a little Lady Gaga? I'm learning how to relate to my younger parishioners."

"I'd love to."

Alex took a handful of peanuts and wolfed them down. He realized that he had not had anything to eat or drink since breakfast. He was famished and parched. Antoine looked at him curiously and handed Alex the bowl. Alex emptied the bowl quickly and helped himself to a bottle of water from the side table. Antoine used the remote to turn off the TV.

The priest gestured to one of a pair of threadbare chairs on the other side of the desk. Alex sat and Antoine walked around his desk to sit in the chair across from him.

"What's wrong, Alex?" the priest asked.

"I'm in trouble, Antoine. I need your help."

"Tell me."

Alex told him everything: his trip with Jonah out to the airport, his suspicions about Henri Saillard and Consolidated Mining, the dissent channel message, and the accusations of espionage and diamond smuggling. When he finished, he rested his elbows on his knees and buried his face in his hands. He rubbed his eyes with his fingertips. He was just about out of gas.

Antoine reached over and gripped Alex's arm.

"You've done the right thing. God in His mystery tests even the righteous man. That was the fate of Job."

"Job was a man of faith. I am not. Not anymore."

"How can I help you?"

"I need a place to stay tonight. Food. And, if you can spare it, some money." Alex was embarrassed by this last request. He knew that the church did not have much. But he also knew that he was not going to last long on thirty thousand Congolese francs, which was what remained in his wallet after the cab rides to Kintambo.

"Don't worry. You are among friends here. We don't have much, but what we have is yours."

"Thank you, Father."

. . .

Antoine did Alex one more favor. He let him use the rectory phone to call Brunswick. The dial-up modem on the computer would not support Skype, so he would have to settle for an old-fashioned phone call. But he needed to hear his daughter's voice. Alex sat at Antoine's desk and dialed Maine on the clunky Bakelite rotary phone. He could not remember the last time he had used one of those. His mother answered on the third ring.

"Hello."

"Hi, Mom. It's Alex."

"Hi, honey. This is late for you. What time is it over there?"

"It's late. Listen, I don't have much time and I can't tell you everything, but I wanted you to know that you might be hearing some things about me in the next couple of days. Disturbing things. I want you to know that none of them are true. There have been some . . . misunderstandings here. It might take me a while to get them sorted out."

"Alex, what's going on? What is it?" His mother sounded deeply worried and Alex wished that there were something he could say to ease her concern. He did not want to tell her too much, however. He did not want his family to know anything that might attract the unwelcome attention of diplomatic security.

"I'm sorry. That's all I can tell you for now. I'll call again when I can, and I may have something more to say then. For now, I just want to talk to Anah."

"Are you safe, dear? That's all I need to know."

"I don't know."

"Alex . . ."

"Put Anah on, Mom. Please."

There was a dull thunk that Alex realized was his mother laying down the receiver. Ten seconds later, his daughter came on the line.

"Hi, Daddy," she said. "How are you?"

"I'm good, sweetheart. But I wanted to let you know that I have to go on a trip and I may not be able to call you for a little while."

"Where are you going? Will you bring me a present?"

"I'm not certain where I'm going to have to go just yet . . . and, yes, I'll get you a present. Sugar, it may take me a while to do everything that I need to do. I'll call you just as soon as I can, and until then, Grandma and Mrs. Mabinty are going to take good care of you, okay?"

"Are you all right, Daddy? Is something the matter?" Anah was exquisitely attuned to the emotions of the people around her. Alex suspected it was a skill she had first learned in the enforced closeness of the refugee camp.

"Everything's fine, Anah." He tried to project as much assurance as he could into the lie. "I just wanted to hear your voice and tell you that I love you."

"I love you too, Daddy."

When he hung up, Alex felt hollow and worn.

There was a spare room behind the chancel, or what would have been called the chancel in a more imposing church building. A set of wooden steps hidden behind a moth-eaten tapestry depicting the martyrdom of John the Baptist led to a small, Spartan room that held a metal cot and a white plastic table with a cheap gooseneck lamp. A mosquito net hung from the ceiling. A small window let in the night air. Although Alex did not ask, he suspected that Antoine used the room to provide one of the Catholic Church's oldest services: sanctuary. He may have hidden Ilunga's political allies here or men running from the gangs or the militias. Now Alex was here seeking his own form of sanctuary.

He stripped off his clothes and hung them on a hook behind the door. Antoine had given him some of his old clothes. They fit after a fashion, and they were at least clean. It occurred to Alex as he was opening the mosquito net covering the bed that this was the night he was due for his once-a-week antimalarial. Moreover, he was not carrying any Zoloft. He would rather deal with a bout of malaria right now than a visit from the black dog. The springs on the cot were shot and the bed squeaked violently when he lay down. He did not mind. Almost immediately, he fell into a deep and untroubled sleep.

What seemed like minutes later, Alex was shaken awake. In the dim light from a flashlight with fading batteries, he saw that his midnight visitor was Jean-Pierre. The boy looked worried.

"What is it, Jean-Pierre?" Alex asked, sitting up on the cot.

Jean-Pierre put a finger to his lips.

"There are men here, looking for you," Jean-Pierre said softly.

These were the first words that Alex had ever heard Jean-Pierre speak. Although somewhat raspy from underuse, the boy's voice was strong and clear. Alex hugged him.

"I wasn't sure you could talk."

"I didn't want to," Jean-Pierre explained. "But I had to . . . for you."

"Who's here, J.P., the police?"

Jean-Pierre shook his head. "Men from the jungle."

Alex knew what this meant. The kind of men who had destroyed Jean-Pierre's village and murdered his family. Guerillas. Bush fighters. Killers.

"*Genocidaires*?" he asked. "Rwandans?"

"I think so."

Alex and Jean-Pierre crept down the stairs. Jean-Pierre moved without making a sound, but the floorboards creaked under Alex's weight. He hoped the tapestry would muffle the noise. The involvement of Ngoca's Rwandans in the hunt for him was very bad news. He had suspected that the police would be looking for him, but sending genocidal goons to hunt down an American officer seemed beyond the pale even for a Neanderthal like Viggiano. Alex realized that he had made a mistake in coming here.

Light was coming in through the thin tapestry. They were too late. The Rwandans were in the church. It was only a matter of time before they found the room and there was no other exit. He and Jean-Pierre were trapped.

"Jean-Pierre," Alex whispered, "can you get out and down through the window upstairs?"

Jean-Pierre was silent for a moment as he visualized the challenge. Then he nodded. *"Oui."* The window was too small for Alex, but the slight Jean-Pierre should be able to make it.

"Then do it. Run and warn the others. Then find a place to hide. Stay away from these men. Do you understand me?"

"Oui." Jean-Pierre ran lightly back up the stairs. His departure was like a load of responsibility being removed from Alex's shoulders.

He lifted one side of the tapestry and peered into the church. Three gunmen were moving toward the altar. One was walking down the center aisle with his Kalashnikov slung over his shoulder. Two others, holding their rifles at the ready, were moving down the narrow aisles along the walls on either side of the double row of pews. There were a few tapestries hanging on the walls, and the gunmen were lifting them with the tips of their rifles as they passed. The church was not especially big, and it would not take long for them to reach the John the Baptist tableau that was the only thing standing between Alex and an untimely death.

If they caught him in the bolt hole he was in, there was nowhere to go. It was only about twenty feet to the side door and the relative safety of the inky black night. The gunmen were now more than halfway down the nave. Alex could not be certain, but he thought he recognized the man in the middle aisle from the arms deal at the military airfield that he and Jonah had observed. Militia leaders were at the top of the food chain in the Congo, and this one was scanning the rows of pews with an air of barely concealed eagerness.

Alex steeled himself to make a dash for the door. Maybe if he took them by surprise, he could cover the twenty feet before they could target him. Maybe. Doubtful. The odds were not appealing, but it was still better than waiting to be trapped like a rat. Just as he was about to throw back the tapestry and make a run for it, the doors at the back of the church opened with a crash.

Father Antoine was standing in the doorway dressed in his full clerical garb. The tall priest made for an imposing figure silhouetted against the darkness outside. He had traded in his cane for a crosier, the shepherd's crook of a bishop. Antoine spread his arms wide, raising the crosier in his left hand.

"Yea, though I walk through the valley of the shadow of death, I will fear no evil." And, in fact, the priest seemed almost preternaturally calm.

"You will fear me, priest," the largest of the militiamen snarled in his distinctive Rwandan French. "Tell me, where is the American?"

Alex slipped quietly out from behind John the Baptist's beheading. With the gunmen focused on the back of the church, he had a chance to make it to the door unseen.

"You have misplaced an American?" The priest laughed. "How careless of you. Do not worry. Americans are as common as fruit flies. There must be millions of them. Be patient. I'm sure another one will show up sooner or later."

"Do not be a fool."

"It's a bit late for that. I've been one most of my life. But in the end, it has been a life of purpose. What is your purpose in life, my Rwandan friend? And how do you expect to explain yourself when the time comes to meet your Maker?"

"Maybe you can help me with that, priest, for you will no doubt see him before I do."

The militia leader drew a finger across his throat and the foot soldiers on either side fired two sustained bursts of automatic-weapons fire into the priest's midsection. Antoine's vestments disintegrated in a fountain of blood and the priest toppled over on his back. The crosier fell from his hand to clatter on the floor.

"No!" Alex screamed involuntarily, as he lunged toward his fallen friend. The Rwandans pivoted, their instincts honed by years of fighting in the jungle driving them to zero in on the new threat. The leader smiled when he saw Alex and slung his Kalashnikov off his shoulder. Alex dove for the exit and just made it outside when a hail of bullets from at least one of the AKs slammed into the door frame.

Outside, Alex scrambled to his feet and ran in the direction of the stables, not because it was safer but because it led away from the dormitory and the children. He had no shoes and was just as glad because his bare feet made little noise as they slapped against the flagstones. He did not have much of a head start. A moment later, the three gunmen were in the courtyard, shining powerful flashlights in a spiral search pattern. The flashlights in the hands of guerillas were now as dangerous as their automatic rifles. A spear of light passed briefly over Alex and swung quickly back to track him. For a moment, he was fully illuminated and he saw his own shadow projected onto the wall of the stables in front of him. He dodged violently to the left just before a burst of weapons fire cut through the night air, crashing into the wall where his shadow had stood only a half second before. He managed to avoid the questing beams of light long enough to reach one of the stable's shuttered windows. Noisily, he slipped the bolt that fixed the shutters together and left them dangling wide open. Then he hid behind a pile of lumber and copper pipes that he and Jean-Pierre had salvaged from the interior. As he had hoped, the gunmen found the open window and assumed that Alex had climbed inside. The militia leader bolted the window and led the two foot soldiers into the stable through the front door. Once they were inside, Alex ran as quietly as possible to the door and closed it. The bolt was on the outside. The building had been designed to keep horses inside rather than to keep intruders out.

It would not take long for the guerillas to realize what had happened, and they would be able to force their way out without too much trouble. Even so, Alex reckoned that he had bought himself a little time. He was tempted to run for the side door in the compound wall and escape onto the city streets, but he could not be sure that the guerillas would not take out their frustration on the orphan boys. Jean-Pierre might have spread the alarm, but Alex needed to be sure. The heavy thump of rifle butts on the door of the stable signaled that the *genocidaires* had discovered that they had been duped. He needed to get to the boys before the guerillas escaped.

Alex ran in the direction of the blockhouses, where the boys slept. The trap did not hold the *genocidaires* for as long as he had hoped, and he could sense, more than hear, the guerillas following close behind him. He had nearly reached the dorm when a commanding voice boomed out of the night. "Mr. Alex, get down, now!"

Without thought, Alex threw himself forward on the ground, skinning both of his forearms on the flagstone courtyard. Rifle fire whizzed over his head, and for a moment Alex was afraid that the guerillas had opened fire on the orphans. In a moment, he realized that he had it backward. The boys, led by a sixteen-year-old veteran bush fighter named Luc, were shooting at the guerillas, using the *genocidaires'* own flashlights as aiming points. Many of the orphans Antoine had taken in over the years had spent time with the militias. They were boys, but they were no strangers to killing. It was over in less than twenty seconds. All three *genocidaires* were dead. None of the students were hurt. Jean-Pierre stood next to Luc, and Alex was grateful to see that he was not carrying a rifle. There had been enough violence in his life.

"Thank you, Luc," Alex said, as he pulled himself up from the ground. His forearms stung something fierce, but he was otherwise unhurt.

"Antoine?" the boy asked.

"I'm sorry."

The boys, veterans of the Congo's wars, some with years in the bush and dozens of notches on the stocks of their AKs, cried bitter tears over the loss of their surrogate father. Alex joined them without shame. The death of his friend was a debt that would be paid in full.

25

Embassies, U.S. embassies in particular, were fortresses. They were castles designed to protect secrets rather than kings, but the principles were not all that different. The American mission in Kinshasa was an imposing mass of stone, steel, and glass. And tonight Alex Baines was going to break in and steal its secrets. He was in desperate need of two things: money and information. And he thought he knew where he could find both of these. The Ambassador's personal safe.

If he made the mistake of thinking about the entirety of what he needed to do, it was a ridiculous proposition. Layer upon layer of security protected what he was after. When he broke it into smaller pieces, however, it was much less daunting. To someone from the inside, many of the layers were gossamer-thin, known codes, systems, and routines that depended on an opponent's ignorance of day-to-day operations and standard procedures. Alex reviewed what he had to accomplish. It was doable. Just.

The first hurdle was the outer wall. It was fifteen feet tall and topped with razor wire. A sophisticated active laser alarm system alerted Post One if anything larger than a chipmunk tried to make it over the top. The wall was impregnable, but it had a weakness. It had a gate and a guard post. More important, that post was manned twenty-four hours a day by a local contract guard. A human being. Soft, squishy, and unpredictable human beings were the weak links in any "impregnable" system.

Tonight the guard on duty was Farouk, a middle-aged man with a pronounced belly and a receding hairline. Farouk carried a 9mm pistol in a holster on his belt, but his most dangerous weapon was a simple green button on his desk that would alert the Marine guard at Post One to call the detachment to a REACT. Within minutes, half a dozen heavily armed Marines would be in the compound wearing ceramic body armor and ready for just about anything. The Marines worked for Rick Viggiano. Alex's challenge would be to keep Farouk from touching that button.

At one-thirty in the morning, the traffic on Avenue des Aviateurs was thin, and Alex kept his head turned away from the cameras on the corner of the compound walls as he dashed across the street to the Embassy.

The gatehouse looked like it had been grafted onto the wall. The outer door opened into a screening room complete with an airport-style metal detector through which the guards could process visitors before buzzing them through the door to the courtyard. The inner and outer doors could not be opened at the same time. Ordinarily, as many as three guards were on duty, but in the middle of the night there was only one guard covering the graveyard shift.

Alex looked through the narrow glass window on the outer door. Farouk was sitting with his feet up on the desk, thumbing through one of the local sports magazines. He tapped on the glass. The guard startled, glanced over at the door, and hit a button on his desk. The door's electronic lock disengaged with an audible click.

"Good evening, Farouk."

The guard looked decidedly unhappy.

"Hello, Mr. Alex," he said. "I wasn't expecting to see anyone at this hour."

"I know. I hope I'm not disturbing you. I'm actually coming back from a dinner that went late and I wanted to stop by to pick something up from the office."

"Just a minute, please," the guard said, picking up the receiver of his switchboard-style phone.

"What is it, Farouk?"

"I need to call Mr. Viggiano. He left strict instructions that we were to call him immediately when you came to the Embassy. He was really quite insistent."

Farouk's index finger was suspended over one of the speed-dial buttons. Although he could not see what was written next to it, Alex was confident that it read either VIGGIANO HOME or VIGGIANO CELL. He leaned forward and pressed the kill switch. The dial tone went silent.

"You don't need to do that."

"Oh, but Mr. Viggiano said it was very important."

"Yes, I know. I lost my embassy ID and Rick found it. He was going to give it to me personally, but we spoke a couple of hours ago and he told me that he would leave it with the Marine at Post One. So it's all taken care of and there's no need to wake him."

"But Mr. Viggiano said . . ."

"That was before he and I spoke. It's okay now. You really don't want to wake him unless it's something serious. You and I both know that he has something of a temper."

Farouk looked confused, torn between his desire to follow the RSO's instructions and his desire not to become the object of the abusive ex-cop's wrath.

"Maybe you're right," Farouk said, putting down the receiver. "No need to bother him at this hour if it's already fixed."

"That's a good call."

The gatehouse opened out onto the road that nearly circled the Embassy compound inside the massive outer walls. To the left, the road led to the big circular driveway of the Ambassador's residence. To the right, it curved around to the front of the Embassy chancery. Closed-circuit TV cameras monitored the courtyard. The Marine on duty at Post One monitored the feeds. Alex walked as close to the wall as possible to avoid the cameras' overlapping fields of view. Talking his way past the local guard at the gate had been one thing. Getting the Marine to let him into the chancery was quite another. The Marine Security Guards seemed to take great joy in their rigid and inflexible enforcement of the rules. There was no way the Marine was going to let Alex into the chancery without his embassy ID. It was more likely, in fact, that the MSGs had orders to detain Alex on sight.

He couldn't just walk inside. With the push of a button, the Marine on duty could lock the doors to the lobby and trap Alex inside. The door that actually led into the chancery was like the door to a bank vault. The heavy steel swung out on pneumatic arms. Three-inch-diameter titanium rods slid out from the frame to anchor the door to the reinforced concrete wall.

In contrast to the steel door to the chancery, the double doors that opened into the lobby had a glass-paned front. From the far side of the road across from the entrance, Alex could see into the lobby and he could just make out the form of the MSG on duty behind Post One's bulletproof glass. Fernando Gutierrez was a nineteen-year-old corporal from San Juan with two great loves, the United States Marine Corps and Guitar Hero. A surveillance camera mounted on the wall right behind Alex was pointed at the entrance. Alex studied the setup for a moment and then disconnected one of the leads that clipped into the camera like a phone jack. He watched the Marine. The feed from the camera had gone dead and it took only a moment for the young MSG to realize that something was wrong. It was standard procedure when a camera went off-line for the MSG on duty to conduct a visual inspection of the equipment. Alex had seen Marines do it many times over the years.

The front door was typically left unlocked. The vault door on the inside, however, was part of the chancery's "hard line" and could be opened only from the inside or by a switch located at Post One. The MSGs could also open the door with a key they wore around their necks. The only other person in the Embassy with this key was Viggiano. From the booth, the Marine on duty could see everything in the lobby, and in the event of an attack he could secure all of the doors and windows with a single master switch. To get outside to check the camera, however, Gutierrez would have to leave the booth and walk around to the vault door. The moment Corporal Gutierrez turned and exited Post One by the back door, Alex ran for the entrance. For fifteen or twenty seconds, the Marine would be both blind and deaf to his surroundings.

Alex eased open the front door and slipped inside, taking an extra few seconds to close the door securely behind him. Crossing the lobby at a run, he threw himself flat against the wall next to the vault door. Moments later, the door clicked open. Alex was shielded from the corporal's view behind the open door. He caught the edge of the door with the tips of his fingers and held it open. Although it weighed at least a ton, the door was finely balanced on its hinges and it was not hard to keep it from swinging closed. When Gutierrez exited the lobby, Alex stepped around the vault door and into the chancery. The door closed behind him with a mechanical whirr as the titanium locking rods reengaged. He had successfully penetrated the Embassy's outer defenses. He was now inside the hard line.

Alex did not want to risk the elevator, which would have shown up as active on Post One's instrument panel, so he took the stairs up to the executive suite. A six-digit cipher lock protected the door to the suite, but most of the senior officers in the mission knew the combination. The lock was intended to keep out intruders and overly curious local employees, not cleared Americans. The suite itself was alarmed, and Alex had thirty seconds to enter the code before it triggered a warning to Post One. A digital timer on the keypad counted down the seconds. He did not have this combination, but Spence was a creature of habit and Alex hoped that nothing had changed since his days as the Ambassador's staff assistant. As Ambassador, Spence was entitled to pick his own codes, and for as long as Alex could remember, he had used the same number for his alarm—100755—his wife's birthday. It was exactly the kind of thing that Diplomatic Security warned you not to do. The blinking red light switched over to solid green. The alarm code had been accepted.

Although it was unlikely that anyone would notice, Alex did not want to turn on the office lights. There was a chance that they could be seen from the street. He had brought a small flashlight from the tool kit that he had been using at Antoine's church and used that to navigate.

Spence's office was crowded with memorabilia from his diplomatic life: awards and honors, ethnic artwork, and various souvenirs. The inexorable accumulation of tchotchkes was one of the lesser hazards of a Foreign Service career. Pride of place was given to Spence's ambassadorial commission, a poster-size document in a heavy gold frame, signed by the President and emblazoned with the Great Seal. The commission began with the words: "The President of the United States, reposing particular confidence in your honesty, integrity, and ability..." Alex feared that what he had come to learn would confirm that the President's trust had been misplaced.

There was a collection of framed pictures on a shelf beneath the commission. Some were professional photos of Spence posing with presidents and secretaries of state. Others were family portraits. One was of Anah. This was her school picture from last year. Alex remembered the care with which Anah had selected her wardrobe for that day, modeling half a dozen outfits for him before settling on a hot pink sweater and the cream blouse with the polka dots that matched the beads in her hair. He felt a sharp stab of loss at their separation.

Impulsively, he slipped the picture out of the frame and into his jacket pocket, stashing the empty frame in the bottom drawer of a filing cabinet. It was, he knew, a foolish thing to do. If Spence noticed the missing picture, he would know right away that Alex had been there. But he wanted the picture and—if he was honest with himself—he did not want Spence to have it. He had broken the bond of trust with Anah as well as with Alex. And he bore at least a share of the responsibility for Antoine's death. Alex could feel the anger and guilt over his friend's murder roiling inside him like a nest of snakes.

In contrast to the clutter elsewhere in the office, Spence's heavy oak desk was almost bare. Peggy gathered Spence's papers at the end of the day and locked them in the safe. The Ambassador had a separate safe that he used for his personal papers. It was the one he had used to lock up the file Viggiano had allegedly found in Alex's house. This was the one Alex wanted to get into. Here again, he was hoping that Spence had not changed his ways. On the desk were two phones, a regular switchboard phone and an encrypted STE, a leather blotter, and a silver paperweight in the shape of Africa. The paperweight was titanium, a gift from Consolidated Mining. Next to the paperweight was Spence's Rolodex.

The Ambassador was something of a Luddite and still kept paper records of his key contacts. He also habitually used it as a kind of cheat sheet. Alex flipped through the names until he found the one he was looking for: "Mr. Mosler." Underneath were the numbers 456-179. Several digits seemed to be missing, but that was because it was not a telephone number. It was the combination to Spence's safe, which like all of the State Department's safes was manufactured by the Mosler Safe

Company. Spence liked to come into the office on weekends, but he was never very good at remembering all of the combinations.

The Mosler safe had an LCD dial that spun without tumblers as a further deterrent against safecrackers. It opened readily to the combination 45-61-79. In the top drawer, Alex found the leather bag of diamonds and the file folder of secrets that had so quickly unraveled his life. He pocketed the diamonds. They were easy enough to convert into hard currency, albeit at significantly less than fair market value, and the money they represented would help him keep running. Even innocent men needed to eat. There was also a handheld Iridium satellite phone and a 9mm pistol with a spare magazine. He pocketed those as well.

In the second drawer, Alex found what he had hoped not to find. A dark green folder labeled simply OPERATIONS contained aerial photographs of Busu-Mouli. He would likely have recognized the village from his own memories of flying over it in J. J. Sykes's Otter, but some faceless drone in the intelligence community had removed any guesswork by labeling key landmarks for easy identification. Small white boxes and arrows identified the mine and smelter, the wharf, the armory, and, most ominously, Chief Tsiolo's house.

Beneath the photographs was a memorandum of agreement on the letterhead of Executive Solutions, a South African mercenary outfit famous for both professional competence and obsessive secrecy. The memo committed the company to provide two Denel AH-2 Rooivalk helicopter gunships to support a raid on the Congolese village of Busu-Mouli on July 23 in exchange for a cash payment of $150,000. That was only five days from today. No matter how brave they were, Jean-Baptiste's village guard would be utterly helpless when faced with armored attack helicopters mounted with high-speed Gatling guns. If they fought, they would die. It was not hard to imagine who would be leading the raid: Innocent Ngoca and the *genocidaires* of the FDLR.

Alex took the folder and closed the safe drawer. With luck, it might be a day or two before Spence realized that his safe had been rifled.

There was a loud click and the room was bathed in a sudden but muted light. Alex turned with a deliberate slowness to find Jonah Keeler sitting in the Ambassador's chair, his feet up on the desk. Keeler had pulled the chain switch on Spence's desk lamp, casting a huge shadow of himself onto the blank wall behind him.

"Pretty grim reading, huh, sport?" he said.

"Hello, Jonah. Been there a while?"

"Long enough. I know what's in that folder, or most of it anyway. You're looking at the Busu-Mouli file, aren't you?"

"Sure enough." Alex set the file down on the desk in front of Keeler and sat down in one of Spence's wingback guest chairs.

"Jonah, they killed Antoine. He was trying to protect me and they shot him. Ngoca's *genocidaires* murdered my friend. He was a good man. What the hell is going on?"

"I'm sorry, Alex. I didn't know."

"Why is this little village so all-fired important that it's worth framing me for espionage . . . that it's worth killing my friend?"

"Do you know how many Westerners there are in the Congo, not counting the UN or the aid organizations? I'd be surprised if it's more than a thousand. How can an organization like Consolidated Mining maintain control over the vast swaths of this country that it claims title to? Fear. The company is giving the Congo and its people a raw deal. As long as this is seen as inevitable, the natural order of things, Consolidated can get away with managing its considerable assets with no more than a pitiful handful of expats. Challenge that authority, however . . . call into question Consolidated's right to rule . . . and you threaten the viability of the entire system."

"You mean it isn't just about the value of the copper. Busu-Mouli was demonstrating that it could mine its own resources and keep the profits. Consolidated needed to make an example of it so that other villages were not tempted down the same path."

"Precisely. Busu-Mouli is an opportunity for Consolidated to make a buck, but there are lots of those to be had. More important, what the Tsiolo family is trying to do is a threat to the company's carefully balanced system. That cannot be tolerated. This country has to be kept dependent on the company."

"But why is the Embassy—why is Spence—not only allowing this but actually facilitating it? Has Spence been bought?"

"It's not quite as simple as that. Have you ever heard of something called the Africa Working Group?"

"In passing. It was some Cold War thing. A network of hard-core anti-Soviet types at State who wanted to step up support for the right-wing sociopaths in Africa in their wars against the left-wing sociopaths. People talked about it like it was a kind of old boys' club."

"It was more than that, I assure you." Jonah took his feet off the desk and leaned forward conspiratorially. It was the kind of body language that the CIA taught in its Psychological Manipulation 101 course at the Farm, the Agency training facility in rural Virginia. "It wasn't just State Department types. The group wasn't big, but it was broad. There were military officers, intelligence operatives, NSC people, and Hill staff from both parties. It was a regular interagency love fest. The Working Group didn't stop with debates in the Georgetown policy salons either. They went operational in the mid-seventies."

"Operational?"

"Yep. They started actively supporting right-wing insurgencies all across Africa. Jonas Savimbi in Angola. RENAMO in Mozambique. Tombalbaye in Chad. As long as you were anticommunist or at least anti-Soviet, the Working Group would back you with money, weapons, and political support. They got into bed with some of the continent's real nut jobs."

"All of this outside official channels?"

"Most definitely."

"So where did the money come from? Underwriting insurrection isn't cheap and the black budgets aren't big enough for something like that."

"Think about it for a minute."

Suddenly it was clear. "The mining companies provided the up-front capital in exchange for drilling and digging rights."

"Spot-on. The Working Group got the resources they needed to support the anticommunist right-wingers, and the mining companies got preferential access from friendly governments to all sorts of mineral goodies, with well-placed members of the Working Group doing most of the political heavy lifting for them."

"Spence was part of this?" Alex asked.

"I think so. Secret cabals tend not to keep official membership rosters, but he's the right generation and he's got the right connections."

"But what about now? The Cold War's been over for twenty years. Anticommunism is essentially a nostalgia act."

"Yes. But once something like this gets started, it tends to survive on sheer inertia. The Working Group found a way to adapt to the post–Cold War world. They persuaded themselves that America's strategic interests lay in securing exclusive access to Africa's mineral resources. They continued to bankroll insurgencies, but now with a twist. They were no longer concerned with the ideology of the groups they backed. They wanted effective insurgent movements and guerilla groups that would keep the states they operated in weak and divided. This made the local governments dependent on the Working Group and their mining company allies. It's become increasingly hard to tell whether the mining companies are doing the bidding of the Working Group or the Working Group is doing the bidding of the companies. At this point, there may no longer be any meaningful distinction between the two."

Alex's pulse picked up as he thought through the implications of what Keeler had just told him.

"So Consolidated Mining is using Innocent Ngoca and the Rwandan *genocidaires* to keep the Congo weak so they can bleed it dry on the cheap and Spence is part of some Skull and Bones–style group of Cold Warriors that is helping them do it. Is that what's going on here?"

"In part. You're still thinking too small."

"How so?"

"Consolidated Mining and the Africa Working Group aren't just using the *genocidaires*. They created the *genocidaires* for the express purpose of destabilizing the Congo, Africa's richest mineral prize."

"How is that possible? The violence in Rwanda was a Hutu-Tutsi interethnic fight that had been building for years."

"Really? What actually triggered the violence?"

"President Habyarimana's plane was shot down trying to land at Kigali airport. The Hutu blamed it on Paul Kagame, who was a Tutsi . . . Jesus Christ. You think the Working Group was responsible, that they somehow shot down the President's plane."

"They do have some of our people working with them," Keeler replied, meaning CIA black operatives. "What was Spence doing at that time?"

"He was the Deputy Assistant Secretary for Central Africa in Washington."

"Did his brief include Rwanda?"

Alex nodded. "Yes." He desperately did not want to believe that this could be true. "What about Sudan?" he asked. "What about Darfur? Was that the Working Group's doing as well?"

"Perhaps. We're not certain."

"We?"

"Not everyone who works on Africa is irredeemably cynical. There are some of us who recognize the continent's promise and its potential. This place can be so much more than a strip mine for U.S. industry.

I am part of another informal group within the government that is pursuing this more positive vision of the future. We are a sort of counterweight to the Africa Working Group, except that we are generally younger, more junior, and not nearly as influential."

"So what makes me a threat to the Working Group? Is it the dissent channel message I wrote?"

"Yep. Secretary Roberts has a track record as something of a goody-two-shoes. The Working Group couldn't take the risk of a formal investigation into their activities. The moment you wrote that cable, you became an unacceptable risk. They needed to discredit you first and then remove you altogether. You're lucky that you got away from Viggiano. You never would have made it back to Washington."

Alex was deep in thought. "That's why Spence chose me for this job, isn't it?" It was a rhetorical question. "Because I was crazy and had lost my clearances, it would be relatively easy to discredit me if it came to it. That's why Spence called me up out of the blue and offered me Julian's job. It wasn't in spite of my troubles with DS, it was because of them."

Jonah shrugged, but it was clear that he agreed.

"Did Viggiano kill Julian?"

Keeler shrugged again.

"Christ on a crutch."

He picked up the Busu-Mouli folder.

"I don't understand why Spence is holding on to this kind of information. It's dangerous to him. Why keep this stuff around?"

"Mutually assured destruction. None of the players in this little operation trust any of the others worth a damn. The paper trail is insurance against one of the partners trying to rat out the others."

Alex put the Busu-Mouli folder back on the desk.

"I suppose I have you to thank for putting the bomb under the Land Cruiser."

"Yeah. Pretty cute, huh?"

"And I suspect it wasn't an accident that my old friends Chaudry and Sharif were manning that checkpoint."

"Nope. That one took some work too. But I figured that your friends wouldn't shoot you in the back. If the checkpoint was manned by some schmoes, they might have killed you when you ran. That would have been unfortunate."

"No shit." Alex slumped back in his seat, trying to come to terms with what Keeler had just told him and what he had found in Spence's files.

"So what do I do?" he asked.

"We can help you, but we need your help as well."

"To do what?"

"Flush out the game. The Africa Working Group has covered its tracks very carefully. Everything is deniable. Nothing is provable. We need them to make a mistake, expose their agenda, and give us an opportunity to destroy them."

"Destroy Spence?" Alex asked.

"I'm not talking about whacking the guy. I'm not even talking about a trial and prison. We're patriots. We don't want to damage the United States. We just need to ensure that the Working Group is stripped of its influence."

"Can't you just go to Secretary Roberts yourselves or even the *New York Times*?"

"Not without real proof. Information and recommendations that make their way to the principals are the result of hard-fought battles, and they always have another agenda. Your cable was dangerous because it would have cut through the layers of bureaucratic defenses that the Working Group has built up over the decades. It would have gone right to the top without an opportunity for the Working Group membership to water it down with caveats and the on-the-one-hand-on-the-other-hand language so beloved of Washington technocrats. If we move against the group without hard evidence, we will be destroyed our-selves. We would be leaving the Working Group a clear field to pursue their amoral strategy. We need the group to make a mistake, expose its flabby belly."

"How do I get my life back?" Alex asked simply.

"You know Spence better than anyone else. Help us find what we need."

"Before I do anything else," Alex replied, "I'm going to Busu-Mouli. I can't let Executive Solutions and the *genocidaires* destroy that village."

"This wouldn't be about a certain farmer's daughter, would it? About five-eleven. Brunette. Foxy."

"Not entirely."

"Thought so."

"I've only got a few days."

"Want to borrow my plane?"

26

I t's not nearly as scary as you might think," J. J. Sykes said, as he banked his aircraft, a venerable Beechcraft Bonanza, to point the small single-engine plane into the wind. "Just don't pull the chute until you're clear of the tail."

Alex shifted uncomfortably in his seat and fiddled with the unfamiliar straps on the parachute. He had spent the four-hour flight hunched over in the passenger seat to accommodate the bulky pack. A smaller pack strapped to his belly held money and diamonds, a change of clothes, and some equipment, including the satellite phone he had pilfered from Spence's safe.

"You sure you can't land somewhere around here? I don't mind a walk."

"Sorry. No can do. This thing has wheels, not pontoons."

Jonah had put Alex up in a CIA safe house and had made the arrangements for Sykes to fly him to Busu-Mouli. Unfortunately, the amphibious Otter was undergoing a major overhaul and would not have been ready until after the planned assault on the village. Sykes agreed to fly Alex out in one of his other aircraft, but none were capable of landing on the river and there was no suitable runway within one hundred miles of Busu-Mouli. Alex was going to have to parachute into the town. To make matters worse, both Keeler and Sykes had been adamant that it had to be done at night. Too many people in too many villages would notice the parachute during the day and there was no telling whom they might report back to. That was how Alex found himself flying at five thousand feet in the dead of night over an inky black carpet of African rain forest, planning to make his very first parachute jump.

"Have you ever done this before?" he asked Sykes.

"What, jump out of a perfectly good airplane? No thank you. I hear tell there's nothing to it. Just count to three and then pull that handle on your chest."

Alex reached over with his right hand and grabbed the handle. He'd been reaching for it obsessively every thirty seconds since they left the ground. It was reassuringly easy to find. When stationary . . . in the well-lit cockpit . . . and under no pressure.

The Beechcraft was too old to have a factory-installed GPS navigation system. Sykes was using an off-the-shelf unit that was not so different from something that might have been mounted on the dashboard of any SUV in any American suburb. All the major landmarks were marked, however, including the vast expanse of the Congo River and the various villages that lined both of its banks.

"Here we go," Sykes said, breaking into Alex's distracted reverie.

"Busu-Mouli?"

"Yep, right down there." Sykes pointed to a spot off the port-side wing.

Alex could not see anything. "How can you tell?"

"I can't, but I trust the GPS. Always trust your instruments. Your eyes will lie to you. Try to get you killed. Your instruments always tell the truth. You ready for this?"

"Uh, no."

"Great. Let's do it."

The Beechcraft leveled out and Sykes punched a red button grafted onto the face of the instrument panel. The button sent a signal to the hard points on the belly of the plane, and a pair of clamps disengaged, releasing two GPS-guided projectiles that looked like oversize lawn darts. Weighted steel tips held the projectiles point-down while fins on the side of the darts responded to signals from an onboard receiver that guided the payloads to a fixed landing point. These particular projectiles carried infrared strobe lights mounted on their tails. Had they been military issue, the projectiles would no doubt have had a macho moniker like "spearhead" or "thunderbolt." These were CIA toys, however, and the Agency's quirky technical branch had christened the projectiles "Sammies" after the engineer who had designed them. They were accurate to within three feet. Tonight their target was the central square of Busu-Mouli.

Sykes put the Beechcraft into a slow banking turn. Reaching behind him into the aircraft's open cargo space, he retrieved a black Kevlar shoulder bag. Inside were two fourth-generation Night Hawk night-vision systems. Alex slipped one on over his head. The straps held the scope, which was about the size and shape of a small video camera, firmly in place. Sykes strapped on the second Night Hawk and dimmed the interior lights. Alex hit the power button on his Night Hawk. Instantly the forest floor came alive, a shimmering green carpet with a flat darker region that Alex knew must be the confluence of the Mongala and the mighty Congo River.

"There's the signal," Alex said, pointing slightly to the right of their line of travel. The twin infrared strobes were invisible to the naked eye, but showed up as bright pulsars through the Night Hawk scopes. There was a jump helmet on the floor by his feet. Alex put it on. It was designed to accommodate the night-vision gear and fit comfortably.

"Get ready to jump." Sykes gestured toward the back.

Alex climbed clumsily between the seats into the rear cargo space. "Let's get this over with."

"Okay. Remember. When I open the door, it'll be too loud to talk. You'll have to do it on your own. Just grab hold of the handles and wait for the green light."

"All of the lights are fucking green in this scope."

"Well, wait for any old light then. You'll know it when you see it. Remember to really jump out that door. If you pussyfoot around, the tail is likely to slice you in half. We're not all that high, so make sure that you're clear of the aircraft and then pull that goddamn ripcord. Got it?"

"Yeah. I'm ready. Mostly."

In between the two front seats was another makeshift control panel with several buttons, dials, and switches that Sykes called the Jump-master. He flipped two of the switches and the side cargo door of the aircraft opened up. There was a loud rush of air. Alex took a deep breath and looked out. He tried not to look at the jungle canopy a mile or so below. Grabbing the smooth steel bars welded to the sides of the door frame with either hand, he crouched down like a sprinter on the starting blocks. He had practiced this on the ground in Kinshasa. It had seemed easy. Over the door was a series of three lights. Alex knew that they were red, yellow, and green, but they all looked about the same color through his scope. The middle light was lit. Yellow. They were approaching the drop zone. Alex felt himself tense.

The middle light went dark. The third light went green. He launched himself into the void.

He sensed more than saw the tail of the aircraft whip by overhead, and then he was falling toward the forest floor, his body twisting violently in the air. Sykes, who had spoken with remarkable authority for a man who now claimed never to have jumped himself, had told Alex to focus on a single spot on the ground. Free-falling in the dark, however, he was having trouble even telling the ground from the sky. Without waiting to count to three, he reached across his chest and pulled the rip cord. Almost instantly, he was jerked roughly upright and the scene before him stabilized as the horizon seemed to reemerge from the jumble of images that had threatened to overwhelm him.

The bright beacons of the Sammies' infrared signals stood out in sharp contrast to the surrounding jungle. They looked to be less than half a mile away. Sykes had dropped him right on target. The parachute he was using was military grade and intended for jumpers with vastly more experience than Alex. Sykes had taught him the basics of steering and warned him that the controls for the rectangular airfoil were extremely sensitive. One thing they had not had time to practice was landings. Alex grabbed on to the two toggles that controlled the pitch of the canopy. It took a moment or two to get a feel for it, but the steering was surprisingly intuitive. There was no wind to speak of, and Alex was able to guide the parachute until he was almost directly over the signals from the twin Sammies. Then he pulled on the left steering line and started a corkscrew descent that he hoped would bring him down right in the center of Busu-Mouli.

According to what Sykes had told him, it would take about four minutes to reach the ground from five thousand feet. It seemed to happen much faster than that. From about one thousand feet, Alex was able to make out the outlines of the buildings in Busu-Mouli and the layout of the central square.

It was difficult to judge distance through the single lens of the Night Hawk. Alex concentrated on keeping the Sammies directly underneath him, making delicate adjustments with the unfamiliar steering controls. The Sammies were embedded in the ground just a few feet apart in an area about forty feet on a side that looked to be mostly clear of debris. That was where Alex hoped to land. For the last two hundred or so feet, the ground seemed to rise up at him with dizzying speed. At what he guessed was about fifty feet, he pulled down hard on the toggles to flare the chute and slow his descent before impact. He must have applied the pressure unevenly, however, because the chute slipped suddenly to the right, and instead of coming down in the clear area, he landed on the sloped corrugated tin roof of a house. The crash of his body against the metal made a terrible noise, but the tin roof was flexible and helped cushion his fall. He did everything he could to protect the equipment in his belly bag. Then the chute dragged him off the roof and he fell in an awkward heap, landing hard on his left side and smashing his head against a fence post. Even with the helmet, the blow left him dizzy and he struggled to strip off the chute before a gust of wind could pick it up and drag him across the courtyard.

The noisy landing had alerted the village to the intrusion, and by the time he was free of the chute, Alex found himself staring through his eyepiece at the glowing green barrel of a Kalashnikov. Someone pointed a flashlight in his face, overloading the night-vision system, which flared white and then went black. It would reset itself eventually, but Alex simply flipped the goggles up onto his forehead. His left side and his left arm hurt like hell.

It took a moment for his eyes to adjust to the light. The man training the rifle on him was Jean-Baptiste. Three of his guardsmen stood behind him. Alex undid his chin strap and dropped the helmet and the Night Hawk to the ground.

"Didn't we do this the last time, Jean-Baptiste? You point a gun at me. Someone tells you that there's no percentage in shooting me and we kiss and make up. Let's skip ahead. Can you take me to the Chief? There's something he needs to know. If you can't tell by my entrance, it's urgent."

Jean-Baptiste lowered the rifle grudgingly.

Only now did Alex begin to realize just how terrifying—and exhilarating—the drop had been. Part of him wanted to scream into the night sky for the sheer joy of being alive, or at least not being dead. Sykes had clearly soft-pedaled the number of ways he could have killed himself on this jump.

"I didn't expect to see you back here," Jean-Baptiste said.

"I didn't expect to be back, at least not so soon. I thought I might even show up on a boat or a plane, maybe even in the middle of the day. But I'm here now and I need to see Chief Tsiolo. Can you take me to him?" The rush from the jump had him keyed up and he was ready to pick a fight with Jean-Baptiste, even though the man was armed with a Kalashnikov.

"The Chief is dead."

Alex felt like he had been kicked in the stomach.

"What about Marie?"

"Chief Tsiolo now." It was Marie's voice and Alex experienced a moment of pure relief as she stepped out from the shadows into the now torch-lit courtyard. She was dressed in khaki cargo pants and a black T-shirt. A long knife protruded from a sheath on her dusty work boots. A wide leather belt with an oversize gold buckle was the only truly feminine touch.

To Alex's surprise and pleasure, Marie hugged him, and he winced from the pain in his side as he tried to return her embrace.

"Are you hurt?" she asked.

"Not seriously. This was my first and, if I have anything to say about it, last parachute jump. I'd say that I need to work on my landings, but if I never do this again then that's really not true."

"You couldn't have flown to Goma and taken the ferry downriver? That's what most people do."

"I was in kind of a hurry, and it'll likely be a while before I can take any commercial flights. It's complicated."

They stood face-to-face for a moment, letting the silence speak for them.

"I'm sorry about your father, Marie. He was a great man."

"Yes, he was. His death is a loss to us all, not least of all to me."

Suddenly Alex felt dizzy and he put out a hand to steady himself on the wall of the house. Marie took his arm and gestured for Jean-Baptiste to help on the other side.

"Come on," she said. "Let's get him up to the house."

"I'll give you one thing," she added, with a hint of mischief.

"What's that?"

"You do know how to make an entrance."

"Just wait until you see me leave."

After a few stumbling steps, Alex shrugged off the assistance. "I'm okay," he said. "I can walk."

He smelled it before he saw it. The acrid odor of smoke seemed to permeate the village. When they arrived at the place where the Tsiolo house had been, there was only a burned-out shell. A few charred beams were all that remained of the Chief's home . . . of Marie's home. Even without the night-vision scope, Alex could now see a number of buildings in the village that had fire damage. Some were still standing, others had burned to their foundations. A few were being rebuilt or repaired.

"What happened?" Alex asked. But he knew the answer.

"*Genocidaires,*" Marie replied. "They attacked us twice since you left. The first time they took my father from me. The next time they took my home. We beat them back both times . . . but the cost was terrible. With time, we can rebuild what was burned. The lives lost can never be replaced."

"I'm so sorry, Marie. What about the smelter?" Alex knew how important that building was to Marie's plans for the future.

"It survived. And we guard it very closely now. Come. I am staying in a house just up the road from here. Jean-Baptiste, why don't you go settle down the guard. We don't want the boys to start shooting at shadows."

With her home destroyed, Marie had moved into the second largest house in the village. The family that lived there had insisted on moving in with relatives so Marie could have the house to herself. Although sizable by village standards, the house was still only a single room with four sleeping pads on an elevated platform covered by mosquito nets.

Near the door there was a kitchen area with a wood-burning stove that vented directly through the wall. A table made of rough-hewn planks and some empty crates served as both a living and dining area. A pair of oil lamps cast enough light to read by. Alex sat in one of the chairs while Marie poured him a generous glass of palm wine. The wine was too sweet and violently strong and exactly what he wanted.

"How is your arm?" Marie asked in her South African–inflected English. Alex liked that she had chosen to speak to him in his own language.

"Pretty banged up," he admitted.

"Let me see it."

Alex hesitated.

"It's either me or the traditional healer in the next village. I think you would call him a . . . what's the word . . . witch doctor? For a few francs he'll mix up a poultice of cow dung and bloodwort that he guarantees will work. For a few dollars he'll break the wing of a chicken and then wring its neck. It's supposed to be powerful magic. So what do you say? Your friends at Consolidated Mining have given me the finest first-aid training available in a five-day course."

Alex unclipped his belly bag and carefully stripped off his jumpsuit. He was wearing a dark blue T-shirt and a pair of tan pants made of some rip-proof but breathable synthetic fabric that Keeler had given him. Zippers along the legs of the jumpsuit made it possible for him to take it off without removing his heavy boots. His rib cage protested the effort and his arm was throbbing by the time he was finished. Marie's touch was gentle and it was clear to Alex that she knew what she was doing. She checked for range of motion and probed his forearm to see how far up the pain went.

"There's no way to be certain without an X-ray, but I don't think it's broken. It is at least sprained, and we should splint it up and maybe put it in a sling for a while."

She put a simple splint on Alex's wrist and gave him a few nonnarcotic painkillers from the small stock of medicines she kept in her rebuilt first-aid kit.

"Now let me take a look at your ribs," she said.

"I'm okay. Really. I just got the wind knocked out of me."

"We'll see about that."

She had to help Alex remove his shirt. Very gently, she explored the muscles and bones along his side with the tips of her fingers until she found a spot that made him flinch.

"I think you may have cracked at least one rib and you're going to have a very large bruise. But it doesn't look serious."

Ignoring the screaming protest from his ribs, Alex struggled back into his shirt. He was still feeling a little light-headed as he sat back at the table. Marie poured herself a glass of the home-brewed palm wine from a plastic bottle that still bore the label of a popular cooking oil.

"Thanks, Doc. I'm glad someone's still making house calls."

"It's not every day that a representative of the all-powerful United States government parachutes into our village in the middle of the night. Onto our village, really, if you think about it."

"I'm afraid that I no longer represent the U.S. government. I'm here on my own."

Marie raised an eyebrow. "What happened?" she asked. "Did you kill someone?"

"Not yet, but I'm seriously considering it."

Alex told her what had happened and about his suspicions regarding Consolidated Mining and Henri Saillard. He told her about his dissent channel message, being framed as a spy and a diamond smuggler, his escape, and the murder of his friend Antoine. He explained what Jonah Keeler had told him about the shadowy Africa Working Group. And finally he told her about what he had found in Spence's safe—the epitaph for Busu-Mouli. Marie asked no questions, but when he described Antoine's death she reached across the table to take his hand in her own.

There was a brief hint of fear in her eyes when he told her about the contract with Executive Solutions that was quickly replaced by a look of grim determination. Marie Tsiolo was a Luba chief from a long line of chiefs, and her people needed a leader.

Her first question took him by surprise.

"Do you want to tell me about the scar on your chest? The circular one. My father had one just like it."

"I know. He gave me this." Alex touched his chest where Marie's father had carved the ritual symbol. "He also made me a citizen of Busu-Mouli and a member of the Luba tribe, which I suppose makes you my chief now."

"So he brought you into his little club, did he? He and Katanga were very secretive about it. What do they call it? The Brotherhood?"

"That's what I understand. You probably know more about this than I do, even though I'm guessing that there are no women in that particular club, chief or otherwise. For one thing, they'd have to change the name and that would mean getting new stationery."

Marie smiled at that, and Alex felt the pain in his side ease as her evident pleasure released a few endorphins into his system.

"You'd be right about that, although I think my father was thinking about making me an exception to the rule." She pointed at his chest. "Is that the reason you wrote that message to Washington, the one that got you in trouble?"

Alex had to think about that. "Maybe in part. But mostly because of what's happening here. Because of what's happening to you and, if I'm honest about it, because of something I did in the past. I had to speak up."

"Thank you for what you've done," Marie said. "We owe you a debt. You have sacrificed a great deal for our village. Your chief . . . your people . . . will look after you. I would tell you that you can stay here for as long as you wish, but Busu-Mouli may not be here much longer. I don't see how Jean-Baptiste's village guard can stand up to helicopter gunships."

"So what are you going to do . . . Chief?"

"Evacuate the town. If we can't find another place to settle, we may become refugees for a while. If I can hold our people together, we will survive, and when the mining company is done with our land, we will return."

They both knew that what the mining company would leave behind would bear little resemblance to the lush green hills of Busu-Mouli. It would be a no-man's-land of broken rock and slurry with acid and poison leached deep into the soil. Nothing would grow here again for generations. Moreover, Alex had the additional perspective of having spent considerable time in a UN refugee camp, and he was not as sanguine that the Busu-Mouli community would emerge from that experience intact.

"There may be another way," Alex suggested. He had not thrown himself out of an airplane simply to tell the Tsiolo family that their village was doomed.

"What are you thinking about?" Marie was curious but wary. "We don't have the training or weaponry to deal with the helicopters. Between the Afrikaners from Executive Solutions and Innocent Ngoca's killers, we'd be slaughtered."

"You don't have the weapons, but we know somebody who does."

"Who?"

There was a pause.

"Our friend Joseph Manamakimba."

"He certainly knows something about burning villages."

"He's no saint," Alex agreed, "but you don't think the label he's been saddled with is true or fair any more than I do."

Marie looked briefly down at her hands and then directly into Alex's eyes.

"No, I don't."

"I think Manamakimba was on the wrong side of a smear campaign organized by Consolidated Mining. The company sees Manamakimba as a convenient fall guy for some of the atrocities their own forces have committed."

"Nothing that company does would surprise me," Marie responded vehemently.

"According to your friendly neighborhood Central Intelligence Agency, Manamakimba has access to surface-to-air missiles, the portable kind that one man can fire from the shoulder. They're not great against jets, but they're death to helicopters."

Marie was quiet for a while as she weighed the options.

"There's not enough time," she observed, after at least five minutes of deep thought. "The attack is set for just four days from now. We don't even know where Manamakimba is."

"No. But we do know how to reach him." Alex pulled a somewhat tattered business card out of one of the deep side pockets of his pants and dropped it on the table in front of Marie.

"He gave us his card."

27

JULY 20, 2009
BUSU-MOULI

Predictably, Jean-Baptiste and some of the more headstrong members of the village guard were opposed to asking Manamakimba for help in defending the village, arguing that they could stand up to both Executive Solutions and the Rwandans without outside assistance. Katanga had been the one to bring Jean-Baptiste around. In his idealistic youth, Marie's uncle had spent some time with the armed wing of the African National Congress. He knew what the Afrikaners and their helicopters were capable of.

Only when Marie felt that she had built sufficient support for the idea among the subchiefs and other notables in the valley did she give Alex the go-ahead to call Manamakimba. This took most of a precious day, but Marie knew that there was no other way. She was Principal Chief, not an autocrat. The politics of decision-making in village councils were complex and could not be hurried easily.

Fortunately, the sat phone had survived Alex's hard landing without obvious damage. The phone required line-of-sight connectivity with at least one of a number of satellites in low Earth orbit, however, and did not work well indoors. So Marie, Alex, and Katanga sat on cheap plastic chairs in front of Marie's new home for one final review of their approach to the Hammer of God.

"Are you sure that your spies will not be able to listen in on this conversation?" Marie asked. "In your movies, they seem to be able to do this pretty easily."

"By now, Spence has to know that I have his phone," Alex admitted. "It depends in part on how deep in the government the Working Group has penetrated. If he has people in the NSA . . . that's the Signals Intelligence Agency . . . they could track the location of the phone and tap into any calls. But a request to do that has to go through the Station Chief, the guy in charge of CIA operations in Kinshasa. That's my friend Jonah, and he's promised to misplace any trace requests that come in for this number."

Alex hesitated. "There's one other thing."

"What is it?" Marie asked.

"I've kept the batteries separate from the phone, but once I put them in, the NSA will be able to track it. Cell phones are not only vulnerable to interception, they are also potential targeting devices. Unmanned aircraft launching precision-guided missiles that home in on a specific cell or sat-phone signal are one of the U.S. government's favorite methods for targeting 'Persons of Interest' in some of the wilder parts of the world. I doubt that the Working Group has access to those kinds of capabilities, but it's a risk."

"Then let's keep this conversation short," Marie said.

"Okay. Who's doing the talking, Chief? You or me."

"I'll do it," Marie said. "I have something he wants."

"What's that?"

"You'll see."

Alex inserted the batteries and punched in the eleven-digit number. He set the phone on a stump that served as a kind of table and activated the speakerphone function so that he and Katanga could listen in. There was nearly a minute of dead air before they heard the phone ring on the other end.

A familiar voice answered.

"Hello, Ambassador Spencer," said Joseph Manamakimba. "It's been a long time."

Marie raised an eyebrow and looked at Alex.

"Mr. Manamakimba, this is Marie Tsiolo. I'm using the Ambassador's phone, although I must confess that it is with neither his knowledge nor his permission." There was a nearly two-second delay between each exchange as the signals bounced back and forth across a constellation of satellites.

"Of course. Excuse me. This number is in my memory and it was the Ambassador's name that flashed on my screen. I should not have assumed it was him. How are you, Ms. Tsiolo? And thank you again for your assistance in arranging medical care for my many children."

"I'm glad that worked out. Our mutual friend from that conversation, Alex Baines, is joining us on this call."

"I'm so pleased. Mr. Baines, I'm afraid that you'll have to tell your Ambassador that I remain uninterested in his proposition."

"What proposition is that?" Alex asked.

"You really don't know?" Even through the tinny speakers Manamakimba's amusement was plain.

"I'm afraid not."

"Now that's interesting. Maybe you are as naïve as you seem."

"Almost certainly. So what was the proposition?"

"To take over the enforcer role from the Rwandans. It seems they've started to negotiate for more than what Consolidated Mining considers the market rate for industrial murder."

"The Ambassador and I have parted ways over this very issue," Alex said.

"I see. Congratulations, Mr. Baines. Welcome to the real civilized world. Where are you calling me from? Kinshasa?"

"Busu-Mouli," Marie replied.

"So your employers have not yet stripped your valley to bedrock? That's good news."

Marie was again struck by Manamakimba's powerful intelligence and the depth of information he possessed. The guerilla leader had a network of informants that any clandestine service in the world would have been proud of.

"Not yet, but that may well happen in the near future. My people are in grave danger. I think you know that. I think you have known that for some time." Marie paused. What she had to say next was not easy to say, although she knew it was necessary. "Joseph, we need your help."

The Hammer of God laughed.

"Of course you do, Marie, more than you realize. I would be happy to discuss this matter with you, but not over the phone." It seemed that Joseph Manamakimba shared Alex's reservations about satellite phones.

"Can we meet somewhere in person then? I'm afraid that we are under some time pressure."

"As luck would have it, I'm not far from Busu-Mouli. No more than half a day upriver."

"We can be there tomorrow."

Manamakimba gave Marie the exact coordinates. The fancy GPS unit that Keeler had given Alex converted the coordinates into a location on a map almost instantly. Marie knew the place. By the expansive standards of the Congo, it was right next door.

Three boats left Busu-Mouli well before dawn for the trip upriver to Manamakimba's camp. If all went well, they would be coming back with full loads of men and equipment. Marie and Alex were in the lead vessel, a thirty-foot converted tugboat that was named *Nkongolo* after the first mythical Luba king. The other two vessels in the flotilla were essentially barges with motors mounted awkwardly on the sterns. They steered like wallowing pigs. The only thing that kept them from running aground repeatedly was their captains' knowledge of the river, its shifting sandbanks, and the idiosyncrasies of its currents.

Marie stood alongside Alex in the bow of the *Nkongolo* drinking strong black tea sweetened with honey. The early morning sun was just beginning to burn away the swirling mist that all but obscured the river. As the boat rounded a bend, Alex nudged her gently in the ribs and pointed to the near bank.

A black panther stood immobile on the shore of the river. Its fur glistened in the morning light. The big cat betrayed no fear, and Marie suspected that it might never before have seen a human being. This was the deep jungle. Humans made no more mark on the jungle here than the *Nkongolo* made on the river. Within moments of their passage, the Congo, both river and jungle, erased any memory of their ever having been there.

"It's an omen," Marie decided.

"Good or bad?"

"Good. Very, very good."

"I hope you're right."

The *Nkongolo* and its escort of lumbering barges plied the waters of the Congo for another eleven hours. They passed a few settlements along the way, but nothing that could reasonably be considered a town. Marie saw a fifteen-foot crocodile slide from the riverbank into the water. About noon, she watched a lone figure pole a pirogue loaded with trade goods of some sort downriver. She could only guess how long the boatman had been traveling and how far he still had to go.

It was late afternoon by the time they reached their destination.

Manamakimba and the Hammer of God had taken over an abandoned village on a spit of land where the Congo was joined by another of its countless minor tributaries. The *Nkongolo* tied up alongside a pier made of floating logs with boards nailed across them to make a rough walkway. Marie and Alex hopped out of the boat and onto the pier. Their weight immediately sank the logs below the level of the river. They waded ashore through muddy water that rose to their knees accompanied by two of Jean-Baptiste's guardsmen.

Charlie, the young boy who had suffered from schistosomiasis, was waiting for them. He looked healthy. The rash that had covered the left side of his face was gone. His eyes, no longer yellow and jaundiced, sparkled with life. A short copper pipe hung around his neck from a leather cord as a talisman.

"You look good, Charlie," Marie said in Lingala. The boy smiled broadly, clearly pleased that she remembered his name.

"The doctor gave me some pills," he replied in the same language. "I feel much better now. So do the others."

"Can you take us to Mr. Joseph?"

"Of course."

The Hammer of God fighters were busy with the mundane tasks of camp life. Some men were cooking a communal meal over an open fire, while others gathered wood or fetched water from the river. Two men were trying to cut steaks from a forest deer that had apparently been killed by large-caliber machine-gun fire. Another man was smoking strips of what was euphemistically known as "bush meat," a catchall term for primates of just about any type. The animal in question looked like a monkey, but it might have been a juvenile chimpanzee. It was hard to tell. Either way, Marie was glad they had brought their own food. There were a few elderly women helping out around the camp, but for the most part the Hammer of God was an all-male affair.

Manamakimba greeted them warmly, clapping Alex on the shoulder as though they were old friends and kissing Marie on the cheek.

With a nod and a gesture, he sent Charlie to join a group of boys playing soccer with a ball that had been patched so many times that Marie wondered if there was actually any leather underneath the duct tape.

"Welcome to the temporary home of the Hammer of God," Manamakimba said with theatrical grandiosity.

"I love what you've done with the place," Marie replied. Many of the buildings still bore the marks of recent violence, including bullet holes and scorch marks. Manamakimba ignored the implied criticism.

"You should have seen it when we arrived," he said. "There were at least one hundred corpses rotting in the sun. It took my men almost two days to bury the bodies."

"*Genocidaires?*" Alex asked.

"Yes. One day they weren't here. The next they were everywhere. It's as though they were sent here." Manamakimba gave Marie a keen look.

In village style, they sat on the ground on reed mats and drank bitter tea that Manamakimba himself prepared over a small fire. For a while they talked about nothing in particular, another important part of negotiating in Africa. After they had finished their tea, Manamakimba got to the point.

"So to what do I owe the pleasure of your company? How can I be of service to you two . . . and to Chief Tsiolo, of course?"

"I am Chief Tsiolo now," Marie replied.

"I'm sorry," Manamakimba said, understanding immediately what this meant. "People across the valley spoke highly of your father. They saw him as a man who would stand up to the Ngocas of the world. I have no doubt that his daughter has inherited his steel as well as his copper."

"We'll find out," Marie said grimly.

Alex briefed Manamakimba on what they knew about the impending attack by Innocent Ngoca and the Front and the anticipated air support to be provided courtesy of Consolidated Mining and the mercenaries at Executive Solutions. Marie explained their need for air defenses and the CIA's understanding that Manamakimba and the Hammer of God had access to Russian-built SAMs.

"When we last met," she added, "you told us about what the *geno-cidaires* did to your family, to your wife and your daughter. I am offering you the opportunity for a measure of revenge."

"That will not bring them back."

"No," Marie agreed. "Revenge is not for the dead. It is for the living."

Manamakimba made another pot of tea. He was quiet for some time, deep in thought.

"This is a nice village," he said finally. It seemed something of a non sequitur, but Marie believed that she understood the direction the guerilla leader's thoughts were taking him. It was a thread that she had sensed running through the negotiations that had freed her and her mining company colleagues from captivity.

"It's a fine place," Manamakimba continued, "but it can be no more than a temporary refuge for us. We have few women and most of us have no real skills beyond fighting. We are not farmers or carpenters or mechanics or doctors. My children deserve better than to live like nomads. We need a place where we can live in peace, a place where the people will embrace us and give my children a chance for a new beginning. Do you know of such a place, Ms. Tsiolo?"

This is what Marie had expected, what she had anticipated Manamakimba would ask in exchange for his support. The Hammer of God needed a home and Manamakimba wanted that home to be in Busu-Mouli. It would not be an easy thing, Marie knew, to integrate this band of warriors used to having its way through force into the more settled and structured village life. It was a gamble she was prepared to take, but not without conditions.

"Help us defend our village," she said, "and we will share it with you. We will teach your men and boys to farm and fish and to mine copper ore from the hills. Your boys may court our girls and marry them if they are willing. Provided," and here her voice turned steely, "provided that you accept me as your chief and swear that you will use violence only in defense of our valley and only under my direction."

"I would be a master of my domain," Manamakimba replied, "rather than a servant in yours. Give me land in the valley on which to build our homes and I will lend you the strong right arm of the Hammer of God to defend what is ours."

Marie did not approve of his choice of pronouns or his evident reluctance to use her title. She could only hope that the gap between her demands and Manamakimba's desires could be bridged.

"I would no sooner cede my land to the Hammer of God than I would to Consolidated Mining. The land of my ancestors is not for sale or exchange. There can be only one Principal Chief in Busu-Mouli. That role cannot be shared and I will not midwife the birth of a two-headed beast. My terms are nonnegotiable. If you cannot accept them, we will take our chances with the *genocidaires* and their mercenary allies."

Manamakimba's face was impassive as he considered what she had said.

"And what is my place in this order?" he asked. "Am I to be a goatherd or a laborer in your mines?"

"Neither," Marie answered. "You are a leader of rare gifts. You will remain a leader should you choose to join us. This does not mean that you will not labor. In Busu-Mouli, we all work for our food and our freedom. There will be a place of honor for you at my table of counselors. But there can be no confusion over who is the Principal Chief. Now do we have a deal?"

There was a tense silence and Marie was all but certain that Manamakimba was going to reject her conditions. Her fallback plan was to negotiate the purchase of one or more of the Hammer of God's surface-to-air missiles. She was about to put this proposal to Manamakimba when the paramilitary commander laughed. His laughter was warm and inclusive rather than derisive.

"I can see that you are your father's daughter . . . and a chief in your own right. Very well. I agree to your terms . . . my chief." And Joseph Manamakimba, the most feared warlord in eastern Congo, even if mistakenly so, got on one knee and bowed before Marie Tsiolo, Principal Chief of Busu-Mouli. He took her hand and pressed it to his forehead. And just like that, Marie Tsiolo had an army.

Marie was anxious to get back, but the sun was setting. So they decided to spend the night and leave as soon as there was enough light to navigate by. The Congo is the deepest river in the world. At certain points, it is well over two hundred feet to the bottom of the river. In other places, however, shifting sand bars make night navigation treacherous, especially on unfamiliar stretches of the river. If they ran aground, they might have to unload the boats in order to free themselves. That could take half a day or more and they could not take that risk.

That evening, Manamakimba gathered his clan. Altogether, there were no more than eighty of them, including fighters with their odd assortment of neckwear, the camp followers, and a handful of men and boys too old or too young or too injured to be of much use. It was a small army, but they were battle-hardened and confident, and they trusted their leaders. This was a rare and precious thing, and it made them formidable. When Manamakimba told them of their new home, there were cries of joy from the rank and file. Not a few grown men wept. One by one, the men and boys of the Hammer of God knelt before Marie Tsiolo and pledged their fealty. One more battle, they hoped, and they could finally lay down their guns.

Inevitably, there was a feast: antelope roasted over piles of glowing coals, and potatoes wrapped in banana leaves and baked in the ash at the edge of the fires. It was a chief's job to provide for his people, and from the *Nkongolo*'s stores Marie contributed salted fish, peanuts, and—most important—palm wine. Manamakimba was a teetotaler, but most of his lieutenants took the opportunity to get rip-roaring drunk. A pair of drums was retrieved from somewhere in the *Nkongolo*'s hold and the boat crew from Busu-Mouli danced with the Hammer of God guerillas well into the night.

At about two in the morning, Alex and Marie took a couple of mosquito nets from the boat and hung them up in one of the huts so they would not have to sleep in the *Nkongolo*'s dirty hold. There were plenty of empty buildings. Even so, and without discussing it at all, they shared a hut, curled up on the floor in thin blankets while the party continued. The rhythmic noise of the drums was oddly soothing and they soon dropped off into a deep and dreamless sleep.

When they woke, the sky was already gray and Marie set about supervising the loading of her modest flotilla. Most of the rifles and small-caliber machine guns were stowed on the *Nkongolo*. A few motorbikes and ATVs were driven onto one of the barges and parked alongside three plastic boxes the size of footlockers with heavy latches. These were the shoulder-fired Igla missiles that Marie hoped would save her village.

Standing on one of the barges, Marie watched as Alex and a young Hammer of God guerilla mounted a .30-caliber machine gun on the *Nkongolo*'s rear gunwale, transforming the vessel—as far as she was concerned—from a humble fishing boat into the flagship of the Busu-Mouli navy. Thick planks served as a loading ramp for the barge. When he had finished mounting the gun, Alex hopped off the *Nkongolo* and walked over to the barge with an easy and confident stride. She liked the way he walked. The American paused at the bottom of the ramp and gave her a lighthearted salute.

"Permission to come aboard, Admiral?" he asked.

"Another job title? I'm going to have to update my résumé."

The trip back was uneventful. Even fully loaded, they made considerably better time traveling downstream. It was midafternoon when they reached Busu-Mouli, and Manamakimba wasted little time in getting to work. They had less than thirty-six hours to prepare for the attack. The efficiency and discipline of the Hammer of God was impressive. At first, Jean-Baptiste betrayed a degree of resentment at having been displaced as the head of Busu-Mouli's armed forces, such as they had been. Even Jean-Baptiste had to admit, however, that the newcomers brought weaponry and practical battle experience that he could not hope to match. Soon enough, he had installed himself as Manamakimba's chief lieutenant and the guerilla leader was politically savvy enough to let him do so. Together they directed the farmers and villagers as they dug trenches and fortified firing positions.

The Igla missiles were most effective if they had some elevation. The Hammer ordered his soldiers to build platforms on the roofs of three houses in different parts of the village and posted two-man teams at each site. One man served as the spotter and loader. The second was the shooter. All three teams knew their business. They had three tubes with two spare rounds for each. The equipment was elderly, however, and the soldiers had neither the training nor the tools to do even routine maintenance. Some of the rounds could turn out to be duds. It was even possible that they were all too old or worn-out to fire. In which case, Manamakimba observed philosophically, they were all likely to die.

By the night of the twenty-third, they had done everything possible to prepare. Marie waited behind the sandbag revetment near the well in the village square where Manamakimba had set up their command post. She had an AK-47 slung over her back. Most of the women and all of the children had taken shelter in the mine. A handful of women had taken up rifles and were prepared to fight for their village. As Chief, Marie would lead from the front, but Manamakimba had insisted that she accept a "Royal Guard" charged with her personal protection. One Hammer of God soldier and one village guardsman stood just behind her, pledged to protect their chief with their lives. Manamakimba had warned them that if Marie was hurt in the fighting, they had better be dead.

Manamakimba asked Alex to take responsibility for battlefield intelligence. The Night Hawk scope offered another capability that the attackers did not expect. He posted Alex on one of the rooftop firing platforms, from which he had a commanding view of the tree line and clear sight lines for spotting the South African helicopters. He could communicate with Manamakimba via SMS text messages sent over the sat phones.

The sky was cloudless and the half-moon cast a dim light on the village. Marie was pleased. It was enough light to aim by. A little after eleven, Manamakimba's phone beeped and he showed Marie the terse message from Alex. "They're here. Estimate one hundred men advancing from tree line to the north."

"Let them come," Chief Tsiolo replied.

The *genocidaires* moved quickly toward the village, understanding from both instinct and experience that they were terribly exposed in the open field. The village promised shelter and safety. It was an illusion. When the lead elements of the *genocidaires* had nearly reached the village square, a white flare arced up from the command post, illuminating the invaders and signaling the defenders to open fire. The first fusillade from the entrenched positions was devastating. Hammer of God soldiers and village guardsmen fired from the rooftops and from shallow foxholes reinforced with sandbags. A score of *genocidaires* fell in the first few seconds. The others sought whatever cover they could and returned fire. The invaders still outnumbered the villagers, but the momentum was now with the defenders. For just a moment it seemed as if the *genocidaires* would break and retreat back into the jungle, but the Rwandans dug in and the fight became a brutal slog.

Lacking any meaningful communication capacity, Manamakimba used the younger men and older boys as runners to carry messages to different groups of fighters and to bring back reports from the front lines. The picture was mixed. In places, they were driving the Rwandans back. In other parts of the fight, however, Hammer of God and village guard forces were pinned down by heavy fire.

Fifteen minutes after the shooting began, a Busu-Mouli teenager, bloody and terrified, raced up to the command post from the northern skirmish line. He was breathing so hard from both exertion and panic that he could hardly speak. Marie remembered holding him in her arms on the day he was born.

"Calm down," she said gently. "Take a breath. Then give me your report."

"It's Katanga," the boy said, when he could speak. "He's been shot. Jean-Baptiste is trying to defend the position, but there are too many of the enemy. He can't hold on. He sent me back for reinforcements."

Marie looked at Manamakimba, who spread his hands helplessly.

"There is no one left to send," he said.

"Yes, there is." She turned to the soldiers who had been sworn to defend her. "Boys. You're with me."

"Dulline," Marie said to the teenage runner, "you must lead us to them."

The boy nodded.

She did her best to ignore the icy ball of fear that seemed to have settled in her stomach. Marie was suddenly certain that she was leading these men to their deaths. She feared this responsibility, as she feared being measured against her father and found wanting. She shouldered her rifle.

Young Dulline led Marie's small unit back the way he had come, using the narrow alleyways of the village to keep as much cover between them and the shooting as possible. Abruptly, the buildings ended and Marie understood the challenge they faced. A .30-caliber machine gun was keeping the defenders pinned down. The villagers had just enough cover to keep the machine gun from tearing them to shreds, but they could not fire back effectively, and disciplined *genocidaire* fire teams were advancing under cover. The gun had to go. Marie pointed at her personal guard with the middle and index fingers of her right hand. Then she pointed at the machine gun.

"We are going to kill those bloody bastards," she said. "Are we clear?"

"Yes, Chief," the two responded.

She turned to the Hammer of God soldier, an older man named François with a four-inch scar across one cheek. He was an experienced jungle fighter. Marie hoped he was a crafty one as well. "What do you suggest?"

"Flank the position and kill the gunner and the loader. Then pin the rest between us and our men on the rise. Keep low."

Without further discussion, Marie started crawling forward to a spot where they could bring flanking fire onto the machine gun. François and his Busu-Mouli comrade were right behind her. Dulline was not far behind them. She was proud of the boy. Fifty meters of crawling gave them the angle they needed. On Marie's signal, all four opened fire on the machine gun. The shooter and the loader collapsed in a twitching heap.

"Katanga, Jean-Baptiste!" Marie shouted over the din. "We've taken out the gun. Help us with the others."

Jean-Baptiste and two unwounded defenders popped up far enough to begin shooting at the Rwandan fire teams. Marie and her small team joined in, catching the invaders in the cross fire. They advanced toward Jean-Baptiste's position.

Through the eerie green world of the Night Hawk scope, Alex watched Marie leave the relative safety of the command post and head toward the thick of the fighting. At high magnification, her face was clearly visible. A small knot of village guardsmen was defending a rise in the field that separated the village from the jungle. Rwandan *genocidaires* had cut off their line of retreat, and they were trapped there.

Alex saw Marie take out the machine gun and begin the advance toward the small ridge. The action was some four hundred meters away, but the starlight scope brought it all up close and personal. Then Alex saw something that made his blood freeze. Five heavily armed Rwandans emerged from the trees behind Marie and dropped to the ground. Alex could see them moving on their bellies through the tall grass.

"Marie!" he shouted uselessly. They were too far away and there was too much noise from the ongoing fighting for her to be able to hear. Without further thought, Alex jumped off the roof, gasping at the pain that ran up his injured side. Abandoning any attempt at stealth, he ran toward Marie, shouting her name. From ground level he could not see either Marie and her team or the Rwandans creeping up stealthily behind them. He could only imagine the worst as he weaved his way between buildings and concentrated on keeping his footing as he raced over the rocky ground. His rib cage screamed at him as he pushed himself to run faster.

Without breaking stride, Alex slung his AK-47 off his back. The State Department had taught him to shoot in the two-day "crash and bang" course mandated for all diplomats going to high-threat posts, but he had minimal experience with the AK-47. Manamakimba had advised him to keep it on semiautomatic. Full auto burned through ammunition too quickly. *To hell with Manamakimba's advice.* Alex thumbed the safety on to full auto. He rounded a corner at high speed and suddenly found himself completely exposed in the open field. The darkness saved him. The buildings behind him obscured his silhouette, while the Night Hawk afforded him a clear view of the battlefield in front of him.

"Marie," he shouted again. "Watch behind you."

She did not seem to hear him and Alex raised his rifle and started firing wildly in the general direction of the attackers, howling like a lunatic. He felt detached from the experience of battle, as if it were happening to someone else. Everything seemed to unfold in slow motion. Alex saw one of the attackers stand up and point a rifle in his direction, zeroing in on the muzzle flashes. He saw his own rounds traverse the target, dropping the Rwandan to the ground. *That's for Antoine, you son of a bitch.* The defenders turned at the sound of the gunfire and were soon taking well-aimed shots at the attackers. Through the scope, Alex recognized Jean-Baptiste among the defenders.

Alex continued his mad dash, reaching the attackers' position at about the same moment that he ran out of ammunition. It had not taken more than fifteen seconds for him to burn through the entire clip. *Maybe Manamakimba had a point.* He still had the advantage of the Night Hawk. And he swung the assault rifle by the straps at the next *genocidaire* who tried to stand. Through luck more than skill, the heavy stock crashed into the man's forehead and the Rwandan fell unconscious. The other invaders, who believed they were under attack by a much larger force, broke and ran for the jungle. Alex thought it was all over, but when he turned back toward Marie, he found himself nearly face-to-face with Innocent Ngoca. The *genocidaire* leader had his rifle leveled at Alex's midsection. A malevolent smile played across his face. The green glow of the starlight scope made it look even more sinister, almost like a Halloween mask. For all practical purposes, Alex was already dead.

Suddenly he was thrown to the ground and he could both hear and feel a hail of bullets flying over his head in both directions. Ngoca collapsed to the ground, but so did Jean-Baptiste, who had just saved Alex's life by forcing him out of the line of fire. The leader of the village guard lay on his back a few feet from Alex. Blood dripped down one corner of his mouth and the bullet hole in his chest was making a horrifying sucking sound. Alex dropped his useless rifle and went to Jean-Baptiste's assistance. It was quickly apparent even to Alex's untrained eye that there was little that could be done for the guardsman. Jean-Baptiste knew it as well. He tried to speak, but could not. Instead he reached up and pressed the tips of his fingers to the circular scar on Alex's chest. Then his hand fell limply to the ground.

A moment later, Marie knelt in the dirt next to Alex and put her hand on Jean-Baptiste's bloody chest. Tears blurred her vision. She had not loved Jean-Baptiste the way he had loved her, but he had been her friend. The entire village would mourn him, assuming that they survived the night.

Just then, she heard the distinctive thrumming sound of rotor blades. There were two deadly Rooivalks in the sky over the village. The navigation lights were lit, giving the helicopters the air of giant prehistoric insects. Red fingers of light, tracer fire, reached out from the twin chain guns mounted just under the canopy. Whatever the beams of light touched, they destroyed. Marie saw three Hammer of God fighters literally cut in half by the chain guns. *Why didn't the missile teams fire?*

Almost as soon as she was able to form the thought, she heard a waterfall-like roar and watched a bright white line arc into the sky from a nearby rooftop until it connected with one of the helicopters buzzing over the river. At first, the Igla seemed to have no effect on the Rooivalk, which turned its chain gun on the offending missile team, killing both men and shattering the platform from which Alex had been monitoring the battle just a few minutes before. Then the South African gunship slipped to the right and pitched backward. The chain guns fired their red tracers wildly into the sky. The Rooivalk spun once in a complete circle before dropping tail first into the river.

Two more Igla missiles shot into the night sky, bracketing the other Rooivalk. The first missile narrowly missed the helicopter, but the second destroyed the back half of the tail. The gunship limped out of the fight with the pilot struggling to maintain flight stability. The helicopter dropped low to the river and flew off at speed.

Disheartened by the loss of air support, the Rwandans started looking for their exit. Small groups of fighters broke and ran for the tree line, pursued by elements of the village guard and the Hammer of God. As many as half of the retreating *genocidaires* were shot in the back. Marie would gladly have shot them all.

28

On the day after the battle, Marie Tsiolo buried her dead. Busu-Mouli had survived the night, but at a terrible cost. Twenty-two villagers were dead and another nine injured, two of them so badly that they were likely to die. Marie knew every one of them. Some had been her playmates growing up. One had been her lover. Others had been mentors or teachers. Some were young enough that she had been a mentor or teacher to them. Those deaths were the hardest to bear. The Hammer of God had lost another eleven men and boys. Marie did not know their names, but she was their chief and she grieved for them. The invaders had lost even more. There were some fifty bodies scattered through the village and the surrounding fields. At least two more were entombed in their helicopter at the bottom of the Mongala River.

The village cemetery was too small to accommodate all of the bodies. At Marie's direction, Mputu and his sons organized work crews to gather the dead and dig their graves. Alex worked alongside Mputu, digging into the rich black earth with a dull spade.

In her anger, Marie had wanted to dump the bodies of the Rwandans into the river or gather them in a pile and burn them. It was Manamakimba who dissuaded her. These were simple soldiers, he argued, not leaders or commanders. Born into other circumstances, they might well have grown to be good men. Moreover, the village could ill afford the risk that the ghosts of the *genocidaires* would return to haunt Busu-Mouli. Still, Marie felt there had to be some distinctions made. The defenders would each get their own grave and marker, but she had Mputu dig a single long trench for the bodies of the Rwandans.

By midafternoon the work was done. Mounds of earth in neat rows served as mute testament to the costs of Busu-Mouli's defense. At the base of each mound was a wooden plaque with the name of the deceased. Later, the families would carve more elaborate grave markers. For now, however, the goal was simply to remember the dead. As Chief, it was Marie's obligation to lead the burial ceremony.

The ceremonial clothes and jewelry that her mother and grandmother had worn before her were kept in a storehouse and so had survived the fire that had destroyed her home. At the bottom of the trunk, Marie found something that first made her smile and then brought tears to her eyes. It was a small wooden doll that she had played with as a child. The doll wore a dress made from scraps of the same material her grandmother had used to make the ceremonial gown Marie had come in search of. Her father had carved the doll from a block of rosewood. She remembered her mother sewing the dress, her nimble fingers making perfect stitches as she worked by lamplight.

Marie was not long past playing with dolls when her mother had died from some nameless fever. Her mother's absence was a dull but persistent ache. The loss of her father was still fresh and raw. For a moment she felt utterly alone. Marie was only now beginning to grasp the essential loneliness of life as a chief. Her father had borne that burden effortlessly. Marie felt less than worthy. She gently placed the doll back in the trunk. *I have not forgotten,* she promised silently, as she closed the heavy lid.

Two of the older village women helped her dress. They braided her hair in a traditional Luba pattern and bound it with a copper chain secured by a gold pin in the shape of a bird. A band of entwined copper and gold sat high on her forehead. Earrings of glass and clay beads and beaten copper disks framed her face. Her dress was made of rich red and black cloth with gold trim that left both her throat and arms bare.

When Marie emerged from her borrowed home, she looked less like a chief than a queen. She stood tall before her people, and she was not unaware of the effect she had on the villagers and Hammer of God fighters who stood in a loose semicircle around the grave site. Alex was there and at that moment she knew that he found her beautiful. That pleased her. Some of the injured were there as well, including Katanga, who sat on a carved wooden chair with his leg heavily bandaged. He had lost a lot of blood and a piece of his thigh, but he would live.

When Marie spoke, her voice was clear and strong, but it also betrayed the anger and profound sadness barely contained beneath her cool exterior.

"My people," she began, and her words took in the Hammer of God as well as the villagers. "We have suffered a terrible loss. Too many of our fathers and brothers, our friends and neighbors, have died defending their homes and families. Their spirits have gone to the next world, from where I am sure they will do everything in their power to keep us from harm. We honor their sacrifice by living. We honor our ancestors by surviving and prospering and remembering their names and their lives and what they surrendered in our defense. This is our burden and we embrace it joyfully, for we are all of us one people."

And Marie sang the opening verse of the Kasala, the lyrical death song of Luba tradition. The mournful call and response of the Kasala invited the village to grieve together as a community for the fallen.

Manamakimba and those of his warriors who knew the Tshiluba language joined in the singing.

The Kasala ended with a long plaintive note that resonated with all of the hope and sadness of the moment. That note, many of the Luba believed, would reach across to the spirit world and serve to comfort the dead. Almost as soon as the echo from the last note had died away, the drumming began. A dancer stepped forward in an elaborate costume made of raffia palm fiber and bark. He wore an oversize round mask painted ochre and red with a beaten copper border and wild raffia hair streaming behind. Marie recognized the dancer as Mputu. As an addition to his traditional costume, Mputu wore what looked like a showerhead around his neck, a gift from Manamakimba. Two of his sons were the drummers, beating out complicated rhythms on drums made of large gourds with goatskins stretched taut over the tops and bound with rawhide straps.

By ones and twos, as the spirits moved them, the mourners joined in, purging their negative emotions in the ecstatic, transportive experience of communal dance. Marie, Alex, and Manamakimba danced alongside the others, and it was nearly dark before the drumming stopped and the mourners started back to their homes, clustered in family groups. Marie had asked prominent families to temporarily "adopt" members of the Hammer of God into their households to speed their integration into Busu-Mouli, and she made sure that everyone had a home to go to.

Marie needed sleep. Just as she was thinking of making her own exit, Alex touched her lightly on the arm and indicated with a nod of his head that he would like a private word. They walked over to the well in the village square and rested on a mahogany log that had been there as a kind of bench as long as Marie could remember. The moon rising just above the tree line cast long shadows on the ground.

"That was a beautiful ceremony," Alex told her.

"Thank you."

"I'm sorry about Jean-Baptiste."

"So am I. He was a good man."

"He saved my life at the price of his own. He's the second man to do that this week."

"Jean-Baptiste died defending his village," Marie protested. "He would have considered that an honor."

"It's still not safe to be around me. I came back to Busu-Mouli because I needed to warn you about the attack. Now my presence here is nothing but a danger to you and the village. I need to leave. The sooner the better."

"Where will you go?" asked Marie.

"Into the heart of darkness."

Marie smiled. "I've read Conrad. This is the heart of darkness. You're on the very stretch of river where Kurtz lost his mind."

"That was Marlow's heart of darkness. Mine is somewhere else."

"Where?"

"Kinshasa."

Alex made plans to leave. It was not as straightforward as it seemed. For one thing, Busu-Mouli was a long way from Kinshasa and there were no airports or major roads anywhere nearby. For another, he was a fugitive and he had no way of knowing how wide a net the Embassy might have cast. At a minimum, there would be a reward. It was Uncle Sam's standard MO.

Air travel was too risky and overland was too slow. The river itself was his best bet. He learned from Mputu that the *Nkongolo* would be traveling downriver in the morning with a load of copper for trade. It could take him as far as Mbandaka. From there, he could get a commercial ferry to Kinshasa.

He was packing his meager belongings when Marie walked into the house where he was staying. She had traded in her ceremonial dress for work clothes and steel-toed mining boots. *Even dressed like a laborer,* Alex thought, *she was still extraordinarily beautiful.*

"I'm going with you."

"To Kinshasa?" Alex asked.

"Yes."

"Why would you want to do that, Chief? Your responsibilities are here."

"My responsibilities are to my people, who will never be safe until the mining company and its political proxies are brought to heel. Ngoca is dead and we have hurt the Rwandans badly, but they will be back. I can sit here and wait for that day, or I can go with you and try to finish this. The snake has a head and that head is in Kinshasa."

"Who will be in charge when you are gone? Manamakimba?"

"No. That would be putting the fox in charge of the henhouse. Katanga is well enough to serve as Acting Chief until I return."

"The mine?"

"Mputu can take charge of it. He knows as much as most mining engineers by this point. I have confidence in him."

"I don't know how long this will take."

"This is the Congo, Alex. We have learned to be patient. Our most important resource is not copper or coltan; it is time."

At least they would travel in style. Marie had the *Nkongolo* scrubbed clean from top to bottom and a fresh coat of paint applied to cover the fishy odor that had worked its way deep into the timbers of Busu-Mouli's most riverworthy craft. As a finishing touch, Mputu had cut the letters of the boat's name out of a thin sheet of copper and hammered them into the wood on the stern. His oldest son had carved a turtle head from iroko wood and mounted it on the bow. In the stories, Lolo Ina Nombe, the founding ancestress of the Luba clan, often appeared in the form of a turtle. The *Nkongolo* was now, Mputu averred, fit to transport a chief.

Most of the village was there to see them off. Katanga, who was sitting on a stool with his injured leg elevated, had brought Marie a gift—a flat, oblong object wrapped in an embroidered cloth that looked antique. Marie took the gift from her uncle with reverence.

"Where did you find the time, Almost Father?" she asked.

"I have not had so much to do over the last few days," Katanga said, looking pointedly at his leg. "I needed to find some way to keep busy."

Marie unwrapped the gift. It was a dark wooden panel with convex sides about two feet long and one foot across. It was elaborately carved, with cowry shells, clay beads, and bits of polished metal set into the wood. Marie gasped for joy at the sheer beauty of the object.

"Thank you, Uncle. I will treasure this. Keep it safe for my return." And she bent to hug her last surviving relative close.

"What is it?" Alex asked.

"A *lukasa* memory board," Mputu explained. "We use them to record the history of our people. This one that Katanga has carved tells the story of the defense of Busu-Mouli. The figure in the middle represents Marie. You are there as well, as am I, Manamakimba, Jean-Baptiste, and others. It is a magnificent tale."

Alex could see the artistry in the *lukasa*, but he could not see what Mputu was describing.

"How can you tell what it says?"

"Some of us have learned to read the *lukasa*. I know how. Marie knows." Mputu turned and looked him hard in the eye. "Someday . . . maybe . . . you will as well. Take care of her."

"You know I will," Alex promised.

. . .

Their first day on the river was uneventful. The captain, a weathered old man named Philippe, was a skilled and experienced pilot. It was almost like a pleasure cruise. Alex and Marie spent most of the day on the fantail talking. That night they tied up at a communal pier a little more than one hundred miles downriver from Busu-Mouli that served as a rendezvous point for traders. The river here was wide and flat and calm, almost like a lake. Philippe had cousins at a small settlement about a twenty-minute walk from where they had tied up. Marie gave him leave to visit, with the proviso that he be back by sunrise. She and Alex ate fish stew and watched the sun go down as they drank Primus beers that had been cooled in the river.

Alex had strung on the fantail a pair of hammocks that they used as chairs, and they sipped their beers as the sky turned from red to purple and the waters of the Congo River from brown to black. A night heron flew over the boat and lit in the shallows, where it could hunt for frogs and small fish. As the sky grew darker, the jungle grew louder. The deceptively deep calls of the tiny tree frogs mixed with the higher-pitched trills of the cicadas and the chattering of a troop of mangabey monkeys.

"Anah would love this," Alex said. "I wish she were here to see it."

"I hope that she visits Busu-Mouli soon. Since my father made you a citizen of Busu-Mouli, that makes Anah one of us as well. She will be most welcome."

"She would like that."

Marie lit a lamp hanging from a hook on the bridge. It cast an orange glow that just barely offered enough light to read by. She used a screwdriver from the *Nkongolo*'s tool kit to open another pair of beers and settled back into her hammock directly across from Alex.

"So what's your plan?" Marie asked. "I realize I should have asked this question before we left, but I was afraid that I might not like the answer."

"I need to find proof of my innocence."

"What about proof of Consolidated's guilt?"

"I expect that they will be one and the same."

"How are you going to do it?"

"I'm not entirely certain yet, but I have some ideas. And I think I have some allies. Do you remember Albert Ilunga?"

Marie smiled ruefully at that. "Of course I do. The only vote I've ever cast was for him as President. I even took a break from my studies to work on his campaign. For a brief moment it looked like the Congo would have a future, and many of us believed that Ilunga was the man who could lead us there. We won that election fairly, and as far as I'm concerned, he is the duly elected President of the Congo. But when the election was stolen from him, I stopped paying attention to politics. It just seemed as if one group of jackals was trying to outmaneuver another group. I haven't heard anything about Ilunga for years. I wasn't even certain if he was still in the country."

"Well, Ilunga has been keeping a low profile, but I'm not sure that he's given up on playing a political role." Alex told her about his meeting with Ilunga and Ilunga's membership in the Brotherhood of the Circle.

They sat in silence for some time as Marie thought over what he had told her.

"And what will you do about your Ambassador?" she asked finally. "You do accept that he's involved in something . . . wrong." The word seemed wholly inadequate. "Evil," she corrected herself.

Alex looked stricken.

"Spence's role in this is the hardest thing for me to get my mind around. He was more than just my mentor. In some ways, he was like a father to me."

"A father who framed you and set you up for murder?"

"I hope that there's another explanation for that, but I agree that it's hard to see one. I owe him so much. When I was at my lowest point after the Sudan, Spence stood up for me. He was the only one."

"What happened to you in the Sudan, Alex? What did you see that had such an effect on you?"

Alex closed his eyes and told her the story. It was the first time he had spoken about the Sudan to anyone other than Dr. Branch. Even Spence didn't know the whole story. As he spoke, the past broke through the walls that he had carefully constructed to separate it from the rest of his life. It rushed forward and tried, as it had tried before, to consume him.

After Alex finished, it took some time for the arid desert to fade from his mind and be replaced by the humid jungle night. He had been running from the trauma of the events at Camp Riad for the better part of three years. In the lamplight, Alex could see that Marie was crying.

She reached across the narrow gap between them to take Alex's hand. Her fingers were calloused from working in the mine, but they were gentle and she stroked the back of his hand, offering him the simple comfort of human touch. Impulsively, Marie leaned forward and kissed him on the mouth, softly and questioningly. His fierce response was a definitive answer to her unspoken question. He reached one hand up behind her head and held her tightly as his lips and tongue explored her mouth.

Abruptly, Marie pulled away. She touched Alex's cheek with the back of her hand.

"Are you sure you are ready for this?" she asked.

"No. I'm not sure. I'm not sure of anything. But I'm willing to take a risk."

Marie stood and moved to sit beside him on the hammock.

29

The port at Kinshasa was unbelievably chaotic. The *Nkongolo*'s captain expertly piloted the fishing boat through the congested waterway and moored at a pier on the edge of the marina. They hoped to remain relatively inconspicuous as they looked into the question of how high a profile Alex had as a fugitive. In penance for his status as an alleged criminal mastermind, Alex stayed belowdecks on the *Nkongolo* while Marie went into the city to look around. He did not relish the idea of a day in the ship's hold. The smell of fish was beginning to work its way through the layer of fresh paint.

Philippe bought a stack of local papers and news magazines at a kiosk near the entrance to the port, and Alex spent the afternoon thumbing through them. There was no mention of the fight at Busu-Mouli. Neither was there anything about the incident at the UN roadblock. Alex allowed himself to hope that Viggiano and Saillard had decided to keep everything under wraps. This hope was crushed when Marie returned from her surveillance mission with several samples of a "wanted" poster that she said was posted prominently around the town. The picture of Alex was from his embassy ID. It was not a particularly good photo, but it was good enough. So was the reward of ten thousand dollars offered for information leading to his arrest. Perversely, Alex was somewhat put out that he did not rate a larger amount. The money was likely coming out of some kind of unaccountable slush fund, either the Embassy's or the mining company's. Ten thousand dollars might well be the largest amount they could offer out of pocket. It was still an awful lot of money for the Congo.

"So what do you think we do about it?" Alex asked.

"I think we need to change your looks, as much as that pains me . . . because you are exceedingly cute."

"How about a nose job? Maybe some Botox."

"Or silicon breasts and a platinum blond wig."

"I prefer my idea."

"I'm sure."

Instead of plastic surgery, Marie cut Alex's hair short and dyed it black before styling it to look more European. He had not shaved since leaving Busu-Mouli, and a week's worth of growth would help to hide the line of his jaw. A beard, a new hairstyle, and a pair of sunglasses was not, Alex knew, much of a disguise. Using the small mirror in the *Nkongolo*'s head, he compared his new look with the picture on the wanted poster. His best defense was almost certainly the low resolution of the embassy ID photo.

"You still look cute," Marie offered, and because Philippe was on deck, she took the opportunity to kiss him. The physical part of their relationship was still new enough that each kiss was a discovery.

"You ready to hit the town tonight?" Alex asked, sliding the back of his hand affectionately across her bare upper arm.

"What do you have in mind?"

"I'd like to take you to a friend's place. Introduce you."

"What friend?"

"Albert Ilunga."

"I'd like that."

With a price on his head that was more than most locals could hope to make in a lifetime, Alex was a marked man. Money, however, was a shield as well as a sword, and he still had a small war chest from the diamonds he had sold before parachuting into Busu-Mouli. Marie did the shopping. For three thousand dollars in cash, she bought a midsize Mitsubishi Carisma with patched seats and a balky transmission.

They waited until after eleven to make their move, on the theory that traffic would be light enough so they would not have to stop but not so light that they risked attracting unwelcome attention from late-shift cops looking for a shakedown and a bribe. Marie parked as close as possible to the *Nkongolo*. Alex tried to look unconcerned on the short walk to the car. He felt foolish wearing sunglasses in the dark, but he was hardly the first hipster or gangster to affect them as fashionable evening wear. There were few other cars on the street and even fewer streetlights. Although Marie drove carefully, she still felt the muscles in her back tense when they drove past a police car idling on a side street like some kind of ambush predator. There were no sirens and no lights, however, and within twenty minutes they had reached Ilunga's villa and the headquarters of the Freedom Coalition. They left the car in the alley alongside the building.

There was a guard at the gate to the villa.

"Good evening, brother," Marie said, as they approached the elderly man sitting impassively on a small stool. He looked them over carefully, but his expression betrayed neither interest nor concern at their presence.

"Good evening," he offered grudgingly.

"We are here to see President Ilunga," Marie said, and Alex saw the guard's expression shift slightly at her use of the title earned but never claimed.

"It is late, madame. Perhaps tomorrow."

"It is most urgent. I assure you that he will want to see us."

The guard was now staring at Alex, who recognized him as one of the men who had been learning how to read when he had visited with Father Antoine. Alex took off his sunglasses.

"You recognize me, don't you?" he asked. "I remember you as well. You know that I am a friend to both Antoine and Ilunga."

"You have friends," the elderly man replied, "and enemies too, it would appear."

"You've seen the posters?"

"We all have. Mr. Ilunga said you might return and that you should be admitted. He is still awake. I'd suggest you try the kitchen. The President likes to eat late."

The gate was opened, and Alex and Marie stepped in off the street.

As the guard had suggested, they found Albert Ilunga in the kitchen eating a sandwich. The kitchen was simple but clean and spacious enough to feed the center's sizable resident population. There were two oversize refrigerators and a six-burner stove. The man who might have been President sat alone on a bar stool alongside a wooden countertop peninsula. He was wearing jeans and a faded blue work shirt. A single light fixture hanging over the counter illuminated the room.

Ilunga did not seem surprised to see them.

"Hello, Alex," he said, wiping mustard from the corner of his mouth with a napkin. He stood up. "You are most welcome. I'm sorry about Antoine. I know he was a close friend."

"To both of us," Alex replied.

"Are you going to introduce me to your charming companion?"

"Albert Ilunga, Allow me to present Marie Tsiolo, Principal Chief of the village of Busu-Mouli."

Ilunga kissed her hand. *"Enchanté."*

"Mr. President," Marie said simply.

"So you were one of my supporters, it would seem."

"I still am. It should be you in the presidential palace, not Silwamba. If it were so, then my village would be safe."

"What is happening to your village?" Ilunga motioned to them to take a seat, and the three of them sat on bar stools around the counter-top. He listened attentively as Marie told him about Consolidated Mining's plan to plunder her valley.

There was a brief silence as Ilunga weighed the implications of her story. "Yours is not the first such report I have heard about the nature of this company and its connections with the government. This is a very serious problem. We will discuss it further. But first, can I offer you something to eat?"

Alex realized that he was famished. Ilunga made them each an overstuffed sandwich with thick slices of ham and Swiss cheese. Pickled radishes and cold beer completed the meal.

"I've seen some not terribly flattering pictures of you around town," Ilunga said to Alex. "You've made quite the impression in the short time that you've been back in this country. I congratulate you."

"Yeah. I suppose I've made more of a splash than I had planned."

"You can judge a man by his enemies. By that measure, you are doing quite well."

Ilunga finished his sandwich and took a swig from his beer.

"So I don't suppose that you've come all this way just to tell me the story of your village," he said, raising one eyebrow and offering Marie a slight smile. When he smiled, the lines on his face smoothed and he looked years younger.

"No," Marie agreed. "We have come to ask for your help."

"My help? I can offer you shelter and a sandwich, but what else do you think I can do to help you?"

"You can take what belongs to you by right and become president of this country," Marie said.

Ilunga shook his head ruefully. "That was a long time ago—"

"Nonsense. It was six years ago. Everyone remembers what happened. I came back from South Africa to work for your election. I believed in you. It's not too late to reclaim what was lost . . . what was taken."

"Thank you for what you did. The Freedom Party was a great movement. But we underestimated both the strength and the ruthless character of our opponents. That mistake cost me three years in prison. Now I do this. I help the veterans of our wars. For now, this is the best way I can help my country."

"You can help your country," Marie insisted, "by getting rid of Silwamba."

"Someday I may get back into politics, but that day, I'm afraid, is not today."

"Why not?"

"It's too soon. We are not ready."

"Really?" Alex asked. "Then what's with the armory in the basement?"

Ilunga seemed somewhat embarrassed.

"I have a small collection of firearms downstairs . . . for contingencies," he explained to Marie with a shrug.

"How small?"

"Not so small, perhaps."

"What are the guns for, Albert, if not to support your political movement?" Alex asked.

"I lost the presidency to a man who could command guns, who could put armed men loyal only to him onto the streets. I had nothing similar. I will not let that happen again. Next time . . . when the time comes . . . I will be ready." Ilunga fished a pack of Marlboros out of his shirt pocket and offered it first to Alex and Marie. When they declined, he lit a cigarette and turned over the bottle cap from his beer to use as an ashtray.

"Let me tell you something of my home," Marie implored. "There are nearly four thousand people in my valley who look to me for security and prosperity. I can give them prosperity. Our soil is rich and there is copper in our hills. Security, however, is beyond me. I have done what I can, but if I cannot break the hammerlock that Consolidated Mining has on this government, my people will never be safe. Only you are in a position to do this."

"It's not that simple," Ilunga protested.

"Isn't it?"

"We are not yet strong enough. I do not have the resources I need. For now, this is my work. I can do more good here with these men than I can in prison . . . or dead. Over time, perhaps, we will grow strong enough to challenge the established order."

"Hardly the most courageous position that you've adopted, Mr. President. I had expected more from you."

Alex had been sipping his beer and observing the exchange between Marie and Ilunga. Now he decided to step in before it got out of hand. Ilunga was still their best hope for finding a way to put pressure on Silwamba, Consolidated Mining, and the U.S. Embassy.

"Albert, there is more going on that Marie hasn't yet told you about. It is bigger than the mining company and it threatens the future not only of this country but this continent." It was clear that Alex had captured Ilunga's interest. As he explained what he knew about the Africa Working Group and the hold this shadowy organization had on U.S. Africa policy, Ilunga seemed to grow both sadder and more thoughtful. When Alex finished, his resistance to the idea of taking up the political banner again seemed weaker, but not yet dead.

"Politics is not cheap in the Congo," he observed. "I have some sponsors who support the work of this institution, but not nearly enough funds to mount a credible challenge to Silwamba."

"When we met the last time," Alex said, "you told me that God would provide when the time came to take on Silwamba."

"Yes. I still believe this."

"Well, He sometimes moves in mysterious ways."

Alex pulled the leather bag of diamonds from his pocket and dumped the stones on the countertop. Even uncut and unpolished, they caught the light and glowed with a warm internal fire.

"That should just about cover the costs."

Ilunga, his eyes wide, did not argue.

"So what would you propose we do?" he asked. "The next round of so-called elections is more than two years away. And that will likely be just another farcical rerun of Silwamba's 'referendum' on his rule. He won't allow anyone to stand against him on a level field."

"You don't need to run against him," Marie replied. "You've already been elected. Silwamba is a usurper with no legitimacy. What we need to do is to persuade the public and the world to recognize the victory that you've already won."

"Can that work?"

"It's been done before," Alex said. "Student demonstrators in Serbia brought down the Milošević regime. Something similar happened in the Tulip Revolution in Kyrgyzstan. I think it's a pretty good place for us to start."

"Take the initiative," Marie implored. "Get the regime responding to you."

Ilunga picked up one of the larger diamonds and held it up to the lights hanging over the counter. It was the size and shape of a cherry. Small rainbows appeared on the countertop as the crystal refracted the light from the lamp. He took a drag on his cigarette. The blue-gray smoke did nothing to dim the brilliance of the stone.

"Very well," he said finally. "Let's get to work."

Although her face remained impassive, Marie squeezed Alex's leg tightly under the counter.

From behind them, a new voice asked, "Can I get a glass of water?" This voice was immediately familiar to Alex, even though he had heard it speak no more than a dozen sentences. He turned to find Jean-Pierre standing at the threshold to the kitchen wearing a pair of pajamas at least three sizes too large with a pattern of blue and red elephants.

The former child soldier squealed with joy when he saw Alex, and ran to hug him.

"I have been working to find homes for Antoine's former charges," Ilunga explained. Some are staying here with me, including young Jean-Pierre. He speaks quite well these days, you know."

"Is everything okay now?" the boy asked.

"Not yet, Jean-Pierre," Alex replied. "But it will be."

30

The morning sun woke Marie before the alarm sounded. She stretched languidly and propped herself up on one elbow to look at Alex still sleeping soundly next to her. They had been sharing a small room on the second floor of Ilunga's house. There was barely enough room for a double bed and a nightstand. Still, the time she had there with Alex was a wonderful luxury. He was a patient and tender lover, but Marie was wary of the strong feelings she was developing for him. He was the first white man she had slept with. Color was not an issue for either of them, but neither was blind to the obstacles to a long-term commitment.

She ran her hand across his chest. He stirred. Reaching up to take hold of her hand, he pulled it to his mouth and kissed her palm lightly. A little electric thrill shot through Marie's spine. She did not know how long they had together, but they had today.

As she thought ahead to what they had to do that day, Marie

frowned slightly. This would be the first serious test of Ilunga's political strength and Marie was nervous that it would fall flat.

Alex must have sensed her anxiety. "Don't worry," he said, pulling himself up into a sitting position on the bed. "It's going to go great today. I'm just sorry that I won't be there to see it."

Although Marie had many of the campaign's foot soldiers distributing pro-Ilunga literature pull double duty by also taking down the "wanted" posters with Alex's picture on them, it was still not safe for him to be near a large crowd in broad daylight. This left Marie in charge of organizing Ilunga's campaign and she had risen to the challenge. She had cut her teeth on byzantine tribal politics. Still, she was nervous about the day and grateful for Alex's support. She forced herself to smile.

"It's going to be fine," Alex repeated.

"God, I hope so."

The campaign to unseat President Silwamba had started online. Some of the more advanced computer programmers in the Freedom Coalition had already been working on a website promoting Ilunga as the real winner of the last election and the best hope for political reform in the Congo. The message was clear: Silwamba was illegitimate. Albert Ilunga was the duly elected President of the Congo.

At first Ilunga had been skeptical of this approach. He had wanted to march to the presidential palace and plant his flag. What good was the Internet, he asked, when less than five percent of the population outside of the capital had access to a computer? Marie and Alex had persuaded him that this was not a normal political campaign. They were targeting the Kinshasa elite and international public opinion. Their goal was to get Silwamba's own supporters to turn against him. If an election was like a boxing match with two heavyweights slugging it out in the center of the ring, Ilunga's political movement had to be more like jujitsu. They had to get Silwamba off balance and let the weight of his position ultimately drag him down.

It had been nearly a week since Ilunga had agreed to challenge Silwamba. Encouragingly, there were already some signs that their campaign was gaining traction. The initial trickle of visitors to the website had not grown to a torrent, but at least it was a steady stream. Marie had reached out to a number of women's groups, including the Wives of Wounded Veterans. Ilunga, meanwhile, had put the word out through the Brotherhood of the Circle that the time for change had come. The secret society was not large, but many of its members were in positions of influence and nearly all were eager to see the back of Silwamba.

They had not yet had any public events, however. Today Ilunga would lead a march from the villa to the ironically named Freedom Square in front of the presidential palace. The turnout would be a key test of his political strength. The website and flyers called on Ilunga's supporters to gather in front of the villa at ten in the morning for the march. Marie had told Albert that they were hoping for five hundred people to show up. Privately, she thought they would be lucky to get half that.

Silwamba's naked power grab in the aftermath of the election had sucked much of the energy out of the Congo's nascent democracy movement. Marie was less than certain that they would be able to revive the coalition that had come so close to propelling a man she considered honest and decent into the presidency.

That is why she found herself holding her breath when she and Ilunga stepped out the front door of the center at ten-fifteen. The bullhorn in her hand was heavy and it would make her feel ridiculous if there were only a handful of people waiting for them on the street. Standing in the small garden between the house and the front gate, Ilunga took hold of Marie's upper arm and turned her to face him.

"No matter what happens today, Marie, know that you have done well. This is just one piece of a larger effort. It is important. But if our supporters are not yet ready, it is not the end. I assure you."

Marie nodded. "Thank you, Mr. President."

Ilunga opened the gate and they stepped out onto the street. The crowd of supporters waiting for him to appear roared its approval. Blinking back tears, Marie surveyed the scene in front of her. There were at least two thousand people in the street, many waving light blue and gold Congolese flags or handmade placards in various languages that read ILUNGA IS PRESIDENT. Ilunga took the bullhorn from Marie and held it up to his mouth.

He made it only a few syllables into "My fellow citizens," however, before the roar of a fired-up and adulatory crowd drowned him out. There would be a time for speeches, they seemed to say, but this was a time for rejoicing.

When they had quieted some, Ilunga spoke for ten minutes. Few in the audience could hear what he said, but no one seemed to care.

While Marie had been working on building up Ilunga, Alex had focused his energies on finding a way to take down Consolidated Mining. He needed two things: information and evidence. So while Marie was leading a march to the front door of the presidential palace, Alex sat down with Ilunga's in-house computer guru, Giles Mbaka, to plot a more circumspect trip through the back door at Consolidated Mining.

Giles was the senior computer instructor at the Coalition. He was also a hacker of considerable skill, who did his work on a beautiful, high-end PowerBook that had "fallen off the back of a truck." Giles did not look the part. His nose had been broken and badly set at least once, and his build was more like that of a professional wrestler than a computer geek. He had big, beefy hands that moved with surprising grace across the keyboard. Most unsettling, however, was that Giles had only one ear. The left side of his head was a mass of scar tissue where the ear should have been. Giles kept his hair cut short, as if to draw attention to his disfigurement. All of Ilunga's inner circle had complicated and often violent pasts. Giles was evidently no exception. For whatever reason, Giles and Alex had clicked almost immediately, and the hacker had taken on the project of proving Alex's innocence as a personal charge.

When Alex walked into his classroom, Ilunga's webmaster was wearing a dark blue Hawaiian shirt opened halfway to his navel and his trademark orange-tinted sunglasses. The left earpiece balanced somewhat precariously on a nub of puckered scar tissue. The glasses, he insisted, helped ease the eyestrain from hours in front of a monitor. Alex was pretty certain, however, that Giles wore them because he thought they looked cool.

In the corner of the room, two TVs were on with the sound off. One was tuned to the DRC's state news channel and the other to CNN. Giles pulled the international programming off a pirated satellite feed distributed through some of the Internet's darker corridors.

"How's it looking, Giles?" Alex asked, taking the seat next to him. The image on the PowerBook monitor was a schematic diagram of Consolidated Mining's website, the back-end configuration accessible only to the company's IT people . . . and now to Giles.

"It's pretty tricky." They were speaking in English, a language for which Giles had boundless enthusiasm but only reasonable proficiency. He was a huge fan of Hollywood movies and American TV, and he used his conversations with Alex as a chance to brush up on his skills. Alex was happy to oblige. He owed Giles. The hacker had spent the better part of two days exploring Consolidated's computer system.

"The firewalls are . . ." Giles paused, looking for the right word before settling on the almost nonsensical "hotter than they need to be."

"Can you get over the walls?" Alex asked.

"Over? Maybe not. Under? Maybe yes. But if they are looking, they see me. No promise I find anything on the other side. Could be a red hand say, 'I sorry I call Mr. Alex a spy. He is a really nice guy.' Maybe nothing. Maybe report on how much money they make last year. It's hard to know."

"What about Henri Saillard's e-mail account? Is that inside or outside the wall?"

"Inside."

"What's on the outside?"

"His calendar. The secretary keeps and her account easy to read."

"That's a start. Let's take a look at that. And if you wouldn't mind poking around a bit more to see if there's any way into the restricted areas that won't trip the alarms, I'd be grateful. At some point, though, if we can't find a quiet way in, we may just need to knock down the wall and see what we find."

"No problem."

Giles needed only seconds to open Saillard's calendar, and Alex spent the next fifteen minutes reviewing his schedule of appointments. The seeds of a plan were beginning to germinate. The sheer audacity of the idea was enough to make it almost plausible.

"Can you get into the maintenance records?" Alex asked.

"I think yes," Giles said, clicking through a series of links and inputting commands with bursts of keystrokes. The records included such routine corporate data as the schedule for the janitors and the maintenance plan for the motor pool. That was not the kind of information that Alex was after.

"What about building schematics, blueprints, that sort of thing?"

"I not think there's no something like that at this system." If anything, Giles's English seemed to get worse with practice.

"Where do you think we might find that kind of information?"

"Maybe they have paper copy somewhere inside. E-copy . . . maybe the . . . *c'est quoi le mot?* . . . *l'architecte?* . . . has on his server."

Alex clapped the giant hacker on the shoulder. "Giles, you are a fucking genius. Do you think you can find out who designed that building and get a copy of the plans?"

"Maybe yes."

"How soon?"

"Tomorrow."

A re you out of your mind?" Marie asked, when Alex explained to her what he was planning to do. She had come back from the march overjoyed and excited about their prospects for success. Even the police had seemed at times to be helping the demonstrators rather than hindering them. Bringing just a few members of the security services over to their side would be a real victory. At the same time, she recognized how fragile their gains were and how quickly joy could turn to bitterness.

"Do you have any idea what's likely to happen to you if you get caught?"

"Unpleasant things. But I can't simply sit on my ass and wait for my good karma to deliver justice. I have to take the fight to these guys. I need to know what they're doing and see if there isn't some way that I can shake them up a bit."

Marie felt a brief flash of anger and there was heat in her response.

"And have you given any thought to what it means for Ilunga and what we're trying to do here if you are found out? They would use you to discredit him. We're working for change that could ultimately heal an entire country. Think about what you're putting at risk because you want to get your job back."

As soon as she said this, Marie regretted the words, but it was too late to unsay them. Instead of getting angry, however, Alex reached out and took her hand.

"I have thought about it. What I want to do is essential to Ilunga's mission. Silwamba and Consolidated Mining aren't simply allies, they are a single organism. We need to know more about them, to find their

vulnerabilities. And as for me crawling back to the Embassy and plead-
ing for my old job . . ."

Marie looked away, ashamed that she had even leveled that charge.

"I'm done with them," Alex continued. "No matter what happens to
Consolidated Mining or to me, I'm finished with the State Department . . . with government. It's over."

"What will you do?" Marie asked.

"I don't know. I'll need to think about that. And I'll need to think
about what's best for Anah. But I won't go back to making the kinds of
compromises that the State Department has demanded of me. I need
something simpler, more . . . pure. You know something? I've slept better since I became a fugitive than at any time since the Sudan."

She kissed him hard on the mouth and he held her tightly against
his body.

"Will you help me?" he asked, stroking her hair.

"You know I will. What can I do?"

He pulled back and looked her in the eye.

"Can you do some shopping for me this afternoon?" he said
seriously.

"Of course. What do you need?"

"I'll make you a list."

Two days later, Alex called the main number at Consolidated Mining and asked for Henri Saillard's office. He was using a prepaid
mobile telephone that Marie had picked up for him on her shopping
trip. Alex did not want the mining company to be able to trace the call
back to either Ilunga or the sat phone he had liberated from the Embassy. The woman who answered Saillard's line had a cheery voice and
a Flemish accent.

"*Allo.* Monsieur Saillard's office," she announced.

"Good morning. My name is Benoit Juneau. I am the new Commercial Counselor at the Swiss Embassy. There is an urgent matter that I need to bring to Mr. Saillard's attention. I know that this is very last-minute, but I wonder if he might be able to see me today. It's important and I will only need a few minutes."

"Mr. Saillard's schedule is quite full today."

"I'm sure that it is." In fact, Alex was holding Saillard's schedule in his hand and knew exactly what the mining company's representative in the Congo was doing with his day. Interspersed with several genuine business meetings were such diversions as breakfast at the Grand Hotel Kinshasa, a tennis match with an executive from British Petroleum, and a massage with "Serena." There was no indication as to whether this came with a happy ending.

"Perhaps if you could let me know the nature of the issue," the cheery scheduler offered.

"It's a communication from my government and I'm afraid it's rather sensitive. I would need to discuss this personally with Mr. Saillard."

There was a pause that lasted long enough that Alex feared they might have been cut off. "I think I can squeeze you in for perhaps twenty minutes right after lunch," she said finally. "Shall we say three?"

"That would be perfect, thank you."

At two-fifteen, Alex stepped out of a rented BMW in front of Consolidated Mining's headquarters on Avenue Kasavubu. He was wearing a blue pin-striped suit from a high-end Kinshasa boutique and tortoiseshell zero-prescription glasses. The tie—red with thin blue stripes—was Zegna. His hair was slicked back with copious amounts of styling gel, and he had trimmed his beard into a designer stubble. In his right hand, he was carrying an oversize black leather briefcase with the monogrammed initials BWJ. It was a self-consciously flashy look.

Certainly, he bore little obvious resemblance to the blurry ID photo on the "wanted" posters. And the posters themselves were growing increasingly scarce as Ilunga's supporters were quietly ripping them down as they were plastering the walls of the city with their own campaign material. Still, his thin disguise would not withstand even a casual encounter with someone he knew.

Consolidated Mining's headquarters was a modernist cube of steel and black glass that seemed out of place on a block dominated by crumbling, Soviet-style concrete structures. The building also seemed somewhat less than proud of its identity. The only reference to the company was on an understated brass plaque to one side of the revolving door that led into the cool, dark lobby decorated in black leather and chrome. The receptionist, a stunning young Congolese woman in a pastel European-designed suit, was clearly also part of the décor. So were the armed guards in dark blue uniforms standing post in front of the glass door that led to the office area.

The receptionist's unobtrusive name tag identified her as Yvonne. Alex told her that he was there for a meeting with Henri Saillard. Discreetly, she checked that the name Benoit Juneau appeared on her list of expected visitors. Mr. Saillard's office, she told him, was on the fifth floor. She did not ask to see any ID. Alex had the right look, the easy arrogance of a first-world diplomat in a third-world country that is surprisingly hard to fake.

The elevator, like the rest of the building, was functional and spare. It opened directly into the waiting area for Saillard's office. The room featured Scandinavian modern furniture and high-quality abstract prints. An attractive woman who looked to be in her mid-thirties sat behind a desk of blond wood in front of the door that Alex presumed led to Saillard's private office.

"May I help you?" she asked. Alex recognized her voice from their conversation on the phone.

"Benoit Juneau to see Henri Saillard."

"You are early, Monsieur Juneau," she said, with just a hint of reproof in her voice. "I'm afraid Monsieur Saillard has not yet returned."

"Am I early? I thought we said two-thirty."

"It was three o'clock, monsieur."

"How foolish of me. Serves me right for making the appointment myself. My scheduler is away this week, I'm afraid. I'm sorry to inconvenience you like this."

"It's no trouble. I hope that you don't mind waiting."

"Not at all. Would you mind if I used the WC?"

"Of course not. It's through that door and down the hall on the right."

Alex knew that. It was on the plans that Giles had acquired for him off the server at Van Der Rhone & Samuelson, the architecture firm in Amsterdam that had designed the unsightly edifice. He also knew that at the end of that same corridor was the entrance to the stairwell that led to the roof. Saillard's office was on the top floor, so Alex had to climb only a short flight of stairs to reach the door to the outside. To his relief, the door was unlocked. He had tools in his bag that might have allowed him to get it open, but probably not without damaging the door in some way. He did not want Consolidated Mining to know that anyone had been up here. Alex pulled a roll of duct tape out of his briefcase and taped the latch inside the strike plate.

The roof was painted white, but it was still hotter than Hades under the midday sun. Immediately, Alex saw something that had not been in the plans. An elevated landing pad had been added to the roof. A red and white helicopter sat parked in the middle of the landing circle. It was a Bell 222, standard-issue transport for self-important executives the world over. This one had Henri Saillard's name stenciled on the door in fancy script.

Alex stripped off his jacket and draped it over a pipe. The satellite dish was right where it was supposed to be. Phone service in Kinshasa was both incredibly expensive and unreliable. It made economic sense for the mining company to use satellite service rather than the state-run telecom. He did not have much time. If Saillard returned to the office before he was finished, Alex could find himself trapped on the roof with no way down. The schematics had given him only a rough idea of the layout. Now he needed to find and access the junction box that controlled the dish. A thick green cable led from the base of the dish along the top of a low wall and terminated in a nondescript gray box protected by a padlock. This is what he was after. But there was a problem. Installing the helicopter pad had forced the company's technicians to move some things around. The junction box was now in the wrong place.

He pulled a map out of the briefcase and laid it on the ground to line it up with the orientation of the building. His target was a half-finished shopping mall a little more than a kilometer from the Consolidated Mining building. The developer had built most of the mall's concrete shell before running out of money and skipping the country one step ahead of the gangsters hired by the bank to collect on the loan. The abandoned property had been hanging in legal limbo ever since. Giles had helped him find it. For what Alex needed, the mall was practically perfect. It was isolated, elevated, and had a direct line of sight to the Consolidated Mining building on Kasavubu. Unfortunately, the junction box had been relocated to the back side of a retaining wall that would block the signals that Alex was hoping to pirate. He could fix it . . . he hoped . . . but it would take time.

A pair of shortened bolt cutters made quick work of the lock. There was nothing special about the system inside. The controls and the wiring were plain vanilla. Alex removed a small metal dish about six inches in diameter from his briefcase. A black plastic box was attached to the back of the dish. A second box, this one gray and metallic, had red and blue wires extruding from the sides with copper alligator clips attached at the ends. It looked ugly and slapdash, and it was. But Alex was reasonably confident that the gear would work as intended if he could line it up with the target. As the minutes ticked off, he could feel himself sweating from both the sun and the pressure. His watch read two-forty. He had hoped to be done by now.

Because he was not sure what he would find, Alex had brought an assortment of tools and parts that he thought might be useful. Linking the gray metal box to the guts of Consolidated Mining's communication system was pretty straightforward. The alligator clips kept the circuits intact, but they allowed a secondary signal to run through a connection at the top of the box. A third wire connected to the power cord drew enough electricity to keep the machinery active. Alex attached a three-foot cable to the connection at the top of the box and looped it over the wall. From the other side, the dish should have line-of-sight access to the abandoned shopping mall. He put the lid back down on the junction box and slipped over the wall to fix the dish in place. The construction site was clearly visible about five blocks away. After securing the cable to the back of the dish, Alex lined it up with the mall as best he could and used the duct tape to tie it securely to one of the pipes running from the rooftop solar water heater. He checked his watch again. Two-fifty-one. Alex hoped that Saillard shared his countrymen's penchant for lingering over lunch.

There was still one more stop to make. He did not want Saillard's assistant to call the Swiss Embassy to see what had happened to Monsieur Juneau who had mysteriously disappeared on his way back from the men's room. After removing the duct tape from the door, Alex returned to Saillard's office. He offered profuse apologies to the personal assistant, but it seemed that he was not yet over the stomach bug that had laid him up for the better part of a week. Unfortunately, he would have to return to his office immediately to see the Embassy doctor and he would be in touch to reschedule the meeting. The secretary was solicitous, understanding, and sympathetic. She could see from Monsieur Juneau's flushed appearance and sweat-stained shirt that he was indeed unwell.

Alex departed in haste. It was two-fifty-seven. The elevator door opened on the lobby level just as Henri Saillard was walking into the building. Alex saw him through the glass door and turned to drink out of a water fountain as Saillard walked through the door and into the open elevator no more than five feet away. Alex kept his face turned away, but he was certain that everyone in the area could hear the jack-hammering of his heart. Saillard paid him no attention, however, and as soon as the elevator doors had closed, Alex straightened up and walked out onto the street.

Later that day Alex invited Giles and Jean-Pierre to join him on an early evening errand. They stowed several boxes of electronics in the trunk of Giles's car and Alex directed the computer hacker to the construction site he had targeted from the roof of the Consolidated Mining building.

Giles drove a beat-up old Citroën that might once have been white. They parked in a deserted lot on the backside of the unfinished shopping mall. The red-dirt lot was dry and cracked. An abandoned panel van stood on blocks in one corner. Everything of value had long ago been stripped from the vehicle. The rusting hulk looked like the bleached bones of an animal that had died on the savannah and then been picked clean by scavengers. They carried the boxes of gear up a concrete stairway. The stairs, like the rest of the building, were only partly finished. They were open to the outside and pieces of rusty rebar jutted out of the landings. When they reached the third floor, Alex noticed a peculiar pungent odor. It reminded him of ammonia.

"What is that smell?" he asked Giles.

"Take a look." The hacker pointed to the next landing and Alex saw a large colony of bats clinging to the wall. They were restlessly stretching their wings in anticipation of the falling darkness. The stairs above were slick with nearly half an inch of guano. There was something unsettling about the way the bats moved on the walls. These were small common brown bats. Some of their fruit-eating cousins had three-foot wingspans. Alex shuddered slightly at the thought. Jean-Pierre was utterly unfazed by the bats and carried his small box of gear past the colony without breaking stride.

They exited the stairwell on the fifth floor. They set the boxes down while Alex looked for the best place to set up. This floor was probably intended for office space rather than retail. It lacked any kind of broad central corridor. A corner office that Alex suspected had been earmarked for one of the project's muckety-mucks offered the best line of sight to the Consolidated Mining building.

There was still some material left on-site from when the developers had called a halt to construction. Alex and Giles built a table from abandoned scaffolding and scrounged a couple of empty crates to sit on.

"What are we doing here?" Jean-Pierre asked, as he helped unload the boxes of electronics.

"We're going to do a little spying," Alex answered.

"That's cool." Jean-Pierre did not have a problem with that. There were no moral absolutes in his world, only friends and enemies.

Alex explained each step to Jean-Pierre as he and Giles set up the gear.

"This is a satellite telephone." Alex handed the phone to Jean-Pierre. "It works a little bit like the TV dish that you and I worked on at the church. But instead of cartoons, this picks up conversations. We're going to listen in on the phone calls of our friends at Consolidated Mining and see what we can learn."

"Show me how it works," Jean-Pierre replied.

It took nearly two hours to build the system that Alex and Giles had designed. It was a Rube Goldberg device that included a broken-off car radio antenna on radial legs made of wire coat hangers, a commercial satellite tuner, and Giles's backup laptop, a clunky but serviceable Hewlett-Packard. Linking up the hardware and software had taken longer than they had anticipated and the system had more steps to it than Alex was comfortable with. None of the steps were especially complicated, however. There was no reason it should not work as promised. Just in case, Alex asked Jean-Pierre to push the power button on the laptop. This was for luck. Given all that the boy had been through and somehow survived, someone somewhere was looking out for him. The system booted up normally. For the next ten minutes, however, nothing happened. Alex was about to reboot and try again when the electronic sound of numbers being dialed came over the sat phone's speaker. The computer identified the number being dialed as Consolidated Mining's corporate headquarters in New York. After three rings, someone picked up on the other end.

"Mr. Jackson's office, may I help you?"

"Hello, Darlene, it's Yvonne in the Kinshasa office." Alex recognized the voice of the mining company's receptionist. "I just want to confirm the proposed travel dates for Mr. Jackson's visit."

The conversation was inconsequential. But its significance was clear. Alex had penetrated Consolidated Mining's security. He had a direct line into their internal communications. Now, like a fisherman, he would have to be patient and wait for a big one to bite.

31

When the CNN camera crew arrived, Marie knew that they had something going. Their reporter was not a local stringer or even the chief Africa correspondent from Nairobi. It was Annette Cartwright, the news network's "Angel of Death." The perky blond reporter was doing a stand-up in front of the parliament buildings where some eight thousand Ilunga supporters had gathered for the fifth straight day of marches. Nearly all of the demonstrators were dressed in white. This had been Alex's idea. Ilunga was now leading a "color revolution" similar to the Orange and Rose revolutions that had brought down corrupt kleptocracies in Ukraine and Georgia or the yellow "People Power" movement in the Philippines.

The world was starting to take notice of the challenge to Silwamba's rule. Annette Cartwright's presence in Kinshasa was proof of that. Cartwright had made her reputation in Iraq and Afghanistan as a tough-minded war reporter, but she had also covered natural disasters,

famines, and bloody revolutions around the world. Wherever the perfectly coiffed Cartwright went, you could be pretty sure that something
dramatic—and most often terrible and frightening—was happening.
Her colleagues had bestowed the Angel of Death nickname in envious
recognition of her flair for disaster. It was a responsibility she took
seriously.

Marie knew that she needed to get Ilunga on global TV to win the
kind of international patronage that could step up the pressure on Silwamba. Cartwright would want an interview with Ilunga, and Marie
would make sure that she got one. In the meantime, however, she had a
rally to run. A chunk of the money from the sale of Alex's diamonds
had gone to the purchase of a flatbed truck outfitted with a high-quality
PA system. Awilo Longomba, a popular *soukous* musician and longtime
Ilunga supporter, was entertaining the crowd with a selection of songs
from his latest album. Longomba had been in self-imposed exile in
Paris for the last five years. His return to Kinshasa was a mark of how
far they had come. There was room on the truck for the full eight-piece
band. Large white banners draped over the cab proclaimed ILUNGA IS
PRESIDENT.

It was Ilunga's movement, but Marie was the ringmaster. She decided the timing and target for each day's march, and built the program
that would keep people both entertained and politically engaged. As
Longomba was winding up his set, Marie was reviewing the next events.
She carried a clipboard with a detailed schedule, which together with
the Bluetooth headset linked to her cell phone and her "Ilunga" T-shirt
made her look a little like a roadie at a rock concert. A former senior
Congolese army general was scheduled to speak next in support of
Ilunga. This was an important endorsement. While Ilunga had found
strong support among the police, the army was still largely pro-Sil-
wamba. Too many of Ilunga's supporters had fought with the militias
that had battled the national army in the bush for the better part of the

last decade. The Congo was still divided against itself and there was a palpable strain of bitterness and resentment that ran through the society.

It was already starting to grow dark. In addition to a PA system, Marie had purchased lights that had been set up around the square to illuminate the stage. She made a quick call to one of her assistants and the lights came on. The effect was dramatic. Marie hoped that it looked half as good on television. Longomba finished playing to loud applause.

The general, an infantry officer who wore his olive drab fatigues rather than the fancy dress uniform dripping with medals favored by many of his colleagues, was good but not great. He spoke too long and Marie sensed that the crowd was growing somewhat restless. The next event on the schedule was a young singer from Goma who had written a song about Ilunga. Marie was worried that it might be too slow or amateurish, and she was tempted to drop it from the program. One of her assistant producers called with the same concern.

"Do you want us to cut the girl?" he asked. "We don't want to lose the crowd."

Marie hesitated. The young woman had come a long way for this and she had come highly recommended by people in Goma whom Alex knew and trusted.

"Let her sing," Marie said. "But tell her to keep it to one song."

The girl, whose name was Melina, was heart-stoppingly beautiful. A black acoustic guitar hung from a strap around her neck in the colors of the Congolese flag. She stepped up to the microphone and one of the assistant producers cut all but one of the lights, leaving her marooned in an island of light. She strummed a few chords and her fingers began picking out a plaintive but powerful melody. Then she started to sing and for the thousands gathered in the park in front of the National Assembly building, it was as though time had stopped. A silence like a physical thing settled over the crowd and Melina sang of the pain and loss of war and the promise of their champion, their savior, who had come to deliver his people from injustice.

When Melina finished, the crowd was absolutely still. Then the sound of a single person clapping pierced the veil that seemed to have descended over them and triggered a wave of applause and cheers that was part a celebration of a spectacular talent and part a gauntlet thrown at the feet of Silwamba. Ilunga himself stepped up on the stage to embrace her. He turned to the crowd and raised a fist in defiance. Eight thousand fists shot into the air in response.

Near the far end of the crowd, on a raised platform that afforded a clear view of the stage, Annette Cartwright whispered to her cameraman. "Please tell me that you got that."

"Every note."

"Get it on the website. Now."

Within hours, the download of Melina singing her paean to Ilunga and Ilunga's own rousing defiance had gone viral. It was a brand-new ballgame.

With Melina's performance, Ilunga's movement gained an overnight international following. It had all the pieces: a charismatic leader, identifiable bad guys, the visually powerful symbol of thousands of people dressed in white, and, as colorful backdrop, a conflict that had claimed more lives than the Holocaust. Foreign ministers in important capitals started asking questions of their Africa bureaus. Embarrassed bureaucrats who knew nothing about Ilunga or the Freedom Coalition sent hurried cables to their embassies in Kinshasa. Embassy officials, who knew little more, did what they do best. They picked up the phone.

The morning after the CNN broadcast, Ilunga's Freedom Coalition offices were flooded with calls from embassies and Western news outlets looking for a piece of the great man's time. The UK, French, and

South African embassies called to invite Ilunga to dine with their ambassadors. Reuters, the *Washington Post*, and *Süddeutsche Zeitung* wanted interviews. Marie deputized Giles to handle the calls and he held the curious at bay with vague promises to arrange something at some time in the future. Shortly after lunch, however, he took a call that flummoxed him. Mark Fong called from the American Embassy. Ambassador Spencer was hoping that Monsieur Ilunga might be available for a meeting. As soon as he hung up, Giles called Alex. Twenty minutes later, he, Marie, and Ilunga were gathered around the kitchen counter, drinking bituminous coffee and weighing the options.

"I don't like it," Marie insisted. "The foreigners are a big part of the problem here." She looked apologetically at Alex. "I don't see them being part of the solution. We need the press, but the embassies are a waste of time. We shouldn't have anything to do with them, particularly the Americans."

"I'm inclined to agree with you," Ilunga said. "But I'd like to hear what our friend Alex has to say. In many ways, this concerns him more than it does either of us."

"I don't give a damn about the French or the South Africans," Alex replied. "They don't bring anything to the party. I do think, though, that you should see Spence."

"Why? I don't have anything in particular that I'd like to say to him."

"No . . . but I do."

Giles called back Mark Fong and offered the Most Honorable Ambassador Spencer an appointment for the next day at four. There were some ground rules. It was to be a one-on-one meeting. The principals would meet alone, with no notetakers. In addition, the American Embassy was requested not to share the fact of the meeting—or its contents—with any of the other diplomatic missions in Kinshasa.

Everyone wanted time with President Ilunga, Giles explained, and they were making an exception for the Americans. It would not do to have this widely known. Fong accepted eagerly.

There was a stark contrast between the ostentatious way Ambassador Spencer had arrived at Silwamba's office and the subdued, almost furtive manner of his visit to Ilunga's house. Instead of the armored Cadillac flying its miniature American flags, a black Lincoln pulled up to the front gate and parked. The police escort was minimal, a single unmarked car. Even so, when he stepped out of the backseat, Spence was every inch the proconsul, the local representative of the most powerful nation in the history of humanity. His crisp blue suit and red tie projected strength and confidence. His hair was expensively styled and his conservative wingtips were polished to a mirrored shine. As Ilunga had demanded, he was alone.

One of the residents, a veteran named Claude, met the Ambassador on the steps and showed him to the room that Ilunga had designated for the meeting. It was a classroom that had been reconfigured into a diplomatic salon, complete with two overstuffed chairs, throw rugs, and a coffee table made of inlaid mahogany. The chairs were threadbare and the carpets were worn, but it set the right tone of seriousness. As he had been instructed, Claude seated Spence in the chair farthest from the door. This chair had three inches cut off the legs to make it slightly uncomfortable and to put its occupant at a level just below the host. Alex had suggested it to Ilunga, as he had suggested making Spence wait as a way of making clear whose time was more valuable. Claude brought Spence a cup of tea that he served from a silver tray balanced precariously on the stump of what had been his right hand. The tea was tepid and too sweet to be anything other than an annoyance. Spence knew all of these techniques. He had taught many of them to Alex. All the same, Alex knew that they would rankle.

Ilunga arrived twenty minutes after the appointed meeting time, resplendent in a traditional flowing *boubou* robe and matching headdress. The white linen robe was crisp and the creases were sharp. Subtle gold embroidery highlighted the richness of the fabric. He looked like a head of state. Alex was one step behind Ilunga to his right, filling the role of aide-de-camp. He was wearing the same expensive suit that he had used to bluff his way into the Consolidated Mining building. A diplomat's uniform.

If Spence was surprised to see Alex, he concealed it well. The Ambassador rose, somewhat awkwardly Alex thought, from his shortened chair to shake hands with Ilunga.

"Thank you for making time to meet with me today, Mr. Ilunga," he said.

"You are welcome in my home," Ilunga replied magnanimously.

Spence turned to Alex and extended his hand.

"Hello, Alex. You look well."

"You too, Ambassador."

"I see you've found a new employer."

"I'm just a consultant, really. Working pro bono for the time being."

"Mr. Baines really is a most excellent adviser," Ilunga chimed in. "You should have taken better care not to lose him."

"My loss, your gain."

"I do apologize," Ilunga said, "but I'm afraid a pressing matter that requires my immediate attention has arisen. Mr. Baines has my proxy. I'm sure that he will be able to satisfy your curiosity about our little movement. I am sorry, and I do hope you understand."

"Of course. I'm sure the demands on your time are extraordinary. Thank you for making Alex available. We have some catching up to do in any event."

Ilunga bowed and left the room, closing the door behind him. Alex took the host's seat. Spence lowered himself onto his chair.

"Nice touch," the Ambassador said, patting the armrest. "Your idea?"

"Hey, I learned from the best."

The two Americans, teacher and protégé, sized each other up. Spence sipped the sickly sweet tea to show he did not give a damn about the little mind games, but he could not help shifting his position in his uncomfortably low seat.

"Alex, I'm surprised to see you here. And I'm pleased that you're alive. I was concerned. Maureen was worried sick. Are you ready to come in out of the cold? I'm sure that we can work everything out."

"You tried to kill me, Spence. That undermines the trust level somewhat."

"Nobody tried to kill you. But you had broken the law and violated your oath; we had no choice but to take you in. I'll support you, but there are serious consequences for what you did. You know that."

"Spence, it's just you and me here. Please cut the crap. I know about the Working Group. I know about Rwanda. Don't you talk to me about breaking my oath. Come on, Ambassador. For once, be straight with me."

Spence reached into his jacket pocket and pulled out a device about the size and shape of a cell phone. He pressed a few buttons and studied the screen before setting it down on the coffee table, where it hummed with a slight high-pitched whine. The LiDSS, which stood for Listening Device Screening System, was the latest tool in the counterintelligence arsenal. It was extremely high-end technology. Alex had heard about it, but he had never seen one before. He knew that Spence had used it to first screen the room for hidden listening or recording devices and then set it on an active mode that transmitted ELINT, or electronic interference, designed to counter any system that the passive search might have missed. Alex took this as a positive sign that Spence was, in fact, willing to talk.

"I'm truly sorry about the way this developed. I didn't want it to come to this. Viggiano was insistent that we had to get you out of the country and this seemed the easiest way. Secretary Rogers is an amateur and a sanctimonious ass. He wouldn't understand what we are doing here and how we are advancing the interests of the United States. I know it hurt, Alex, but there was never any intention on our part to follow through on the espionage charges. After a few weeks, they would have gone away. You would have lost your clearances, of course . . . and your access to the dissent channel, but nobody was talking about killing you."

"Even if you cut me out of the department, what was to stop me from going to the *New York Times*?"

If Spence's look of sorrow was an act, it was an impressively convincing one. "Let's face it. You don't have a lot of credibility at this point. I don't think any serious journalist would touch your story. The only thing that would happen if you did that would be that the espionage charges would likely resurface, only this time in a more public and permanent way."

There it was. The threat. No negotiation was complete without one. Diplomats talked in terms of incentives and disincentives, carrots and sticks. They were abstract, value-neutral terms. At least until they were applied to you.

"I don't think I was ever going to make it to Washington," Alex insisted. "Whatever you thought was going to happen, I'm pretty confident that Viggiano intended to kill me and dump my body in the jungle."

"Oh, don't be so fucking dramatic, Alex. You're not that important."

"What about Julian? Did Viggiano kill him?"

"No. That was an accident." Spence leaned forward in his chair, the picture of sincerity. "Julian worked for me, Alex. For us, I mean. He was a member of the Africa Working Group. He had been for more than a decade. Julian was an integral member of the team here in Kinshasa. We didn't kill him. We needed him. I know that you have qualms about our methods, but the Working Group is operating in the best interests of the United States."

"What are those interests? Mass murder? Civil war? Genocide?"

"Grow up. Sub-Saharan Africa is a basket case. I've been working here for the better part of my adult life and it is, I am sorry to say, beyond salvation. It is, however, rich in energy resources and minerals that our country needs. If we don't secure access to them, the Chinese will; and, like it or not, we are engaged in a global struggle for power and influence with Beijing. I want our side to come out on top. If the Chinese lock up the rights to coltan in the Congo or palladium in Zambia or the deep-water oil of Equatorial Guinea, what do you think that means for our economy and our society?"

"Tell me one thing. Darfur. Did you do that? Was the Working Group behind Al-Nour and the Janjaweed? I need to know."

The Ambassador looked genuinely sympathetic.

"I know what happened there was hard on you. It was a bad situation and we were all called on to make difficult choices. You had your instructions and you carried them out as was expected of you. If you want to blame someone, blame the intel analysts who said there was no danger that the Janjaweed would attack the camp. Blame the policy makers who made promises that they couldn't or wouldn't keep. It's not the first time that's happened. It's not the last. And it's not your fault. I'm sorry that I wasn't there when you needed me. You've been like a son to me and I've tried to be like a father to you. So believe me when I tell you that I had nothing to do with what happened to you in Sudan. I would never do something like that to you."

Alex wanted that to be true, but he no longer knew what to believe.

"Sudan was hard. And I'll have to live with what happened there. But there's still a chance here to do what's right and I'm going to see it through to the end."

"With Ilunga? He had his moment, but he's the past, not the future."

"I wouldn't be so sure. This country is hungry for change. For peace. I think Ilunga can deliver that and I think the Congolese will be with him."

"It's not going to go down like that. Silwamba is too well entrenched. There's still time to fix this. Come back with me. We can work this all out."

"It's too late for that, Spence."

"What makes you think I won't report you to the police? You're a wanted man after all."

"I don't think the police would do anything. They're largely on Ilunga's side. The army . . . maybe. But Ilunga's men are pretty heavily armed and I don't think Silwamba wants to start a firefight with CNN's new golden boy. No, I think I'll take my chances on that one."

Spence nodded, his expression respectful.

"You really think you can beat me?" There was no hint of anger in his voice. The experienced and worldly U.S. Ambassador seemed more bemused than anything else.

"I don't need to. This is not about you and me. You're on the wrong side of history. That's all there is to it."

Spence stood. "I supposed that's it then."

Alex rose. They did not shake hands. They exchanged no more words. There was nothing more to say.

32

A lex had gotten used to the rustling of the bats. It was oddly soothing in some ways. At least it meant that he was not completely alone in the dusty shell of the construction site. He had spent more than a week listening in on Consolidated Mining's satphone conversations. Once a day he reconfigured the system to allow for Skype calls to Anah. So far no one had shown up at the family home to accuse Alex of either espionage or diamond smuggling. This was an enormous relief. His daughter was still enjoying herself, but she had also made it clear that she was eager to be reunited with her father. At one point Alex tried to broach the idea that Anah might need to start the fourth grade in Brunswick. She was having none of it. Alex knew that he would have to revisit this issue soon. It was unlikely that Ilunga's revolution would be so accommodating as to fall in line with the school calendar.

He had already learned a great deal about Consolidated's operations. The company was a sprawling conglomerate with interests in everything from nickel smelters in Siberia to iron mines in Australia to South African gold and diamond mines. Many of the conversations related to complex financial instruments designed as hedging strategies against swings in volatile commodity prices. Some of it he understood; much of it was simply too arcane. The most interesting conversations had been between Henri Saillard and Grover Jackson in New York. Jackson, Alex had learned from a quick Google search, was Consolidated's head of global operations. This was one of those fuzzy titles that offered only a vague sense of what the person in the position actually did. What Jackson seemed to do was solve problems, and he had come to look on the Congo as a problem.

In particular, the head office was growing worried about Ilunga's political movement and the threat he posed to the pliant and cooperative President Silwamba. Since the rally in front of the parliament building, Ilunga had continued to gain strength. His protests now drew tens of thousands to the streets and the international media outlets had sent their heavyweights to Kinshasa to cover the power struggle. Jackson was planning to come out to Kinshasa to see for himself what was happening and Saillard had been trying to stonewall him, coming up with increasingly flimsy excuses for why it was a bad time for a visit. The dates and the excuses kept changing. Alex kept notes. The more useful conversations he recorded directly onto his laptop's hard drive.

So far there had been no smoking gun. Late in the afternoon of his eighth day of electronic eavesdropping, however, Alex listened in on a conversation between Saillard and Jackson that changed everything.

At four-fifteen, he heard the long series of beeps that indicated someone in the company was placing an international call. The hacker program told him that the call originated from Saillard's extension. A moment later it informed him that the call was being placed to Grover Jackson's office. Alex perked up and activated the subroutine that would record the conversation to a specific file on the hard drive labeled "Jackson-Saillard."

The secretaries took a moment to establish the availability of their respective bosses and then connected the call.

"Hello, Grover." Saillard's voice was as smooth and oily as ever, but Alex thought that he detected a small hint of tension. "Thank you for taking my call."

"Always a pleasure, Henri." Grover's tone made it clear that it was anything but.

"I have a rather delicate matter that I need to discuss with you."

"Of course. Is this something that should wait until I get out there at the end of the month? We seem to have a great deal to discuss."

"No, I'm afraid this issue is rather more urgent than that and appears to require some action on our part that really should be approved at your level."

"Ilunga?" Jackson offered.

"Well, yes. I'm afraid that his challenge to Silwamba is more serious than we had anticipated. The man has been out of politics for years, and it seemed reasonable to conclude that he was something of a spent force. For whatever reason, that has not proven to be the case. His support is growing rapidly. The President is starting to panic and I believe that he is considering martial law. That would be disastrous from our perspective. It would likely trigger a call for UN sanctions and possibly one of those divestment movements that made it so difficult for us to operate in South Africa under apartheid."

"Are you thinking about the Uzbekistan model?" Jackson asked somewhat skeptically.

There was a long pause.

"I am," Saillard offered finally.

Alex felt the muscles in his shoulders tense and he leaned forward slightly as though that might help him to hear better. He reviewed what he remembered of the failed "Cotton Revolution" in Uzbekistan. A democratic opposition movement with a charismatic leader named Ibrahim Alijevic had threatened to unseat the Moscow-backed Limonov government. The opposition movement, keying off of labor unrest in the country's cotton industry, had adopted a strip of white cotton cloth as its symbol, and tens of thousands of protestors had paraded in the streets of the capital city. Just when it appeared that Limonov would join the growing list of ex-dictators in exile in Russia, Alijevic died. The official cause of death was a heart attack, but it was widely believed that he had been poisoned by the Russian security services. There had been no autopsy.

"Uzbekistan was extremely expensive," Grover reminded Saillard. "And extremely risky. Are you sure this is necessary?"

"I'm afraid so. But I also believe that we can do this for much less than the Uzbek operation cost. We had to bring in outside talent there and the Russians had us by the balls. I think this situation can be managed with local assets."

"Local? Surely you don't mean Silwamba's people."

"Of course not. They'd make a public hash of it. I'm thinking of our . . . partners." Saillard's choice of words was careful and deliberate.

"Really. Do you think they're up for something like that?"

"Some of them appreciate the value of direct action . . . on occasion, that is. I wouldn't want to make a habit of it."

"Have you talked to Silwamba about this?"

"Of course not."

"Good. Don't. That clown couldn't keep a secret if his life depended on it."

"So you agree then?"

There was another long pause while Jackson weighed the options.

"I don't like this," he said finally.

"Neither do I. But I do believe it is the best of an unpleasant set of options. Letting Ilunga take power would undermine everything that we've worked to achieve here."

There was yet another long silence.

"Do you need to seek approval from the board?" Saillard prompted. It was a clever move, Alex suspected, to challenge Jackson by making the decision a test of his authority.

"No," the global ops chief replied. "I agree that this is necessary. Talk to the 'partners' and make the arrangements. But Henri . . . I'm not at all happy that you let things get to this point. We need to have a serious discussion about recent developments when I get out there at the end of the month. Anything that threatens our position in the Congo threatens our control of the coltan trade and that is something that the company cannot accept."

"I look forward to it," Saillard replied in his smarmiest tone.

Alex was certain that he had just heard Henri Saillard and Grover Jackson negotiate the assassination of Albert Ilunga. This development reordered his priorities. Alex's immediate goal was no longer proving his innocence, it was saving the life of a friend. He unhooked the laptop from the receiver. He slipped the phone into his pocket and powered off the computer. Tucking the laptop under his arm, he turned to leave and froze.

Rick Viggiano was standing in the doorway, his Sig Sauer automatic in his right hand.

"I really wish that you hadn't heard that," the RSO said. The menace in his voice was unmistakable.

It was instantly clear to Alex what Saillard had meant by "our partners." Viggiano was going to kill Ilunga. He did not doubt for a moment that the RSO was capable of what the intelligence services referred to euphemistically as "wet work."

"And I wish you hadn't found me," Alex replied. "Looks like we're both shit out of luck."

"I have a couple of questions that I need to ask you now, smartass. Answer me nice and I'll kill you quick. Otherwise, I'm afraid this is going to hurt."

"How did you track me here?" Alex asked. He knew the answer to that. Consolidated Mining's technical staff had found the satellite shunt. It was pretty easy to figure out from the direction the dish was pointing where the receiver was likely to be located. He was simply stalling for time.

"You misunderstand the nature of our new relationship. I ask you questions and you fucking answer them. Dick me around and I will demonstrate this by shooting you in the kneecap." Viggiano seemed cool and unhurried.

"Why don't we start," Viggiano continued, "with the laptop. Give it up." He held out his left hand at waist level to receive the laptop and simultaneously elevated the Sig Sauer to point directly at Alex's chest. "Move slow," he suggested unnecessarily.

There was about a fifteen-foot gap between them. Alex stepped forward, holding the laptop low in his right hand. He moved with exaggerated caution even as he rapidly reviewed the options. Viggiano's clearly articulated intent to kill him had a substantial impact on the risk-reward calculus. As he approached, he looked over Viggiano's shoulder, hoping to fool the RSO into believing that the cavalry had arrived. The old Newark street cop did not fall for it, but it may have distracted him just enough as Alex swung the laptop up as suddenly and as violently as he could. The heavy HP smashed into Viggiano's gun, which discharged almost simultaneously. Alex fully expected to feel the punch of a 9mm round in his chest. Instead, the laptop disintegrated in a cloud of plastic, metal, and glass as the slug tore through its insides.

The gun went skittering across the floor to the corner of the room. Rather than try to bull past Viggiano and escape through the door, Alex turned and threw himself out the window. The scaffolding on the outside had been only partially disassembled. It was about an eight-foot drop to a layer of wooden planks that had served as a workspace when this had been an active construction site. He landed hard. The fall knocked the wind out of him, and the ribs he had injured parachuting into Busu-Mouli screamed in protest. He scrambled painfully to his feet and stumbled along the narrow planks to put as much distance between himself and Viggiano as possible. The row of planks was only about three feet wide and the drop on the far side was five stories straight down. A series of green nylon sheets intended to keep the sun off the workers hung loosely from the scaffolding. The light coming through the sheets was green and sickly. A bullet whined past his head and ricocheted off a piece of scaffolding with a metallic ping. There was no side-to-side movement possible on the planks. Alex could only run straight ahead and he felt like a sitting duck. A sudden heavy thud behind him signaled the RSO had jumped down to join him on the planks. The scaffolding wobbled from the force of his landing. Alex looked over his shoulder. Viggiano was crouched low and bringing the handgun up into a firing position. He was no more than twenty feet away and could hardly miss from that distance.

Without thinking about it, Alex stepped off the plank and dropped. As he fell, he grabbed for one of the nylon sun shades. The sun-damaged material ripped clean through, but it held long enough to allow him to swing onto the row of planks one story down. He looked around wildly. There were few windows on this level. Finally, he spotted an opening about thirty feet away that had been only partially bricked up and he clambered through it. The scaffolding continued to shake as Viggiano climbed down.

The room Alex had climbed into opened onto a center atrium. There was little light at this level, only what came in through a few holes that were waiting for ventilation shafts and power and sewer lines to be installed. The interior was dark and gloomy. A broad walkway ran in an oval around the atrium. The inside of the oval was hollow and dropped down four stories. It was a fairly typical shopping center setup intended to create the illusion of open space and give shoppers a view of the multiple layers of stores in the building. No doubt the workers would have added a guardrail around the walkway if they had finished construction. Now, however, the core of the building was just empty space with nothing guarding against a forty-foot fall. The stairwell was on the other side of the building. Alex looked across. It was about a fifteen-foot jump from where he was to the opposite walkway. Too far, he decided, even with a running start. The alternative was to run all the way around the walkway to reach the entrance to the stairwell. He could hear Viggiano behind him starting to scramble through the opening in the wall.

Alex took off. He wanted to be on the far side before Viggiano made it inside. He was only slightly more than halfway to the stairs when a piece of the concrete wall exploded three feet from his head. Small pieces of the wall grazed his cheek and concrete dust clouded his vision. *Shit.* Fortunately, Viggiano seemed uncertain about whether he wanted to shoot Alex or run him down and question him. The RSO was trying to do both, so he was shooting on the run in the dark. In movies, the good guys always seemed to be able to do this effortlessly, but Alex remembered from his "crash and bang" training just how difficult it was to fire on the move with a handgun. He had a good chance of making the stairs. Two more wild shots sped past. Alex heard them hit concrete, but nothing came as close to hitting him as Viggiano's previous shots had.

He reached the stairs and started down them three at a time. The stairwell was unfinished and open to the outside. Viggiano was close now, maybe fifty feet behind him. Alex heard the squeaks and rustles of the bat colony as he ran past and retained enough presence of mind to slow down as he crossed the landing covered in the slippery guano. Viggiano was not as careful. The RSO took the landing at full speed. His right leg went out from under him as his foot slipped on the oily bat shit. His arms windmilled wildly and he fought to regain his balance. The pistol went flying out of his hand into the darkness of the building's interior. Viggiano did not stand a chance. He had built up too much momentum, and Alex watched the man who had tried twice to kill him hurtle headfirst into the air.

He fell thirty-five feet to the parking lot below. The packed dirt was as hard as concrete.

Even three stories up, Alex could hear the dry-branch crack of the RSO's neck breaking on impact.

33

It is not an easy thing to tell a man that there is a contract out on his life. For Alex, this task was further complicated by the sense of responsibility he felt for having persuaded Ilunga to reengage in the Congo's rough-and-tumble politics. Outside of South Africa, there were few retired elder statesmen on the continent. The losers in political power struggles tended to die untimely and often violent deaths. In challenging Silwamba, Ilunga had put himself in the firing line. Adding multinational business interests to the equation further increased the level of risk. Even with Viggiano dead, the threat against Ilunga was both real and immediate. First Antoine, then Jean-Baptiste, and now Ilunga. Alex could feel the guilt gnawing at the back of his mind.

"I'm sorry, Albert," he said, after explaining what had happened at the construction site and what he had learned listening in on the call between Saillard and Jackson. Alex, Marie, Ilunga, and Giles were sitting at the small table in the courtyard of the villa. A few smoky torches did a tolerable job of keeping the mosquitoes at bay. Ilunga seemed unconcerned by Alex's report.

"You have nothing to apologize for. I knew exactly what I was getting into. I knew it when I was languishing in solitary confinement. And I knew it when I agreed with you and Marie that now was the time to make this move. It was my decision and I am prepared for the consequences. Why do you think I've spent three years building up my personal army? Your friends from New York will not find me such an easy target."

"Maybe not," Alex agreed. "But they have essentially unlimited resources and I'm afraid that they'll keep doubling down until they succeed."

"Well," Ilunga said philosophically, "it doesn't seem like there's very much that we can do about it. We have come too far. We need to keep moving forward."

Alex was impressed and just a little surprised by Ilunga's determination. The coalition leader had been manifestly reluctant to launch this challenge to Silwamba's rule. Alex now suspected that Ilunga had been playing the devil's advocate, arguing the other side of the issue to tease out all of the problems and pitfalls and to make sure that they had considered the issue from all angles.

"Maybe there is something that we can do," Marie suggested. The three men looked at her expectantly. Marie was wearing a plain white blouse and black slacks with a thin gold chain around her neck. Her hair was tied back with a white ribbon. She looked both luminous and fierce.

"What do you have in mind, my dear?" Ilunga asked. His eyes sparked with an amusement that was somewhat incongruous for a man who had just been threatened with assassination.

Marie leaned forward slightly and looked straight at Ilunga.

"We can move faster. We can go from calling for change to making change. Pressure has been building on Silwamba and his cronies. The regime is slowly hollowing out. Now may be the time to crack it open. They think that they're coming after you . . . let's turn the tables and go after them."

It was hard to read Ilunga's expression, but his eyes narrowed and his brow furrowed in concentration.

"How would you propose to do that?" he asked, although it was pretty clear that he understood what Marie was suggesting.

"Take over the parliament, take over the airwaves, and force Silwamba out of the country. Let him live out his miserable life in Switzerland or under Castro's protection in Havana. I frankly don't give a damn where he goes as long as it's not here."

"A coup?" Ilunga suggested mildly.

"Justice," Marie replied confidently.

"Marie is right," Alex chimed in. "The core of our argument is that you are the legitimate winner of the last election. We don't need new elections to reaffirm that. Silwamba has stolen this country with the help and support of our friends at Consolidated Mining and . . . it pains me to say . . . at least some parts of the U.S. government. A coup is, by definition, unconstitutional. It's Silwamba's regime that is an affront to the Congolese constitution and the will of the people. The public is sick of the corruption and violence. This government is ready to fall."

Ilunga still seemed skeptical, or maybe he was just playing devil's advocate again.

"We've built up considerable moral capital," Ilunga observed. "We risk squandering that if we resort to violence."

"I absolutely agree with you," Alex replied. "This country has seen enough violence. But there's a difference between force and violence. I think we can do this without having to fight."

"And how much experience do you have bringing down governments?" Ilunga was not being unkind, but he was challenging Alex to make the best possible case for an idea that was, at best, controversial.

"Me personally, not so much," Alex admitted. "But I know a guy who does."

"I think we are going to need some beers for this next part," said Giles. He went to the kitchen and returned a few minutes later with four ice-cold Heinekens.

"Now let me tell you what I have in mind . . ."

Giles approached the U.S. Embassy with a certain degree of trepidation. The building was imposing and forbidding. There was nothing welcoming about it and that impression was further reinforced by Giles's knowledge that the people who worked inside were conspiring against a man he loved and admired, a man who had rescued him from a life of desperation. He would do anything for Albert Ilunga, however, and if that meant walking into the belly of the beast, then so be it.

Following Alex's instructions, he went to the main gate and walked up to the local guard, who eyed the two-hundred-and-fifty-pound Giles suspiciously.

"Can I help you?" the guard asked.

"I have certain information that would be of value to the United States. I am interested in discussing this with the American authorities."

The guard seemed unimpressed.

"The visa line is around the corner," he observed. "You won't help yourself by making up a story. Why don't you go wait in the line like everybody else."

"Imbecile. I am not here for a visa. I have information that is so hot it's radioactive. You have exactly ten minutes to get me in with the CIA or so help me I will take what I know to the Chinese. They pay in cash."

"Your name?"

"Is of no use to you."

The guard shrugged. "Wait here, please."

"Make it quick. The Chinese Embassy is three blocks from here."

The interview room was all white. The walls were a plain white with no pictures or decorations of any kind. There was a cheap-looking white table and half a dozen metal chairs, all painted white. The chairs were uncomfortable and the room was too warm. This was deliberate. Giles sat alone in the room for some time. This too was deliberate. Although there was no obvious "mirror" like those that were found in every interview room in every police station in the United States, carefully hidden cameras allowed case officers to observe the walk-in's behavior before going in to speak to him. Forewarned, Giles sat quietly and waited.

After some twenty minutes, Jonah Keeler opened the door. The CIA Station Chief was wearing a blue suit with thin white pinstripes about an inch apart. His club tie was done up in a Windsor knot. His embassy ID hung from his neck on a lanyard in the cherry and white colors of Temple University. Giles recognized him from Alex's description. This was the man he needed to speak to.

"Jonah Keeler?"

Keeler raised an eyebrow and took a seat opposite Giles at the Formica table. "Yes. And you are?"

"A messenger."

"How interesting. From whom?"

"Your friend from Busu-Mouli."

"Well, well. And how is he?"

"Alive."

"The list of those who would wish otherwise is growing longer."

"Are you among them?"

"No." Keeler pulled a pack of Marlboro Lights from his pocket and offered one to Giles, who declined. Keeler lit the cigarette with a gold lighter and returned both the pack and the lighter to his breast pocket. There was no smoking allowed in any U.S. government facility. That was only one of the many rules commonly breached in this room.

"So why send you? Why not just pick up the phone?"

"I believe that he has learned to distrust telephones."

"I can imagine that's true. What message do you have for me?"

"He would like to meet you tonight at ten."

"Where?"

"He told me to tell you to meet him on Green Dolphin Street."

Keeler smiled and tapped his cigarette on the corner of the table to knock the ash onto the floor. "I know the place."

M arie and Alex got to the Ibiza by nine. With his light disguise and the gradual disappearance of the "wanted" posters from around town, Alex was less fearful of being recognized. Even so, they took a table in the back, where the shadows were the deepest. It was a different band than the one that had been playing on Alex's last visit. This band had a female lead singer who looked—and sounded—remarkably like Cesária Évora. The backing band was small, just guitar, drums, and piano, but the woman's voice needed little adornment.

Marie had found time to go shopping, Alex realized. She was wearing a sky blue silk blouse that he had not seen before and a coral necklace just the right shade for her skin. The top two buttons of the blouse were open, and when she leaned forward, there was just a hint of her black bra. She wore small gold hoops in her ears and had let her braids hang loose. It was a younger look for her, less "chiefly" and more carefree. She noticed him staring at her.

"What is it?" she asked shyly.

"Chief Tsiolo, you are absolutely fucking gorgeous."

"Such language." Marie rubbed her foot suggestively across his calf underneath the table.

A teenage waitress brought them a bowl of heavily salted peanuts and took their orders. Marie asked for a glass of pinotage. Alex ordered Dewar's on the rocks.

For the next hour, they tried to forget the enormous risks they were taking. There were many more ways that things could go badly than right. At the moment, however, the music was good and they were enjoying each other's company.

"You know," Alex observed, "this is almost like a date. I think it's our first."

"I'd say so. It's a nice spot for a first date. Think you'll get lucky tonight?"

"Hope springs eternal."

"That it does."

About five minutes before ten, Jonah Keeler walked into the Ibiza. He spotted Alex and Marie immediately, but went to the bar and ordered a drink. With a studied nonchalance, Keeler surveyed the room, looking for any patron or employee who appeared out of place. When he was satisfied that no one in the bar raised any red flags, he made his way casually to the back tables, where Alex and Marie rose to greet him.

"Chief Tsiolo, I presume," he said warmly, taking Marie's hand. "It's a pleasure. The pictures in your Consolidated Mining personnel folder do not do you justice. You are truly lovely."

"Thank you," Marie replied. "The staff photographer at the mining company used to moonlight at the city jail taking mug shots."

Keeler turned to Alex and unexpectedly enfolded him in an embrace.

"God, I'm glad to see you alive. I don't think I told you that J.J. had even-money odds you were gonna break your neck on landing. That was a hell of a thing you did."

"There's a first time for everything . . . and a last. I'm just glad they weren't one and the same that night."

"So did you hear about Viggiano?" Keeler asked, after they had sat down.

"Yeah, a tragedy. He was a beautiful human being."

"A real sweetheart."

Jonah's eyes darted briefly in Marie's direction and then back to Alex, who understood the implicit question.

"It's okay. Marie knows everything that I know. Without her, I would have been dead some time ago."

Keeler nodded his acceptance of Alex's endorsement.

"So what happened?" Jonah asked. "All I know is that I have a dead RSO with bat shit on his shoes and gunpowder residue on his arm. I also have a little hobby den inside the abandoned building where he died . . . with your fingerprints on just about everything, by the way . . . and a laptop computer more or less gutted by a 9mm bullet from the dead guy's gun. Do I have that about right?"

"Pretty much. What's the fallout like?"

"Un-fucking-believable. Viggiano didn't tell anyone where he was going and the cops didn't find his body until the next morning. It wasn't, by all accounts, a pretty sight. The dogs got to him. Spence had me leading the investigation, which lasted all of three hours before they shut it down. The official cause of death is 'accidental slip and fall.' Somebody got to Spence, and I have a sneaking suspicion it was a foppish Belgian with a soul patch and a bad attitude. Tell me I'm wrong."

"No. I think you've pretty much got it nailed. Did you keep the computer? There's some data on it that could prove extremely useful."

"I sent it to our tech guys in Jo'burg. Not much hope that they'll be able to recover the data from it. The bullet absolutely eviscerated the hard drive. What was on it?"

"You'll need a little background first."

"I got time."

Alex gave him a brief rundown of the events since J. J. Sykes had taken off from Kinshasa with Alex on board as a reluctant skydiver. He told him about the decision to partner with Manamakimba, the assault on Busu-Mouli, their successful efforts to recruit Ilunga back into politics, and Alex's parallel efforts to pry open the locked doors of Consolidated Mining's secret chambers. When he told Keeler about Saillard's conversation with Grover Jackson, the Station Chief's eyes widened in disbelief.

"You had that conversation recorded on the hard drive?" Keeler asked.

Alex confirmed that he had.

"Fuck!"

Alex also explained to Keeler the circumstances surrounding Viggiano's death. "In a way, 'accidental slip and fall' isn't that far from the truth. I certainly didn't kill him. Which didn't stop him from coming damn close to killing me. I will admit that I'm not exactly sorry he's dead. The guy was dirty. I just hope that his being dead doesn't wind up making it harder for me to clear my name."

Keeler polished off his Jack and Coke and signaled the server for another.

"So what can I do for you? You asked for the meet."

"If we had time, I think we could succeed in ousting Silwamba purely through political pressure and installing Ilunga. But we're running short on time. Even with Viggiano out of the picture, Consolidated Mining has the resources and the contacts to kill Ilunga. That would obviously put something of a damper on the movement."

"So you're thinking that you need to push the pace a bit?" Keeler asked. "Are you talking about a coup?"

"A bloodless one," Marie interjected. "We want a change of government, not a civil war."

"I wanted to see you, Jonah, because we need your advice. I suspect that you've had more experience with this kind of thing than I have."

Keeler nodded. "Mozambique in '93, Côte d'Ivoire in 2002."

"That was us?" Alex was genuinely surprised. In the Ivory Coast a kleptocratic pro-Russian dictator had been swept aside in a surprise putsch that had installed a kleptocratic pro-American, or at least pro-ExxonMobil, strongman. There had been no hint of Agency involvement in those developments.

"Hey, we can keep a few secrets."

"So is there a set of instructions for this kind of thing?"

"More a collection of generally accepted principles."

"How would you apply them to these circumstances?"

"I have some ideas."

"A moment," Marie said. "Before we take this further, I need to ask a question. I know that you have helped Alex. I know he considers you a friend. But you work for the American CIA. Why would you want to help us in this?"

"If Alex has told you about the Africa Working Group, then I expect he's also told you that there are other factions contending for influence over policy that have very different views and different priorities. I happen to represent one of those groups that sees tremendous positive potential in Africa. We need to invest here, not just extract. So we want the same things. I wouldn't have thought to go to Ilunga to try to bring about change, but I'm happy as hell that you did. Now that you've come this far, I want to help you finish this and get it done right. Does that seem fair?"

"Fair enough," Marie agreed.

"So how do we do this thing?" Alex asked.

Keeler pulled a government-issue ballpoint pen out of his suit pocket and reached for a dry cocktail napkin. "Here's what we need to do," he began.

And on the back of a bar napkin, they began to sketch out a workable plan for revolution.

34

We're getting close, Albert," Alex said confidently. "We just need another couple of days to make sure all the pieces are in place." Alex, Ilunga, and Keeler had just left a planning meeting with key lieutenants and were walking to the car that would take Ilunga to a student rally at the University of Kinshasa. Ilunga's new personal assistant, a twenty-something engineering student at the university named Pascal, walked two steps behind, talking animatedly on one of the three cell phones he carried on his belt. In only a few short weeks, Ilunga had begun to acquire some of the trappings of power and privilege.

"What I'm most concerned about," Alex continued, "is the media. State-run TV is going to back Silwamba without question. That's still the single most important and influential source of news, especially in the big cities. Seizing the station is an option, but the risk of violence is high. I want to give this one some more thought."

"Don't worry," Ilunga replied. "I can take care of RTNC." This was the acronym for Radio-Télévision Nationale Congolaise, the only truly national station in the country. "I've put the word out to the Brotherhood."

"It's not clear to me how that's going to take care of the problem."

Ilunga shrugged. "Just don't worry about it. RTNC is not going to be an issue. I'm more concerned about Silwamba's personal guard force. If the Black Lions come out of their barracks and fight for Silwamba, I'm afraid that many people could be killed."

"Don't worry about the Lions," said Alex, deliberately echoing Ilunga's own vague assurances about the RTNC. "I think I've got a solution to that problem."

Ilunga looked at him shrewdly. "Do I want to know what your solution is?" he asked.

"Probably not."

"Then I won't ask. Just make sure the Lions stay in their den."

They walked through the front gate and turned right down the tree-lined Rue Lukengu. Ilunga's car, a dark blue Peugeot, was new, purchased with some of the money that Keeler had made available to the movement. Alex's diamond money was nearly exhausted and the influx of CIA cash was welcome, but Alex could not help wondering what strings that assistance might come with.

Ilunga moved to the door closest to the curb and his young aide scurried around to the other side of the car. The driver was just about to open the door for Ilunga when Keeler yelled "Stop! *Halte!*" Everyone froze in an almost comical tableau.

"What is it, Jonah?" Alex asked.

Keeler pointed at the hood of the car. "Do you see that?"

There was a small loop of wire, no more than an inch across, sticking out of the seam where the hood joined the body of the car.

"That doesn't belong there," Keeler continued.

"Is it a bomb?"

"Maybe. Albert, step away from the vehicle, please."

Ilunga complied. Like a good aide-de-camp, Pascal stayed close to his principal.

Keeler took a closer look at the wire loop.

"You," he said to the driver, after a moment's inspection. "I'd like you to open the hood, please . . . but do not, under any circumstances, start the car. Do you understand me?"

The driver nodded in the affirmative, his eyes wide.

When the driver pulled the latch on the inside, Alex turned away instinctively, half expecting the car to blow up in a violent Hollywood-style explosion. Nothing happened. The hood popped up half an inch and stopped. Keeler explored the area under the front of the hood with his fingers, looking for something out of place. When he was satisfied, he disengaged the latch and allowed the hood to swing open on its springs. Alex could see immediately that there was a device on top of the engine block that was not part of the car. A greasy brick of what he suspected was plastic explosive was packed alongside the fuel pump. Copper wires coated with plastic in various colors connected the bomb to the starter, but one of the wires had come loose and had been caught in the small loop that Keeler had seen on the outside of the car.

"It looks like someone was in one hell of a hurry," Keeler explained. "They didn't have time to do a good job. With this loose wire, I'm not even sure this thing would have gone off."

"It's still a pretty serious attempt on Albert's life," Alex observed. "It looks like our friends at Consolidated Mining have found a stand-in for Viggiano."

"But one who is not so experienced, perhaps," said Ilunga, who had abandoned the visibly shaken Pascal to join them in inspecting the bomb.

"Looks like it," Keeler agreed. "Viggiano was an asshole, but he was a competent asshole. If he was still alive, we'd most likely all be dead."

"Even so, they will come back and try again," Alex commented. "They only have to get lucky once."

"Agreed." Keeler looked searchingly at Ilunga. "I think we need to accelerate the timetable for the operation."

"What are you thinking?"

"Do you have plans for tomorrow?"

35

François Mwambe glanced nervously at his watch. It was ten minutes before eight. He was sitting where he sat every morning at this time, in the Senior Producer's chair for RTNC's influential morning news show *Wake Up, Kinshasa!* The eight o'clock news program was the most watched show in the city. François understood that this had less to do with the show's seamless production values than it did with the extraordinarily beautiful newsreader, Adrienne Ngambe.

On the studio floor, Adrienne was already sitting behind the anchor desk with the hair and makeup people fussing over her. *She was*, Mwambe thought, *absolutely stunning.* She was also, he knew, a real bitch who would run over her own mother to advance her career. Cameras two and three centered in on Adrienne from different angles, and her perfect face appeared in stereo on François's monitor. Her lips were moving as she reviewed the material for the morning newscast, but François kept the sound turned off. He found her voice irritating.

The RTNC systems were highly automated. When it came to propaganda, Silwamba insisted on only the best. They ran the show with only two producers, François and his assistant. Bosco Lumala was the cousin of a senior official in the Ministry of Information. Although he had gotten the job through family connections, Bosco was a hard worker and was learning to be a competent producer. He had also proven to be a good colleague. François felt bad about what he was about to do to him.

At seven-fifty-five, François looked up from studying the monitor. "I stayed out too late last night, Bosco. I'm afraid I'll pass out halfway through the show. Would you mind getting me a cup of coffee."

"Sure. Two sugars?"

"You know it."

The young assistant producer stepped out of the booth and started down the hall toward the break room, where an aging Italian machine produced execrable coffee. François locked the door behind him. From his briefcase, he produced a CD and dropped it into a slot on the console. At eight o'clock on the dot, the *Wake Up, Kinshasa!* logo appeared on the screen accompanied by the program's theme song, an amped-up bass line intended to convey a sense of urgency and immediacy. It was François's responsibility to cue the feed for Adrienne's morning news brief. Later in the program, she would do a stand-up in front of a map of Central Africa as she reported on the weather. It was primarily an excuse to show off her magnificent legs.

This morning, however, instead of hitting the green button that would have broadcast Adrienne's beautiful face to Kinshasa's eight million people, François pressed a black button on the other side of the console. The *Wake Up, Kinshasa!* logo was replaced by a close-up of Albert Ilunga.

"My fellow citizens," Ilunga began. "Now is our hour . . ."

François touched his chest. Through the thin layer of cotton, he could feel the ridges of a circular scar no more than two inches across.

It took security more than half an hour to break through the thick steel door of the producer's booth.

A thanase Bononge came by his nickname honestly. Everyone called him Sparky, largely because he spent a good portion of every day hunched over a massive bong smoking low-grade, jungle-grown cannabis. Sparky hosted a popular syndicated radio show specializing in cutting-edge AfroPop. His heavy pot habit gave him a distinctively raspy voice that was instantly recognizable across the country. He was also a regular in the Congo's popular gossip magazines. His long dreadlocks and the aviator sunglasses he was never without gave him a look that was nearly as famous as his voice. Unsurprisingly, Sparky was a night owl and his show ran from eleven to one or two in the morning as the mood struck him. But when Sparky suggested to the suits at Radio Kinshasa that he'd like to try his hand as a morning DJ, it seemed like a no-brainer. It was a one-off show that would be broadcast live by Radio Kinshasa affiliates across the country. After that, Sparky would return to his late-night ways.

"Good morning, Congo. I know that those are words you never expected to hear from me. And I'll admit that it came as something of a surprise to me that there are two eight o'clocks in a day. Who knew? We'll still be playing some of the finest contemporary African music and exploring the music scene in our very own capital city, but I'd like to begin with one of the most powerful pieces of music that I have heard in a very long time. I think that all of my listeners know what I mean."

Sparky cued up a recording of Melina singing at Ilunga's rally in front of the parliament building. Even removed from the emotions of the moment, it was a powerful and stirring song. It was also an unmistakable political statement.

When the song had finished, Sparky spoke to the more than two million Congolese across the country listening to his show. "The days of corruption and oppression are at an end. Take to the streets, my brothers. Take back our country. President Ilunga is taking power today. Be a part of this. Meet him in the streets. I'll be there and we can share the moment."

The owners and managers of the radio station did not actually listen to their own programs. Sparky's political discourse went unnoticed by management for a good fifteen minutes. Then they scrambled to shut him down, but it was too late. Whatever damage he was going to do had been done. "How is it possible," one of the executives asked, "that Sparky Bononge would turn out to have a social conscience?"

36

AUGUST 29, 2009
12:00 PM
KINSHASA

It began as a trickle and became a stream and then a flood. Ilunga's
hard-core supporters were the first on the streets, wearing white
and waving homemade banners. They were soon joined by thousands more. Some came because they had supported Ilunga in the last
election. Some came because they were angry. Some came because they
were curious. By noon, their ranks had swelled to the tens of thousands
as the Congolese people, weary of oppression, corruption, and crony-
ism, took to the streets of the capital. The scene was repeated in Ki-
sangi, Goma, and other cities across the country.

Alex was heartened to see a large number of police officers among
the demonstrators, not seeking to control the protests but to join them.
Historically, the enormous unknown in "people-power" revolutions was
whether the security services were prepared to fire on their own citizens
in defense of the status quo. Where they were, as in Turkmenistan, the
revolutions faltered and died. Where they were not, as in Serbia or

Georgia, the protestors could—and often did—prevail. The police were solidly behind Ilunga. The army, however, was still a question mark. The significant presence of clergy on the streets was also a good sign. Ministers and priests were tremendously influential in this deeply religious society. From his vantage point at the Victory Monument, Alex saw the Archbishop of Kinshasa, who had been a close friend of Father Antoine's, marching down Avenue Kasavubu in his scarlet robes.

Street musicians, food vendors, and small children mingled with the protestors and the demonstrations began to take on a festival atmosphere. Having set everything in motion, Ilunga and his advisers did little to try to direct or control the protestors. The demonstrations grew organically, and inevitably they began to respond to the magnetic pull of the presidential palace. Starting from different parts of the city, thousands of ordinary Congolese converged on Silwamba's grand residence.

"It's a beautiful sight," Marie said to Ilunga. Pascal and Giles had set up a de facto command post at the Victory Monument, complete with maps, a dozen cell phones, and a networked laptop. The monument was less than a kilometer from the palace. It was also slightly elevated on an artificial hill, which gave them a good overview of the protests. It was an impressive scene.

"It is," Ilunga agreed. "But I'm still worried about the Black Lions." He turned to Alex. "Do you think they'll come out of the barracks?"

"No way to know," Alex replied.

"We're ready for them if they do," Marie said reassuringly.

"What's the next step?" Ilunga asked.

"Now you get down off this hill and join your people in the streets. Lead them."

Ilunga nodded, his features set in a look of grim determination. "Walk with me, Chief Tsiolo."

37

The Angel of Death adjusted her skirt. Yesterday Annette Cartwright had been on assignment in Johannesburg when she had gotten a tip from a source she trusted that something big was about to go down in Kinshasa. She and her crew were on the late plane that night.

Her producer had found a spot on a rooftop with a panoramic view of the crowded and chaotic street scene in front of the presidential palace. Annette used a pocket mirror to check her hair and makeup. She straightened her back, looking into the camera with the deadly serious expression universal among foreign correspondents.

Her producer stood behind the cameraman and held up his hand, signaling that the anchor in Atlanta was about to cue their story.

"We go live in three . . . two . . . one . . ." He lowered his hand in a cutting motion.

"Good afternoon from Kinshasa. As many as a hundred thousand

Congolese supporters of opposition leader Albert Ilunga are marching on the presidential palace, demanding the immediate resignation of President Silwamba. So far the demonstrations have been peaceful, and the police and the army have been letting the protestors march. Ilunga's support has been building rapidly in the few short weeks since he re-emerged, seemingly from nowhere, to stake his claim to the presidency on the basis of an election six years ago that he is widely believed to have won."

"Annette, can you give us a sense of the mood in the capital? Is the Silwamba administration worried?" The baritone voice of Jim Gregory on the anchor desk in Atlanta sounded tinny through her earpiece.

"Well, Jim, at least among Ilunga's supporters there's a definite sense of optimism. They feel that this is their moment. These demonstrations are simply enormous. I've never seen anything like this in all my years covering Africa. It's still early, but I'd have to say that the Silwamba administration is facing its most serious test ever."

"Thanks, Annette. And now to Afghanistan, where coalition forces are continuing a major push into the Kandahar region . . ." The Angel of Death switched off her earpiece.

Then Annette Cartwright turned and looked out at the still-growing mob on the streets below. For a moment she allowed herself to observe the scene not as a reporter but as a human being.

"Give 'em hell, Albert," she said.

"What did you say, Annette?" her producer asked.

"Nothing."

38

The President of the Republic was a mean drunk. Silwamba picked up the cut-glass tumbler half full of Johnnie Walker Blue on the rocks and threw it at the head of the messenger. Colonel Nkongo of the Black Lions did not duck. He simply shifted his weight almost imperceptibly and let the heavy glass sail harmlessly past his head. There was nothing he could do, however, to dodge the cloud of expensive whiskey that soaked his face and chest.

"How did you let things get to this point?" Silwamba screamed. "I am surrounded by disloyal incompetents and fools!"

Nkongo said nothing. This was far and away the safest course of action. On his best days, Silwamba had a hair-trigger temper and a penchant for violence. Nkongo had once seen him beat a man to death with a bottle of scotch, and then drink the scotch. As commander of the Black Lions, however, it was Nkongo's duty to advise the President on his personal security. The crowd gathered in front of the palace was nonviolent so far, and the forward observers had not seen any weapons among the demonstrators. But, as Stalin had once observed, quantity has a quality all its own, and the sheer numbers gathered in front of the palace represented a clear and present danger to the President. It was Nkongo's job to guard this man, as repugnant as he might find him. The commander of the Black Lions was nothing if not professional.

"You are useless to me, you idiot! I don't know why I waste my breath talking to you."

Silwamba picked up a red phone on his desk. There were no buttons on the phone, no way to dial an outside number. It was serviced by a dedicated operator on call to the President twenty-four hours a day.

"Get me the goddamn American ambassador," he shouted into the receiver. "And you," he said, looking at Nkongo. "You . . . get me a drink."

Nkongo walked over to the bar and poured a generous measure of Johnnie Walker Blue into a crystal tumbler that matched the one lying in pieces on the other side of the room. He added a handful of ice from the bucket and set it down on a coaster on Silwamba's desk. As he did this, Nkongo touched the handle of the M9 Beretta pistol in his belt holster, just to remind himself that he was a soldier and not a valet.

The President drained half of the glass in a single swallow. When he set it back down, he missed the coaster by at least six inches. Although the air conditioner in the office was turned to an aggressively cool setting, Silwamba was perspiring heavily. It was hard to tell whether that was from the booze or the fear. The President loosened his Hermès tie and undid the top button of his sweat-stained collar. A third chin that had been kept prisoner under the collar leaped out to freedom. Almost contemptuously, Silwamba pointed at the extension on the side table, inviting Nkongo to pick it up and listen in.

A click indicated that the call had gone through.

"Mr. President, you are connected to Ambassador Spence," said the voice of the operator.

"Spence? That prick Ilunga is marching on the palace." Silwamba was now slurring his words badly. "There are a hundred thousand low-lifes on the street in front of my house, Ambassador. My own soldiers are too scared to let go of their dicks. I need the cavalry. Marines, Green Berets, SEALs, I don't give a shit, but I want your boys in here now to straighten this all out. They can work with the Lions on the details. They'll need helicopters and tanks. You have my permission to shoot as many of those assholes as is necessary."

"Mr. President, I'm sorry, but it doesn't work like that. I cannot snap my fingers and call up a brigade of Marines. That's our President's decision, and frankly, I don't see anything like that happening. Politically, it would be . . . controversial . . . at best. I'm afraid that you will have to rely on . . . indigenous assets to manage your security challenges."

"What do you fucking mean I'm on my own? After all the business we've done together, you take a walk when things get tough? Is that how it's going to be?"

"From what my people are telling me, the demonstrators are not violent. If you feel you are in imminent danger, however, you may want to think about Switzerland. That's where most of your funds are in any event, and I'm sure our Swiss friends would welcome you for an extended stay in your villa on Lake Constance."

"I don't want the Swiss Guard in their fucking pantaloons." Silwamba was now shouting into the receiver. "I want the U.S. fucking Army here to protect me."

"That's not going to happen, Mr. President. The United States military is not coming to the rescue. You need to think about other options."

Silwamba hung up. He drained his glass.

"Call out the regular army," he said to Nkongo. "And get me another fucking drink."

39

P rivate First Class Issama Bangala loved his Soviet-era armored personnel carrier, the BMP-1, a clumsy but powerful piece of Eastern Bloc machinery. Sergeant Kabila was the BMP commander and his superior, but it was Issama who controlled their movements.

As commander, Kabila stood in the center hatch, from where he could see everything. The gunner sat in the turret to his left. The BMP-1 mounted a 73mm automatic cannon that packed a considerable punch. The driver's chair was just in front of the commander's seat. Issama looked out through a periscope viewing block that gave him a slightly fish-eyed window on the world. In the crew compartment behind them, eight soldiers sat with their knees touching and AK-47s propped muzzles-up on the floor.

Ordinarily, there was nothing Issama liked better than driving his BMP. Today, however, he would have been happy to stay on base and play cards rather than politics. At Kabila's behest, Issama pulled the BMP out of the shaded staging area and onto the road that ran from the main gate through the middle of the camp. A dozen BMPs were lined up on the road with their engines running. Clouds of diesel smoke choked the air. Issama's seat was made of steel. He had wedged a small pillow into the back of the seat that helped cushion the jolts somewhat, but it was still far from a comfortable ride.

By good fortune, Issama's BMP was first in line. This meant that they would not have to breathe in the dust of the BMPs in front of them. It would take at least twenty minutes to reach the palace. The poor loser at the end of the line would spend the entire trip cloaked in the dust of a dozen thirteen-ton killing machines.

"All right," Kabila said from the turret. "Let's move out." It was clear to Issama from the flat tone in the commander's voice that he was no more enthusiastic about this mission than Issama was.

Issama engaged the engine and gave it just enough power to move forward at a sedate five kilometers an hour. As they approached the gate, however, he saw something through his view block that forced him to brake. An eighteen-wheel flatbed truck loaded with cement blocks pulled up sideways in front of the gate and stopped. The driver turned off the engine and jumped out of the cab. Without so much as a backward glance, he ran off into the alleyways of the city. Almost immediately, another heavily laden truck pulled up alongside the first and parked. At least ten more heavy trucks followed, boxing in the gate and trapping the BMPs inside their own base.

Issama waited for orders. Kabila got on the radio and called in their situation to the base commander. It took a long time for the commander to make a decision. Finally, word came over the radio with instructions for the BMPs. *Stand down. Return to the staging area.* It was with a degree of relief that Issama pulled his BMP under the canopies, where the armor was parked out of the sun.

Some of the soldiers returned to their leisurely afternoon pursuits. Others, including Issama, huddled around a shortwave radio listening to the news on the international Radio Sans Frontières. Many of the soldiers sensed that they were on the cusp of an historical event. But whatever happened today in Kinshasa, it would not involve the 15th Mechanized Brigade. Issama was not at all unhappy about that.

The team was small, only ten men, but they were veterans of the fighting in the bush. And while half of them were missing significant parts, including one man with both a prosthetic arm and a wooden leg, they were disciplined and experienced. This counted for considerably more than being of sound body. They were all armed, but they kept their rifles on safety and they were under instructions to fire only in self-defense.

Paul Mbane, a skinny thirty-year-old who had spent half his life under arms, was in command. Mbane's left sleeve was rolled up to his shoulder and pinned off. The Freedom Coalition had taught him to read and write, and helped him find a job in a shop owned by one of Ilunga's supporters. He would have had no compunction about killing for the man who had given him a new lease on life. But that was not his mission.

A truck pulled up in front of the state-run Telecom Congolaise in Kinshasa's Kintambo district. Mbane and his "squad" dismounted. The two private security guards at the main gate with pistols in their belts were only too eager to surrender their sidearms and make themselves scarce. Mbane led one team of five to the President's office. A second team took control of the central telephone exchange. Confronted by a team of heavily armed men, the president of the national telecom, an ally of Silwamba, was surprisingly gracious. Other than holding him, Mbane and his men made no demands of the telecom executive. Everything was calm and orderly. No one was hurt.

That scene was played out across the city at carefully chosen locations: TV and radio stations, newspapers, and government office buildings.

Paul Mbane did not know it, but it was all straight out of the CIA's playbook.

40

I want you to exercise judgment," Colonel Nkongo told his second in command.

Captain Azarias Zola saluted smartly, but it was clear that he was not entirely certain what to make of this ambiguous instruction.

"The President's decision-making is growing increasingly . . . erratic," Nkongo explained. "This unit has a proud reputation and every man in it earns the honor of being a Lion every day. We are the President's guard, but we are also the guardians of our traditions. I will not have this unit or its members stained with accusations of dishonorable or criminal behavior."

"Yes, sir." Zola understood what Nkongo was saying to him. The Lions had received orders to arrest Albert Ilunga for treason and subversion. This would require moving through a crowd of tens of thousands of Ilunga's supporters, seizing him, and then making their way back through the same crowd carrying Ilunga in shackles. With armor support and hundreds of disciplined troops in full riot gear, the mission was straightforward. With the fifty soldiers that Zola could deploy, no matter how superbly trained they might be, the most likely outcome was a massacre of civilians that would focus the disapproving attention of the world on the Black Lions and its commanders.

Zola was a leader of men. He took no small pride in that, and if he had a weakness it was that pride. At six-foot-four and two hundred and fifty pounds of muscle, the captain was an imposing physical figure. But it was the force of his personality and the strength of his will that allowed him to lead men such as these. The Lions were precise on the parade ground, but they were not a ceremonial force. They fought. Their claws were bloody as well as sharp.

In the concrete barracks building, the Lions were getting ready for their mission. They donned body armor and Kevlar helmets. Zola had instructed the men to carry nothing larger than a Kalashnikov or a shotgun. He would not use machine guns or rocket-propelled grenades in the crowded plaza. As always, the men were thorough in their preparations. Even so, Zola detected an undercurrent of unhappiness that was a potentially serious concern. The Lions did not welcome this mission.

The barracks were located in a largely residential area half a mile from the presidential palace. The narrow one-lane street that led from the barracks to the palace was closed to all but official vehicles. This was the only route to the palace from the barracks. It was contrary to good security practices, but the President preferred to keep his Lions close at hand rather than basing them at a more secure facility farther out. On most days, the route was a lively pedestrian street with a vibrant market scene. When Zola led his soldiers out of the barracks, however, the street was nearly deserted. The metal shutters and grates that secured the shops in the evening were pulled down and locked tight. This activated Zola's internal-threat radar. He scanned up and down the street, but did not see anything else out of the ordinary.

The captain led from the front, setting a quick pace that would bring them to the plaza in less than ten minutes. At about the halfway mark, Zola saw a man standing alone in the middle of the street. He was armed, but he held his Kalashnikov in his left hand with the barrel pointed at the ground. Even if Zola had not recognized his face, the brass kitchen faucet around his neck would have marked him as a member of the feared Hammer of God. Joseph Manamakimba stood between the Lions and their designated target. With a clatter of metal, shutters on either side of the street swung up on their rails, and thirty men and boys from the Hammer of God rushed out to stand behind their leader. All wore at least one magical talisman around their necks and all were armed.

Manamakimba smiled broadly in welcome.

"Brave Lions," he said loudly enough for all of Zola's men to hear. "Go back to your den. Today is not a day for hunting. Today is a day for change. By sunset you will have a new president, one worthy of respect and the service of such fine men."

"We have our orders, Joseph Manamakimba. We will pass."

"Whose orders? The orders of a tyrant, a thief, and a murderer? You are better than that, Captain Zola."

Zola considered his position. In addition to the soldiers deployed at street level, the Hammer of God had placed two .30-caliber machine guns on second-story balconies. If Zola's troops tried to bull their way through the Hammer of God forces, the machine guns would rip them apart with enfilading fire. Even if the Lions won the fight, they would be so badly cut up that they would have almost no chance of carrying out their primary mission. And while Zola hated to admit this to himself, part of him agreed with Manamakimba. Silwamba had done nothing admirable in an office he held but did not deserve.

For a moment the two sides stood poised on the point of conflict. Then, with a hand signal, Zola turned his forces around and marched them back in the direction of the barracks. He did not look back at

Manamakimba and the Hammer of God. He was uncertain as to whether this was the right course of action, but there was no going back from this decision. The Black Lions had taken sides.

The humidity was doing brutal things to her hair, and Annette Cartwright thought about covering it with a head scarf. It was not a particularly good look for her, however, so she quickly brushed her hair out and freshened her makeup. While she was not completely satisfied with her appearance, her story was hot. Over the course of the day, the crowds in front of the presidential palace had swelled to hundreds of thousands.

"What's this bit for again?" she asked her producer.

"CNN International. Renee is anchoring." Renee Maksimova was an Oxford-educated Russian and one of a bevy of young attractive women the cable station had hired in an effort to hold on to viewers who were getting more and more of their news online. Annette had never met Renee, but she disliked her on general principle.

"And we go live in three, two, one . . ."

"Good afternoon, Renee. Here in Kinshasa, the pressure on the Silwamba government continues to build. We estimate that there are now more than a quarter million people crowding the plaza in front of the presidential palace demanding Silwamba's immediate resignation. Opposition leader Albert Ilunga has made an appearance and will be addressing the crowd. His primary challenge will be to maintain control of his own supporters and to keep this situation from becoming violent. Serious violence here could bring the Congo's wars home to the capital for the first time, and the fighting that has plagued eastern Congo could take root here as well. Ilunga has to be sensitive to this challenge even as he continues his efforts to topple the weakening Silwamba administration."

The cameraman swung the lens away from Annette and focused

in on the flatbed truck that served as a platform for the speakers. Ilunga was climbing the stairs to the stage accompanied by an attractive Congolese woman whom Annette recognized from earlier rallies. A source had told her that she was a tribal chief from the east and that she had Ilunga's ear. Annette made a mental note to seek her out for an interview.

"Renee, it looks like Ilunga is ready to speak. Let's hear what he has to say."

"Silwamba," he shouted into the microphone, the speakers carrying his voice clearly to the crowd gathered in the plaza while CNN carried it live around the world. One of Giles's more advanced students was part of the team that had taken over RTNC, and he was patching the CNN feed into the RTNC broadcast. Across the country, Congolese citizens with no access to international news were able to listen to Ilunga's speech via the CNN feed.

"Silwamba," Ilunga continued. "You are trapped like a rat in that grotesque palace of yours. You command nothing. You rule nothing. We the people have taken power. Come out, Silwamba, and the people will be merciful. Do not think that you can wait us out. For we have waited long enough . . ."

41

President Silwamba threw a heavy crystal ashtray at the three-thousand-dollar plasma television in his office. The glass shattered and the picture of his hated rival went dark. That did not solve his problem because he could see Ilunga and his growing mob of supporters through the picture window in his office. He could even hear the taunting of the crowd as they called for him to step down. Nkongo and Zola stood ramrod straight on the carpet in front of his desk.

"I send you out to do the simplest damn job and all you come back with are excuses. I asked you to arrest one unarmed little man and you can't even do that. You two are a disgrace."

"Mr. President," Colonel Nkongo said. "The risk of civilian casualties and the unexpected appearance of the Hammer of God in the city made the costs of the operation too high. We regret that we could not carry out your instructions in this instance, and we urge you to consider evacuating the city."

"Evacuate?"

"Yes, sir. We have a helicopter on call, ready to ferry you to a military airfield and a Gulfstream standing by with a flight plan for Switzerland. At this point, Mr. President, this is the best available option."

"I will not hand my country over to that rabble. If you cannot take him alive, I want him dead."

Silwamba walked around his desk and stood looking Nkongo right in the eye. The whiskey smell of Silwamba's breath was almost overpowering and his eyes were bloodshot and angry.

"I asked you if you understood me, Colonel."

"Yes, Mr. President, but the Black Lions cannot support you in that. We have our sworn duty to you, but we also have sworn an oath to our country. We have found the balance between these responsibilities. I urge you to take our advice and evacuate . . . sir."

On the wall next to the broken television, there was a gun rack. Silwamba selected a wicked-looking Russian Dragunov sniper rifle and held it out for Zola.

"Captain, I trust that you know how to use this."

Zola nodded. He did not, however, take the gun.

"Take this rifle, Captain, and shoot Albert Ilunga."

Zola did nothing.

"Shoot him!"

Zola stood stock-still and looked out into the middle distance. Nkongo stepped forward as though to take the rifle away from Silwamba. The President raised the gun in a menacing fashion and Nkongo stepped back. He had no doubt that Silwamba stored the gun fully loaded.

"Goddamn you. Never send a boy to do a man's job. I will kill him myself."

Silwamba was visibly drunk and it took him a moment to get one of the side windows open so that he would have a clear field of fire. It was not more than five hundred meters to the target. For Zola or any other experienced sharpshooter, it was not a difficult shot. Even sober, Sil-wamba would have had a difficult time. Since the President was drunk, Zola did not fear too much for Ilunga's safety. But even if he missed his target, he was going to hit somebody. There were simply too many people in the plaza. When he squeezed the trigger, someone was going to die.

Silwamba raised the Dragunov to his shoulder and lined up his shot. He took time with his aim, but Zola could see his arms shaking. The President was so drunk it was a wonder he could stand, let alone shoot.

The two shots were like thunder. For a moment Zola blinked . . . not certain if he could believe what he had just seen. Colonel Nkongo had drawn the pistol at his belt and the President of the Republic was dead.

42

The ring tone, a snippet of King Kester Emeneya's "Everybody," indicated that the call had come in from a specific number. It was the agreed-upon signal. The two men standing on the corner of Kasavubu and Rue de Lisala walked casually down the street until they reached the headquarters of Consolidated Mining. Each man had a duffel bag slung over one shoulder. The straps on the bags were taut. Whatever they were carrying was heavy. The windows at street level were smoked glass. This both helped keep the interior cool and lent the operation an aura of mystery. Reaching into the bags, the two men pulled out lengths of iron pipe that they threw at the windows, shattering them into thousands of smoke-colored fragments. The men then pulled four grenades from their bags and tossed them through the window into the lobby of the building. The grenades did not explode, but they quickly filled the lower level of the building with thick, acrid smoke. Before the security guards could even make it outside, the attackers were gone.

Inside Consolidated Mining's headquarters, alarms were blaring and emergency lighting tried to cut through the smoke that was now filling the building. The Head of Security ordered the building evacuated. It was all done according to standard procedures . . . which were available on the company's intranet site and easily accessible to anyone logged on to the Consolidated Mining system.

The crowd in front grew quieter when the great doors of the palace swung open and two soldiers wearing black berets that marked them as Lions marched confidently down the steps. One of the soldiers was carrying something under one arm. They stopped at the base of the flagpole in the circle and lowered the gaudy gold and white flag that was Silwamba's personal banner. There was an almost eerie silence as the crowd waited to see what would happen next. The two soldiers fixed another flag to the ropes, and when the crowd saw the blue and gold flag of the Democratic Republic of the Congo ascending the pole, they broke into loud and rapturous applause. "Ilunga *is* President!" they shouted.

Standing proud and straight, the two soldiers opened the gates to the palace and let the flood of people onto the grounds.

"And there you have it, Renee," Annette said, as her cameraman captured the spectacle for a global audience. "The Silwamba government has fallen. Albert Ilunga has taken power. And we await the reaction of world leaders to these stunning developments."

"Thank you, Annette . . . and now over to Jim Stevens for an update on world sports . . ."

From the Victory Monument, Alex and Jonah had an unobstructed view of the flag-raising that signaled the change in government. An enormous wave of relief swept through Alex's body. The people had spoken and Ilunga was their choice. Internationally, the fact that the movement had been nonviolent would make it possible for the United States, Europe, and leading African nations to embrace the new government.

A helicopter flew in low over the crowd as though it was looking to land. Alex recognized the Bell 222 that he had seen on the roof of the Consolidated Mining building. As the helicopter banked over the crowd, Alex had a clear view inside the cockpit. Henri Saillard was at the controls.

Instead of landing, the helicopter made a single pass over the crowd and circled the presidential palace. Then Saillard flew out over the Congo River in the direction of Brazzaville.

Jonah Keeler pulled a cell phone out of his pocket and started to dial a number. He dialed by touch, his eyes fixed on the helicopter. It was a long sequence of numbers, longer than was necessary for a simple call. Keeler's intention suddenly seemed clear.

"Don't do it, Jonah," Alex said forcefully, reaching for the phone just as the Station Chief hit the green "transmit" button. Halfway across the Congo River, where the water depth was greater than one hundred feet, Henri Saillard's helicopter exploded in a bright ball of flame. It was later rumored that a fortune in diamonds was scattered on the riverbed along with the wreckage of the Bell and the unrecovered body of Henri Saillard. The currents on that stretch of the river were especially treacherous, however, and the bottom was a ten-foot bed of silt. Those few treasure hunters who tried were never able to prove that the rumors were true.

43

Getting out of the Foreign Service was a damned sight easier than getting in. It had taken nearly a year and a half from the day Alex took the first written exam until the day he took the oath of office as an FSO. Getting out had taken about five minutes with the Embassy Management Counselor. He had signed half a dozen forms, turned in his badge and his hard drive, and handed over the keys to his house. His RAV4 sat in the Embassy lot, stripped of its diplomatic plates. After eight years of service to the United States, Alex was on his own.

He had no regrets about leaving the Service. The events of the last few months had changed him, and there was simply no going back to the life he had once thought was all he wanted. Alex was pleased, however, that he was leaving on his terms. Shortly after Silwamba's fall, Spence had been recalled to Washington for "consultations." It was understood that he was never coming back to Kinshasa. Meanwhile, the charges against Alex had not only been dropped, they had disappeared. As far as official Washington was concerned, nothing that had happened had ever happened. The director of the Africa Bureau's executive office had even called to ask if Alex wanted to throw his hat in the ring for the Deputy Chief of Mission opening in Tanzania. It was surprisingly easy to turn down this plum assignment. He had plans that did not include the Department of State, and he was eager to embrace the future. Before he could do that, however, there was one more stop to make. His fixer, Leonard, had insisted on driving him.

"You know, there's a certain irony in this," Leonard observed, as he forced his aging Citroën laboriously through Kinshasa's tangled traffic. "God alone knows that I would rather be living in California than the Congo . . . and I suspect that you would be happier here. Man plans, God laughs."

"I reckon you might be right about that. I don't really know what's going to happen to me next, but I do know that it's going to be my decision and not Uncle Sam's."

They pulled up to the gate in front of the presidential palace.

"Security won't let me park here," Leonard said. "I'll wait for you in the lot across the street. Give the old man my regards."

"Thanks, Leonard. I appreciate this. You've been a good friend when I needed a friend."

The guard at the gate seemed unimpressed when Alex told him that he had an appointment with the President. But his name was on the right lists and he was buzzed through the small pedestrian entrance next to the larger gate that admitted vehicle traffic. He walked around the circle to the massive front steps. The Congolese flag flying on the flagpole at the center of the circle was just one concrete example of the changes that were under way in the city. The palace itself felt like a very different place. On his first visit, the building had seemed empty and lifeless. Now it was bustling with government officials and staff, visitors, and even, Alex was amused to note, what looked like a tour group. That was definitely not something you would have seen under Silwamba.

A harried-looking receptionist behind a desk at the far end of the lobby apologized because the President was running late. She asked Alex if he would mind waiting in the salon on the second floor.

"It won't be for long," she assured him. "I'm sorry to ask this of you. The President has been overscheduled today, I'm afraid."

The waiting room was across the hall from the President's private office. It was spacious and well appointed with comfortable chairs and tables stacked with newspapers and magazines. There were two other people in the room. One of them was Jonah Keeler. Alex focused on the second man in the room. He recognized him immediately. Garret Lockhart was the head of Africa operations for Altera Natural Resources. ANR was one of the largest minerals-and-mining companies on the continent. Consolidated's success at the political game had kept ANR frozen out of the valuable Congo concessions, but Saillard's death and Ilunga's rise to power had stripped the company of its primary patrons. The Congo was once again wide open for competition.

Lockhart was a large, beefy Texan whose homespun aphorisms disguised a nimble mind and a deep knowledge of Africa. He was based out of ANR's regional headquarters in Johannesburg but traveled widely. His fluent French and Portuguese had never quite lost the twang of West Texas and Lockhart liked it that way. For his audience with Ilunga, the mining executive was wearing a four-thousand-dollar Italian suit and cowboy boots. It was the boots rather than the suit that seemed like an affectation.

ANR was part of a family of companies that included Altera Petroleum. It was Altera that had won the rights to explore for oil and gas in Western Sudan after the genocide in Darfur. Although only a second-tier player in the energy industry, Altera had outmaneuvered a number of the major multinationals to claim the prize. There had been rumors of payouts to senior Sudanese officials, but nothing could be proven. Now ANR's Senior Director for Africa was here with Jonah Keeler to see the new President of the Congo. A number of disconnected pieces began to snap together in Alex's mind. He did not at all like the shape that was emerging.

Jonah seemed completely at ease and not at all concerned about the conclusions Alex might draw from his apparent partnership with Lockhart.

"Hello, Alex," Keeler said with genuine warmth in his voice. "I trust you know Garret Lockhart."

"By reputation. What the hell is going on here, Jonah?"

"Garret, would you excuse us for a few minutes?" Keeler asked his companion.

Lockhart obliged without complaint, tipping a thankfully imaginary cowboy hat in Alex's direction before leaving them alone in the waiting room. Keeler pointed at the chair Lockhart had been occupying. Alex did not sit down.

"What's this about?" he asked again. "I'm getting the idea that you have not been straight with me about the people you represent." Alex kept his cool, but the undercurrent of tension in his voice was unmistakable.

"I have twenty-five years with the CIA. Straight's not really our thing." Keeler smiled.

"Tell me more about the people you work with in Washington, the ones who have been trying to take down the Africa Working Group. They're not really so different in their goals, are they?"

"Nope, not really. They're more like rivals to the Working Group than mortal enemies, I'm afraid. Mind you, we like to think of ourselves as a little more subtle and a little less brutal than our competitors. The Working Group had some class-A talent, but they got greedy."

"You used me. You used me to destroy your competition and open the door to your friends at ANR. And you almost got me killed in the process."

Keeler rose and stood at the window looking out on the plaza in front of the palace. It was crowded as always, but nothing like it had been in the heady days and hours leading up to Silwamba's demise. The Station Chief was quiet for a moment as he considered his response.

"That wasn't my intention. I did hope that I could use you to get Spence and Saillard and the rest of the Working Group off balance. I thought that if I could get the Working Group to overreact, we could take advantage. Turns out, though, that you're a resourceful little bastard. I can't really blame Saillard or Viggiano for misjudging you, but Spence really should have known better."

"So you hung me out as bait."

"I helped you. You were the one who came to me about Busu-Mouli. You wanted information and I helped you get it. You were the one who wanted to know what Consolidated Mining was doing in eastern Congo and I helped you see that. You came to me to help you plan a coup and I helped you with that too. Let's not forget who the *demandeur* was in this relationship. Your interests and mine happened to coincide, that's all."

Another piece of the puzzle clicked into place.

"You put the Busu-Mouli file in Spence's safe, didn't you?" Alex said. "You broke into the safe before I got there and left it for me to find."

Keeler shrugged.

"We have a source in Executive Solutions, so we knew what was coming. I wanted you to know it too, so I wrote up a letter describing the arrangements and left it for you along with a couple of satellite shots I ordered up from Langley. It was all true. It just wasn't real. I figured you'd go looking for answers there. If you hadn't done it yourself, I was going to make contact with you and steer you in that direction. You did it all on your own, though. I've got to hand it to you."

"That's pretty self-serving, Jonah."

"And if I hadn't left that file for you, your girlfriend would be dead right now and every building in her village burned to the ground. Is that really the way you would prefer things?"

"No. You're right about that."

"Listen, Alex, most of what I told you *is* true. We and ANR really do look at things differently than the Working Group. Most of us aren't old Cold Warriors, for one thing. We're younger, more flexible, more business oriented. We can do a lot of good in the countries we operate in, and all we want in return is a certain level of preferential treatment from the powers that be. That's all. If you're not greedy, there's enough to go around for everyone."

"Except the people."

"There's something for them too. We build clinics and schools. We try to contribute to the societies we operate in. It's part of our long-term approach."

Keeler stepped closer to Alex. It was a gesture of intimacy, but it also seemed somewhat mannered, like another tip from the Agency's training manual "How to Win Friends and Influence Them to Betray Their Country."

"Alex, I think there'd be room for someone like you in our organization. You're smart and connected, and you know this continent better than just about anyone else in government. You could do great things with us . . . meaningful things. You could stay with State if you want or, if you prefer, Garret would be more than happy to find a place for you at ANR. Marie too, I suspect. Good mining engineers are in high demand right now. Consolidated was a rotten organization. We're not like that. We're different."

"Is that what you're going to tell Albert?"

"Hey, he's just moved up from double-A ball to the major leagues. He's going to need some friends to help him learn the game. We're ready to do that for him. Plus, he owes me. I saved his life after all."

Alex was suddenly certain that Jonah had planted the bomb in Ilunga's car himself and left a loose wire that he could conveniently and dramatically "spot" just in time. He was equally certain that the CIA man would never own up to that particular stunt.

"Albert is not like Silwamba, you know."

"I know."

"He's not looking for an easy score. I don't think you'll find him corruptible."

"We'll see . . . You know what they say about power."

The door opened and Lockhart entered, accompanied by the aide who had shown Alex to the waiting area.

"The President is ready for you," the aide said to Keeler.

"Thank you."

Alex stepped between Jonah and door.

"One last thing, Jonah." Alex kept his voice low to keep the exchange private. "The Sudan. You told me the Working Group was behind what happened in Darfur."

"No. That's not correct. I told you that they might have been."

"But they weren't, were they? Altera Petroleum got those contracts. You were behind that. Everything you just told me was bullshit."

Keeler's smile reminded Alex of a crocodile's.

"You figure it out, kid. I gotta go. The head of state is waiting for us. My offer's still good. You know how to reach me."

The door closed and Alex was alone in the waiting room. The room felt oppressively hot. There suddenly seemed no point in his meeting with Ilunga. Albert would know soon enough what he was dealing with and he would make the decisions he had to make.

Alex walked down the hall and down the stairs to the lobby. He stopped at the reception desk to tell the scheduler that he had been called away for an emergency and would be back in touch to reschedule the meeting. Then he walked out into the tropical heat.

As he had promised, Leonard was waiting for him.

"You ready?" he asked. Alex's bags were in the backseat of the Citroën. He had three hours before his flight.

"Yeah. Let's go. There's a girl I've been dying to see."

EPILOGUE

Amazingly enough, the satellite phone still worked. At some point, someone in the State Department's administrative offices would realize that no one could account for the phone, and they would stop paying the bills. The department's budgeting process was so fragmented and incoherent, however, that that day could be a long time coming. Alex would keep using the phone until it stopped working, giving thanks for once for the inherent inefficiencies of government.

He was sitting in the shade of his porch with a cold beer perched precariously on the railing. It was all new construction and the wood still smelled of sap and sawdust. For the first time since Darfur, he felt at peace. The dreams were not gone, but they came less frequently and were less intense. Psychologically and emotionally, he was in a good place. Still, he had deliberately been putting off this conversation. It would be painful, but it was something that he felt he had to do.

The number that he dialed was familiar. The phone connected with an Inmarsat-3 satellite in geosynchronous orbit that bounced the signal to an Intelsat satellite crossing over North America that beamed the signal down to an earthbound receiver. Three seconds after Alex hit the "call" button, a phone rang in the library of an eighteenth-century farmhouse on Maryland's eastern shore. Ambassador Spencer answered after only three rings.

"Hello, Alex. I've been expecting your call. Of course, my caller ID just identified you as me . . ."

"That's all I ever wanted to be."

"I understand. I'm sorry that I disappointed you in the end. That's only supposed to happen with the children you raise. Not the ones you choose for yourself later in life."

Although he had steeled himself for this exchange, Alex struggled to keep the catch out of his voice.

"I've been trying to understand why you did this, not just to me but to yourself. I don't know that either of us is ever really going to know the answer. You're a better man than that. I hope that you're willing to try to prove it. There's a lot of life ahead of you in which to make amends."

"That's kind of you. But I don't believe that I've ever felt quite so . . . old."

Alex had spent several vacations with Spence and his family at their farm in Oxford, Maryland. It was right on the Chesapeake Bay, with a big sloping lawn that led down to the water. From the back porch, you could see the sunset over the bay. For a man such as Spence, however, for whom the exercise of national power had been his whole life, retirement was simply a short prelude to death. The word had gone out in foreign policy circles in Washington that Spence had been forced out because of some mysterious malfeasance on his part. It did not take more than that for the invitations to seminars and soirees to stop coming. Spence was not only out of government, he was also out of public life and there was no immediate prospect of rehabilitation. No matter how beautiful the surroundings, Alex knew that this would gnaw at the soul of his former friend and onetime mentor.

"Spence, there's something I need to ask you. Were you part of the decision to kill me? Did you agree to that?"

The pause was considerably longer than the two-second satellite delay.

"I had nothing to do with that," Spence said finally. "I hope you believe me and I know that you have every right not to. I agreed with the others that we needed to get you out of the Congo and back to the States. But that's all. The espionage charges were a placeholder. They would have kept you out of circulation for a while. Then they would have gone away. It was Viggiano and Saillard who had other ideas. I thought I was in control of the operation, but it turned out that it was in control of me. You're as much family to me as my own girls. If that slippery bastard Keeler told you that Viggiano was acting on my orders, that's another of his damn lies. He's Agency. It's a habit. They lie even when it's easier to tell the truth."

"Thanks. I needed to know."

"Did you get the news about Al-Nour? He's dead. The Sudanese killed him. It looks like he had become too much of a liability."

"It doesn't really matter, does it?"

Alex felt nothing at learning of the death of the man whom he had seen murder his daughter's grandfather. This surprised him somewhat. Al-Nour's death would make no difference in Darfur. Someone else would take his place. The problem was the system that created and rewarded men like Al-Nour. That system was bigger than all of them and that system had not changed.

"I heard from those few of my 'friends' who will still talk to me that you left the Service. I was sorry to hear that. You're a hell of a diplomat. I know that Mother State will take you back in a heartbeat. I hope you'll change your mind about that."

"It's too late. I'm done with that life and there's no going back. I'm ready for what comes next."

"Are you going into business?"

"I suppose I am."

"Consulting?"

"No, Spence. I'm going into the mining business . . ."

A lex hung up. From the porch, he could look out over almost the entire village of Busu-Mouli and admire the progress the villagers had made in rebuilding from the battle with the *genocidaires*. Since Manamakimba and the Hammer of God had come to Busu-Mouli, the various rebel groups still battling in the bush had given the town a wide berth. The village was peaceful and growing more prosperous as the mining operation had become more efficient and productive. Alex had been a part of that. He and Mputu were constantly tinkering with the equipment while Marie managed the overall mining operation. It was the most satisfying work that he had ever done.

In the village square, some kids were playing soccer with one of the new balls that Alex had brought with him from Kinshasa. Charlie and Jean-Pierre were among them. Anah had been kicking the ball around with the boys earlier. Now she was sitting under a nearby mango tree playing with a wooden doll that Marie had given her. The doll had a head of coarse goat hair and a beautiful dress that looked like the one Marie had worn to the funeral after the battle with the *genocidaires*. The three children, all newcomers to the village, had become close friends. Charlie lived with Manamakimba and his new girlfriend, a local Busu-Mouli girl. Jean-Pierre lived with Alex and Marie, sharing a room with Anah. He was family now. The Luba adoption ceremony had been a simple affair, but the party that followed had lasted for two days.

Alex sipped his beer and watched the children playing. The sheer exuberance of the game was a reason to feel joy. Anah put her doll down and rejoined the soccer game. He looked at his watch. Marie and Mputu were expecting him at the mine in a little less than an hour. They were planning to test some new commercial-grade equipment that they had picked up for a song when Consolidated Mining had been forced to liquidate its operations in eastern Congo. It was good, solid gear that should make it possible for them to reach much deeper into the hills. The irony was icing on the cake. He decided to join Anah and the boys for some soccer before heading up to the mine. Even if he was a little late, Alex was sure that Marie would not mind. After all, they had plenty of time.

A NOTE FROM THE AUTHOR

THE DEMOCRATIC REPUBLIC OF THE CONGO:
THE REAL STORY

This is a work of fiction. None of the main characters in the story are real, although I do think the world would be a better place if there were more Albert Ilungas in it and fewer Silwambas. What is not fiction, alas, is the immense suffering that has been inflicted on the people of the Democratic Republic of the Congo over the last twenty years. The Rwandan genocide was the precipitating event that triggered the First Congo War (1996–1997). During and immediately after the genocide, more than a million people from Rwanda crossed into what was then Zaire as refugees. Among them were many of the perpetrators of the violence in Rwanda: the *genocidaires*. Rwandan forces crossed the border to battle *genocidaire* militia groups and the conflict widened, ultimately involving troops from half a dozen countries. The Congo is a baroque cathedral of violence.

The First Congo War was followed quickly by the Second Congo War, which began in 1998. By the time it ended (at least on paper) in 2003, more than five million people were dead, most of them from disease and starvation. The official end of the war brought neither peace nor prosperity to the country, which had changed its name from Zaire to the Democratic Republic of the Congo in 1997. Violence, hunger, and disease still claim an estimated 45,000 lives a month. Nearly three million people have died as a direct or indirect consequence of fighting and political unrest since the signing of the so-called Global and All-Inclusive Agreement on Transition in the DRC. A massive multibillion-dollar UN mission in Congo has done little to provide peace and security.

Cross-border trade in what came to be known as conflict minerals—including gold, diamonds, tungsten, and coltan—fueled the fighting in the Congo. The country's vast mineral wealth gave all of the parties to the violence, Congolese and foreign, both the motive and means to keep fighting. One recent study estimated that armed militia groups control more than half of the mines in the Congo's eastern region. The mines often rely on forced labor, with miners—including children—working shifts up to forty-eight hours long under dangerous conditions. The militiamen use casual violence and rape as tools to control the civilian population.

As of this writing, the DRC is once again under threat of a wider war. M23, a rebel group based in the eastern province of North Kivu, seized control of the city of Goma and its one million inhabitants. The M23 is a relatively new group, but the scenes of widespread fighting in the DRC's wild northeast are all too familiar.

This is necessarily a shorthand sketch of an incredibly complicated and deeply saddening situation. There are numerous resources available, however, for readers who would like to learn more about the DRC's tragic modern history—www.refugeesinternational.org and www.crisis group.org are good places to begin. For those who would like to take a deeper look at Congolese history, I recommend the incomparable *King Leopold's Ghost* by Adam Hochschild.

Readers looking to do something to help the people of Congo can consider making contributions through one of the reputable international aid agencies operating in the country. Caritas, CARE, the International Committee of the Red Cross, and Oxfam International are just four of the many organizations active in providing relief and development assistance to those in need. Ultimately, of course, the people of that beautiful but embattled country need more than aid. They need a chance.

A disclaimer: The views expressed here are my own and do not necessarily represent those of the U.S. Department of State.

DEMOCRATIC REPUBLIC OF THE CONGO

© 2014 Jeffrey L. Ward

CHRIS LYNCH

SPECIAL FORCES

GOOD DEVILS

BOOK 3

WITHDRAWN

SCHOLASTIC PRESS ★ NEW YORK

Library of Congress Cataloging-in-Publication
Data available

ISBN 978-0-545-86168-7
1 2020
First edition, December 2020

Printed in the U.S.A. 23
Book design by Christopher Stengel

CHAPTER ONE

Gabe-Real

This is how I got here. As for exactly where *here* is, more in a bit.

Love is what got me here. I love and respect my brother so much that I became him.

Borrowed him. Stole him, some might say.

Dallas is my older brother. He's not my big brother, because I'm twice his size, give or take. On the inside, he's every bit as large as me, if not larger. We'll never know what would have happened if he'd grown to full size, but he never did, largely due to a severe case of something called scoliosis, which he's had since he was about eight years old. It means his spine is so twizzled around that his ribs are squashed on his left side and his shoulder blade pushes to the right.

That spine snakes up through him from tail to throat. It even speaks for itself, since much of the time Dallas's voice wheezes, on account of his squeezed heart and lungs.

My name is Gabriel. Or it used to be, anyway. I'm six feet three inches tall and weigh 220 pounds. Up until not long ago, I was a two-way star for my high school's football team. I started at quarterback—because why bother with anything else if you have the choice?—and middle linebacker. Played nearly every down, every game. I also threw things—javelin, hammer—for our track and field squad. Throwing things can be very satisfying.

Good as I was at all that, I may have been an even better skier. My town has the tallest ski jump in the whole United States, and I sacrificed many bones, ligaments, teeth, and what have you to mastering that thing.

But I mastered it, eventually.

Everything I did, my brother was there, clapping and huffing me on. He wanted me to be better and better and best at everything. It also gave him his own special style of joy to participate alongside me. Through me.

My father was there for a lot of it, too. Pa. Even though he spent most of his waking hours working. He worked full-time at the paper mill in town. He worked part-time up farther north, logging all over the Great North Woods, providing timber to feed that mill and several others in the area. Even his play was kind of like work: hunting, fishing, and trapping things to eat or sell in order to make life that little bit better for us. (Though not exactly better for the things he'd hunt, fish, or trap.)

That life was lived primarily in Berlin. That would be the Berlin in the great state of New Hampshire, as opposed to the one that exists in the depraved state of evil and chaos on the other side of the Atlantic Ocean.

We had a second home, too, which made us lucky indeed. That was the result of all that hard work my pa put in—though I helped, too, by working as much as I could. The big house, the one with two bedrooms, was in Berlin. The second had no bedrooms, because it was more of a hunting, fishing, trapping shack. It was sixty or so miles north in Pittsburg, also in the great state of New Hampshire and hard by the border with Canada. Close enough that you could hit a golf ball from Pittsburg to Quebec. Which I would do if golf wasn't such a jerk sport.

Very international, that northern arrowhead of New Hampshire is. We've got a lot of French Canadians in Pittsburg, and a lot of Norwegians in Berlin. That's how we wound up with the Nansen Ski

Club, and then the jump, "The Big Nansen." That was one of Berlin's big claims to fame and where I wound up claiming my own piece of fame when the first Olympic trials in ski jumping were held there in 1938.

I was almost thirteen years old.

Technically, I was too young to participate without parental consent. But I was more than ready in every other way. On the other hand, Dallas *was* old enough . . .

So, at the age of almost thirteen, I qualified for the United States Olympic team by jumping as Dallas Greene. Team selectors were none the wiser.

Problem was, everyone else in town was plenty the wiser. Including my father, who thought I was still a child and ought to be living the life of one.

I was an Olympian for about five days.

It was a tasty five days, however.

No matter how much high school football and track and field I participated in, nothing ever quite matched that feeling again. I was restless, always restless. Got in lots of fights, too. Life seemed to be coming up unsatisfying and unfair. Life needed to be punched.

Dallas was also restless. And while he didn't get in

a lot of fights, he was more and more in a fighting mood. If *I* felt life was unsatisfactory and unfair, he had six thousand times more right to feel that way.

Then came December 1941. And everyone everywhere was in a fighting mood.

The first Saturday after Pearl Harbor we were in a regional playoff game down in Franconia. We were killing them. Slaughtering them. If we were still little and had the slaughter rule, where you stopped the game when one team was mauling the other, this game would have been mercifully stopped.

Fortunately, there was no slaughter rule at this level. So we slaughtered them. Then slaughtered them some more.

Don't know if I was angrier than everybody else, but what I do know is that, on this day, I was better than everybody else. I was throwing passes so hard and bullet straight that eventually my receivers were missing catches on purpose to protect their delicate hands. But no matter, I took it all on myself after a while. Three out of every four offensive downs became running plays, run by *me*.

And run *at* me. Since I was also our team's middle linebacker, I got this thing in my head. I felt like if I took it to the other team's ML—took it to him

consistently and ferociously—I was somehow winning a battle with myself. Like he was me, only I was
the better me. I ran at this poor sap so relentlessly it
became like the guy with the ball was pursuing the
defender. I guess I was. Pursuing and *trampling*.

And on defense, I was the disrupter general. In my
mind, my teammates were on the field just to hold
their positions. But the job of attacking the opposing
team was mine. That is the beauty of middle linebacker, when you do it right. If you want the thing,
it's yours.

And I wanted it.

Pass plays, run plays. If I was blitzing or stuffing
the run or harassing the sad little quarterback they
fielded, none of it mattered. I sacked the QB more
times than I could count. (That's a lie. I can actually
count to seven.) I saw running backs practically tack-
ling *themselves* to avoid being forced into contact
with me. I even intercepted two passes, the first two
of my life. I was embarrassed for them.

Dallas was there, cheering me along as best he
could. Pa was there, thundering his love at me above
all other sounds just by calling my name. There was a
small traveling contingent of Berliners barking out my
pretty great nickname, *Gabe-Real! Gabe-Real! Gabe-*

Real! so persistently that eventually the Franconia fans had to succumb and join in.

The final score was probably 65,000 to nothing, but the scoreboard only went up to two digits, so we left it as an indistinct yet comprehensive victory.

One would think that it would have been an unbeatable day. Short of something along the lines of making an Olympic team, say.

"That was the greatest thing I ever saw" was Dallas's recap of the game.

"Son," Pa added, simply shaking his head in wonderment. It would be fair to say my father was a man of few syllables, so that counted as a mouthful.

So everybody was satisfied, right?

Thing was, to be fair, dominating in this game, in this region, at this level, was not a herculean feat. I knew what I was achieving, and what I wasn't.

So that was the day I quit.

Quit football. Quit track and field. Quit skiing. Quit school. Quit New Hampshire. Quit being a kid.

I waited until the first week of May 1942 to make it anything like official, however. That was nothing to do with finishing out the school year, though, and everything to do with fishing.

Spring fishing season starts when the lakes all ice out and start dumping their bait fish into the Connecticut river, with the salmon running right behind them.

I don't even like salmon, but that's not the point. The point is that fishing is the one outdoor activity my father, my brother, and I all enjoy together. And that means we hang around riverbanks and inside the shack for good long hours, talking about stuff if we have stuff we want to talk about.

I had stuff I wanted to talk about in May 1942. So did Dallas.

"I would kill to be able to fight," Dallas said, seemingly to the fish he was casting for.

Pa and I said nothing right away. Neither did the fish.

"I want to fight," I said eventually, making a point of addressing my father directly in the way my brother had not.

Pa looked at me while continuing to cast. "Me?" he said, straight-faced. "You saying you want to fight *me*, boy?"

"No," I said, "not you, Pa."

"Good," he said. "'Cause, big as you are, we both know I'd still kick your butt."

"Yeah," I said, "we both know that."

"Ahem," Dallas said, raising a hand in the air.

"Right," I said, "all three of us know that."

We all went silent again for a bit. He was a genius at that, my father, sniffing out a conversation he figured he did not want to have—which was most of them—and derailing it before it got any traction. But this one was too important, so I had to persevere.

"I have an idea, Pa," I ventured.

"Oh, don't do *that*, Gabriel. Your ma had an idea once, and where is she now?"

"I know, Pa, I know—"

"You do? Tell me, then, because I have no clue. And she owes me money."

Evidently, the old man had sussed out my seriousness on this one and was prepared to employ his full powers of digression. I would have to soldier on.

"Listen, Pa," I said.

"I am listening," he said. "What else have I been doing here but listening? And maybe a little fishing when you give me a chance—"

"Pa," Dallas rasped. Dad pays heed when my brother speaks up. And he was speaking up now, because he knew what I was doing. We'd only passed a few words between us regarding my big idea, but he knew what I was thinking before I even knew I was thinking it. He always knew.

"If Dallas could go to war, he'd be in it already," I said. "That's right, isn't it, Dallas?"

"Yup. And I'd be good, too, if they'd just let me. I'd be a killer killer against those Nazis."

"Right," I said, "you would."

"He can't, though," Pa said. "And that is that."

"Maybe that doesn't have to be that," I said.

"What would that be, then?" Pa asked. "If it wasn't that?"

"Maybe it would be this . . ." I said. "Maybe I could do his fighting for him."

"You're too young, boy. And *that* is that."

"I could pass for old enough. You know it."

"But you are *not* old enough."

"He is if he's me," Dallas interjected.

Now a real silence descended. Even the Connecticut seemed to cease its burbling.

Long silences were nothing unusual in this family, but this one was making me squirm.

"Pa," I said, attempting to get the jump on him. "Remember when you wouldn't let me be an Olympian ski jumper?"

"Oh, again with this?" he said.

Back to silence. It was a solid fifteen minutes, which is nothing in fish time but a lifetime in my time.

"So, what? I'm supposed to let you join the Army as Dallas, while I keep Dallas with me, as Gabriel?"

"If you like," I said.

Another fifteen minutes.

"Well," Pa said with a hint of somberness that was just detectable below his normal tone, "he *is* a lot cheaper to feed than you are."

CHAPTER TWO
Dallas Alice

I wanted a fight that mattered. One that mattered to me, and to my brother, and ultimately to my father as well.

I got that fight. And a good many others to boot.

Fair enough, since I had joined a fighting force. With my proud name and the birth certificate to prove it, I left Gabriel Greene behind in the capable care of my brother and signed on at the recruiting office for the United States Army Infantry.

Dallas Greene's dream was coming true.

Sent down to Fort Benning in hot, sweaty Georgia, I took on my basic training with an eye toward the Jump School and eventually advancing to the airborne infantry.

But my goodness, was Georgia roasting, humid, and irritating.

Being told what to do, all day and every day, also turned out to be an annoyance. Especially in the swelter. Probably should have considered that earlier.

Basic was pretty basic—straightforward and undemanding if you showed up in halfway decent condition. Lots of runs in the sun, the infernal sun, with and without full packs. Obstacle courses. Hand-to-hand combat training. Rifle range. Endless and pointless marching drills. Truth is, except for the brutal weather, it was the kind of stuff a guy might do on his own just for fun. I had been to summer camps that felt pretty similar.

And like summer camp, I even sort of buddied up with a guy. I was usually good for just one buddy at a time, whatever the situation, because that's just how I am. In basic, I lined up with a bunkmate chosen for the brilliant reason that he looked something like me. Big as me, linebackerish like me, and kind of outgoing, which I kind of definitely am not. That made him an ideal pal to sit with at chow and line up alongside for silly drills.

"Silly drillies," my pal, Kelvin, said as he grabbed my foot one morning during the second week of camp. I was lying on my bunk, digesting breakfast, when he nearly dragged me off and onto the floor.

"All right," I said, kicking him halfway across the room, which he seemed to enjoy.

"My, but you Texans are feisty in the morning," he said, laughing.

Because the Army is the Army, nicknames are a big deal and often have to do with a guy's place of origin. Because my name was Dallas, even though it wasn't, the boys concluded I was from Dallas, Texas, which I wasn't. And anyway, why would a guy show up from any city already with the nickname of that city? Did they just conclude that everybody in Dallas, Texas, went around calling everybody else Dallas? That would be one confusing city right there, I can tell you that.

And it would have gotten my comrades every kind of mixed up if I dared try to enlighten them about my being from Berlin, and Pittsburg, and that neither of those places were actually where they would probably think they were.

So I didn't bother mentioning the great state of New Hampshire. Let them think I was a Texan for all I cared. Accent's pretty similar anyway, right?

"I'll show you a feisty Texan," I said. (I was perhaps by now losing all connection to what was real or not.) Kelvin and I squared up for our turn as the feature match in hand-to-hand combat.

We really were well-matched. He was as strong as

I was, and as tough. And from the helpless grin on his face as we waded in toward each other, he relished the fight every bit as much as me or anybody else.

As we approached, arms raised in attacking posture, I was thinking about my brother, the real Dallas. How badly he would have wanted to do this himself. How great he would have been with a rigid spine up him. How great he probably still would be, fighting on heart alone.

This was why I was here.

Fighting for Dallas. Fighting *as* Dallas. I swelled with—

Bam!

Stupidity, I guess. I swelled with stupidity. It wasn't like it was a sneak attack or anything. Kelvin came right at me, crouched low and then driving up with an open hand jam right up my chin.

I took a trip. First up off my feet, then backward and down, right onto my backside.

The crowd loved it. One full platoon of boots there on the field burst into a combination of laughs and whoops at my crashing to the ground.

Frankly, I thought I was more popular than that.

The Black Hat—that's what skills instructors were called—came rushing over before I could even raise myself off the ground, and screamed me flat onto my back.

"What is wrong with you, soldier? Walking straight into a shot like that, very first thing? He never even faked you. You wanna be dead or somethin'? 'Cause if you really wanna be dead that bad, I'm of a mind to kill ya myself, right there where ya lay right now! Now, you are gonna get your sorry self into upright position and wade back in—wading with your eyes *open* this time—and give this fella waitin' patiently behind me something at least *worthy* of having him beat the crap outta. Can you do that for me, son?"

I wanted to shout that I would gladly do that *to him*. Maybe some other time.

So instead I went with "Yes, Sergeant, I can!"

"Good," he said, stepping back and clearing me to reenter the fray.

Kelvin and I were all business now. This kind of unarmed training was as serious as it got. Getting knocked on my can like I did was not only humiliating, it was genuinely lethal. What we were doing here was developing moves for actually killing, or at least debilitating, another man. Hands and feet were flying from the get-go, Kelvin landing another and then another chin jab on me. The Army's version of the jab was open-handed, with the heel of the hand making the impact, quicker and more accurately than the boxing jab. He was really good at it. But prepared as I now was, I could absorb the blows and snap back with the same speed and force.

Bopping him with three straight jabs of my own, I dazed Kelvin into backpedaling three steps. I followed him and, as he braced for the next jab, shocked him with an almighty stomp kick with my right boot to his left knee. That knee bent so far in the wrong direction it was almost as if he had a two-way hinge in there instead of a normal human joint. He nearly fell over backward, and I was poised to pounce on him if he did. Instead, he caught himself and jack-knifed straight into my face with a double tiger claw. The blow not only snapped my head back—I expected to see most of my face flesh dangling off his talons at the end of it.

This was not the schoolyard fighting we all knew and loved. This was dirty, nasty, necessary fighting. Rules? The rules—and this was the lesson more than anything—were to kill and don't get killed. Whatever it took.

He went for my eyes with another claw.

I kicked him between the legs so hard I heard a gurgling of internal organs from his gaping mouth.

This could not go on forever. We were throwing and kicking, chopping and clawing, so furiously that if one of us didn't land a death blow of some kind we were both likely to drop from exhaustion.

By now, every boot in the area was roaring us on. We really were well-matched for size and strength, not to mention speed and stamina and grit.

But in the end, I realized, I had the thing that separated us. I had him for balance.

Balance is the thing. The thing of all things. The rest of all that is valuable and important. But if you have all that *and* natural balance, you have everything. You have everyone.

I gauged just about how much I had left in the tank. Ten or twelve hard shots, maximum. I laid into him, *bam*, *bam*, *bam*, and *bam*. Left, then right, then left, then right. I bounced hard-knuck shots off his sharp cheekbones faster than he could react, until he had to start anticipating the next shot, looking left when I didn't aim there, looking right after I'd already been there.

Until—swishing, sweeping, shadow-dancing—I worked my way around to behind his left ear and *unloaded.* All the power of my final six punches was poured into one thunderous right cross that pitched him headlong into the dusty Georgia ground that was waiting to embrace his face.

"Well, that's a bit of an improvement!" the Black Hat bellowed into my face. The words were far more encouraging than the delivery.

More encouraging still was the little wave Kelvin directed my way, as a couple of other boots half dragged him away from the parade grounds. I waved back at him just as the Black Hat stepped aside, revealing my next mean-looking adversary.

I wasn't even getting a chance to catch my breath. I guess in a system of tests and challenges this represented a step up.

I was okay with stepping up.

"Dallas, huh?" the guy said, standing six inches away, and three inches taller, from me.

I hesitated briefly. My new identity still didn't feel *entirely* natural, plus I had the added complication of several robust rattlings of my brain in the recent past.

"That's right," I said.

"We got a lot in common, me and you," he snarled.

In my experience, there were two kinds of situations where someone says that to you. One of them was when the someone has a lot in common with you. The other was when the someone doing the saying was a loathsome jerk.

I loathed him already. Jerk.

"How do we have a lot in common?" I asked.

"Well, I'm from Dallas. Texas. For real. Nobody calls me Dallas, though. I'm called Malice."

Of course you are is what my brain said. Wouldn't want to give him that satisfaction, though, so my mouth said, "Hi, Malice."

He looked a little surprised. My guess was that he wore that look a lot.

"Hi," he answered awkwardly.

Then he attacked me. Which, okay, he was supposed to do, but yikes.

He surprised me by opening with a roundhouse kick, a big boot to my right hip that caused a lot more trouble than I would have expected. Quick as the strike was, he managed to dig the hard toe of his boot deep into the joint, in a way that caused my hip to go all weirdly out of line. As he followed up to throw a few shots at my head, I did all I could do to get my right leg to support my defensive evasions at all. I moved like a newborn giraffe with one missing leg. It was like I spent the first thirty seconds of the fight chasing myself in a wobbly circle.

The only thing that saved me was that Malice couldn't figure out where I was going, either. I just kept moving in desperation, trying to hold on until the feeling came back in the joint and I could mount something like a counterattack. All the guys circled around us were laughing as Malice pursued and I scrambled, and by the time he caught and lined me up, he couldn't help catching a little contagious laughter as well.

I mean, I very nearly joined in the yucks myself.

Instead, I did the smarter—and funner—thing.

Bang!

Taking advantage of Malice's momentary lapse of focus and his understandable overconfidence, I managed to plant my good leg rigid and explode up into his face with an open-hand jam straight to the nose.

It caught him so perfectly, there was an explosion of blood that made it look as if he'd had a ripe beefsteak tomato planted in the middle of his mug.

Now *this* was fair. I couldn't move properly and he couldn't see properly.

It was gonna get pretty. And all the boys knew it.

The screaming grew deafening. Hey, how much worse might it get if we both went deaf?

His puffy, watery, blood-spattered eyes were turning him into a blinking fool, but that didn't stop him from pursuing me. In fact, he charged harder, swinging wildly at where he thought I was. He came closer, working out my game-leg pattern until finally he cut me off at every turn as I desperately tried escape, evasion, delay.

Until, inevitably, he caught me. I had my arms raised to defend the certain hammer blow that would knock me safely into next week.

But he was too cute for that. And too cunning. And above all, too cruel.

With inhuman precision—and, yes, malice— Malice took advantage of my defensive cover-up to roundhouse me again and *bang!*

The toe of his boot, again, deep into the tender center of my hip joint.

I went crashing down as hard as if he'd taken an ax to my leg.

I grabbed at my hip, trying to scream, trying not to scream. Then, perhaps foolishly, trying to get to my feet again. I needn't have bothered with that. Two seconds later, Malice landed like a giant bird of prey on top of me. He put me in an almighty choke hold from behind and squeezed and squeezed with his huge right forearm.

My hip almost stopped hurting. Not that it was some kind of miracle. The feeling in my legs was fading, along with my breath and my consciousness. My quit was rising in me. I was giving up.

"Maybe you don't belong here, Alice," he hissed in my ear.

The crowd noise had mellowed considerably, unless it was just another of my senses checking out. But at the same time, as Malice applied more pressure to my throat while repeating again his taunt of my— my brother's—name, I found my quit was suddenly quitting.

"Alice," he said. "Are you with us, Alice?"

I was consumed then, with thoughts of Dallas back home in Berlin. I could feel him with me, as he was with me always, no matter what I did. He wanted so badly to be the one doing what I was doing right now.

Well, not exactly what I was doing *right* now.

Both of my arms shot like pistons up behind me, finding Malice's face, hammering and hammering. He squeezed harder then, and I stopped punching. Instead,

I started reading the terrain of his features, poking at him with my palms, fingers, thumbs. I felt him shaking his head like a drenched dog, trying to jerk me loose, his strength running down at the same time. That's one of the drawbacks with the big muscly guys—they get fatigued quickly.

I went for his eyes. Found one of them. Sank my thumb in there practically up to the nail.

Two massive thoughts flooded my brain, and they both produced the same intensity in me. One was *They taught us that hand-to-hand combat was all about kill and don't get killed—forget about being polite because there are no rules in this.*

The other thought was *You do not mock my brother's name, no matter who you are.*

As he howled at the eye gouge, Malice's grip on me loosened just enough. I took advantage of the moment to reach all the way back and seize ahold of his big blocky head. With a mighty whip, I chucked him right over my shoulder and into the dirt, face-down in front of me. We were even now, my hip no longer a handicap with us both fighting crab-style on the ground. I liked my odds better, now that they'd evened.

I was biting ferociously into his ear, snarling

through a pulpy mouthful of his blood and skin and cartilage.

"What's my name, boy?"

"Rrrrorrrr," he spat.

I put my own choke hold firmly around his neck. Then toggled my head, his ear still in my teeth, like a dog killing a rat.

"What's my name?" I said again.

I knew we were exceeding the limits of our combat training. I also knew we were being allowed to test the limits here, because for some reason, they seemed extra interested in testing ours. Still, I could sense the Black Hat inching closer, and with him the end of hostilities. Sort of.

"Say my name!" I snarled once more. "Or I swear I'll rip this thing off and swallow it. You'll be listening to me digest it before anyone can stop me." Not sure how garbled most of that sounded with me speaking through a mouthful of Malice mulch, but he seemed to get the gist of it.

"Dallas!" he screamed. "Dallas, Dallas . . . Dallas!"

The Black Hat was on me then, with a hand on my shoulder that was firm enough to communicate his message.

But not firm enough to stop me from putting one last two-handed shove to the back of Malice's head, slamming his face off the ground.

Next thing I knew, a couple of boots had me by the upper arms, lifting me up out of the dirt while two more did the same for Malice. I took a little bit of pride in noting what a semiconscious, gooey mess he was. They pretty much dragged the two of us single file off the grounds, toward what I figured was the medical building. Until, suddenly, I was no longer dragging. I watched Malice drift away as the boys abruptly stopped, spun me around, and planted me.

In front of yet another big ugly beast. Bigger, uglier, and more beastly than the previous two, even.

Apparently, I wasn't off the clock yet.

Everything inside me hurt, and I had all the energy of a spent car battery. No matter. I raised my hands into fight-ready position and planted my feet wide for stability.

And promptly fell over sideways, as my hip gave out entirely. I looked like I was playing an especially reckless version of "I'm a Little Teapot."

CHAPTER THREE

Whaju Do?

I was fairly woozy when they brought me in, so I wasn't quite aware what the building even was. There were cots lining each side of the barnlike wooden shack, several with battered-looking boots occupying them. And since I, too, was a battered boot, I gathered that this was one of the base's medical facilities. Didn't matter all that much to me, since I got to lie comfortably, with nobody coming around to boss me into action. In fact, it felt like I was going largely unnoticed.

Which suited me just dandy.

"So, whaju do?" said the guy in the cot directly opposite mine. We were aligned in such a way that if our beds were on wheels, we could have a sort of bumper car smashup feetfirst.

Not only did I have no idea what the guy meant, I was instantly irritated that he was asking me anything at all.

"Whaju mean, whaju do?" I mimicked him in a way he seemed not to recognize.

"I mean," he said, "whaju do to get yourself jammed into this box?"

The only reason I bothered answering was to get him to stop asking.

"I got kicked in the hip," I said.

"What? They don't put you in here because somebody did something to *you*. What did you do to somebody else?"

"Nothing. Fought back a little bit, I suppose."

"Betchu did more than just that."

"Why are you saying that? I'm a patient in the infirmary because I'm injured. Doesn't matter how I got this way."

"It matters in *this* infirmary."

"Oh, does it? Well, as a matter of fact, I'm feeling better already. So, any time now I'll be out of here and you can go back to talking to yourself, ya bedbug."

"Yeah? Well, I might be a bedbug, but you ain't just any ol' patient in any ol' infirmary." He pointed to the far end of the place, where a guard stood at the main door.

"So what?" I said.

"So, if you're feeling so much better, then why don't you just skip on out of here?"

"Maybe I will," I said.

"Well, go, then," he said.

Never one to shy away from a challenge—no matter how childish and/or stupid that challenge may have been—I rolled off my perfectly safe and comfortable cot, and began the long hobble over the bare wood floor toward the exit. And because I was somehow locked in this competition with somebody I didn't even know, somebody with two black eyes and both arms in plaster casts, I used approximately 50 percent of my current strength pretending that my hip didn't feel like somebody was working on it with an ice pick deep into the joint. A flaming ice pick, actually.

By the time I had walked the seventeen miles or so to the spot where the guard was, I wished I had never gotten up. Too late for that, though.

The guard raised his rifle at my approach. He had it across his chest in such a way that if we were playing ice hockey I'd have been bracing for a wicked cross-check.

I happened to be a great ice hockey player, and something of an expert at both delivering and absorbing cross-checks.

"You can stop there, soldier," the guard said.

"What?" I said. "Oh, there must be a mistake. Surely you are here to guard for us, right? Keep us safe and all while we recover."

"Please return to your cot."

"Ah, c'mon," I said, and took a step forward.

This was no cross-check. I felt the sharp poke of a rifle nozzle catch me right in the solar plexus.

"Please return to your cot, soldier. Now."

Having received the message, I slowly removed myself from the barrel of the guard's gun. I backed away, pivoted crisply and painfully, and marched back in the direction of my assigned cot.

Laughter from the other half dozen or so inmates followed me like a dishonorable honor guard all the way up the aisle.

When I got to the cot, I did a sort of barrel roll maneuver down into prone position.

The laughter subsided, and the place went silent.

"So," the guy with the arm and eye issues said, "whaju do?"

When I didn't reply, another guy a few spaces down joined in. "I heard he ate a guy's face."

"I did *not* eat anybody's face," I snapped. "Whereju hear that?"

"I heard it from a guy," the guy said. "He was just in here. Didn't you see him? He didn't have no face."

"Ha-ha-ha," I heard somebody say. The somebody may actually have been me. All the guys up and down the rows started laughing about the man with no face, and I had to admit it felt pretty good to me to be laughing along with them. There are worse things in the Army than to develop a reputation as a snarling, face-eating beast, and it seemed that here I was, developing just such a reputation.

Next thing I knew, the place went quiet and I had company, right beside my bunk.

"How you feeling, soldier?" the Black Hat from the training ground asked me.

"Not too bad, sir," I said, "all things considered."

He took a seat on the corner of my bed, adopting a much more conversational tone compared to the screaming-up-my-nose he was doing earlier.

"Now, you see, Greene," he said, "that's what I'm here for. To consider all those things."

"Sir?"

"Right, I'll be clear. You did a commendable job out there, at the hand-to-hand. A very impressive job."

"Thank you, sir. Ah, sir?"

"Yes?"

"Am I under arrest?"

"What? Oh, yeah. Technically, yes, you are."

"But, all I did was . . . fight."

"Well, yes. Fight, and tear strips off another recruit. Literally."

"All right. But, with respect . . . nobody stopped me."

Black Hat let out a little laugh and shook his head while looking down at the floor.

"True. And, more importantly, you never stopped yourself, either."

I paused, trying to catch up to the logic, or slow down to it, or whatever was required to get me out of the muddle my head was in.

"Is that the way it's supposed to work?" I asked.

"No," he said cheerily. "Not in an ideal world, or an ideal fighting outfit, anyway."

I was getting no closer to figuring things out, so I settled in to just listening and hoping until it all fell together eventually.

"Anyway, Greene, you showed a lot of grit out there today—resourcefulness, toughness, skill . . . and, well, viciousness."

I had never thought of myself as vicious. All those other things, grit, resourcefulness, toughness, skill . . .

sure, they sounded like me to me. But I never would have used the term *vicious* on myself.

Now somebody else had used it on me. Somebody in a position to know a thing or two about these things.

And it felt pretty good.

"Maybe most impressive of all," Black Hat said, "was that after two grueling fights, when you practically could no longer even stand up properly—"

"'Scuse me, sir," I interrupted, "no practically about it . . . I *couldn't* stand up . . ."

"Indeed, when you couldn't even stand up, son, you still stood *in*. You stood tall, ready to go again without pause."

I thought about it, ran through the scene in my own head again, then nodded at the basic accuracy of the man's version of events.

"Yes, sir," I said, "I did that."

"You sure did. Thing is, Greene, you possess an accumulation of qualities that would be of value to . . . well, any fighting force, frankly."

"Thank you, sir."

"But I had in mind a specific force you might be uniquely suited to. An old buddy of mine is currently out recruiting for a new outfit that's being formed from scratch. He's traveling the country looking for just the right men, and he's coming through here next. I'd like to have him talk to you, if you are at all interested."

Black Hat handed me a flyer.

"But aren't I under arrest?" I asked before reading the paper.

"For the moment," he said, standing up and smiling down. "So you'll talk to him?"

"Sure," I said, gently stroking my convalescing hip. "What else have I got to do?"

The answer to that, of course, was not much.

I enjoyed army training and was learning new stuff every single day. There was plenty to keep a guy on his toes mentally, learning everything about weapons and ammo and map reading and the whole strategy of warfare and the crappy state of the entire world as we knew it—which seemed to change profoundly on an almost daily basis.

But the truth was that a soldier's life was a physical life. And if you were laid up and out of that, then a soldier's life was a tormented life.

If, that is, you liked the physical soldier's life.

And I *loved* the physical soldier's life.

So this game of hospital limbo I was playing while waiting to get back in the real game was a pretty boring thing. I started looking forward to medical intervention just to get me out of the dark regarding my condition. The only information I'd so far been provided came directly from the hip itself, with occasional jolts of searing pain that sometimes reached all the way up to my ear.

That first evening, the doctor made his rounds, and when it was my turn, he gave my hip a deep poking with his thumb, finding so many entry points I never thought that joint could have. My leg might as well have been connected to my body by a bony pinwheel. Then, with both hands clamped to points high and low on my thigh—and I had to admit I did not think that the medicos would have the mightiest talons in the Army, but they sure enough did—he maneuvered my leg every which way until that hip became my enemy within. My enemies without had nothing on this torture.

"Grrrrwwrrr . . ." I said, as low and manly as I could for a guy who seriously felt like crying.

The doc rotated the thing a second and third time, through all the positional possibilities, until he was satisfied. At least one of us was.

"Three, four, five days, tops," he said, making a bunch of pencil scratches on my chart. "Then you'll be eating faces again in no time."

It was a small world here at Fort Benning. You eat one face and you're labeled for life.

"So it's just, what, a kinda bruise or something?" I suggested.

"My guess is a small tear in the labrum," he counter-suggested. "That's the cartilage that cushions the ball of the hip joint."

"Oh. And that only takes a few days to heal?"

"More like weeks, actually. For normal people. But soldiers are not normal people. And also, that kind of time on the shelf is a luxury we—meaning you—do not have."

Truth was, I had no problem with this prognosis. I was happy enough to do some limping in order to get more or less directly back into action.

"Fine. Thanks, Doc. In the meantime, is there anything I can do for this? To help me get better, quicker?"

He looked like he was giving my question serious consideration. Then he spoke, and I concluded that he wasn't.

"See the guy who delivered this perfectly executed,

malicious kick? That boy knows exactly what he's doing. Unless he is just preternaturally lucky. Either way, my professional advice to you is not to stand directly in front of him again."

"Good advice," I said. "Thanks."

It was, in fact, very sound advice. Thing was, I didn't intend to take it. I was going to stand in front of Malice . . .

And stand in front of *malice* next chance, and every chance, I got.

That was simply how things were here, and how they were now.

And how I liked them.

Gabriel (or whatever it is you are calling yourself these days—I cannot keep up with you),

It has already been an adventure, I can tell you that. For starters, contrary to their image, the Army lets you do practically anything you like, without limits.

Maybe I should clarify that a bit. They let you do anything you like, as long as you like to fight. All kinds of fighting, with and without weapons. And what do you know? Turns out I like fighting. Who'd a thunk it, huh?

I suppose maybe I should qualify that a bit further still. Seeing as I am writing to you from a version of military jail. Yes indeedy, big brother, I got busted for fighting a little better than they are used to seeing around here. And I hope you will be pleased to hear that I got busted for defending YOUR good name.

Okay, our good name.

Anyway, here is a thing I have learned. And yes, it turns out I can learn. Actually, I have learned a good many things, but this one rises up to near the top already. If people—particularly people in an organization full of rowdies and agitators like the military—find out that there is a name, an insult, or a sore spot that gets right under your skin, you can expect to hear it a lot. A whole lot. And up close and personal, too.

People here seem to think it's funny to

call a guy named Dallas "Alice." Cause it sort of rhymes, see?

If you listen closely, it doesn't even rhyme. Not really.

And yes, I am educating people to this effect, one wise guy at a time, so don't you worry.

I seem to be suddenly popular. Gotta go, write back soon.

Me (you, whichever)

CHAPTER FOUR

Wrong in All the Right Ways

Black Hat was back.

With company.

"Greene," he said as the two of them stood over my bed, "this is Lt. Col. Fisher. He's the man I told you about."

I saluted the colonel, as I had been taught. He nodded, dragged up a chair to my bedside, and smiled at Black Hat.

"I'll leave you two to get acquainted," Black Hat said. He made his departure.

When he was gone, I waited, as I had also been taught, for Col. Fisher to speak first. I didn't have to wait long.

"As I believe you heard, Private," Fisher said, drawling out the word *heard* for a particularly stretchy time, "we are assembling a brand-new outfit. New in that it does not yet exist in any form. There's nothing remotely like it in the United States' armed services, or anybody else's for that matter."

"I did hear a little bit about that, sir," I said. "But only *very* little."

"Well, there's a good reason for that. It's still classified, an early-stage operation. Until we get just the right personnel into position, this operation doesn't officially exist."

"Sounds like fun, sir," I said.

"I was hoping you would say that. Or at any rate, words to that effect."

"Can I ask what it is that makes you think I might be among 'just the right personnel' for your outfit?"

"You may indeed ask, soldier. But let me answer by way of asking *you* some questions first. That sound all right?"

"I'm game, sir."

"Yes, we already know that much."

Who's *we*? Best to let him ask the questions for now.

"Ever do any hunting, Greene?"

"Yes, sir."

"Fishing?"

"Yes, sir."

"*Ice* fishing?"

"Yes, sir."

"Logging?"

"Yes, sir."

"Skiing, skating, contact sports, mountain climbing, eating people's faces . . . ?"

"Yes, sir. Yes, sir. Y—ah, sir . . . ?"

"Yes, Private Greene?"

"Am I correct in thinking that you already know the answers to the questions you're asking me?"

"You are correct in that assumption, Private."

"Am I correct in thinking that you know more than just those answers?"

"See there, soldier, that is another important factor. You are not just a brute force—though we do like that . . ."

There's that *we* again.

"You've also got a keen, deductive mind."

It was like a reverse job interview, and I'd already nailed it. My confidence grew by the second.

"Did you also know, sir, that I made the United States Olympic ski jump team?"

If I thought I was going to catch him with that itty-bitty tidbit, I'd miscalculated. Conversationally, I went down the ski jump on my face.

His smile was both warming and chilling as he leaned down to me—July and January in the Great North Woods at the same time.

"Of course we know that, *Dallas* Greene," he said.

Oh. Oh, holy hippopotamus.

He knew. *They* knew.

"You know."

"We know. Private, we know so much, we don't even know what we know. We know so much we forget half of it. How's that kid brother of yours, anyway? Gabriel, is it? Bet you've made him awfully proud . . ."

"As punch, sir."

"As punch. We like that. We like pride. It does not cometh before a fall, by the way, so just forget that nonsense right now. Here, you can be proud all you like."

"It's forgotten, sir."

"There, you're learning already. The *strategic forgetting* will come in handy in this outfit, soldier, I can promise you that."

"No doubt, sir, no doubt. Have we come far enough along in the process where I can ask what exactly the outfit we're talking about *is*?"

"We have, and you can. It's the First Special Service Force."

I let that roll around a bit. In my head. In my mouth. Tasted a little like ear.

I liked it.

First Whatever Whatever Force appealed to me right away.

I liked being first.

By the end of the week, I was still in pain. But I was out of jail, hospital, and Georgia.

My sore hip still caused me to walk around as if I was Gabby Hayes toddling behind some invisible sheriff in a B Western movie. Didn't bother me much, though, as it was only pain.

I tended to feel like, if you didn't have some kind of ouch getting at you, then you probably weren't working hard. If you weren't nursing at least a low-level injury, how would you even know if you were accomplishing anything in life?

Personally, I'd probably be lonely without it.

A limp, though, tended to attract the attention of grunty pig soldiers who were bored and boarding a mystery train to who-knew-where.

"Hey, where's the posse at?" somebody yelled at me as I made my way through the first very full car. He said it with that "cowboy movie–sidekick" voice and flapping his lips like he had no teeth.

"Thataway," I said, jerking a thumb toward the

rump-end of the train. "If you hurry, you can catch 'em."

"Ya don't catch a posse—they catch you," somebody else yelled out, as if this was a serious debate. "Dummy."

Didn't think I was going to miss New Hampshire this much, this quickly. But I'd had snappier exchanges with a salmon on the Connecticut River.

"Catch this," I said, slapping myself on the behind hard enough to pink up my hand.

"Woo-oooh-hoo!" was the general consensus of the audience I left behind. Couldn't tell if they were woo-hooing for me, about me, or at me, but I was happy to be on to the next car.

Just then the engine piped up its long, sad whistle and the locomotive bucked and chugged gradually into motion. I swagger-staggered my way forward through a car nearly as full and rambunctious as the first one. The heavy bag I had slung over my shoulder certainly didn't help with the wobbling, and neither did the guy who stuck his leg out into the aisle to trip me up. Or, I should say, *guys*. One from each side extended a booted hoof into my path at the same time, coordinated to take both legs out from under me simultaneously. I dropped hard onto both knees, with my kit bag driving me harder to the floor.

As I held my ground there on the ground, amid the screeching laughter raining down all over, I actually took a moment to consider that I had never experienced the double trip before in my life. Hadn't even seen it in person. Huh. Wasn't that a thing?

This was another thing.

My brain was still engaged with the double-trip notion when I made my selection out of pure instinct. I leaped left at the louder of the two trippers. He just about saw me coming and attempted to get the drop on me first, but my timing could not have been better. The boniest part of my skull, up at the very peak, made contact with the guy's nose with such a satisfying crackle it almost made me hungry. The momentum of my leap carried us up and over, until I knocked him back over the lap of the guy in the window seat next to him. As I had my quarry firmly pinned down with both my hands on his collar, I sensed a twitch coming from the direction of his seatmate.

While holding the one guy down, I turned to my side and leaned so hard into the window-seat fella I could have told you what he had for lunch two days ago.

It was bologna and Swiss. With brown mustard. And a pickle.

Even though I was subduing one guy, the other had my undivided attention. An accomplishment of which I was rather proud.

"Fold your hands," I snarled.

He folded his hands like a good boy, on top of the other guy's belly.

"In your lap," I said, 'cause I felt like being a jerk.

He took his folded hands and worked them burrow-like under the man in his lap, through the kidney zone, until they were wedged between his lap and the other guy's back.

Oh, I was feeling it now. Power can be such—

Bang.

The guy on his back caught me right on the tip of the chin with a good whistler of a straight right hand.

The trip from cocky to stupid is a very short tumble, it turns out.

As he straightened me up with that shot and I banged into the seat across the aisle, I became more aware of the wildness of the guys all around. They were having the time of their lives—unless they'd had otherwise ridiculously fun lives. Even the guy with the blood running out of his nose was smiling at me at this point.

"What?" I said to him. I felt like I was in the middle of some big game where I was the only one who didn't know the rules.

The guy looked dramatically around in all directions, holding his hands wide and palms up, like he couldn't believe what he was seeing. The boys all loved it and screamed as much.

Then he looked back at me. "You're supposed to punch me now, numbskull."

Oh.

He looked truly haunted, the grin too wide, the teeth too tall, the blood dribbling down over his lips and into the wide dental spaces of his gums.

What does one do?

One punches, is what one does.

Not sure if I ever did anything with the same force as I put into this punch, but the guy absorbed it, keeping his feet and wib-wobbling all around like the Scarecrow from *The Wizard of Oz*. Once he righted himself, he flashed me that demented blood-soaked smile again, and we were at it.

The two of us stood squarely toe-to-toe, in a way you never did anywhere other than in a packed and swaying clunker of a train. All the other guys were pressed in so close, we practically had to shove left and right to clear space every time one of us tried to belt the other.

This was fighting. I mean, obviously this was fighting. But unlike anything out in the known world, this was close in and stuck in and hard-knuckle. There was no maneuvering, no avoiding, just taking shots and throwing shots for all you were worth.

We were worth a lot, too. I'd been in my share of fights and more back in New Hampshire, but every hammer this guy caught me with was harder than anything I had ever weathered before. At the same time, I was hitting him with punches that were landing so heavy and clean, the most distressed part of me was my aching hands. I tasted the tang of my blood in my mouth, felt a couple of bottom teeth start to wiggling.

And all the while, the guy smiled that smile. And here's a thing—you can't help smiling back at a smile like that. It's like the yawn reflex, only with seriously more dire consequences.

After about a minute of this, my associate and I were tiring noticeably, the haymakers making less hay. The guys all around were crowding ever closer, to the point where I accidentally clocked one of them behind my opponent's ear. Then he did the same, seemingly on purpose, like this was now part of the scorekeeping.

Then, without warning, the crowded feeling loosened up. The deafening holler-storm moved away, and the two of us fighters watched as the whole rotten mob migrated up toward the front of the car.

It was clear pretty quickly. There was another fight. One that was capturing what little imagination this bunch possessed. Our moment in the spotlight was done.

Momentarily, it hurt my feelings.

I turned to my guy, who promptly hurt my stomach's feelings. He hadn't gone for the body before that, so it was quite an effective move. I doubled over and went *oooff*, almost loud enough to bring our audience back. But while I was down there I figured, *Why not?* And I hit my man solidly below the belt.

He dragged me into the booth behind him. He was still smiling at me, but it was more smiley smiling now. It must have taken him half his energy to keep that grin up, so I was glad he did it. Who knows how it would have gone otherwise?

His friend remained in his seat next to his pal and opposite me. I reached into the aisle with my foot and dragged my kit bag under my seat.

"This train is bound for glory," he said, offering me his hand to shake.

I scooped a palm full of blood out of my lower lip, then took his hand.

"Gory, glory," I said.

"Gory, glory, hallelujah," he said.

For fifteen, maybe twenty minutes, we sat there, the three of us making our way toward God-knows-where. All the windows were blacked out, and yet, all these hard-nut bad boys were willing to fly blind to wherever it was we were going. Turned out my dance partner's name was Sacks, and his friend was Bergeron.

"And what do they call you?" Sacks asked me.

"Ah . . ." Maybe it was all the shots to the coconut I'd taken, or just my tangled web of stories catching up with me, but it was several long seconds before I could manage an answer to this seemingly straight-forward question. "Gabe—" I started, then stopped. "Dal—" I started, then stopped.

"Interesting name you got there, Gabe-dal," Bergeron said.

"What's that, Norwegian?" Sacks asked.

"It's not," I said. "Or maybe it is, I don't know."

"You don't *know*?" they said in singsong unison,

highlighting the absurdity of the situation. And I agreed, too. I was absurd.

Flustered by my own dopeyness, I blurted, "Alice. Just call me Alice."

They looked at each other solemnly. Then Sacks gave me the big flesh-eating grin once more.

"Alice. You want us to call you Alice."

"Yeah," I said confidently, like this was somehow my well-thought-out plan. "The guys at Fort Benning called me that. It grew on me. Also, I like to fight. Builds character and skill and resilience. And I'm pretty sure that, as Alice, I'll have a lot more fighting to do."

This, surprisingly enough, was just the right thing to say to these kinds of people.

"I like the way you think, Alice," Bergeron said, pointing and grinning at me.

"Absolutely," Sacks added. "You're a real man, Alice, coming up with a thing like that."

"Oh," I said, feeling pretty good about myself right now. "Really, I'm just making it up as I go along."

It was unlikely I would ever speak a truer statement.

The fighting and noise went on unabated for another hour, with no signs of slowing down. It became more apparent every minute that whoever we were and wherever we were headed, this train carried a population of mad marauding maniacs who all liked to fight every bit as much as I did. It became clear in no time that, while brawling had its many attractions, sitting around listening to it really didn't.

"What's the story with all the cars up ahead of us?" I asked my seatmates.

"Well," Bergeron said, "I think the one a couple of cars up has snacks. And I heard that the one a couple of cars beyond *that* has music. Like a jazz trio or something."

I was stunned.

"Well then, what are we doing in this dogcatcher's wagon?" I asked.

"There's a process," Sacks said wearily. "You gotta fight your way up. Every carriage, the more amenities and amusements they got, the more guys you gotta take on to gain admission."

Just the notion of it made me tired.

But it wore off quickly.

"Do they have Planters peanuts?" I asked.

"Who doesn't have Planters peanuts?" Sacks said, shaking his head.

"Fig Newtons?" I asked.

"Now you're pushing it," Bergeron said to me. "Now he's pushing it," he said, turning to Sacks.

"Guy's a big dreamer," Sacks said. "What's wrong with that?" He stood up.

I stood up, too. "Nothing," I said. "Not a thing wrong with that."

Bergeron stayed slumped in his chair. He let out an exhausted sigh.

"I don't even *like* Fig Newtons," he said. "And I'm not too crazy about peanuts, either. That Mr. Peanut guy looks like an idiot, by the way. Who wears a monocle, honestly?" Then *he* stood up. "But you're not leaving me here on my own."

It took almost four days for that train, that rolling thunder carnival of testosterone, to get to our destination. The smell was exactly what one might guess. Take every dead thing you've ever been close to, mix that with curdled milk and cabbage, have your dog eat all that and then throw it back up again and then roll in it. That was us.

We were more than just the smell, though. We battled and blustered and blowharded our way across the country, to the point where we got to know and hate and appreciate and sometimes like and fear one another like no group of people I had ever encountered.

We became—or maybe always were, but hadn't discovered it before—one big, violent family. We were just beginning our journey into the battle, but this train full of lunatics was already at war. We were simply being transported to the next phase of our training and organization, but the train ride itself felt dangerous. Traingerous. Was that a word? It should've been. We'd make it one.

Maybe that was the plan all along? Fighting men forged through traingerousness.

Finally. Finally, finally, finally, we came to a stop. *The* stop.

Helena, Montana, was what it said over the sooty, dilapidated train station building.

Holy moly.

Nobody on Earth would try and tell you that northern New Hampshire was anything less than rugged. So I was no dainty flower when it came to such places.

But.

Holy.

Moly.

When the lot of us were puked out of the train cars and onto the stony turf of Helena, I heard every last man hiss with the crispy crackle of the dusty wind that snapped us to attention.

And big? I nearly made myself fall down with the dizziness of turning in circles trying to find out where this big sky ended. It was disorienting enough that I'd have been less nauseous if I climbed back on the train with every last one of those warthogs and sealed the doors behind us.

But a few minutes later, I realized this was as beauteous as the good Earth was ever likely to get. I went from feeling sickly to having my breath taken away in the best possible way.

There were uncountable acres of majestic plains, leading to mountains in three directions that sang at you to climb them up and ski them down.

Montana was what New Hampshire wanted to be when it grew up.

And in the fourth direction was what must have been the town itself, just a few miles east. It had one big, beautiful double-spire cathedral, surrounded by bunches of smaller buildings, like a mom with her cubs.

Fort William Henry Harrison itself was a strange thing. It was like a big militarized version of one of those old Wild West ghost towns that emptied out once the gold stopped rushing. It had obviously been a fort for a long time but had not been up to much lately. There was a hospital that still seemed to be functioning, people filing in and out, and some other long, low wooden buildings that probably housed officers. There was a primitive disused airstrip that looked like it now serviced nothing but America's mighty fleet of tumbleweeds.

Once we'd dismounted the train, every man was given a sleeping bag, boilersuit, and a pair of jump boots. I was amazed that they would presume to know everybody's size, but as we were marched to wherever we were going, it became obvious that they presumed no such thing. Guys all around started immediately horse trading, based on body size, in an effort to make sure nobody was left with a pair of boots three sizes too big or small.

And then we were home. In the middle of this great ghost town of a fort, across an expanse of flatness, a tent city sprang up before our eyes. Shaped like shoeboxes with pointy hats on them, these tents at least seemed fresh and new, as if they'd been thrown up just for our arrival. Which they most likely were.

"There ya go, boys," barked our noncommissioned escort as he directed us one by one into our tents. The one that was to be my home address was about a dozen along, down what was basically the main street of the camp. There was no obvious method to who was assigned to bunk together, other than each next bunch was shoved into the next available tent.

That worked out well, actually, since the guys I was naturally walking together with were the guys I had already gotten friendly like with. So Sacks and Bergeron, along with Wallace and Bruce, who the other two knew from boot camp, were my roommates in Montana.

Spirited lads, every one of them.

"Hey, I don't have a mirror," barked Bruce, acting like this rated as a minor catastrophe. He had dumped his gear on the ground against a tent pole. His chosen spot looked exactly like every other spot in the big empty tent.

"Nobody has a mirror," Wallace snapped, dropping his own gear nearby. "Stop yer bellyaching."

"Wait, hold on," Bruce said. He rushed right up to Wallace, stared into his face intently. To be more specific, he stared into his forehead intently. He leaned in and steamed it up with his breath, then buffed it up with the sleeve of his shirt. Then Bruce backed a few inches away, seeming to admire himself in Wallace's forehead. He even picked something out of his teeth for extra dramatic effect.

It was, to be sure, a vast and shiny expanse of forehead.

To his credit, Wallace stood impassively through it all. Maybe that encouraged Bruce, because he smiled broadly. Possibly at his own reflection, though.

Once we were settled into our quarters, mail call came along impressively quickly.

While I had not the faintest advance notice where I was headed, apparently my brother knew better.

Actually, he knew nothing of the sort. We were so top secret that nobody anywhere knew what we were up to, other than the Special Forces folks themselves.

But it was still kind of fun to think that Dallas had everybody beat. When I arrived at Fort William Henry Harrison in Helena, his letter was there already.

It wasn't his doing, really. The Army knew where we were headed all along. Everybody's mail was forwarded.

Big Little Brother,

You must be one very important young ruffian. It is nearly impossible to get any information on what you are up to. I know this because—while I do not particularly care—dearest father keeps trying to get answers about what you are up to.

I will keep this short, since I know you have a very limited attention span. But I want to tell you, Dallas (or Alice, or whoever), how proud and overwhelmed I am about what you are doing. I know you are going to kill. And kill people who need to be killed.

I would kill to be able to kill like you are going to do.

Write to me when you can, what you can. I know there is more to what is happening. I just know.

And I should be allowed to know more, whenever you can tell me. Know what I mean, Dallas Greene?

Signed, with admiration and stuff,
Gabriel Greene

I knew he knew. He always knew.

I was destined to kill, starting pretty soon. Sure, everybody in the service in wartime should be expecting to do some killing, except maybe the cooks and motor pool guys (even though there are lots of jokes that they kill more soldiers than anybody). But we were different. We could feel it already. We were being honed and sharpened like the human equivalents of the commando daggers we all carried. Every last guy here in camp had a danger about him that you couldn't miss the moment you met them.

But also, weirdly, you couldn't miss that most of them were good guys at the same time. Good guys who could also be good at being bad guys.

I was a good guy. But I was also, maybe, a bad guy now.

And I was kind of okay with that.

This was something new that maybe my brother also already knew about me.

CHAPTER FIVE

Love and War

I fell in love in Montana. I had never really been in love before.

It was with a knife. Does it count if it was with a knife?

We had a special commando dagger that was with us at all times, even times when we were technically unarmed. I found myself unsheathing my knife in any quiet moments, running my thumb up and down its sharp, sharp edge to the point, where even I was sure my flesh was about to part over the blade, like the Red Sea.

And the beauty didn't have just the one sharp, sharp edge. It had two, running from a needle-pointed tip. It was a double-edged shard of high carbon stabulous steel. The blade itself was near wafer-thin, designed to slip between ribs with a minimum of resistance. It was seven inches long, made specifically to reach all the vital places inside a torso. The profile was vaguely dolphin-shaped, narrow at the nose, widening to the cross guard, and then tapering off again all the way to the back end of the hilt. It was balanced so well that you could rest it with the cross guard on the tip of your finger and it would simply perch there without tipping one way or the other.

Both edges were kept honed to the degree where you could slice a boiled ham with it and still read all the way down an optometrist's chart with the thin slices covering your eyes.

On the flip side, if a guy didn't train sufficiently or pay proper respect to the commando dagger at all times, he could quickly find himself fingerless—or worse.

It was all about thrust. Stab and jab and stab and stab and stab again. The thrust—hey, there's that word again—of our training was about establishing dominance over the enemy by stealth. And then once we got the jump on the guy, about killing him so thoroughly that even if there was an afterlife there would be nothing left of him to send on to his spiritual forwarding address.

We had to kill quietly. And we had to kill comprehensively. No enemy soldier who saw us could be left to tell about it, because we were not equipped to stand

and fight like regular infantry. We were hunters, plain and simple.

That meant we crept up on these poor saps, gave them no chance to prepare themselves, then stabbed. Stabbed, stabbed, stabbed, neck, neck, chest, kidney, lung, heart. It was like a proper medical procedure, only in reverse, in that we were extracting life from a body rather than preserving it.

Once I realized that, I actually started making a straw-drinking, slurping noise whenever I multi-stabbed our practice dummy. Like I was drinking his imaginary life away. Like it was a game. A harmless, deadly game.

"Again? Again, Alice?" came the voice from the next stall over in the latrine.

It was Bruce. How did I know it was Bruce? Because everybody knew when Bruce was on the toilet seat, since as soon as he had some success over there, he called out, "Pilot to bombardier! Pilot to bombardier! Opening bomb bay doors. Dropping load!" Same routine every time.

Bruce, you see, came to us from the Army Air Corps.

Everybody, of course, loved it. Including me. Except that this time I was too preoccupied with my knife to notice that Bruce was there the next hole over.

Apparently, my straw-slurping noise was too much even for Bruce's bombardiering.

"Sorry," I said. "I'll be quieter now."

"Um, no," he said. "Not quieter. Finished. Stop loving your knife now, and let's go. And that slurping stuff . . . what are you, a kid or something?"

I suppose the true answer would have been yes. But I didn't feel comfortable with the true answer. Also, this was coming from the toilet bombardier, so c'mon, now . . .

But he was right. We had to go. And where we had to go was the mountains. Even though this was our off time, our gang was keen to do something. Something not unlike what everybody had been doing since the moment we had arrived at Fort Harrison. If it wasn't shooting and stabbing, it was mountain climbing. If it wasn't humping across plains for two days with 120-pound packs on our backs, it was jumping off towers or from the backs of full-speed trucks. (This was to simulate parachute jumps in all kinds of weather, to practice landing on our feet in such a way as to not shatter our shins, or unhinge our knees, or rearrange our ankles from their natural configurations.)

But what did we do with our days off?

More of the same, naturally.

We had already become a unit of our own, even though officially nobody authorized us to do any such thing.

Me, Sacks, Bergeron, Bruce, and Wallace. In no time, we had formed a platoon, or company, or whatever it was five like-minded guys amounted to in an operation like this.

Fortunately, as we were eventually to find out, the Special Forces kind of liked it when bunches like us went rogue. Unlike the rest of the military organization, Special Forces were not only tolerant of guys who weren't dedicated rule followers—they encouraged them.

Lots of the time it appeared that the Force (which was what everybody came to call the First Special Service Force) was just barely following any rules of their own. It would have been a mistake to come to that conclusion, though. Because unlike the individual mad mugs who did the Force's dirty work on the ground, there was nothing at all haphazard about the way Force operations were structured. Anything that appeared chaotic about our activities was, in reality, carefully orchestrated chaos.

We were supposed to be ready for anything, at any time. And our training reflected that.

Which was how we wound up headed for the airstrip on our day off.

When Bruce and I had tromped from the latrines to the edge of camp, we were greeted by a line of trainers handing out packed parachutes as if they were hot lunches back at high school.

"This must be pretty comforting for you, Alice," said Bergeron, "since this is what you should be doing right about now anyway. You know, getting your sloppy joe in between Phys Ed and Biology?"

Everybody within range laughed robustly, even though it wasn't funny. Why was that even funny?

"Why was that funny?" I called out to everybody, or anybody.

I answered myself. It was funny because it was a remark about how everyone on the whole base knew I was just a kid, when I thought I was pulling off my full-grown-man routine quite convincingly.

Bergeron could tell I was bothered.

I could tell that Bergeron did not care that I was bothered.

"Calm down, kid," he said calmly, as if to show me how it was done. "I'd love to be as young as you again, and fighting these rotten so-and-sos with all that energy. A young man's fury is one of nature's most glorious forces."

By now, we had all collected our jump packs and were moving along the line to board the modified C-47 transport—a plane we'd been given no notice to expect.

"I'm hardly any younger than you," I said with such a lack of force that it may have left a trail of spittle down my shirt front.

Bergeron could not have been happier with this gift.

"Alice," he said, "the boxer shorts I'm wearing right this minute have got stains I made before you were born."

"Yeah?" I said, not quite rising to the challenge, or the delight of pretty much everyone. "Well, I don't believe your stains are even *as* old as me, never mind older."

There are some assertions, and some audiences, where it doesn't matter a whole lot how factually correct you have been. You have already destroyed your own argument just by virtue of having attempted it.

The plane had cranked up its engines by now, but you might not have known it due to how deafening the laughter of the Forcemen was as they boarded.

Within minutes, the big old boat of a plane had a belly full of ruffians. Despite having no advance warning of what we would be doing, all the guys were jabbering and jostling away as if this was the big day out that we'd all been promised by our parents for ages. There was some silly jockeying for position along the two queues of jumpers stretching fore and aft of the mid-craft exit door. The jump order was hardly going to be decided by the success or failure of which goons muscled their way to the front of the line. Two jump masters roared at all of us even louder than the plane's engines to fall into line or risk not jumping at all.

That was a threat to be reckoned with. Because we had been told all along that this was an acceler-ated, intensified, condensed jump course. If any of us failed to hurtle out of it midair, we would be leaving Fort Harrison on the next train eastward.

Nobody wanted that. We were all so rabid to be part of whatever this military madness was that we behaved like actual dogs over it. A few years earlier, Dad had taken me and Dallas way up into northern Quebec for a vacation, and my favorite part was when we went dog-sledding. I had always heard that these musher dogs were simply *mental* for the mush-ing, that they flat-out loved to pull sleds to the ends of the frozen world and back. I took that to be one of those grain-of-salt things, because goody-goody types were liable to say the dogs were overworked and exploited and whatnot. How else would the sled-dog set respond, but to say that, oh, no, these boys just love to run their guts out? Then I saw it with my own eyes. As the dogs' master came and selected the team one by one from the cage, the rage flying off all the dogs that *weren't* picked was some-thing I had never seen the likes of before. Happened over and over, with each dog selected. If the bench-warmer dogs could've gotten any closer, they would have certainly torn the throats out of the chosen ones. Then, as we took off on our sledventure, we had to veer close by the tall chain-link fence that held all the tough-luck pups. I was truly scared for our safety as the entire pen of dogs threw themselves at that fence, almost hard enough to tear through it. Dog spittle, and some bits of blood, and possibly a couple of canines came raining over the other dogs, the musher, and Dad and me and Dallas. These dogs wanted to *run*.

And that was pretty much us, the Forcemen.

In our case, run and jump and fly.

We all did, sort of, what the jump masters told us to do. As the C-47 roared and rumbled its way down the strip and off planet Earth, we all continued jostling for positions near the open door of the plane, anxious to be as near as possible to first man out and into the sky.

One of our daffier men, a wiry doofus called Whalen, somehow managed to get himself positioned second in one of the lines. Right behind him was possibly the toughest individual I had yet encountered, named McLaughlin.

Nobody messed with McLaughlin, ever.

Nobody told this to Whalen, apparently.

From behind, McLaughlin put a double death grip on Whalen's shoulders, squeezing and crunching until the effect was to buckle Whalen's knobby knees.

The jump masters acted as if they neither saw nor heard any of this, one of them calling out a half-hearted "Knock it off, boys" as he stared out to the sky above and the terrain below.

In short order, Whalen was shorter than he had been before. Then he was splayed awkwardly, one leg out in front of him and the other behind. McLaughlin finished his move by yanking the guy flat onto his back with a sort of rowing motion, then stepping on him as he stole his spot in line.

I had the best spot in the house, now right behind Whalen, as he hopped up to his knees and made the strategically questionable move to shove McLaughlin forcefully in the small of his back, dangerously close to offloading him at about one thousand feet high.

McLaughlin whipped around and took hold of Whalen by the throat with his left hand. Whalen, still on his knees, managed to wheeze out, "Go ahead, Mac, hit me. Go on."

"Well," Mac said, "I wasn't planning to, but okay."

And with that, McLaughlin dropped an almighty right hand straight onto Whalen's forehead, just above his left eye.

It was hard not to be impressed when wiry Whalen whiplashed backward, banging his head on the deck and then bouncing straight back up like one of those inflatable punching toys.

McLaughlin had by then turned his attention away from Whalen and toward his goal of hopping out into that wide, howling sky. Whalen, bless him, went at McLaughlin with both hands, raining what were presumably supposed to be punches over the harder man's back, neck, and head. All the while he bobbed around on legs that looked like his knees were mounted backward. If McLaughlin even noticed, he was being very brave about it.

It was only when Whalen veered perilously close to toddling out of the plane that the incident was finally concluded. Having no intention of surrendering his not-terribly-hard-won first position, McLaughlin grabbed Whalen by the back of his collar and slung him backward, into the wall opposite the jump door. Only then did one of the jump masters decide to intervene(ish).

"Whalen," he barked, "you are in no fit state to jump out of an airplane. Now, get to the back of the line so that you can be ready when your turn comes up!"

As Whalen made the walk of shame toward the rear of the craft, every other man whaled on his back, propelling him ever faster. He finally crashed into a heap before bouncing right up again and taking his rightful place in line.

We were slightly less furry than those huskies in Quebec, but otherwise indistinguishable.

It was clear by now that this kind of thing was as crucial to the Forceman's training as calisthenics, map reading, or demolitions.

The two jump lines had essentially sorted themselves

out when the plane reached altitude. It was time to start tossing happy maniacs off the side of the aircraft. We were all saddled up and tethered, clipped to the clothesline-type setup that ran the length of the plane's interior above our heads. Once each man jumped, his personal line would be yanked up by the clip, and his parachute's cord would be automatically pulled, releasing the silk that would cradle him all the way back to Mother Earth.

In theory.

But how much ever works out in practice quite like it does in theory?

The guys were all so excited to jump, it took all the strength the two jump masters could muster just to keep us from tumbling out as one great mass of goon. When the master gave McLaughlin a slap on the back, it was as if the guy had been shot out of a howitzer. He sailed an impressive distance horizontally before gravity and the cord ganged up on him, shooting him downward until the chute opened above him. We could all hear the joy of his whooping as he swung under it, pumping his fists and kicking his feet. It was utterly contagious; the very same whoop echoed around the belly of the C-47.

A plane full of wild huskies, for sure.

The way it was planned was an alternation of the two lines: left-right-left as jumpers took their spots and sailed smoothly into the sky. We were intended to function the way the teeth do on gears and flywheels. But in all the excitement after McLaughlin's leap, the number-two guy opposite me rammed right into the number-one guy. Number One actually half turned to give Number Two a shot in the chops with his elbow, when nature and circumstances conspired to hurl the two of them together through the door and into the almighty crosswinds.

When their cords pulled taut against the clothesline, they were too close together. Bang up against each other, in fact. So tangled were they that only one of the chutes opened. The unlucky chuteless guy grabbed on to the other one—literally for dear life—as if they were the most loving of brothers you could imagine. I, like everyone else, was stunned into immovability at the sight of this, until my jump master, two inches from my ear, bellowed, "I said, *jump*!"

The guy at the top of the other line made an exaggerated, mannerly "after you" gesture. I didn't need to be told a third time. I hurled myself out into the shocking wind, and the next thing I knew, *pop,* my cord was pulled and my parachute was deployed and I was enjoying the greatest thing I had ever imagined. And I had imagined this very thing about two hundred and fifty million times since I was four years old.

I was flying. Or floating. Or something.

The distinction did not matter.

I stared straight up at first, amazed at the billowing pillow of lightness above me—my chute, my own personal cloud. Then I looked down below me to see a sight just as powerful and wondrous in its own way.

The comedy double act who had stumbled out right before me were now in a midair punch-up. The two guys flailed and hammered away ferociously at each other, even as the ground was rushing up in their direction. The one without a working chute had his legs wrapped around the waist of the guy who did so that he could use both hands to inflict maximum damage to his only link to survival.

I may have seen more ungrateful acts in my time, but I couldn't think of any. Because of the extra weight of two of them on the one parachute, those guys hurtled to the ground extra fast. When they hit the dry August crust of Montana, they looked like one compact dust devil with arms and legs whang-dangling every which way. The chute dragged them for another hundred feet or so beyond the crash, and I believe they were still fighting when—

Bammmmm!

If there's anything more comical than two knuckleheads so caught up in midair fisticuffs that they forget about the approaching ground, then it's gotta be the *third* knucklehead who's so caught up in watching them that he forgets about the hard earth rushing up to smack *him* even sillier.

Fortunately, I had the training and muscle memory to recall the right way of giving in to violent physical reality. Just as I was hitting ground, I went into shock-absorption mode, bending my knees and rolling forward like a big dumb boulder, just the way I'd been taught all those times I'd jumped off the tower or out of the back of a moving truck.

Towers and trucks, though, could never fully prepare a guy for the force of *this*. I went over onto my face and heard my neck crack loudly. My forehead and nose scraped the ground hard enough that I feared I was leaving my face behind. I went tail over top once, then twice, and then three times, making stops along the way to bash one of my shoulders, both knees, and of course my still-delicate hip. When my rotten traitor of a parachute had finished dragging me halfway across the state, I think I must have had nearly half of Montana ground into my pants.

It was probably the most fun I'd ever had in such a condensed amount of time. I rolled over onto my back to see my mad batch of teammates following me down out of the sky. There were no more punch-ups but quite a few spectacular wipeouts and a lot of howling with the sheer joy of the business.

I would defy any single kid in the whole of New Hampshire to try and tell me he was having a better time than I was having right here.

Even if the next part of the exercise was to gather up our parachutes and repack them the best we could. Then to start the long, nomadic trek back across the plain, and the mountain, and then more plains, over the five- or six-mile distance back to camp.

Even if every inch of me hurt like the devil.

Especially that wicked hip.

And even my uncontrollable smile.

CHAPTER SIX

Mutton Head Said

It felt almost like cheating that we only had to make one more live dive from a C-47 to earn our prized jump wings. Every man in the outfit would have been happy to leap fifty more times on the way to making the grade, but this accelerated program was indicative of how things were going to go for us. While none of the enlisted men had the slightest idea what our ultimate assignment and destination would be, there seemed to be an all-fired hurry to get us trained up and dangerous enough to go anywhere and do anything to anybody.

The first Canadian recruit I got to know fairly well was a guy who called himself Mutton Head.

To be fair, he called himself Mutton Head only after everybody else started calling him Mutton Head.

To be even fairer, everyone else started calling him Mutton Head only after I started calling him Mutton Head.

And that's enough with the being fair for now. He had a head of hair like an honest-to-goodness sheep. It was all yellowy-white and bushy like a wool halo. It had to be something special, because the Canucks were as groomed and clean as it was possible for soldiers to be. So the fact that Mutton was allowed to go unsheared was testament to his amazing mane. It was ultimately a great source of Canuck pride.

Turned out they didn't much like to be referred to as Canucks, by the way.

Which I didn't understand, because it was a friendly-sounding nickname to my ear.

Unlike, say, *Yankees*, or the more popular derivative, *Yanks*, which so much of the world—including those same Canucks—seemed to think was a great fun term. This might have been okay with me were it not for the diabolical New York Yankees, who were not at all from New England and therefore were disqualified from *being* actual Yankees or even *Yanks*, but stole the word from us anyway.

Anyway.

"Anyway, *Alice*," Mutton Head said pointedly as we humped it back to base from the second jump that earned us our wings, "it's not about which side of the border we started out from. It's about what's the same about us, the qualities that brought us together here."

I had to say that got me pensive. I wouldn't have thought that one of these northern woodchucks could make me think about stuff the way ol' Mutt had me thinking. But he was doing it.

"I think," I said, "that what brought us into this band of mad and merry men is our determination to do ultimate damage to the wicked people peopling this world of ours today."

"Of which," he said, "there are many."

"There are indeed many," I said.

"And whom," he said, "we are ready to smite, by any means necessary."

"By any means, the smiting," I said.

I could sense that he was fingering the edge of the commando dagger at his hip as we talked. I knew for certain that I was.

"Why are you walking like that?" he said after a quiet bit. "If you don't mind my asking."

I limped on, staring straight ahead.

"And if I do mind you asking?"

"I don't know," he said. "Frankly, I don't care enough to be too bothered about it. I just figured since we have probably close to two miles still to go—a long way to be hobbling along like Boris Karloff, by the way—I might make some conversation. I could shut up, though, if you'd rather."

I sized up the two miles before us.

"C'mon, Mutt," I said. "You know that anybody who's ever listened to you for five minutes would vote for *shut up*."

"Wellll," he said, "somebody's neck bolts are a little too tight today. But have it your way. I'll be quiet from here. But you're gonna miss me, I promise you."

I like a lot of quiet, generally. The sound of our jump boots hacking across the dry October turf would figure to do me just fine.

But amazingly he turned out to be right. It wasn't long before I did miss him. He was a yapper but an engaging one.

Less amazingly, though, he couldn't manage silence beyond the first hundred yards or so.

"You can lean on me the rest of the way," he blurted, "if that helps you any."

For a Canadian sheep, Mutt was a pretty great guy. It was hard to justify making him keep quiet. If that was even possible. Which it wasn't.

"Thanks anyway, Mutt," I said. "But I'm sure it looks worse than it is—"

"I hope so, since it *looks* like your leg is gonna fall off before we reach base."

"Yeah," I said, "well, it's not. I just got a little tear in the hip area somewhere. It was almost healed, but I think I tore it a little bit again. No big problem. It'll be fine. I'll be fine. Long as I can still do my job, this doesn't even count as a problem."

Everybody here had already worked out that tolerance for pain was one of the minimum requirements for sticking with this outfit. The pain I was enduring was even becoming something of a thrill. I knew that every last member of the Force was feeling the same stuff, and that nobody else was going to complain about it.

So. *Nobody* at all was going to complain about it.

"C'mon, Mutt," I said, maybe a bit more stoically than I really felt, "everybody is hurt to some degree at this point. *Everybody.* Aren't you dealing with any injuries right now?"

"Nope," he said with an exaggerated shrug.

I made extra effort to keep up with him, and to try and minimize my limp. Not that I had a limp.

"Oh," he finally said, as if it were just occurring to him. He held out his left hand to me like a big dog giving me his paw. It was a basically normal-looking paw, or hand, except for the part running down the outside edge, from the base of the pinkie to the wrist.

It looked like what was running beneath the surface there was less a stretch of bone than it was a small gnarled tree branch, with a big knot protruding from the midpoint of it.

"Well, I broke it," he said. "I punched this guy who I thought was a meathead. But he turned out to be a boulderhead. Also, I should have used my right hand. Left's just for setting a guy up. So really I got what I deserved."

He held his hand up like that for a surprisingly long time as we continued marching. So long, in fact, that I got tired of looking at it before he got tired of holding it up. I looked determinedly away. Then, when I looked back at him, it was still there.

"Mutton Head," I said, "how is a broken bone in your hand *not* an injury?"

"Pfffft. Look at us, Alice. Are we walking on our hands?"

"You got me there, pal. That's an excellent point. We are not walking on our hands."

"Exactly. That's why this isn't an injury any more than a bee sting would be. This is nothing."

And *that* was the position of the Forcemen on what did and did not constitute an injury.

"Gotcha," I said. "As long as we walk on two legs, then a broken hand is not an injury around here."

"But hey," he said as if I'd given him some great idea, "how 'bout I *do* walk the rest of the way on my hands? Even with the broken bone, I could probably still beat you into camp, what with that sad little hip thing you got happening."

I pretended to consider the offer for three seconds.

"Shut up, Mutton Head" was my reply.

"No, come on," he said, backpedaling so he could face me. "It'll be fun. We'll take bets from all the guys. Betcha nobody bets on you."

I could swear that no matter how much we walked we were getting no closer to the camp.

There was a cluster of about twenty guys marching about a hundred yards behind us. Mutt broke away from me and ran toward them.

"Boys," he called out, "we got a great bet going here . . ."

Ah crap. It hurt more than I would ever be able to tell anybody, but I double-timed it the rest of the way to camp. I had to put as much distance between me and him as possible, before he figured out what I was doing.

Because while this was excruciating, nothing was going to hurt as much as the humiliation of Mutton Head beating me back to base, walking on his hands, with one of them broken.

Nobody would have bet against him.

Not even me.

CHAPTER SEVEN

The Kid

There was plenty of rivalry between the Americans and Canadians of the First Special Service Force. Despite the fact that they were our next-door neighbors and little brothers all wrapped up together, this experiment we were undertaking was basically unprecedented. The two armies had long fought side by side, through way too many conflicts to count. But not under one command.

In fact, technically speaking, while common sense would say that Canada was joined at the hip to the United States in every way that mattered, there was one way that probably mattered most of all.

They were actually British.

Or Britishish, anyway.

As part of the Commonwealth, the Canadians had been involved in the war since the beginning, in 1939. You could often hear references to American forces as Johnnies-come-lately, since we didn't get in until after

Pearl Harbor in December '41. There was a lot of fighting that happened before we jumped in, and a whole lot of it was done by Canadians.

So really, if you squinted hard, it wouldn't be too difficult to see them as the senior partners in this new Forceman Firm of ours.

Nobody was about to squint that hard, however. The command structure was top-heavy with American officers, we were training on America bases, and even the Canadian recruits we had on board were issued with American uniforms for the duration of the First Special Service Force adventure.

This was indisputably our show, even if those guys were key players within it.

Didn't mean they didn't have plenty to contribute, based on their broader experience of this war. Or that they didn't have hard-won lessons to pass on to us. If we weren't too full of ourselves to accept them.

To be sure, there were a lot of pigheaded Yanks (yes, those were the *Yanks*) who were. I was not one of them.

It was sometime in early November when Mutt came bouncing into our tent feeling all generous. The Montana air was already turning slightly spiteful, and viewing snow on the top of the not-too-distant peaks had become commonplace. Late mornings like this one were prime time for catching a crucial nap before lunch, and then whatever wicked activity they had planned for us for the afternoon. We had all been up since the usual reveille squawked us awake at five o'clock. Then we had chow in the mess hall, calisthenics, and our beloved mile-and-a-quarter obstacle course all designed to heat us up before they slowed us right down again by lying us down on our bellies on the cold, cold ground for target practice out on the range. That would be the *rifle* range, not to be confused with the Range, which pretty much described the whole state of Montana.

That hot-cold-hot-cold routine was one of the great surprising challenges of our training so far. Getting tired and sweaty while pushing your physical endurance all over the camp, only to follow that with the seriously unpleasant sensation of lying flat on the chilled serving platter of the rifle range was a near-certain way to encourage cold and flu, bronchitis and pneumonia, in every last man we had.

One might almost think they were doing it to us on purpose. Just to see.

So it was no surprise that when Mutt ambled in, our gang was hunkered down and bundled up for whatever kip we could get ourselves. Sacks, Bergeron, Wallace, and Bruce were sound asleep. It always took me longer to drop off, especially in daylight. So while they were snoozing, I was relaxing by reading all the mail they'd left unattended under their bunks. Which meant I was free to indulge.

It wasn't like any invasion of privacy or anything, since I'd read it all already. A couple of times.

"Hey, hey," Mutton Head bleated, waking nobody and only just about getting my attention.

"Yes, Mr. Mutt," I said without lifting my eyes from Bergeron's letter from his girlfriend—who had a sister my age, by the way.

"I'd heard about the shortage of fresh reading material in this tent, so I brought you a present. You can only read other guys' mail for so long before, y'know, you go a little goofy."

"Who told you I do that?"

He ignored my perfectly reasonable question.

"In my civilized country, that's actually against the law, reading mail addressed to somebody else without their permission."

The clumsy way I was stuffing Bergeron's girl-friend's letter back into the envelope was more incriminating than a full confession would have been.

"I wasn't . . . Anyway, it's illegal in my country, too. So shut up."

"Right, pal, that's putting me in my place," he said, shaking his head and laughing at me. Then he dropped into a seat on the side of my cot. Right onto my very sore hip.

"Ahh, jeez!" I yelped.

"Sheesh," he said. "You New Hampshire guys are so fragile."

I wondered for a few seconds what good it would do me to make the point that nobody had ever referred to me as fragile, not once in my whole life, and that probably nobody from New Hampshire ever had to listen to such guff. The answer, coming swift and clear, was *none*. It would do me no good at all.

"So where's my present, Mutt?" I growled through gritted teeth.

He was beaming when he reached into his inside shirt pocket—which lots of guys learned to sew into their clothing—and pulled out a book.

"Happy birthday," he said. "What are you, twelve now?"

"It's not my birthday," I said.

"Still eleven, then. Good. Because I'll need you to give me that back after you've finished reading it.

Maybe even before you've finished. It's kind of top secret."

"Yeah, right," I scoffed.

"Okay, maybe second or third shelf from the top. But we're definitely not supposed to give them to our barbarian brethren to the south."

I checked the book over. It was small, maybe six inches high by four inches wide. And it had a very homemade feel to it. Like somebody's mom had hand-stitched the spine and reinforced the covers with heavy-duty board and hessian fabric to hold it all together. Despite all this, the book looked like it had been through war—literally, I assumed. It was bent and dented and crackled every which way. Still, it didn't look like it was giving up the fight any time soon.

Across the bottom of the front cover was a slash of heavy cloth tape with precise handwriting over it, saying,

YOUR MANUAL
Not for Circulation

"What's this?" I asked.

"So, it's true," he answered. "New Hampshire cavepeople can't read, either."

"Mutt," I said, "I swear, I will beat you to death with this book before I even attempt to read it."

"I knew you'd say that," he said. "Reading is so much harder than beating."

Turned out, Mutt was an inspiration.

"I bet I could read this book *and* beat you with it while I'm at it."

"All right, all right," he said, hands up surrender-style, laughing but clearly defusing me at the same time.

"So," I said, "you gonna tell me all about this little book or not?"

"I am," he said.

I had flipped open to what looked like the first serious part of the text.

COMMANDO TRAINING
INSTRUCTION NUMBER 1

I didn't venture any further than that heading. Every man in camp was speculating on a daily—no, hourly—basis just what it was we were up to. What were we being trained for, and where were we going to be dispatched?

This, at least, felt like an answer of some sort. Or

maybe the beginning of a possible, partial hint at one.

"Commandos," I said to Mutton Head, who was still essentially parked on my bad hip. "Are we actually commandos?"

A huge and unsettling smile unfurled across his crazy mouth.

"Yes," he said, "we actually are. Of course, I got bounced out of the British Commandos, and so . . ."

"Why'd you get bounced?"

"I was too tough. Kept breaking all their soldiers."

"So you're not going to tell me, then."

"No. But the important part is, things are different now. I'm ready this time. I am gonna be great this time. I have all that experience behind me— which you'll take advantage of, if you're smart. And also I have the Book. I wasn't supposed to hold on to that once they dumped me, and I'm *sure* not supposed to be waving it around to every Tom, Dick, and Alice out here on the Great Plains. The Brits really love their cloak-and-dagger, secret-secret stuff, I can tell you that."

"And you actually trained with them?"

"Yes, sir, Mr. Alice. They had me up there roughing it in a place called Lochaber, in the wild Highlands of Scotland. I'd call it Godforsaken, but I'm pretty sure God never got near enough to the place to forsake it. It's too wet even for God, that area."

"Mutt," I said wearily, laying in a phony yawn for emphasis, "thanks for this. But right now, I think I need to get a few winks in before the opportunity escapes me. I will read it, though. Later."

"Okay, sure, of course," he said, hopping up off my bunk. "But you remember to take extra special care of that book. If you let it fall into the wrong hands—or any hands—I'm afraid I'm obliged to kill you."

"Have you ever killed anybody?"

"Not actually. Not all the way, anyway. Not yet. But I'm gonna. And so are you, by the way. Don't forget that."

I had no idea why, but there was something in the warm and friendly way Mutt said it, even though warm and friendly was the way he said everything. It made me thoughtful about the whole killing thing, in a way I hadn't experienced before. And it made me sad.

"I won't forget it," I said as he stepped halfway out of the tent.

He stepped back in.

"Unless something happens to my book," he

added. "Then I *will* kill you, before you get a chance to kill anybody else."

"Well, in that case," I said, "I guess I won't lose your book."

"Wise," he said, and was gone.

I read for probably fifteen minutes before I started feeling the droopy eyelids. Still, my tiredness had battle with the compelling text I held in my hands.

In war, resolution, Winston Churchill had urged in supporting the formation of commando units. *In defeat, defiance.*

All the guys loved Churchill. We all aspired to be like him. Except maybe in better shape. I could almost hear his voice, urging me on, while at the same time reading me to sleep.

Commandos intended for "smash and grab" operations, behind enemy lines . . . Small units covering large areas . . . Emphasis on speed and cunning . . . Individuals deciding own course of action without being told . . . Esprit de corps . . . Offensive, not defensive spirit . . . Destruction of the enemy . . . Silence and secrecy . . . Self-reliance . . . Inquisitiveness . . . Opportunism . . . Open-mindedness . . . Physical fitness . . . Intelligence . . . Stalking and concealment . . .

*Creation of diversions . . . Street fighting and
rioting . . .*

My reading had been bleeding into my dreaming,
and maybe then to my sleep speaking, leading to my
bunkmates gleaning what I was supposed to be keeping to myself . . .

"Miscellaneous," said the voice that was neither
my own nor Winston Churchill's. It took me several
seconds to get it, but the voice belonged to Wallace,
now sitting on the side of his bunk and reading aloud
to the others. "Miscellaneous, which is unquestion-
ably the most significant category of all, separating
commando training from all other service training.
Because the commando is all about miscellany, about
improvisation and adaptability. What to do if taken
prisoner. Silent movement over all types of ground.
The various stages of a raiding operation."

I sat up like a jackknife. Wallace passed the book
over to Sacks, who then picked up the narration.

"The bayonet should take precedence over all
other weapons . . ."

I didn't know how long I was out for, so I couldn't
know how long this bullyboys book club had been in
session. But undoubtedly much of what I thought had
been running through my mind was what was being

directly read into it. A story time of jamokes was taking turns reading out loud the top(ish) secret commando manual that my good friend Mutton Head had insisted nobody could know about. I only prayed that Mutt himself wouldn't know about it.

"Oi, Yanks!" came the unsettling shout as Mutt slammed the makeshift wood-frame door of our tent into the makeshift doorframe.

"Listen, relax," I said, rising to my feet to greet him.

"What're you doing with my book?" he said as he made his way toward Sacks.

"Reading it," Sacks said. "What else are you supposed to do with a book?"

Enraged, Mutt leaped at Sacks and yelled, "I'll show you one possibility right now!"

Sacks just managed to unload a desperation pass, like a quarterback under a heavy rush, over Mutt and into the waiting hands of Bruce.

As Mutt wrestled Sacks off his bunk and onto the floor, I approached Bruce with outstretched hands. "C'mon, guys," I said. "The book doesn't belong to you."

"Oh," Bergeron called out, "but my girlfriend's letter belongs to you, does it?"

Ah, right.

"Sorry about that," I said. "I was bored. But you'll have to get me back some other way. This is Mutt's book."

Bruce peacefully handed the book over to me. Then, before I could even turn, Mutt snatched it far less peacefully away. He shoved it back into that inside pocket from where it came.

"What's the big deal, anyway?" Wallace asked. "It's just a book. I mean, it's a fantastic book, but still . . ."

"The big deal," Mutt huffed, "is secrecy. I don't know how far you read, but secrecy—"

"Silence and secrecy," Sacks called.

"Right," Mutt said wearily.

"And stalking and concealment," Bruce added.

"Yesss," Mutt hissed.

"Smash and grab," I added without even knowing where that came from.

"Sorry," I said as Mutt wheeled in my direction. I shrugged at him. "I wasn't awake for most of it, I swear."

Mutt growled. "I'm not even supposed to have that book with me here. And it *sure* isn't supposed to be circulating. So you can see why an outfit like this—"

"Commandos, right?" Wallace chirped, and the rest chimed in happily.

"Yes, commandos. You can see why secrecy is vital to an operation like this. And why somebody who clearly disregarded that sacred secrecy might find his sorry butt on the next cold train to Saskatchewan, dumped right out of the Special Forces altogether."

That was when I got even more unhelpful.

"Again," I said. I thought I was being sympathetic.

"Ya know, Alice . . ." Mutt grumbled, punching one big hairy fist into one big meaty palm as he stared me down.

Fortunately, Wallace took charge, since Wallace is our take-charge guy.

"So, why'd you give it to Alice, Mutton Head?" He was using the term as both name and accusation.

Mutt looked just a little bit sorry as he continued looking my way. At least he stopped the palm punching.

"He's still just a kid," he said. "And he seemed like he could use some help. We need to look out for him."

"Hey!" I objected. Probably fittingly, everybody ignored me.

"*Kid,*" Wallace said, pointing at me repeatedly. "*The Kid.* I like it. Better than Alice, anyway."

"Yeah," yelled somebody, then another somebody, then another piled on with "*The Kid, the Kid, the Kid!*"

I objected strenuously.

They ignored me strenuously.

Actually, maybe I didn't mind all that much. And the guys sure were enjoying it.

Suddenly, *bap*, and the book smacked me right in the face.

"You got the whole thing started, Kid," Mutt said, plunking down on the edge of Bergeron's bunk. "Might as well read on."

"Yes, excellent idea," Wallace said. "Read out loud to the rest of the class, Kid."

This was supposed to be nothing like what I left behind at school.

CHAPTER EIGHT

An Army Travels on Its Stomach

The guys were getting restless.

At least demolitions training was fun and instructive. We blew some old miners' buildings on the edge of camp so sky-high they may finally have come to a landing in Alaska.

There was a lot of hiking, marching, mountain climbing, and simulated cross-country skiing in anticipation of the ample snows surely to come soon.

The highlight of the autumn was a marching competition. This pitted the three regiments of the Force against one another in a sixty-mile race with full packs.

And if that was the highlight of the autumn, then surely the highlight of the highlight was lunch at the halfway mark. We brought nothing edible with us at all. This was part of the exercise. They were always preparing us for the times we would be cut off and on our own, unable to contact any other living souls to assist us. We had to learn how to make our way, orient ourselves by compass, by stars, by moon or sun or whatever was available, to establish our destination.

And get to that destination without being detected.

This included not dying of starvation—which obviously would have spoiled everything.

So this day, after thirty miles of hiking away from camp, our first nourishment since breakfast was?

Foraged.

We dumped our full packs in an impromptu mini camp formation. Then we went out into the hills with nothing but our knives, to bring back any edible, potentially edible, or remotely possibly edible things we could find. And we had exactly twenty minutes for each man to contribute his bounty to our potluck meal.

Miss the cutoff, even by a second, and you missed the meal. You would walk *another* thirty miles on an empty stomach.

When the feast came rolling in, it was an impressive spread indeed. Each one of us was using his shirt as a sort of apron/shopping bag, and Montana did not skimp on the treasures it offered up. Worms and salamanders and wood lice, crickets and beetles and grasshoppers. For vegetables, we had a cornucopia of wildflowers, scrubby tough green weeds, and varieties of grasses and bushes that would make any bison's mouth water.

It would have been nice if somebody lured in a bison with that. But they'd take too long to cook.

We were instructed for that reason not to take anything bigger than a rodent. And not a big rodent, either. Time was short if we truly wanted to compete in this race, and who wants an undercooked prairie dog or rat, huh? Certainly not us, since we were not barbarians, and we didn't have any ketchup.

It was, of course, all the enlisted men doing the foraging. But the kindly noncommissioned officers were back at camp when we returned, there to give instruction and help with prep and presentation in any way they could.

As a matter of fact, they even cheated a little on our behalf. Turned out that, to make one of the main dishes a bit more palatable, they'd brought along what passed for takeout food in this operation.

Hundreds, thousands of earthworms, which had been presoaked in water overnight. Apparently that's the first stage in making earthworms not only nutritious but delicious.

That was just the first stage, mind.

"Gentlemen, unload all your findings into these buckets over here," Lt. Morrison said when our little gang reconvened with the collected goodies. Morrison was the NCO assigned to show my company the ropes of this particular peculiar dining experience.

"All into the same buckets?" Bruce asked, sounding indignant.

The lieutenant laughed. "Private, are you worried about spoiling the meal by mixing up all the different flavors?"

Bruce laughed back. "I think I see your point, Lieutenant." He quickly emptied his worms, beetles, crickets, and assorted weeds into the nearest bucket. Laughing along, all the other guys stepped up and did the same, until we had a lineup of pails loaded with writhing, teaming, slithering, crawling, hopping . . . lunch.

"Now," Morrison said, "comes the easy, but no less important, part." He reached his hand down into the bucket of presoaked worms and drew out one that was as long as a bootlace but four times as fat. He held the worm in one hand and with the other began stroking, squeezing, massaging the disgusting mass from one tip to the other. Gradually, stuff came out the far end.

Stuff came out.

"See," the lieutenant went on, "if you don't work all the mud and partially digested worm food out before you consume it, then you are most likely eating mushy worm *poop*. I can assure you, you do not want that. And we do not want that *for* you. So everyone, step up here and do some squeezing."

There were muffled retching sounds as a few guys unwisely allowed themselves to start thinking about it, but mostly everyone just got on with it. Watching the slimy brown goop ooze out of each worm and fall to the ground was quite gross if you thought much about it, so not thinking much about it was the only way to go.

It also got us working fast.

The pile of whistle-clean worms accumulated so quickly that within minutes the lunch bucket was full to brimming.

"Excellent," Morrison said. "We'll get to the next phase of preparation momentarily. First, over here." He led us back to the other pails of accumulated grub, where he immediately went into bug prep. A lieutenant from another group sidled over and dropped a metal bucket that had a fire burning within it.

"Thank you, Lieutenant," Morrison said.

"You're welcome, Lieutenant," the other lieutenant said. Then he popped something in his mouth and started smile-chewing vigorously. It sounded crunchier than any potato chip I ever heard.

"Look," Morrison continued. He pulled a large cricket out of a bucket, then impaled it on a pointed stick roughly the size of a pencil. Cricket didn't like it very much. It paddled its legs in the air.

It liked the next bit even less. The lieutenant grabbed the bug's head in a pincher movement with the nails of his thumb and index finger. Then he pulled.

The cricket's head came right off in the lieutenant's grip, like a loose cork. That was followed by a load more looseness. What appeared to be the entire contents of the internal insect came slurping out, trailing loyally behind the head.

"Right, soldiers. If it has got an exoskeleton, then we clean it out in this fashion, like gutting a fish. Then we flash-fry them, for no more than four or five seconds, like so."

Morrison held the stick-impaled creature over the bucket flame for the designated time. Satisfied that the deed was done, he removed the snack from the fire, looked all around at us for extra effect, and then chomped the cricket off the stick like it was a toasted marshmallow.

Didn't sound like a toasted marshmallow, though.

Karrunnch-crunch-crunch was all the cricket had to say for itself at this point.

Guys howled and moaned, mostly to be dramatic. But they jumped right to it when the lieutenant barked, "Chow time! Each one of you has seven minutes to consume enough nutrition to get you another thirty miles back to camp. When I whistle, you are to stop, no matter what you have or have not had to eat. Then you will pick up your pack and start marching immediately. Go, go, go!"

There was all manner of unsettling noise at that point. There was groaning and retching. Crunching and crackling. Some guys barfed things up, but with Lt. Morrison swooping on every guy who did, nobody was prepared to do it twice.

Another lieutenant came by with another bucket. "These worms have now been boiled, for hygiene purposes. You are welcome!" Every man he passed was ordered to dig in. "You must, repeat, *must* squeegee out the remaining worm poop and guts before consuming this delicacy!"

Nobody argued; nobody hesitated. When it was

your turn, you just scooped, squeegeed, and swallowed. I believed this type of dining was known as *family style*.

I'd eaten worse, when my father did the cooking on fishing trips. And since we were eating pretty much the same stuff we made the fish eat on those trips, it was probably only fair.

More than once, Bruce came over and shoulder-bumped me. "You gonna finish those worms, pal? Got any spare wood lice?"

"Shut up and eat," Wallace said. He was taking this very seriously, which was how he took most things.

But you haven't lived until you've seen a very serious fellow talk very seriously with his mouth full of legs, heads, wings, and a couple of squidgy squiggles of leftover life.

By the time Lt. Morrison whistled and started screaming at us to saddle up and march, I had eaten at least eight worms, a fistful of assorted exoskeletons, and more gritty, fibrous greens and wildflowers than a cow probably puts away in a week. I kept waiting to feel sick.

But I never did. As the whole Force set out like clockwork to complete the race, all I felt was . . .

strong. Fit and ready and anxious for whatever came next. Bergeron and Sacks were clearly feeling the same, as they spearheaded the march toward home, going way faster than we had on the way out.

My regiment came in first. For this, each winning man was awarded a new spork.

CHAPTER NINE

Pop Goes the Weasel

There were rumors everywhere, every day, about where we would be deployed and in what kind of mission. Then those rumors would change to something new. Then they would change back again.

Knowing the way the military worked, I was convinced that somewhere there was one office dedicated exclusively to generating and disseminating rumors—the Department of Rumormongering, perhaps—to keep the minds of the troops occupied until the real thing came together.

But by December 1942, the situation had gotten full-scale maddening. We were all pretty new to the machinations of army brass, but even we could tell that this was not the way things were supposed to work. We'd been trained so hard, we were officially a threat to all creatures great and small, including ourselves. If things were working right, we'd have been dispatched someplace by now, or at least told what to expect. We were already at the very peak of preparedness.

And Pearl Harbor was exactly one year ago.

It was more than time for us to get in the game.

Additionally, all the stuff we'd taught *ourselves* through the commando manual had us convinced we were in for some soldiering like the world had never seen before.

Unfortunately, we were starting to wonder whether the world *would* ever see it.

Then the long-promised Montana snow started falling.

And falling.

And falling.

It was fairly hypnotic, staring at the fat flakes tumbling out of the impossible Montana sky. The distant and not-so-distant hills were already covered in white. The sky was camouflaging itself, joining with those hills and the ground just outside to make one uninterrupted wipeout of white, everywhere you cared to look. Bergeron and I had lingered in the mess tent long after breakfast, equal parts bored and enchanted as we watched winter smother the whole base.

"Guys," Sacks said as he swooped into the tent.

"What are you doing? We've been called out. You need to come out to the strip. We've got work to do."

With that, he was gone again, scurrying like some arctic fox across the parade grounds and away to our assigned gathering place.

Reluctantly, with our expectations dampened by experience and our senses softened by December, Bergeron and I made our way out to the spot.

"Listen," I said, having taken months to work up the courage, "about your girlfriend's sister . . ."

"No, kid," he snarled, "just, no."

Through the heavy coating of snow that had been falling for several hours now, we found the rest of the team already gathered at our rendezvous point.

Our team plus two, that is.

Our regular crew was there, but with the addition of Munch—our Norwegian ski instructor—and a dog. Looked vaguely like a dog, anyway. He was pony-size, with a coat of gunmetal-blue fur over his shoulders and back that looked to run about eight inches thick. My initial thought on seeing him was that this was the first creature I'd met since receiving my knife that I might not be able to kill with it. If it came down to that.

It *probably* wouldn't come down to that, though.

The dog came bounding toward Bergeron and me, and I instinctively drew the dagger out of the scabbard strapped to my hip.

"Don't be an idiot," Bergey said before stepping directly in front of me and allowing the animal to leap and tackle him right onto his back.

Bergeron lay there flat, looking up at me, letting the beast play at gnawing through his neck. "Kid," he said, giggling through the less-than-ferocious mauling, "I'd like you to meet Otto. Otto, this is the Kid."

"Otto," I said, bowing in his direction.

Otto interpreted this to mean that I was calling him.

I watched the whole big snow-swirly sky of Montana whip up and over me as Otto bounded and pounced, leaving me slammed to the ground.

Bergeron, evidently not fearing for my safety or his own, threw himself on my attacker. The three of us rolled merrily around on the cold, hard winter wonderland of ground.

Shaggy like a rambunctious haystack, Otto was clearly delighted with the wrestling. Not that his face was giving much away, since the mass of fur hanging down from his head, snout, and ears made it anybody's guess whether he even had a face.

"Otto's our boy," Sacks called as he rushed over to join the fun. He gave the dog a double forearm cross-check in the ribs. Seemed like he put all of himself into it, but Otto barely flinched. In fact, Sacks more or less bounced right off him before tumbling over onto his back. "He's basically a canine version of us," Sacks continued. "Can't be sure, but we figure he's a refugee escaped from the military guard-dog training center on the other side of Helena. Must have just broken away, and since nobody's come looking for him, I guess he's an unwanted desperado. Which makes him ours, right, guys?"

Everybody whooped and howled their approval, to the point where Otto himself had no option but to join in the howling.

We were very much a wolf pack now.

"And after all," I said, "he did choose us of his own accord. A volunteer no-good, just like the rest of us."

"Ooo-ooo-whoooo," somebody howled, or everybody howled. "Playtime's over, boys," hollered Wallace, our possibly-official-but-possibly-not company leader. He was standing up behind the controls of a nifty little machine we'd only glimpsed a couple of times so far, the T-15 all-terrain transport vehicle.

Affectionately known as the Snow Weasel.

The Weasel looked like a small tugboat mounted on top of tanklike tracks. It was actually designed to carry a maximum of four men and a modest amount of supplies. But since we ourselves were designed to ignore design and make up our own, this beast was now packed and stacked, with six men, one abominable snow mutt, snowshoes, ski gear, and weapons and supplies that indicated we were possibly planning for an overnight excursion . . . or longer.

I'd been camping a million times back home, but this was the bivouac of my dreams.

We rocked and bounced and tumbled around the small space afforded by the Weasel, as we hightailed across the flat on the way to Pine Mountain and yet more training. Otto repeatedly threw his great furry mitts over Wallace's shoulders, as if he wanted to take over the driving. Thirty to thirty-five miles per hour might not sound like hightailing in most circumstances, so maybe the dog could actually handle the controls. But this felt like we were rocketing, what with all the boys, the gear, and the massive animal all skimming together across the bleach-white frosty surface of planet Helena.

It sure seemed like we were headed to something big. Maybe it would turn out to be just one more disappointing training exercise in preparation for not much more than another training exercise, and then another.

But it didn't feel like it.

As we skittered across the landscape, this started feeling like a different beast.

Even if the powers that be had simply given up on sending us into the conflict overseas, and decided to settle on allowing Montana to finally declare war on Wyoming, that would be just fine with us.

Personally, I was happy to follow our Norwegian friend wherever he thought we should go. When Munch first showed up, though, I was highly skeptical. Why did I need instruction from *anybody* when it came to anything ski-related?

Then Munch came along, with his cool way about him and his quiet certainty about snow and ice.

I was a convert. For the first two months or so, all he did was train us in the best available methods of traversing the Earth's surface by way of cross-country skiing—without snow under the skis.

To put it mildly, I was unimpressed.

First, as far as skiing went, cross-country was for grandmas and people who had no idea what snow was actually good for.

Second, how could this guy have anything to teach someone from *New Hampshire* about sliding down slippery slopes?

To get this out of the way as quickly and painlessly as possible . . .

First, wrong.

And second, ah, also wrong . . .

Norwegian people had to be the best skiers in the world, judging by Munch's skills.

I was dumbfounded from day one by what he could do. He achieved speeds on completely flat terrain that I could barely make while barreling down the jump during the Olympic trials.

Now he led us out to the base of the magical frozen mountain for one more session of trying to make us as good as him.

I was nearly there. But I would be foolishly lying if I pretended that I could combine cross-country and alpine downhill and ski jumping into the full package that Munch had mastered. So now that we were here—

Norway!

"Norway!" Somebody shouted out as we were handed our gear. Our gear, which now included something we'd never even seen before.

White camouflaging.

This was great beyond imagination. Not unlike when we were given our parachute packs before boarding the plane, each of us was now handed a pack that opened up into a sort of otherworldly, giant white weatherproof poncho. We each immediately draped ours over the full kits we'd already donned.

"What about Norway?" Munch asked as he pressed gear into my hands.

"We're really being sent to Norway?" Bruce hollered as he opened up his pack of equipment like a kid tearing into Christmas presents.

In addition to the brilliant white poncho, each man received his skis, big goggles, and a pair of poles that looked like they had large round waffles attached to the bottom.

Oh, and a new weapon.

"Congratulations," Munch said. We were all standing more or less in line—facing him but not looking at him. We were too preoccupied with our

Christmas presents. "You men are among the first to be issued the M3 submachine gun, fresh from the factory."

It was a handsome thing . . . short, light, just stubby enough to be easy to carry but still potent from the look of it. It was sort of halfway between a sidearm and a full-size machine gun. We'd trained on the Thompson M1, but this was feathery by comparison.

Munch continued. "You will see that you have just one spare magazine to carry, so be sure to conserve rounds when the time comes. It is fairly easy to operate this gun, therefore be mindful not to get carried away."

Live ammunition? *Spare* live ammunition? Things were finally getting serious.

I wanted to get carried away. I very much wanted to get carried away.

Munch did his Munchy thing, attacking Pine Mountain as if it was nothing more than a game of hopscotch. Now, this gang of ours was not inclined to take a challenge lightly, and anytime we were left in Munch's snowy wake, we couldn't help but take it as a call to arms.

Just by being as good as he was, he made every last one of us better.

Even Otto.

Otto stood still for about thirty seconds as Munch ascended Pine Mountain. He looked back and forth and then back again between us and him, deciding where his loyalties were.

They fell, unsurprisingly, upward.

He bounded—there really wasn't a better word for how Otto did anything—in the direction of our Norwegian superman, daring us to hop along and catch up.

Sacks, Bergeron, Wallace, Bruce, and I pulled ourselves together, strapped all the gear on, slung the guns over our shoulders . . . and stared at one another like dopes.

In the half minute it took us to do that, Otto and Munch had surely put another quarter mile between them and us.

"Roaaarrr!" we all cried as we made our initial assault on the innocent mountain.

It was seriously hard work to ski your way to the top of even a *small* mountain, like Pine. It was only possible now because of our previous cross-country training, combined with the insane level of physical fitness that came of our endless Force training. Still, by the time we found one Norwegian soldier and one mound of dog perched at the summit, you could see the clouds of our collective breaths all the way back to Helena.

"Now we are going to race back down," said Munch, without even waiting for us to recover. Otto seemed to understand just what he was saying. He ran excited, bouncy rings around the instructor. "Otto and I are going to take off ninety seconds ahead of you. You must track us and attempt to catch up and capture us, before we return to the bottom and steal your Weasel."

Munch was the master, no doubt about it. But I was confident that, now that we were down-hilling it, I would be able to make up that minute and a half and catch him before he could make off with our vehicle. Especially with that crazy bear dog dogging him the whole way.

In fact, it seemed almost too easy.

"Are you all familiar with the sport, the biathlon?" Munch added with a satisfied grin. "In my native country, we call it *skiskyting*."

"Skiing and shooting, right?" Wallace said.

"In crudely simple terms, yes," Munch answered.

"Crudely simple, I'm your man!" Bruce yelled, punctuating it with an entirely superfluous "Woo-hoo!"

"That outburst will cost you, Private Bruce," said Munch. "I realize this is just an exercise and, yes, you guys are probably overtrained by now, and overanxious. But that's all the more reason not to lose your edge now. Stealth and self-control, these are going to save you over and over again. You must keep your emotions in check at all times. Therefore, Bruce, you will hold your position for another ninety seconds behind the rest of the group, before finally setting out."

"Unfair," Bruce moaned.

"Considering that *woo-hoo* would likely earn you a sniper's bullet in a real combat situation, I'd say it's more than fair. And since I'll be giving out prizes based on order of finish, perhaps you'll be motivated to ski faster than your teammates."

"Yeah," Bruce scoffed, "thanks, but I already have a pretty nice spork."

Everybody laughed out loud—though not *overly* loud—at that. But we all also knew that Bruce was going to break his neck to try and beat us all to the bottom.

"So it's basically just a downhill race," Sacks said, "with you cheating a little bit."

"Well," Munch said, "I get to cheat a lot. You see, I was out here earlier, mapping out a route for myself. There was only half as much snow then, so it already looks a lot different. But I know what's what. You will be able to track me, of course, through the ski marks in the snow. But my trail through the pines won't be as easy for you to follow as it will be for me to make it. Also—and this is where the biathlon aspect comes in—there will be points along the way where you'll find enemy sentries. You are to stop and eliminate those sentries with gunfire before moving on."

Bergeron decided to voice what everyone was thinking. "How will you know we've accomplished that?"

"Well," Munch said, "I happen to be a big fan of the honor system."

"Me too," Bruce said. "That's my favorite system of all. Easiest to beat."

Munch sighed dramatically. "What kind of instructor would I be if I hadn't planned for *that*, Private Bruce?"

"The generous kind?" Bruce responded, incorrectly.

"You'll know the real answer when you find the targets," Munch said. Then he hitched himself up to hit the trail. A trail only he knew. "You'll go in teams of two. After Otto and me, ninety seconds later you two go, Sacks and Bergeron. One minute later, Greene and Wallace will follow. Ninety seconds after that," he said with a grin and a dismissive wave, "the rest of you will go."

"The *rest*?" Bruce said with a laugh. "Sheesh, even the dog got mentioned by name."

"By the way," Munch added, "if you shoot me, or Otto, or one another, then you automatically lose."

But of course.

It took the Otto-Munch team about a second and a half to cover the fifty yards out of the mountaintop clearing and disappear into the woods.

Wallace was keeping time.

"Go, men!" he called.

Sacks and Bergeron dug hard into the snow with their poles, launching themselves down the slope.

"Can we trust you to time yourself properly once we take off?" Wallace asked Bruce.

"No," Bruce responded casually.

"Ah, you're a man of honor," Wallace said to him.

With all seriousness, or at least as seriously as Bruce could say anything, he responded, "The First Special Service Force does not require men of honor. In fact, it discourages them. What it requires is men who *will get the job done*, no matter what."

Wallace and I looked at Bruce, then at each other.

"He's got a point," I said.

"I suppose he does," Wallace said.

"See you at the bottom," I called over my shoulder as we started our descent.

"Oh, you'll see me before that," Bruce said.

Munch knew just what he was doing when he ordered us the way he did. He had no intention of losing this competition. While Sacks and Bergeron were great all-rounders, capable of rising to any task set before them, they were no serious threats to catching the Norwegian in a ski race. The only genuine threats here were me and the straggler Bruce.

Munch did his best to put impediments in our way. It was going to be our job to overcome those impediments.

Wallace led, because Wallace leads. He was a gifted tracker, and there were no hesitations as we slalomed our way through the first stretch of fairly dense forest. I was right on his heels, sometimes literally. Occasionally he had to look back over his shoulder to chew me out for running the front tips of my skis right up and over the backs of his.

It would be important for me to quit that. The woodland was so thick with trees, and the required turns so sharp, that the biggest threat to anyone in this exercise would have been Wallace breaking his neck in a collision while having to turn and yell at me.

There were shots. I nearly stopped in my tracks at the surprise sound of the M3 popping off round after round in such a concentrated burst. But when I realized Wallace was bearing down even harder to make tracks downhill, I dug my poles in and chased after him.

In another couple of minutes, we plowed to a stop at a treacherous spot in the trail. It was a small clearing, overlooking a steep drop-off to the left. Sacks was just then elbowing Bergeron out of the way to shoot at something in the distance.

There was a small flag near where we stood, a flap of white fabric waving from a flexible willow stick jammed into the ground. Written in heavy marker on the fabric were the words:

BERGERON—HAT
SACKS—VEST

Looking over Sacks's shoulder as he aimed, we could see the snowman. He stood at attention about thirty yards down the slope, and he was wearing a vest that was frankly embarrassing on him. There was a clump of dark something on the snow several yards farther down the hill.

"That's his hat there on the ground," Bergeron said, with a childish excitement that made me feel like the grown-up of the bunch for once. "Blasted it right off his head."

"Good for you," I said.

"Shut up, everybody," Sacks snapped before squeezing the M3's trigger and peeling off a bunch of rounds.

The snowman looked almost lifelike—or more like deathlike—as the bullets tore into his vest in roughly the heart region. The shots chewed him up in such a way that he partially collapsed leftward and onto the ground.

"Nice shooting," Wallace said.

"Yee-hah!" Sacks yipped as he shoved off with his poles to launch down the hill toward his prize.

"Grab my hat while you're down there," Bergeron called after him.

We watched for several seconds as Sacks made the trip to the bottom, as if he was catapulted out of a chute. Once there, he ripped what was left of the vest off the snowman, turned, and began the much more arduous upcountry trek back to where we were.

"Hey," Bergeron grumbled. "The hat. He forgot my hat!"

"Ha," Wallace said. "It's a race, dummy. He didn't *forget* anything. You're on your own, my friend."

"Argghh!" Bergey shoved off down the slope.

At almost the exact same time, there was a swoosh behind us, and we turned to see Bruce flying past.

"Heigh-ho!" he whooped—sounding just like all seven dwarfs—as he left us in his powdery wake.

Wallace and I saddled up and lit out after him.

The trail got a lot faster through this next stretch, straighter and less packed with trees. While I was good at the slalom, this was really my game— straight, steep, and fast. Out on the open flat, I turned on the speed and passed Wallace like one of his tires was flat. Way up ahead, I saw Bruce turn hard right into a thick copse of trees and disappear from my view.

Behind me, I heard the unexpected gargle of Wallace expressing some frustration. I glanced back just long enough to catch him working his way back uphill for some reason.

Not my problem. This was a race.

I followed where Bruce had just entered the trees, when I heard what had to be Wallace's M3 going off uphill. His burst of fire was much shorter than the other two guys' were, reflecting the fact that Wallace was a more patient, and more accurate, shooter.

But what could he have been shooting at? I saw no signs along the way.

My answer greeted me a short way inside the wood. Strewn straight across the ski tracks was a willow flag just like the one where the other guys had been target shooting. I jammed on the brakes and picked it up. The letters read,

WALLACE—GAS MASK
GREENE—HELMET

The stinker. The absolute skunk.

Bruce had removed our flag so that we would sail right past it. Wallace, because he is Wallace, caught sight of our enemy scarecrow in the distance. I, because I am not Wallace and was traveling at the speed of sound, didn't.

There was no way I could make it back up to my intended target and have any chance in this competition. So, plan B it was.

I took off downhill like a human torpedo. I practically wiped out four different times, as I achieved ski-jump speeds over moguls, down into ravines, and one time even around a family of deer crossing my path.

But eventually I caught sight of him. I saw Bruce disappear into a glacial dip, followed him down and then up, and by the time we were on the flat again, we were almost neck and neck. I would have caught him in another couple seconds, but then he jammed on his brakes at the sight of yet another of those infernal flags.

He snowplowed, with the toes of each ski pointing inward, which was the proper way to come to a halt—if we'd been going at maybe a quarter the speed we were traveling. At *this* speed, he had no chance, and I had even less.

When we collided, my chin hammered the back of his head the way a woodpecker would decimate a tree. The crash was spectacular, with arms and legs and poles and goggles and guns blasting into a big, dusty snowy mess.

As we crawled around on the ground regathering our stuff, I said, "Bruce, I have met some dirty dogs in my life, but you are the dirtiest and doggiest."

He had just collected his goggles, and plunked himself down in the snow like he was about to watch a picture show. He pulled his goggles over his eyes and grinned at me with all of his fifty or so teeth bared wickedly in my direction.

"And that, Kid," he said, "is why you should hope you always have me right by your side, whenever they get around to inserting us into this war."

He looked mighty pleased with himself. As I supposed he should have. He was dead right, actually. Not that he'd be hearing it from me.

"Nah," I said, "I think I'll be just fine on my own."

He picked up the flag with his assignment on it, which had gotten flattened in our crash. "Suit yourself," he said, reading.

His M3 was still lying in the snow, a couple feet from me.

"Thanks, I think I will," I said.

I picked up the weapon, dangling by the strap. I flashed back to my high school track and field days . . . and my beloved hammer throw.

"No," Bruce said, looking up just in time to see what I was doing. "No, Kid, no, don't!"

One, two, three swings over my head, and . . . release.

I was pleased to know that I still had my form. The gun sailed in a beautiful arc, up and up and up and down and down and down onto the side of the hill, where it landed probably forty yards back in the direction we'd come from. Then it skidded to a stop after another ten yards or so.

I snatched the flag from Bruce and read it: BRUCE—BIB

I looked down the slope to where the snowman was wearing a red bib, like he was going to be dining on barbecue or lobster or something. This would be a cinch.

"Hey!" Bruce called when he saw all three of the other guys shushing our way, led by Wallace. "My gun. Right there. Grab my gun."

Wallace picked up speed, digging in hard with his poles until he was just about to breeze past us.

"Heigh-ho," he sang to Bruce as he left us there.

As Bruce began his ascent to retrieve his firearm, I lined up and aimed mine. Everyone else was likely approaching the Weasel as I blasted away at that sad little lobster bib. I had to restrain myself in order to save enough of it to bring back with me.

Nobody got a new spork. Or any other prize, for that matter.

"Dead men," Munch said to us when we'd gathered back at base. We found him and Otto all cozied up in the mess tent. The Weasel was long stolen and returned to wherever the Weasels congregated. There were no winners in the race. "Every one of you," he elaborated, "dead. Do you guys have any idea how much racket you were making up there?"

"They're submachine guns, Munch," Bergeron said, "they're bound to make a little bit of noise."

"No, fool," Munch responded, sounding like he was taking this personally—like he was taking *our* jeopardy to heart. "Not the gunfire. The banter, the childish horseplay. If there were any real enemy fighters within five miles, they would have hunted you all down before you even got a chance to fire."

"Yeah," Sacks said, "but everybody knew there were no enemy fighters within five miles of us. Or five hundred, or five thousand, for that matter."

"Well," Munch said sternly, "that is *absolutely* no

reason to get sloppy and stupid. This is where you learn not to get yourselves killed for no good reason. Come on, boys, you were all trained better than that. Even Bruce."

Everybody laughed but not as much as we would have if we didn't know he was right. And if Munch didn't look so truly sad about it. Otto, too, looked sad, in that general area where his face must have been located behind the hair curtain. Might have been his body language, with him slumping a little bit.

"Because," Munch said extra solemnly, "from this point on, it really is going to matter. It's a shame that you guys have gotten so punchy waiting to be deployed, but it's exactly the time now to pull yourselves together. Gentlemen, you are shipping out tomorrow."

For once, just briefly, we were stunned into silence.

Unlike when we first arrived in Helena, the train we boarded in the morning wasn't all blacked out. We were headed back east, and it didn't matter that we all knew it. We were still hoping that our eastward travels would extend all the way to Norway, but there was no confirmation of that. We all silently hoped that was where we'd wind up because it was the best place to pour all our specialized training into a terrain and an objective to give the Nazis a lot more than a black eye. I suppose it was because I was still sort of a kid, like they all said, but I found myself dreaming over and over about being dropped from an airplane. I imagined descending from a great height with my M3 over my shoulder, crossing a mountain range onto an icy plateau with great big oil refineries behind it. In my dream, I always killed hundreds of German soldiers, and the Norwegians—all of whom looked just like Munch and had Otto dogs bounding along beside them—came swarming to greet me like their all-conquering hero. There may have been other guys helping, but mostly it was just me.

I told Bruce about the dream and asked him if he had anything similar.

"Yeah, Kid," he said with one eyebrow raised pretty much above his hairline, "that's exactly my dream." The sarcastic way he said it made me feel like a five-year-old picking my nose through the whole story.

The train jerked into motion, chug-chugging us the first few yards out of Montana and into the big war. Munch, with Otto leaning hard into his thigh, was waving with his left hand and saluting with his right. Gathered at the window like a bunch of pups, we all did some version of saluting him—them—back.

We almost never saluted anybody before. Quite possibly would never do it again.

CHAPTER TEN

Spoiling for a Fight

Brother,

I don't know if you will believe this—I am not sure what I believe myself these days—but I'm coming Rome.

Okay, so maybe that one you should not believe. I am not, strictly speaking, coming Rome.

Close enough, though. Well, of course nothing but the real thing would be close enough to Rome.

But Vermont isn't very far off, is it?

I know, I know. Vermont is stupid and ridiculous, and isn't fit to fetch water for New Hampshire. However, it IS in the vicinity. Fort Ethan Allen, to be exact. And I AM going to be there. Even if it's just for a little while. Do we know why we are going to be there? No, we do not. But we will go, and we will master some other form of warfare there, and THEN we will go somewhere to use it on our enemies.

Or not.

But if not, my brother, we are ready to start using all this expertise on one another. If they do not do something with us soon, some of us—myself included—just might wind up back in the stockade.

I will be closer than I thought I was going to be, anyway. I, along with pretty much everybody else, was convinced they were going to ship us off to Norway.

Norwegians are pretty good skiers, it turns out. As in, REALLY good skiers. The ones we knew around Berlin were no flukes. Our ski instructor in Montana was amazing and taught everybody enough to qualify as a bunch of experts in every type of skiing—even the boring parts were kind of interesting with him.

Anyway, we did not go to Norway. We went to Norfolk. You can see the confusion there, yeah? First three letters are the same.

And that is where the similarity ends.

We thought we were going to Norway because of all the mountain and snow training we were doing, and because the rotten Nazis have got themselves so dug in there since they went and occupied the place. Between the North Sea coastline, the mountains, and all the oil, there was quite a lot for Adolf and his pals to get excited about. So we got all worked up thinking that we were just the boys the Allies needed to parachute into the country, shoehorn the jerks, then ski right back out again.

We were slightly mistaken.

Norfolk, Virginia, doesn't have much in the way of oil, mountains, or snow.

Coast, though, they have got. The harbor is massive and beautiful, and right now with the war on it's as busy as any place I have ever seen. We are just a tiny part of everything here, as they sent us to this very spot for a crash course of amphibious training. That was pretty much the only type of training we hadn't swallowed whole during our program so far. The aquatic scene *in ol' Montana was, shall we say, limited. But now, in addition to all our infantry and artillery know-how, and our airborne expertise, our explosives and mountain and ski and intelligence-gathering education, I would have to say that this amphibious icing makes our outfit the deadliest, most complete cake anywhere in the world. A world that we can master regardless of where we are, what we need to do, and what type of earthly conditions surround us as we do it.*

Land, sea, sky, snow, nobody is going to have the edge on us.

Nobody.

Funnily enough—though to us it was not at all funny—it seemed like that was exactly who we were going to be fighting.

Nobody.

We went from Fort Ethan Allen all the way across the country again. To San Francisco, California.

Hey, fellas, Norway is back that way. Along with Germany and all the rest of Europe!

Yes, sarcasm was now getting the better of us.

But for once it seemed there was an honest-to-goodness plan.

From San Francisco, we were dispatched northward. We weren't being sent after the Germans after all. We were going after the Japanese, who had been occupying the Aleutian Islands.

Right there on our doorstep.

Over our doorstep, in fact. The Japanese had overstepped.

This was the only spot on the globe where this fight actually looked like it was threatening our American home. The Aleutians were a string of islands extending out into the North Pacific from the tip of Alaska. They were officially Alaskan territory, and therefore American territory.

The Japanese had been occupying the Aleutian islands of Attu and Kiska for a full year by the time we were sent up there to take them back. This was the very definition of *too close for comfort*, and everybody was talking about the likelihood that the Japanese were going to use their position as a staging point for attacks on America's northwestern cities. It took us two weeks to chug northward from California until we reached our destination off the coast of Alaska. Every last man was building up his tension and rage with every hour we sailed. By the end, we were salivating to engage.

Then, off the coast of Kiska, the fleet settled into preparation for invasion.

For another two solid weeks, we listened to the bombastic symphony of American naval firepower pounding away at the known entrenched positions of the Japanese.

Finally, on August 15, 1943, the enemy had been deemed softened up enough to send in the ground troops.

First of those troops were to be the First Special Service Force. This kind of spearhead, let-me-at-'em charge was precisely what we had been trained to do all along. It was just a bonus that Kiska in August presented all the specialty challenges that made us perfect for the job. Rough, rocky harbor, snowy or icy ground conditions, mountains, the works. We were in our element. Rather, we were in *all* of our elements.

And we were first among firsts. As part of the FSSF's first regiment, we were the lead attackers when we assaulted the beach.

Ferried into shore on all manner of landing craft, we were too charged up to be either scared of the unknown in front of us, or sick at the crazy chop of the surf that was threatening to throw us up on the beach. (While we simultaneously threw up on the beach.)

When the big front ramps of the landing craft slapped down into the water like great whale tongues spitting us into the face of the enemy, I had just enough presence of mind to suddenly fear a bullet-hail barrage of Japanese gunfire. Or even worse, one of those insane banzai charges that everybody talked about and that terrified even the hardest-bitten of our guys.

But . . .

None of it.

None of anything.

The load of us—guns at the ready, looking for trouble—were instead greeted by silence. We splashed and thrashed through the shallow, lapping waters, up onto the frozen beachhead, and on over the small dunelike barrier that ringed the beach.

There was nobody home.

Maybe we had just pounded them entirely out of existence with the naval firepower we bestowed. But the lack of splattered bodies suggested otherwise.

We were dispatched to the surrounding area to

investigate whether there was some elaborate trap set for us. Creeping around was just as tense, peeking into every dip in the terrain, around every little hill that could turn out to be some mad warrior's lair, as it had been jumping into the water expecting to get machine-gunned facedown into the soup.

Sometimes, *not* fighting could be as draining as the real thing.

Not that we would know, really.

Turned out, we wouldn't know for a while yet. The Japanese had abandoned Kiska some weeks before. So after securing the island for the good guys once more, we steamed our way south to California all over again.

Unbelievably, from California, we were shipped cross-country, retracing our steps all the way back to Fort Ethan Allen in Vermont.

As we stepped off the train in Vermont, Sacks said it pretty well for everybody when he growled, "If I don't get to kill somebody pretty soon, I'm gonna *kill* somebody."

Amen to that.

CHAPTER ELEVEN

Travel Sickness

I never thought I would say this, but was I ever glad when I finally got out of the United States of America.

From Vermont, we trained it down to New York, where we boarded the troop ship *Empress of Scotland*. The *Empress* then took us to Newport News, Virginia, where we collected another bellyful of soldiers and sailors for the Atlantic crossing. It was November 1943 by the time we landed in Casablanca, in Morocco.

Finally we were delivered into the thick of the action when a smaller ship brought us into the heart of the Italian campaign.

Naples.

"If you count the Aleutian Islands as part of Asia—which I think we have every right to do after all our sightseeing," Wallace said as we settled into our barracks, "then we have been on four continents within the last three months. And that's without even factoring in that we crossed North America, what, *four* times?"

"And we haven't stabbed or shot or blown up one single enemy combatant yet over all that mileage," Bergeron said.

"Exactly," Bruce said. "Our reputation must be mud by now. The per-mile kill rate we should be accumulating ought to be in the dozens, at least. And what is it?"

"Zero," I said, proving that I may have been the Kid, but the Kid could do some math.

"Somebody's got to pay," Wallace said.

"And we have got to start earning ours," Bruce added.

It might have sounded like a lot of blowharding, but this group was at this moment as seething with anger as anybody I had ever been around.

I would not want to be the first bunch to come up against us. I was a *part* of us, and I found us a little bit scary.

The lucky fighters turned out to be the German 104th Panzergrenadier Regiment.

Yes, they were as awe-inspiring and fearsome as their name sounded. Even if the name more or less translates as infantry on wheels.

"It translates as more like *armor-plated mobile artillery troops*," Wallace said. We were being unloaded off trucks at the foot of some mountains that, on second glance, were just the foothills of some other mountains, which were just stepping stones to the truly adult mountains beyond *those*.

"Ah, they don't sound so great," Bruce said, giving the enemy an exaggerated wave-off. He pretended like he was just going to hop back up on the truck and go home rather than waste his time.

"Make no mistake, men," our company leader, Lt. Morrison, said, "this is about as serious as it gets, and so are those troops up there. The Allied Armies— British and American, Polish, French, New Zealanders, Indian, Moroccan, you name it—have been trying to pry these guys out of these mountains for months."

"I thought the Italians surrendered months ago?" Sacks asked.

"They did," Morrison said, "but either nobody told the Germans or they just chose to ignore it out-right. For all intents and purposes, this is Germany right here."

"Excellent," Bergeron said. "Just where I wanted to be all along."

"Let's see if you still feel that way once the killing starts," Wallace said solemnly.

By this time, we were all really big on talking up the killing stuff, as if we were going to have our way everywhere we went. We had even developed this gesture among ourselves when we practiced hand-to-hand combat, especially knife fighting. The guy who won the bout would stand up tall, take his knife—real or imaginary—and run his tongue along the length of the blade like he was slurping up some victim's blood.

Except Wallace. He treated this seriously from day one, like he had already seen what was coming. And what was coming was unappetizing.

We were traveling light, but the world was heavy all around us.

There was a surreal aspect to the whole scene. We Forcemen were doing just what we had been groomed to do, silently scaling the geographical rise directly in front of us. And scaling it was. The rockface of Monte la Difensa was as sheer, steep, and imposing as anything I'd seen in *National Geographic* magazine, never mind what I had seen in person with my own eyes.

Even though we never made it to Norway, it was a good thing that we had trained as if we would. The cold, the ice, the wind of these Italian mountains in winter had to be the equal of any Nordic devil-challenge the war offered up.

The ferocious mountain test before us now was a climber's dream, and a soldier's nightmare. It was as if we were climbing up the spine of a sleepy but vicious giant serpent. We had to keep every last thought or breath to ourselves, as we'd been taught. Despite the fact that the whole time we ascended the serpent's scaly back, all manner of bombastic brutality was playing out along either side of it. Traditional infantry and artillery warfare was progressing along the right and left flanks of the mountain we were climbing. It was somewhat crazy to think that we had to go about our business in total silence in the midst of all that.

But we did.

The primarily British infantry to our left and American to our right had no such restrictions on them. Nor, notably, did the artillery companies off a few miles directly to the back of us. These guys were pummeling this hill, as well as several others in the area, with such ferocity that it was an open question whether there would even be a mountaintop to take by the time we got that high.

If we got that high. It was a very, very big *if*.

"There's no sugarcoating this, men," Lt. Morrison said as he gathered us and several more companies around for final instructions. "The regular army types have been trying and dying on these very hills for three solid months now. We've lost enough fighters to completely fill up some of the small towns a lot of you probably come from."

Just then, for the first time in a while, I thought about where I came from.

Berlin. The one I was born in. Population around nineteen thousand.

Berlin. The one I was aiming for. Population four million or so.

Bet we could take 'em.

"Rome," he said, pointing straight ahead *through* the mountain, "is up there. We need Rome. You can get there by going that way, or that way." Now he pointed to where vast armies were marching grimly ahead on either side of this hill. "But none of it makes a blind bit of difference, because the Germans are sitting cozy on the top of every strategic piece of high ground in this whole region. Those armies you see advancing on either side of us are gonna keep advancing, no matter what. And all that artillery behind us is gonna keep trying to blast all Nazi hides clear off these mountains and out into the sea.

"Things are going to happen to you right now, soldiers. Going by the numbers, this is the last time I will speak to many of you. German bullets are gonna get you. This beautiful steep beast of a mountain might well get you. Our own artillery might even get you. However, they will never get all of us, which means we're going to win this thing.

"The truth is, boys, it's all gonna come down to us. There is nobody like us. That is a fact, and it's precisely why we're here. If the First Special Service Force doesn't cut the head off this snake, it's looking like the snake just could win it all. Right now, we're snake hunters. Every last one of you needs to consider yourself the very guy to get this job done, to infiltrate the snake's nest and decapitate the beast. Then we'll have the pleasure of standing atop this mountain, and many more beyond it, waving the boys on the ground through. All the way to Rome. And to Paris. And to Berlin.

"In the meantime, those guys"—he pointed to the top of the mountain—"are slaughtering these guys"—he pointed at all our boys marching into the Nazis' path.

If every man there was feeling like me—and I knew well that every one of them was—we wanted to jump and roar and scream bloody murder now. That was what was happening on the insides of us.

The outsides?

Man after man after man silently put his head down and thumped forward to assault that hill.

All four hundred-odd men of the First Battalion were put on this mission, with the Second held in reserve for if—when—we needed relief. The Third was scheduled to advance on another mountain, Monte Sammucro, as soon as our mission was accomplished on La Difensa.

As much as the air was filling with the smoke and boom of all that was going on alongside us, it still felt right to be going about our business stealthily.

We were trained, after all. Overtrained, some might say. No matter what we were doing at any given time—dropping from a plane, landing on a beach, sliding down a mountain, or, like now, climbing up the face of one—it had been drilled into us that we were at all times sneaking up on somebody.

And that when we reached that somebody, they would be quickly and quietly dead.

So while Difensa was not beyond what we had

already trained for, there were sound reasons why it now held our rapt concentration.

For one thing, we'd learned that in clandestine operations there were two kinds of soldiers—the focused and the dead. There was no third or fourth option.

For another, no matter how superb the training was, there would always be a difference between preparation and real-live action.

In short, how did we know we were going to perform once the combat got real? To be honest, there was no way to tell 'til you got there.

I believed I was a killer. I was convinced I could kill. From the sound of it, everybody else felt the same way.

"The only thing that disturbs me more than killing," Bruce said one day over lunch on the *Empress of Scotland*, "is *not* killing. They've taught us how to do it, they've convinced us of *why we* need to do it, but they've taken forever to put us in position *to* do it. Honestly, no joke—I really, really, really want to do some killing now. We all know who the bad guys are by this point. Now just let us get out there and deal with them."

That ship trip to Europe was truly the turning

point. Bruce wasn't being nutty—wasn't *just* being nutty. He was voicing essentially the same feelings we all shared. We were highly trained killers. We needed to kill, wanted to kill.

Or so we thought.

"I don't know," Wallace said at that same lunch, "I'm pretty sure I'll be able to slit a man's throat when the time comes. But I have to say I won't know for certain *until* that time comes."

Wallace was the only one among us with the guts to say *that* out loud.

Myself, I *had* started to wonder seriously whether I'd have what it took to do the deed when the deed needed doing.

I *believed* I could kill a man who needed killing. I actually *liked* the notion of myself as a bloodthirsty cutthroat.

Could I actually cut a throat, though? And thirst for the blood?

I just didn't know. Nobody knew. Nobody could know. Yet. And this ocean voyage into the war everybody in the world was talking about brought all these thoughts to the fore.

Every decent and sane person on earth agreed our cause was just.

But did that matter? Would it matter when the time came?

We were sure going to find out. And soon.

Our ascent was basically up the mountain's spine. The opposite side, where the Germans had initially mounted their claim to the peak, was a far more gradual slope than what we were attempting. Setting out in a cold, raw mist that shrouded the lower mountain and seeped right into our bones, the conditions had the oddly helpful effect of making us want to keep on moving.

It was easy at first. Guys were practically sprinting up the first several hundred yards of hill. Then it got quickly and noticeably steeper and more arduous to claim each piece of upwardly mobile ground. Cold hunks of semi-frozen turf would come loose in my hand or kick away beneath my feet. More than once a guy lower down growled at me to stop dumping rocks on his head.

Bergeron, parallel with me and five feet off to my left, was the equivalent of my climbing partner. He voiced it for all of us when he asked, "Is this the same mountain we started on, or did we take a wrong turn somewhere?"

My response to *him* was a grunt. Even though I agreed with the sentiment, a grunt was the best I could do.

"Pick it up, guys," Wallace hissed at us. He had paused up ahead and apparently decided we were lagging. "We only have so much time to reach the top. Then our artillery cover ends. We'll be sitting ducks if the Germans get wind of us down here."

"Kind of like musical chairs," Bergeron quipped.

Wallace glared.

"You know," Bergey elaborated, "like, when the music stops . . ."

Wallace glared some more. "Joke like that, I should shoot you myself," he said, then waved for us to double-time it skyward.

"He's a little tense," I said to Bergeron.

"Yeah," he said. We picked up the pace.

I couldn't help picturing it now. Hearing the sudden, complete cessation of our artillery cover and then looking straight up the cliff to see a whole battalion of German soldiers peering down over the top ridge. Smiling first, then opening up with a roaring wall of gunfire sweeping down and wiping the whole load of us right off the cliff face.

I don't know what you'd call having spring in your

step while traveling vertically, but that vision put it straight into me.

The farther we got up the mountain, the colder it became. The misty rain started turning to snow and sleet. The terrain became less stable beneath us as it froze. The relentless battle sounds that had been so close by gradually muffled as the troops rounded the base of the mountain. I took the rare opportunity to check out the other guys nearest to me, and above and below. We were all progressing with a cold grimness, putting more earth behind us and gaining more on the sky above.

Once in a while, somebody would slip, skittering a ways downward—ten, twenty, thirty feet—before catching himself and getting right back to it.

Until one didn't.

Probably six rows of climbers above me, there was a mini rock slide. I heard a desperate scramble, and then a man crashing downward.

Everybody along the way tried to catch him, but he just kept bouncing like a pachinko machine until finally he'd slipped away from the hillside. The man flew backward for fifty feet and then crashed into a protrusion of rock, then another, then away to a pulpy landing at the bottom.

It felt like everybody had stopped. Because everybody had.

Then there was a low bark from up ahead, maybe from Lt. Morrison, maybe from Wallace. But it acted like a bracing face slap to all of us. Every man did a sort of shimmy shake, like a dog shedding water. We got back to the business of climbing.

A short stretch later, and again, pachinko. One of our own shells fell short of the peak. This, we could tell, was happening more the closer we got to our destination.

The shell blew a hole in the cliff face big enough to park a jeep in. The shower of fat angry rocks came bounding down toward us. Every man braced, pulling himself as close as possible to the hillside. The first wave of rocks bounced over with minimal damage, until, above me, I heard a sickening *thunk-crack*. I watched a man backflip right off the mountain. A half second later, he crashed into the climber below, and the two of them bounded in a howl of bellow-moaning down and down and down to the bottom of Difensa.

It was becoming apparent that the Germans at the top of the climb might be less dangerous to us than the time we spent here.

Nobody needed to be told to move this time.

Our greatest challenge yet came when we had reached about the three-quarters mark of the climb. The gradient went from steep to sheer, to backward.

There were a lot of great climbers in this outfit, but only a handful were up to this kind of thing. The bulk of us aligned along the safest ridge as our best dozen spider monkeys jumped fearlessly into the task of climbing the unclimbable.

It was almost hard to watch. These guys would progress two or three feet up. Then reposition hands and feet so carefully you'd think they were performing delicate surgery on a giant gallbladder. Then they would advance another couple of feet and do the whole thing all over again.

All the while, the bombardment went on over their heads.

Only, now there was an added feature. We could clearly hear the Nazi troopers up and over the ledge as they directed their own artillery on our exposed troops at the bottom of their long, visible slope.

At each stage of the climb to the top, a few of the elite climbers backed off. The job became more precarious by the foot. After about a half hour, when most of them had advanced as far as they could, we could see the group approach change. Three of the men heaved grappling hooks with ropes attached, until two of them hooked the great fish that was Difensa.

The two men raced up their ropes, finally reaching the top lip of the mountain.

Though I wasn't directly included in the climb, this was honestly the most anxious moment of my entire life.

The two paused, looking at each other momentarily, then swung up and over the ridge.

Nothing. We heard nothing from up there. Which could mean a lot of things—like they landed on waiting German bayonets, for instance—or it could *mean* nothing.

We had our answer in just a few more seconds, as grappling ropes came sailing over the ridge. The first two guys from the level below scaled to the top like pirates climbing a mast. Then more ropes came down and more men went up. Longer ropes started snaking down the distance from the very top to where the bulk of the Force, including myself, were waiting anxiously for them.

When the rope reached me, I was shaking so hard I could have dislodged enough of the cliff face to create my own cozy cave.

I hadn't realized just how cold I was. After all the nervous energy and sweat that went into climbing vigorously up the first three-quarters of the mountain with a full pack weighing me down, I hadn't even considered how the stillness would cause those frigid conditions to catch up to me. I stared dumbly upward.

I also hadn't realized just how nerve-racking watching other guys who are not you scale a mountaintop could be.

I was terrified.

All of which might add up to some pretty robust trembling, eh?

I attacked that rope and the final ascent like I'd never attacked anything. I needed to shake the cold out of my bones, the inactivity out of my spirit, and the fear out of my soul. This climb was the only solution.

I made a conscious decision as I climbed . . .

Hand over hand, over hand, over hand, over hand, over hand . . .

I was leaving my terror behind. I was condemning it to eternal death, right there on that sad little jut of ridge where I'd stood and nearly frozen watching better men do the job for the rest of us.

When I got to the top of the climb, I looked back.

I stared down at that spot of earth where my fear would die right now. Stared at it so hard I could see my footprints, could make out the actual grille work of the boot soles in the ground.

So long.

The silence became truly critical now.

As scheduled, the bombardment was slowing noticeably now. We crossed the surprisingly broad plain of the mountaintop. It was as if Difensa had a big bald spot at the top of its head. The regiment crept like one great organism across this flattened landscape, toward the opposite slope, where we knew the Germans were operating from.

The whole of the region had been under siege for months. The Germans had set up their defensive line like a trouser belt across the waistline of Italy, in response to the Allied landings in the south of the country and Sicily. So we were late to that party generally, and to this one specifically. The fight to take Difensa—this attempt, anyway—had already been raging for three days by the time somebody had the bright idea to unleash the First Special Service Force on them.

Honestly, it was only the exact kind of thing we were designed, built, and trained for.

There was a lot of blood all around this mountain. We were here to put a stop to that.

But not before we caused a lot more of it first. As long as it was the *right* blood being spilled.

With a minimum of audible commanding, Lt. Morrison surveyed the scene over the far lip of the mount. Like a bunch of kids, we all scooted up behind him to see what we could see.

What we could see were German soldiers. And their firepower. A whole lot of firepower.

They were mostly hunkered down in a series of bunker-like defensive postures on a great big shelf about fifty feet down. But between us and those positions, there was another, shorter shelf sparsely populated with more lightly armed guards who were marching back and forth and occasionally taking scans up in our direction. They clearly didn't think too much about the possibility of anybody making that absurd climb we just did and getting the jump on them. But Nazis being Nazis, they were not about to leave anything totally to chance.

They'd been sheltering from the onslaught of our artillery, but that was now finished, so gradually the Germans were coming out and forming what looked like more aggressively offensive setups, peering down the north slope of the mountain in the direction of Allies positioned east and west of them. It looked for all the world like a shooting gallery setting up at the start of the grisliest carnival you could imagine.

Time mattered. There were untold numbers of Allied lives we might be able to save if we could engage this nest of Germans in the few minutes between the artillery pummeling and when they'd turn fearlessly on the troops below.

With a series of pointing motions and reptilian hisses, Lt. Morrison dispatched man after man along the path that ran just below the lip of the mountain. It reminded me of the old Western movies, where the Indian scouts would recon a battlefield and smartly stake out all the most advantageous high ground.

Without words, every man knew just what he was being told to do, where he was being told to go, and how he was supposed to set up once he got there.

That was where proper training got you. For all the days we'd hated it, we sure loved it now.

It was tough to keep any kind of formation going in this situation, but somehow Sacks and Bergeron, me and Wallace and Bruce, found ourselves single-filing it along to our designated spots together.

And I couldn't have been happier about that.

Especially Wallace. Wallace had followed his natural instincts and assumed the role of leader of our small platoon, and we had all had the good sense to follow where he led.

There was little margin for error. We crept along and then finally settled in behind that short wall of ledge separating us from potential Nazi fire. Once there, with many more platoons already positioned down-ridge, we settled in for a spell of observation and awaited further orders.

After watching and timing the guard patrols on the nearer ridge, it was apparent that we could coordinate an attack to arrive silently behind the guards and take them out before their comrades below even knew. The lower troops were concentrating so hard on our boys below, it was as if the world behind and above them was a nonexistent thing.

Rising up slightly on his haunches, we saw Lt. Morrison signal up and down the line, pointing roughly into each platoon one at a time. The signal was relayed along to the next group, when Wallace rose up and made the same gesture. There were five sets of two-man guards visible from where we were. Morrison motioned to Wallace, pointing two fingers up at him and then off to one of the pairs. Wallace then turned and performed the same choreography for the leader of the next platoon down, who then passed it on to the next. Five platoons in all—us and two more to our right and left—were designated for this next move.

I took it all in like everybody else was. Like a spectator.

Until.

The hand on my shoulder.

Wallace, who everybody would have figured was going to go, had selected *me* to go with him.

Among the many things we learned in Force training, the ability to take our own pulse without looking at a watch was one. We knew seconds instinctively and could feel with the tips of our fingers between ribs how many beats we were drumming. As a highly trained athlete and an even more highly trained commando, I was used to my heart rate being fifty or below.

I placed my fingers between ribs.

When I concluded I could not trust these ribs, I tried another spot.

Same. Going about 170 beats per minute.

"You ready for this?" Wallace asked.

"I'm ready," somebody with a voice that sounded like me answered.

I started to get up, but he pushed me back down. He reached over and removed my M3 from my shoulder and handed it over to Bergeron. Then he drew his knife and held it up between us.

Message received.

Bergeron looked at me hard, shook my gun, and nodded, to assure me he would be getting it back to me.

Then, as the guards made their turns, all five pairs of Forcemen flipped over the wall and slid down into the miniature valley between us and them.

Practically bumping shoulders the whole way, Wallace and I prowled across the short space. When we reached the rise, we started the nine-foot climb.

This was *it*. As far as climbs went, this was nothing compared to what we'd just achieved. But this maneuver wasn't about the difficulty of the climb.

With every second, I was closer to *the* moment. I was about to find out. If I had it. If I had *it*.

That is, if I was lucky, I was going to find out. Since this was literally a blind leap into the unknown, I may not have the chance to find out anything.

We paused, all ten men, hanging on to whatever

piece of rock was available along that ledge. Just hanging there for those few seconds was a lot harder than I would have guessed.

Going on some nearly invisible sign from Morrison, Wallace hissed at me, "Go!"

As I shot up and over that wall, I would have killed for the carefree days of a mere 170 bpm pulse. Suddenly I landed chin-to-chin with a young Nazi who looked both hateful and every bit as petrified as me. He reached around for his gun, but the training— the beautiful, repetitive, brutal training—kicked in without my even noticing. My hand, holding that commando knife hard enough to crush the handle into sand, was pumping, pumping that blade into the guard's stomach, then pumping it right into the space between those two ribs I had just been examining on myself, then pumping into his neck, his gullet, and up. When his jaw hung open, I saw through the roof of his mouth with a crunch.

By the time the guard fell, by the time I allowed him to drop off my dagger, I looked left and right to see the same scene playing out down the line.

Turned out I had *it*. We all did.

Just as quietly as we had stalked and killed these other killers, we went back to the lip of the ridge facing down over our own anxious forces. We gave them the signal to rush up and join us.

Within seconds, they'd swarmed and stormed up the wall, and stood with us now, ready for next moves. As promised, Bergey reunited me with my firearm, whispering as low as he could, "Well done, Kid," while surveying the bloody mess we'd just created.

One by one, the other members of the platoon made a point of saying the same thing to me, surprise mixing with the admiration in their voices.

"Well done, Kid. Well done. Really, well done."

Only Bruce had the nerve to diverge from the script, and I was so relieved when he did.

"Ah," he sniffed, "I've seen better work. But you'll get there, Kid."

We clearly didn't have the firepower to stand toe-to-toe with these hardened troops. They'd been dug in and swatting away our guys so successfully for so long now. Our only chance was to do what we were created for.

Stealth. Stealth and ferocity.

Once again, the lieutenant began coordinating us, leading other companies away from our center line with the other officers. What we needed was to achieve maximum chaos and destruction, at least long enough that the regular troops down below could finally mount a credible offensive.

The Germans had already started their assault in earnest, so we scrambled madly into position to do them the most harm. It was only a matter of minutes until the Germans attacked, and we had eliminated their rear guards. Now we were breaking up into largely autonomous groups to take out individual batteries before they could rain too much more death down on our guys.

Our assignment was a large mortar company dug into the top of a high outcropping of rock, back a ways from the forward edge of the German position. This spot, along with the trajectory of the mortar fire, gave them an almost sickeningly privileged battle position from which they could presumably kill without fear of being killed in return. The setup looked like an exaggerated eagle's nest, and they appeared so comfortable I was sure I saw something like a picnic going on even as they commenced their bombardment.

"Hit 'em!" Wallace yelled, slapping Sacks on the arm. Sacks went into fire mode, unleashing a rocket-propelled grenade from the launcher on his shoulder.

At least four Germans—or their constituent parts—blew like confetti up and out of that nest before the shouting and scrambling began. The remaining mortar group flustered around, trying to establish where we were. But we were well-embedded into a crevice-blessed arrangement of boulders that made us hard to see, while leaving generous gaps to attack through.

All along the mountain encampment now, our guys were making scores—with rifle and machine-gun fire, grenades and mortars, explosives of all kinds.

Within minutes, we'd achieved our first objective—chaos. It was a giddy feeling, watching the crack-efficient Nazi fighters flailing and screaming as we invaded their household, killing them almost at will.

I fell quickly in love with the capabilities of my M3 submachine gun, employing it more in those first few minutes than I had during all the time I'd previously held it combined.

"Not so random," Bergeron snapped at me. "It won't be nearly so much fun if you run out of bullets before those jerks finally find out exactly where you're sitting, will it?"

That was one of the best pieces of advice I'd received in my whole army life.

The initial rush of battle was hard to describe. How was something so destructive so exhilarating?

Yes, those were the bad guys and everybody knew it, so we had right on our side.

We did, right?

Right?

But this, the thrill of the fight, was beyond what I had expected.

It occurred to me that I might never be able to say this out loud to anybody who wasn't here with me along this line this minute, but . . . war . . . could be kind of incredible.

Suddenly, I felt a smack across the back of my helmet, sharper than anything that had ever happened to me on the football field.

"Kid!" Bergeron yelled. "I told you to conserve ammunition, not to stop fighting altogether. What are you daydreaming about? Knock it off already. Get in the game, will ya? Jeez, you really are a *kid*, Kid."

He let out a warm little laugh as he turned his attention back to the enemy. He was still laughing as he squinted and went to squeeze off a few rounds through the space in the rocks.

But they found him first. A single shot came

through the hole, fired by one of those sharp-eyed Nazi marksmen we'd heard so much about.

It was a big shell—went straight through his eye and pinged the back of his helmet as it carried through.

Bergey dropped his gun, dropped his arms, dropped onto his back.

I swung around to see to him, but Wallace had already scrambled over and was up close to his face.

"Back to work, Kid," Wallace said harshly.

"But he was just—"

"Kid!" he snapped again. "We've got a job to do. Take Bergey's replacement cartridges."

"What? No," I said, despite it making all the sense in the world.

"Do it," Wallace commanded, his voice going a little bit softer just when I might've expected it to get harder. "From what I've seen of your shooting, you're gonna need all the rounds you can get. And take his grenades, too. He sure doesn't need them anymore."

I stared for a bit longer than was helpful, at Bergeron and at his stuff, which I was reluctant to touch.

"Fine," Sacks said, butting in all businesslike.

Even though he was undoubtedly closer to Bergey than any of us. I remembered then, meeting the two of them together on that fateful train to Montana.

I watched as Sacks stripped his friend of his grenades and then went into his knapsack for some other stuff I didn't see before he socked it away in his own bag.

"If you guys and your sewing circle are all done now," Sacks snarled, "we've got some animals to slaughter."

Sacks, his face cracking with emotions I didn't recognize, went finally to take Bergeron's spare ammunition.

"No," Wallace said, grabbing his hand, "the Kid will need it."

"Ah, he will," Sacks allowed, then handed the cartridges to me.

"Heads up!" Bruce yelped, then lunged into our area, his M3 blazing.

One of the Nazis had just breached our less-than-airtight perimeter, scaling the stone circle fortress. Bruce caught him at the top of the rock and shot him all the way down 'til he was dead on the ground. The dead Nazi actually fell on top of me, careered off, and landed on our own fallen soldier, Bergeron.

Bruce went straight over, peeled him off, flung him to the ground, and then plunged his dagger in—between the correct ribs, for good measure.

The rest of us were still staring as Bruce withdrew the commando knife from the enemy, brought it up to his mouth, and licked it clean. Both sides.

Somebody probably should have objected.

As Bergeron lay there, holed straight through, nobody did.

It was truly exhausting madness as we engaged these guys in the kind of stand-and-deliver warfare we were never expected to stand and deliver with anybody—never mind the most accomplished infantry and artillery troops in the world. But we had the will to do this, and the cunning, and the physical fitness to match up to anybody's army.

The hours dragged on, and the bodies mounted. We had effectively drawn the attention—not to mention the fire—of the Germans. They wheeled around to start fighting uphill against our jolly band of cutthroats in a way they'd never bargained for.

When you formulate your entire game plan around being the big bullies punching downward against smaller foes half your strength, you aren't prepared when you have to turn on your heels and start punching up.

Good things had begun happening alongside bad ones. The heavy-duty battle stations that had been battering our side from up here for months now had to turn fire on us.

That was a good thing, because that was the plan.

That was also the bad thing, because . . . well, because obviously.

A rocket sailed over our heads, the noise loud enough to take my breath away and stop me from doing my job, if even only temporarily. That was one of the intended consequences, of course. However, it was unclear if even the enemy knew how effective that sound was when it was sailing through the small nests of fighters.

To be honest, it was a horror in every direction. Whether we got hit or not, it hurt.

We traded mortars with them, but as a mobile army compared to their entrenched one, this was a gradually losing proposition. They simply had more reserves of everything, since they didn't have to carry it all on their backs. We were holding our own in the fights, but this, too, was a game we ultimately were destined to lose.

What we were getting right was the divide-and-conquer strategy of pulling the Germans out of their long and unfair battle against the troops on the ground. We were requiring them to carry on a 360-degree fight, which they hadn't previously had to do.

More and more, we could feel the might of our own team's firepower as they grew closer and bolder. The north slope of the mountain was trembling with rocket and mortar fire from our own guys.

And if the occasional life-threatening burst of hillside was delivered to our own neighborhood by our own people, I thought that was a bargain every member of the First Special Service Force was more than happy to make.

Okay, maybe not *more* than happy.

But happy enough.

Everyone was becoming aware that we were running low on supplies. We were up on the crown of this bald beast of a mountain—by our own design, granted—and a war of attrition didn't seem to favor the FSSF over the Nazi machine. But we figured if we could just hold out long enough . . .

Then Lt. Morrison was in our little stone circle, and in Wallace's face.

"It's all we've got," Morrison said.

"You're right," Wallace answered.

"It's like boxing, right?" the lieutenant said. "The smaller fighter—shorter guy, shorter arms—can't just let the bigger guy stand back and take the measure of him. Smaller guy's got to rush him, crowd him. Get inside and chop him down to size with relentless, hacking shots that don't let the bigger guy get his own punches off."

Wallace looked like he had no problem understanding the concept completely.

He also looked saddened beyond sad to be considering it.

"But there's a price, Lieutenant," Wallace said.

"Yeah," Morrison said, "there is that."

The price, put bluntly, was carnage. We were going to have to get in closer, behind, up and under the enemy in order to be able to land any more telling blows in this bout.

Lt. Morrison left orders with us to keep doing what we were doing, holding the line and keeping our heads down, while he went platoon to platoon to personally deliver the message of just what he was asking of everyone.

We'd come to know that was the kind of man the lieutenant was.

As Morrison made his pilgrimage, we conducted our holding action as instructed. But it was becoming quickly obvious that we weren't going to hold up much longer under these conditions. The Germans suddenly seemed to be unloading twice the ordnance right in our faces. The hum and whoosh of rockets was everywhere in the air, and the exchange of machine-gun fire was now being conducted almost completely through a thick haze of smoke.

It seemed like an eternity before Lt. Morrison returned to us with his orders.

"Half of each platoon remains in place; the other half will advance. I've had a couple of my men scouting both flanks of the hillside. Half of the advancing troops will slide down the left and right flanks, into the patchy tree line. Then they'll come up underneath, where the artillery batteries are working the troops on the ground. The Nazis won't be looking. Those guns are concentrating on the ground far below, and on us up here. We can sneak right into their nests and gut them like fish as they man their infernal guns."

"Sir?" Wallace asked. "Where do the other half of the advancing Forcemen go?"

Morrison did a half turn in the direction of the German stronghold.

"Straight into their teeth," he said boldly. "Obviously, it's volunteer-only."

Every one of us put his hand up immediately.

"You sort 'em out, Wallace," Morrison said, heading back down the line. "We go in five."

More and more rounds were coming, pinging off our little rock formation as the Nazi shooters figured out where everybody was nested. The sound was very much like a ticking time bomb for us, but even more immediate.

"Okay, quickly, who wants what?" Wallace asked the group.

Out of nowhere, an unexpected extra body dropped in and piped up.

"If I may, I'd like to lay down the covering fire for you boys."

The visitor was our old Canadian friend, Mutton Head.

"Appreciate the offer, Mutt," Wallace told him, "but you're supposed to be sticking close to your own unit for this one."

Mutt sounded as matter-of-fact as if he was giving a weather report.

"I don't have one anymore. So, if you don't mind . . ."

"We don't mind at all," I insisted.

"Great," Wallace said. "I can't ask anybody else to do what I won't do, so I'm going straight up the middle. Anyone else?"

"No," Bruce snarled.

"Fine," Wallace said evenly. "I understand. I can do—"

"No," Bruce repeated with a bit more pepper on it.

"We don't have time for your malarkey, Bruce. What are you saying?"

"I am saying you are not going up the middle. You're better than the rest of us. We need you. So, no, request denied. You can have the trees bit, but that's my final offer."

It was a terrific moment. The thought of Bruce going all officer class on us gave everyone a surprised chuckle.

But we all knew instantly this was right.

"So I'm going," Bruce said.

"And I'm going," my mouth said without consulting my brain or my knocking knees.

"No!" said Bruce, seeming very much like our fearless leader all of a sudden.

"Why not?" I said. "I'm not better than everybody else?"

"That's true," Bruce said, "you're not. But you are the youngest. By a long way."

I made my weak protest. "I am not any younger than—"

"Save it, Kid," Bruce said, patting me kindly on the cheek. "You're going with Wallace. He gets extra babysitter pay."

"Then I'm going," Sacks said.

"I guess that's you and me, taking the long way around, Kid," Wallace said to me.

"I guess it is," I said, happy enough with my lot in this life.

"You gonna be all right, holding down the fort yourself?" Wallace asked Mutt.

As Mutt was nodding an enthusiastic yes, a big fat mortar arced up into the sky from the German camp and came whistling down onto one of our other makeshift posts.

Bu-hoooom! The explosion, inside a setup like our own, rocked the whole mountain. Stones rained down on everybody, guns and boots and bodies flying every which way. Helmets, some empty, some not, came bouncing across the terrain not far from us.

It was as if that was a signal; in some ways it probably was.

We all slapped hands as we sprang into action. I ran along our line to the left, hard on the heels of Wallace. Mutton Head, after collecting every ammo cartridge the rest of us could spare, leaned into his job of providing covering fire while Sacks and Bruce and the luckiest guys from every other platoon advanced like a bunch of urban raccoons out on a nightly garbage hunt.

The level of small- and medium-caliber gunfire somehow managed to escalate tenfold over the next forty seconds. It was clear that everybody on both sides was appreciating that the fight had reached a stage unlike anything this hill had seen since action began.

Today, somebody was going to win this hill for good.

Follow the bouncing helmet was the name of the game. I stayed right in Wallace's lane until we finally found our way into the scrabby tree cover. Morrison was right that nobody would be looking for the likes of us. The firefight raged, between the Germans and our guys on the lower ground, and between the Germans and our Forcemen on the higher ground. But *we* didn't draw anything other than the odd round of stray bullets and one wayward haywire mortar shell. That shell felt no less lethal for being accidental as it sucked away all the air between Wallace and me, just before crashing in a fireball in the woods.

Several other two-man teams had entered the sparse wooded patch ahead of us, with a couple more pairs bringing up the rear. We were all aligned as close to the open as we dared. Wallace and a few others sized up the scene before us. It was a relatively compact array of awesome firepower, arranged in nests in a sort of amphitheater setup. Anti-tank guns, antipersonnel cannons, machine guns, and various brands of mortars filled each nest so that the Germans could get every bit of ordnance into the air as soon as their targets were spotted. The one novel piece of kit that caught my eye right away was one I'd heard lots about but never seen before.

The Nebelwerfer.

Everybody had heard *of* it. This was the first time we got to hear *it*. It had been literally screaming across the skies since we had arrived in the region. The Nebelwerfer was an artillery piece but in a class of its own. It was mounted on what looked like a Civil War–era cannon carriage, making it highly mobile. It was actually a bundle of *six* cannons all bound up together.

The nest closest to us, which would be Wallace's and my responsibility, contained one long-range anti-tank gun and two Nebelwerfers. One was pointed into the battle area downhill. The other faced our pals on the cliffs above.

As we watched, the downward-facing beast was unleashed. Each of the six massive shells, packed with high explosive charges, also contained another small gift. An ear-piercing siren announced itself to waiting victims with a diabolical screech that you couldn't get out of your head once you'd heard it.

Every man covered up, wincing like we were all going to scream just as intensely, as the six murderous shells sailed their way downward.

Then the silent orders went out. Each pairing was set to be released toward their targets. The Germans had turned toward prepping the other Nebelwerfer in the direction of the Forcemen.

"Machine gunners first," Wallace reminded me. "Nobody else can touch us. Ready . . . go!"

There was never such a *ready, go* anywhere. The two of us exploded like we ourselves were coming out of the business end of rocket launchers.

With an M3 in one hand and an automatic pistol in the other, I shot up each one of the five Nazi soldiers on the right side of the nest. Busy with all the heavy machinery, they were only giving cursory attention to anything within small arms' range. The two-man Nebelwerfer team were dead before they fell, one folding backward over the evil multi-barrel monster, and the other staggering toward me and making the job that much easier.

Wallace was having his same way with the left side of the nest, gunning down the two shell handlers on the ground before they could draw weapons. The gunner sitting in the operating seat of the heavy tank gun had been in the middle of setting his aim and, preoccupied, took a couple seconds to react. He turned on Wallace, who was by now up in the gun seat with him. Wallace stuck his pistol in the soldier's throat, aimed up, and with a *pow* filled his pointy helmet with pulpy tomato soup and gray brains. They pooled there as the man slumped forward.

I'd put my handgun in my waistband just as one of the barely living ammo handlers slowly reached for his gun, aiming it at Wallace's back. I leaped across two other dead men with my dagger drawn and landed behind it, jamming the blade up to the hilt in the German's neck, right where the esophagus tries to hide behind the breast bone.

"Thanks," Wallace said. "I was wondering if you'd be helpful."

I was hyperventilating so hard by now that the Nebelwerfer shells had nothing on me for scream-whistling.

Wallace slapped me hard several times on the back, a sort of Forceman's way of calming a guy down. Then he gestured at the other gun nests where fighting was still hot.

We'd accomplished our objective, but much was still to be done. We leaped out of the Nebel nest just in time to avoid a mortar shell from our own team slamming into it and exploding. There were gunfights and knife fights raging all over this encampment, but we could feel it as it went from being theirs to being ours.

Wallace and I jumped in on two more battle nests, joining the shooting and stabbing. Every other nest was a pot roast of human gore and gravy. There were dead Germans, Americans, Canadians in every hole as the FSSF, or what was left of it, came cascading down the hill from above. The boys below still didn't know—or couldn't believe—that after all their trouble the hill had been taken from the Nazis by this raggedy bunch of hoodlums.

Our biggest hazard now was the odd burst of Allied artillery still flying up the mountain from the disbelievers below.

I suppose it was something of a reward when the brass told us our next assignment was going to be holding Monte la Difensa. The Allies had learned many hard lessons over the course of the war—as difficult and imperative it was to *take* a hill, it was equally so to *hold* it.

It felt like a near-death experience, spending the night on Difensa. The cold was deep and oppressive, despite everything all of us had experienced previously elsewhere in our lives.

We treated the former Nazi stronghold as our personal camp now and spent the night settled into as many of their prearranged shelters as we could. We ran skeleton guard watches so nobody could do to us what we'd just done to them.

It was something of a reunion as we all milled about, waiting to see who made it. Wallace and I obviously made it. So did Mutton Head. Bruce made it. Sacks did not. I now had no friends left from the original train into camp.

Of the four hundred guys who assaulted that

mountain, about one hundred were still around to defend it until we were relieved the next morning.

Relieved by regular troops, who did this kind of thing.

Because we were not regular troops.

CHAPTER TWELVE

Bumps in the Road

The experience of Monte la Difensa turned out to be a template for how the war was going to go for the First Special Service Force. We continued as a vital component of the Italian Campaign, fighting north across the various east-west defensive lines constructed by the Nazis to slow the Allied forces down. It was a long road to reclaiming all of Europe, one that they had been taking, ravaging, destroying since their spree began in 1939.

Mount Sammucro. Mount Arcalone. Mount Majo. Mount la Chiaia. The heights kept getting higher, the orders taller, the fighting more brutal.

We consistently did what was asked of us, which was to take the top off a mountain, kill or capture (mostly kill) all the German soldiers necessary, and then move on.

Once we captured a peak, we would wait for coverage to arrive, then start the joyless march back down the northernmost hospitable face of the mountain on the way to the next one.

In between, we would hike through towns and villages that seemed largely happy to see us.

Fair enough. You'd be happy to see anybody, if the previous tenants were the Nazis.

We ate well along the way. No chewy worms and crunchy wood lice in Italy, that was for sure.

And we saw some sights.

We fought on moonlit snow, which was a vision of heaven in spite of the frostbite nibbling our toes.

We saw concrete pillbox structures, constructed by the Germans on the unlikeliest places. Some were glued to nearly vertical rises just for the purpose of shooting directly down on us.

We climbed some of the most stunning peaks in the world. People must have come from all over the globe to scale these peaks—before it became likely you'd get shot right off them.

We traveled, when we could, on mule trains provided by sympathetic local farm families. With all the miles we were logging and all the gear we were humping, there were times when my best friend in the universe was a stubborn cuss with a hairy, snorty mug about three feet long.

We painted our hands and faces camo black for night maneuvers when there was no moonlight. We conducted raids this way, and without a doubt, this was my favorite operation of all. We couldn't see even one another, though we knew we were right there. And so the look of shock when we revealed ourselves to whatever Nazi murderer or sympathizer had been marked for assassination was reward in itself. The few survivors of these raids—the very few we took as prisoners—were the ones to give us the nickname Devil's Brigade.

The real prize of this bunny hop of mountains was Monte Cassino. There was a fourteen-hundred-year-old monastery sitting way high on a peak above the town of Cassino. The mountain was the Nazi's prime-among-prime observation and assault post on the road to Rome. Thousands of our guys had died already trying to move this particular mountain. Nothing and no one could make it through the valley of the river Liri without being hammered by the forces above Cassino.

Not until we showed up, anyway.

Of all the physical challenges and extremes I had encountered since leaving New Hampshire, nearly every natural wonder of my youth had been eventually surpassed by what I found out in the wider world.

But as I jumped with sixty of my nearest and dearest friends into the Liri on a chilly dead of night in May 1944, my first thoughts were *Well, it's got nothing on the Androscoggin back home.*

Home. Thoughts of home were coming more and more, like the whitewater that floods the northern waters in May.

We did the thing we did best, again at Monte Cassino. We floated downriver until we found convenient staging areas to get out of the water and mount our hillside assault at night. By the time we got there, however, the monastery had become a former monastery. The Allies ran out of patience and bombed the thing out of existence, believing the Germans were using it as a staging post for attacks.

But in a move that actually brought admiration from the Forcemen, it turned out the German soldiers treated the bombardment as a gift. The fall of all that ancient stonework on a mountain so high served the purpose of creating an unlimited number of small battle stations for them to wage war on us.

And the only guys to take them on at that game were us.

Brother Mine,

Italy is incredible, but I am tired.

Sorry, wrong way around. I am incredible, but Italy is tired.

Honestly, there is so much to see here, so much natural wonder it makes New Hampshire look like a giant shoe box filled with wet rocks. I want to come back here, D, when it's all over, and bring you with me so I can show it to you.

If there is anything left of it when we're done.

We are breaking this place, pal. Those other guys are breaking it, but so are we. They take it, break it. Then we take it back, break it some more. It's a shame is what it is.

There are rumors, too. That all this is for nothing. That Italy is just a diversion while other stuff gets done, and that the land gained here has no meaning.

Wait 'til you see it, brother. No land could have more meaning than this.

I didn't know, at first, if I could kill. I can. I very much can.

Now I don't know if I can stop.

I done good, huh? Made something of myself.

In the quiet times between assaults, everybody kills the time by doing the exact same things.

Writing letters.

Sharpening knives.

Oiling guns.

Sharpening knives even sharper.

Hey, I just got that. Killing time between killings. Maybe I even got funnier since being over here.

I am looking forward to seeing Rome, though. And you. And Dad. Won't be long now.

Love, The Kid

p.s. They call me the Kid here. You cannot, though, because I am the big brother now.

CHAPTER THIRTEEN

Final Destination

When we'd finally completed our work at Cassino, we were sent to assist with the breakout from the beach landing at Anzio. It was a brutal operation, and the weakened forces were taking much longer to break out and join the push to Rome than expected. We came in and did what we do, creating fear and havoc. Mostly we worked at night so the enemy could get no rest and was useless for the fighting once the sun came up.

With our help, the forces moved inland, and everybody was on the same road to Rome.

This was something lots of people had been looking forward to, since the early days when Hitler and Mussolini began their reign of terror across the glorious capitals of Europe.

I'd dreamed of this very march when I was still a schoolboy in Berlin.

Dreamed of marching into Berlin, as well.

Almost there now.

"Greene," Lt. Morrison said, surprising me at chow one of the last mornings before we were to arrive in Rome.

I must have looked as startled as I felt, because he tried it again.

"You are Private Dallas Greene, yes?"

"Yes. But everyone calls me the Kid."

He nodded, kind of fatherly.

"Then I'll call you Kid, too."

I just then noticed that Wallace was behind Lt. Morrison. Bruce was behind him. Mutt was behind him.

"Is there a problem, Lieutenant?" I asked.

"I'm afraid there is."

"Please, sir?" I nearly begged.

Wallace put a hand on Morrison's shoulder, getting permission to step up and take over this uncomfortable mission.

"Kid," Wallace said, "it's time for you to go home. You're going home."

"Home?" I said, befuddled. "You mean, Rome. I'm going to Rome. Then Paris. Then Berlin."

"Berlin, Kid. You are going to Berlin, New Hampshire. You've done your job here, and then some. Now you're needed at home."

"I'm needed here," I insisted.

"You are. We surely need you. But your father needs you more. Kid . . . Dallas is dead."

I stared and stared and stared and stared into his clear and kind hazel eyes. I said nothing.

"He had health problems. Yes?"

"Yes," I said, looking around all corners of the tent, then up. "He did. That's why . . ."

"That's why you were here instead of him," Lt. Morrison interjected. "You did a fine thing, son, and a fine job *of* it."

"And now Dallas is dead," Wallace said as gently as a person could say that. "Dallas is dead, and Gabriel is needed. Back home. Your family has contributed enough to the fight already."

I was thinking about what my next defensive maneuver was going to be. I took my breath and was close to delivering it.

Then Wallace opened his arms.

And I fell in.

About the Author

Chris Lynch is the author of numerous acclaimed books for middle-grade and teen readers, including the Cyberia series and the National Book Award finalist *Inexcusable*. He teaches in the Lesley University creative writing MFA program, and divides his time between Massachusetts and Scotland.